Praise for Adèle Geras

' book is a great read ... which leaves you with
ing that there is something right with the world
ll' *Daily Express*

'll be hooked from the start and when you finish
you'll wish you hadn't' *Company*

'Geras assuredly draws the reader into this deeply
ng, grade A saga which has a grip that's impos-
shake off' *Woman & Home*

'lose-yourself-in-it book, *Facing the Light* has
hing ... a not-to-be-missed treat'
Penny Vincenzi

'yable and entertaining read from an accom-
toryteller' *Time Out*

'W 1 perceptive' *Sunday Express*

'dèle Geras at her best: a family drama, secrets
past, romance, complicated relationships. A
y, very skilfully told' *Good Book Guide*

'It est, acutely observed writing which has
relat ps spot on' Scott Pack, The Friday Project

Adèle Geras was born in Jerusalem. Since 1976 she has published many acclaimed books for children and young adults. She lives in Manchester with her husband and they have two daughters. *A Hidden Life* is her fourth novel for adults, all of which are available in paperback from Orion. Visit her website at www.adelegeras.com.

By Adèle Geras

A Hidden Life
Made in Heaven
Hester's Story
Facing the Light

For Sophie and Dan

Acknowledgements

Thanks to Caroline Wood for telling me how a movie production company works; to Edward Russell-Walling for help with choosing wine; to Jane Gregory and Emma Dunford; and especially this time to my editor Jane Wood for handing me the last piece of the jigsaw.

Thanks, too, to Dina Rabinovitch and Sally Prue for reading the novel so carefully and enthusiastically.

As always, I'm grateful to my family for their help and support.

'Are you quite certain that this is what you want to do, Mrs Barrington?'

Constance lay in bed with her eyes closed. Could she muster the energy to answer this young man she hardly knew? She was very close to death. There was no point in deceiving herself and, besides, she was completely calm at the prospect of leaving this world. What irked her was the fact that she would no longer be in control and that was why she'd summoned Andrew Reynolds to her bedside on a day when she knew there was no danger of her son and his wife visiting her.

How the world had shrunk lately! She hadn't left this bedroom for months and was now too weak even to enjoy the distant view of the Channel. She'd loved sitting on her little balcony on summer mornings, looking out over the sloping lawn that ran down to the bank of spotted laurels near the gate. I won't see the garden in spring ever again, she thought. And the house could do with some redecoration. This room, especially. The cream velvet curtains had almost had their day, the William Morris Willow wallpaper, which had once been pretty but which she had tired of about two years ago, had definitely faded ... but what did it matter? Everything could be left for someone else to deal with. What would become of her silver hand mirror? The crystal perfume bottles on the dressing table? They would go with the rest of the glass, she supposed, to Phyllida. Her daughter-in-law was the kind of person who'd know what to do with items like that; how to distribute them where they'd be appreciated. I don't really care about any of it, Constance thought. Not about the bits and bobs of my life.

'I'll sign the new will,' she told him. 'And you must promise to take it to Matthew's office as soon as possible after I'm gone.'

'He won't be very ... happy with what you've decided, you know.'

What business is that of yours? Constance wanted to ask. She'd paid quite enough to buy this man's silence till she was safely out of the way. Let Matt continue to think the will he'd drawn up was valid. He'd realize his mistake soon enough. They all would. She tried to smile, but the effort was too much for her.

'I think I have to warn you,' Mr Reynolds went on, 'that this document is bound to create certain ... well, ill feeling.'

I don't care, Constance thought. How can I convey the depth of my not-caring to this foolish young man who knows nothing? Everyone deserves exactly what they're getting, and they'll soon find out that I don't forget anything – and I don't forgive either.

Constance believed in the afterlife. She always had, and now that she was getting closer and closer to discovering whether she was right to do so, she comforted herself with the notion that she might very well be there, watching from on high as Andrew Reynolds told Matthew that no, the will he'd drawn up for his mother was not the most recent. Not by any means. The heaven of her imagination hadn't changed very much since she was a child, and she saw herself on a cloud, hovering somewhere near the ceiling, listening as her son read this interesting new will out to the rest of the family. She'd worked out every detail of her funeral years ago – they'd all gather for the reading of the will straight after the burial. That was how it was supposed to be. She summoned up what remained of her energy to speak once again. What had he called it? Ill feeling. According to him, she was going to create ill feeling.

'I know,' she breathed at last. 'That is my intention.'

I

Lou Barrington had stopped loving her grandmother when she was eight years old. There had been times lately when she'd hoped that something could be done to improve the chilly relationship they'd fallen into, but now Constance was dead and buried and it was too late. Lou had done her best, but she'd waited years for some indication of a softening, of a change of heart from her grandmother and none had come.

Milthorpe House, Lou reflected as she made her way across the hall, had changed. In her opinion, it had lost its heart and its warmth after her grandfather died, and now there wasn't even Miss Hardy, the housekeeper, to remind her of her childhood. She'd been in charge of everything up until a few years ago, but since her death Dad had arranged agency staff to look after both the house and his mother. Miss Hardy had been pleasant enough, not in the least like Mrs Danvers from *Rebecca*, but you knew that anything you said in front of her would be instantly relayed to Constance. The two of them were very close, so you had to be wary in her presence.

Lou had been told to wait in the library. The room was dark on this cloudy day and she switched on the lights as she went in. Vanessa and Justin, her brother and sister, were in the library already. Why hadn't they noticed how gloomy it was and turned on a light? Burgundy brocade curtains hung at the tall windows. On either side of the fireplace stood the vases which she'd loved when she was a small girl. In those days, they towered over her head. She'd thought they were beautiful, admiring their narrow necks, rounded middles and the mess of dragons, flowers and assorted chinoiserie painted all over them. Looking at them now, they struck her as verging on the hideous: too large, and impractical in every way. Justin turned to greet her with a smile.

'Oh, hello, Lou,' he said. 'I was just saying to Nessa that Constance hardly ever came in here, did she?' Justin was running his hands over the backs of the books without really looking at them. Lou loved the window seat in this room. Its cushions hadn't been re-covered since she was about ten. Sitting there as a child on rainy days, looking over the flowerbeds and then at the apple tree with a bench built round it near the back gate, and beyond that at the slopes of the South Downs, had made her feel as though she'd strayed into the opening pages of *Jane Eyre*. There was always a small slice of sky between the curve of the hill and the frame of the window, and clouds drifted across this luminous space, making pictures that she found entrancing.

'No,' Lou answered. 'She wasn't much of a reader, really.'

Nessa came over and peered at one of the shelves, her dark hair falling forward over her brow. She looked more ethereal than usual in grey jersey, with a filmy scarlet scarf round her neck. She was not exactly pretty but she was slim, and always beautifully dressed and elegant; she made Lou feel large and a little clumsy. Now she said, 'Where are Grandad's books? They used to be down here, didn't they?'

6

'Yes, next to the collected Dickens,' Lou answered. 'Aren't they there?'

'She must have given them away. Not that anyone read any of them, did they? Not now and not when he wrote them, poor old Grandad!' Nessa smiled. 'I think you were the only person who ever opened them since the day they were published. Putting him next to Dickens was wishful thinking on Constance's part.'

'I've got them all at home,' Lou said. What she didn't say was that she treasured them. John Barrington had left his own copies to her in his will and now, even though she hadn't yet read them properly, they reminded her of the hours and hours her grandfather had spent with her, talking about the sorts of things no one else seemed to be interested in: countries far away and times long gone and astonishing people. Stories and more stories. She remembered him reading parts of his first novel, *Blind Moon*, aloud to her when she was quite young. All she could bring to mind now was that it told the story of a young boy called Peter having adventures in a Japanese prison camp. There were other children shut up there with him and the book was about the hero and his gang and the narrow shaves they had with the guards. Most of all, she recalled the atmosphere of what Grandad had read to her: heat and darkness and the image of the moon, which frightened Peter because it seemed to be like the glowing, pale eye of a blind person looking down at them out of a black night sky.

Grandad had still been handsome even though he was old, and one of Lou's favourite pastimes had been looking with him at the albums full of images of someone tall and strong and young. She said, 'I expect Constance has binned the ones that used to be here.'

Justin laughed. 'She reckoned books were dust-collectors. That's what she told me. I'm surprised she kept the library as a library at all. She could have turned it into something else. I would have.'

Lou was shocked at this remark, but then she often found herself taken aback by some of the things Justin and Vanessa came out with. Perhaps that wasn't surprising, considering that they weren't related to her, not really. They were the children of her father's first wife, Ellie, by her first husband, who'd died very soon after Justin was born. Dad was Ellie's second husband, and all her life Lou had been taught to think of Justin and Vanessa – to behave towards them – as though they were her elder sister and brother, and as far as she was concerned, most of the time, that was what they were. They even shared her surname, because Dad had adopted them as soon as he married their mother. But Ellie had taken one look at Haywards Heath and the life she'd be living there and had immediately done two things. She'd had an affair with someone who lived in London and then run away with him, leaving Dad holding the babies, who hadn't been babies but children. He'd married Phyllida, Lou's mother, a few months after Ellie's departure and once she was old enough to know about such things, Lou had sometimes wondered whether help with the shouldering of the childcare burden was part of the attraction.

But no, she knew that wasn't fair to either of her parents. Mum wasn't glamorous like Ellie but she was kind and good-humoured, and even if no one would have called her beautiful, her face was one you were quite happy to look at and if she smiled at you, you couldn't help smiling in return. Lou was born a year after Mum and Dad married, when Nessa was ten and Justin six. Now here they were, the three of them, killing time, waiting to be summoned for the reading of Constance's will.

'You can come through now.' Matthew, Lou's father,

put his head round the door, looking flustered. They followed him across the hall to the drawing room, and Lou looked down at the beautiful Turkish carpet with its pattern of blue and red birds on a fawn background, flying with rectangular wings in and out of glorious, imaginary trees covered in strangely shaped leaves. There it lay on the parquet floor, looking just as it always had, welcoming every visitor to Milthorpe House.

How typical of Constance to have stage-managed this event, Lou thought as she looked around. Mum was being attentive to Dad as usual. She hadn't been too fond of Constance but would never have shown her true feelings. Lou felt most sorry for her father. He'd been completely devoted to his mother and it was clear he'd been crying, which wasn't like him at all. Poor Dad ... Lou had been surprised at how sad she, too, had felt at the graveside. It struck her, all at once, that this really *was* the very end of someone; of everything they'd been. However hard she tried, she couldn't believe in a life anywhere else. *Imagine there's no heaven* ... Lou had never thought there was one, even as a child. The tears that came to her eyes unbidden weren't about any residue of love for her grandmother, but to do with her regret that they hadn't been closer in life; hadn't managed to get over the jealousy, or resentment, or whatever it was Constance felt that had come between them.

The weather (grey, windy, with occasional gusts of horizontal drizzle) had seemed appropriate to the way everyone was feeling. Some of Constance's elderly friends were in black hats with veils. Gareth, Nessa's husband, looked uncomfortable in his dark suit, his round, cheerful face not suited to this setting. Dad had seemed in some strange way *absent* during the service and burial; preoccupied, as though his mind were on something else. Even though his hair had been grey for some years, he still looked young: tall and thin and with very blue eyes, now slightly red-rimmed, behind his glasses. This must be such a sad day for him. What had he been thinking of while his mother was being lowered into her grave?

Lou sat down in one of the armchairs and felt ashamed as she acknowledged that she was feeling calmer now; even beginning to enjoy herself a little. There was a kind of closure about all this, a putting away of a person's life, so to speak, and perhaps it was time for her to stop fretting about the bad relationship she'd had with Constance. If you looked at it in a positive frame of mind, the funeral meant a day off work, and a day and night away from childcare. Poppy was staying with Lou's friend Margie, who, poor thing, was in for something of a culture shock, not to mention probable sleep deprivation. You couldn't imagine a one-year-old, you had to experience her, Lou had told her, and Margie announced gamely that she was ready for anything. Lou smiled to herself. The only question was, would she be ready for a repeat performance? Most likely not, but you could always hope ... Lou would have died for her baby. She adored her beyond all reason and more than anyone else in the world, but how blissful it was to take a break from her for a few hours, even though she missed her.

It was good to be back here, too. Milthorpe House looked from the outside like one of the smaller hotels you saw as you drove here from Brighton, which was just a few miles away along the coast road. Someone had thought of adding turrets to the roof in several places. The front was cream stucco and there were balconies on those rooms that faced the sea. This was some way off, but still visible because the house was quite high up, built on a gentle slope that became the

South Downs once you'd left Barrington land. It wasn't really *Barrington*, Lou reminded herself. Constance had brought the money and the property to the marriage. Her father's family had owned Milthorpe for three generations. John Barrington was a provincial solicitor and Constance was rich and very beautiful and, true to form, she'd never let him forget how lucky he was; how much further up in the world he'd travelled simply by falling in love with her. Lou felt tears coming to her eyes. She still missed her grandfather, who'd loved her, and she'd never stopped loving him even though he'd been dead for more than two years.

'Louise, darling ... how lovely! Years since I've seen you! You've grown up surprisingly pretty!'

What was one meant to say to that? Ellie was well known for speaking before she thought, and even though her tone was quite friendly what Lou heard was *for someone who was such a plain child*! She stood up and kissed Ellie on both cheeks.

'And you look fantastic!'

That was true. It always had been true about Ellie. She had a flamboyant, exotic style that had seemed quite out of place in Haywards Heath, where Dad and Mum still lived. She was wearing a black velvet cloak over a short black satin dress, which caught the light and shone – rather inappropriately, Lou thought, for a sombre occasion. Her matching hat was wide-brimmed and covered in black feathers. It would have been ridiculous on anyone else, but Ellie, with her wide red mouth and dark eyes, looked terrific. One of Constance's memorable pronouncements was made about her first daughter-in-law: *She's a flamingo who wandered into an aviary full of nothing more exciting than sparrows and thrushes.*

Dear old Gran! Always ready with a neat belittling remark. And guess who the thrushes and sparrows were! The rest of the family, of course. Lou was the only person who'd ever called Constance Gran and she did it because she knew how much it irritated the old woman. The war between us, she thought, had been going on for so long. Am I sorry it's over? I suppose not, not really. But while Constance was alive, Lou had never shrunk from a fight, and she'd never changed her views, even though her father was obviously deeply unhappy that his darling daughter didn't get on with his mother.

The last time I saw Constance, Lou thought, I really let her have it, but she'd brought it on herself. It wasn't anything unusual. Lou had been asked down to Milthorpe to show Poppy off to her great-grandmother, and she'd been pleased to oblige. She'd thought the baby would offer some protection from Constance's sharp tongue, but not a bit of it. *I'd have thought that for the sake of the child, you'd have made peace with her father ... so important for a child to have a father ... grow up wild without one, you know ... Any possibility of a reconciliation? You're very young, you know ... How old are you? Only twenty-three? A mere infant yourself. You should grow up and realize that life can't be a bed of roses all the time, dear ...*

And I answered quite politely at first, too, Lou remembered. Tried to explain what it was like to live with being on guard all the time, every minute. What it was like to be always waiting for the next blow to fall, the next overwhelming fury that came out of nowhere and made straight for her. How she'd found she couldn't stay with him once she discovered she was pregnant. He was a man who didn't see anything wrong with using his fists when he felt like it, and no child of hers was going to be exposed to someone like that. But how hard it had been to leave him for ever, in spite of the way he behaved. How awful it was to live somewhere that was too small and where she also had to try and do her work. How sad it was to be alone, but frightened of meeting anyone new. How crippling it was to be anxious and panic-stricken at the very thought of someone kissing you. Above all, how daunting it was to be responsible for a vulnerable creature she barely understood. She'd tried to convey what her life was like, and then back Constance had come with *are you sure you hadn't done anything to provoke him, dear? Some men are very jealous at the thought of a child and we have to understand that, don't we?*

She'd lost it altogether at that point. Sobbed, yelled at Constance, called her names, told her she had as much understanding of anything as a shrivelled old onion and stormed out, banging the door behind her and shouting that Constance was wicked and had no feelings that a proper grandmother would have. She didn't regret making a scene. She should have told her grandmother years and years ago that she was on to her, that she realized Constance didn't love her; quite the reverse. Constance would have denied it, of course. She was good at lying and she'd have trotted out the blood-is-thicker-than-water clichés. But it was true. Constance hated Grandad and me being so close. She knew there was stuff we talked about that he wouldn't have discussed with anyone else, least of all with her. She was just plain jealous.

A man Lou didn't recognize came into the room, and Dad coughed to stop everyone talking. He was very pale and there was a tremor in his voice as he spoke.

'Everyone, this is Andrew Reynolds. He works for Reynolds and Johnson, solicitors. He's got something to say, I'm afraid.'

Afraid? What did that mean? Justin looked bemused. Lou saw Nessa glancing at him with the slightest shrug of her shoulders as if to say *I've no idea what this is about either*. The man, who was gingery and skinny, was holding a large folder. He coughed, clearly embarrassed, and his face went red.

'I was instructed by Constance Barrington shortly before she died to draw up a new will—'

'What on earth—?' Justin interrupted him and Lou saw her father put a hand on his arm to shut him up. Justin looked like someone from a Calvin Klein perfume ad and reckoned that, because of his appearance, he could do exactly what he wanted, when he wanted. He'd been like that ever since Lou could remember, relying on his charm and looks to achieve his ambitions. The strategy had seemed to be working quite well so far.

'I know Matthew' – Andrew Reynolds nodded at her father – 'is his mother's executor and had been in charge of her legal affairs. There is a will, dated May the eleventh, 2003, drawn up by him shortly after the death of Mrs Barrington's husband, John, but I was called in to see her only two weeks ago, very shortly before her unfortunate death.'

The silence was so thick you could almost feel it in the room. Lou wondered whether it was the waves of a still-stormy sea she could hear, or simply a roaring in her ears. Mr Reynolds went on, 'This document is very brief. There's a great deal of the usual thing – being of sound mind, making all other wills invalid, etc., etc., but the actual bequests are very swiftly dealt with. I'll read them at once.' He coughed. 'I took this down at Mrs Barrington's dictation, you understand. And the will is witnessed by the two nurses who were looking after Mrs Barrington at the time of her death:

'This is my last will and testament. The will I made when my husband died is superseded by this one. I

14

know what I'm doing and have not been influenced by anyone. This is what I wish to leave to my son and my grandchildren and others after my death. To my son, who owns his home outright and has control of the law firm Barrington and Son, I will not burden you with looking after a house you've never really liked and endless trouble with the taxman. Milthorpe House and the lands attached to it I am bequeathing to Justin Barrington, who is young enough to benefit from it for a very long time to come, even after taxes have been paid. To his sister, Vanessa née Barrington, now Williams, I leave half of my estate. The other half I leave to my only son, Matthew. This includes stocks, shares and so forth and I calculate that each of you will come away with a fairly substantial sum, again even allowing for the present crippling rates of taxation. To Eleanor della Costa, who has been like a daughter to me, I leave any of my clothes which take her fancy, and all my jewellery, which she has admired for years. She will wear it with style. To my granddaughter Louise, I leave the copyright in my late husband's books. To my daughter-in-law, Phyllida, I leave my collection of china and glass …'

Mr Reynolds went on speaking, but Lou heard nothing. The roaring in her ears had subsided. She was sharply aware, as one is in a dream, of everyone looking at her, staring at her. Nessa had a hand over her mouth. She would just be coming to terms with the fact that Justin had done much better out of this than she … no surprise there. Constance had been besotted with him since childhood. Justin was managing to look gleeful and horrified at the same time. Dad's face was chalk-white and Mum was holding his hand. Ellie's mouth was open. Lou thought: copyright in Grandad's books ... they'd been out of print for decades. They were worthless. Constance had disinherited her, and Lou could almost feel her grandmother's malevolent presence in the room. *I've won*, she'd be saying, from that special hell reserved for the unkind, the jealous, the unforgiving, the endlessly resentful. *I've punished you for years of not loving me. I've given everything to Ellie's children. She was closer to me than your father, or you, or anyone related to me by blood. Serves you right.*

When the solicitor left the room, after what seemed like a very long time, everyone started talking at once.

'I'll fight it, Lou,' her father said. 'She must have gone mad. I'm sure that ...'

'Oh, my poor child!' That was Ellie.

'I don't know what to say ...' Nessa sounded tearful.

Lou heard her mother's voice cutting through the babble.

'What's the matter with all of you? Don't you understand what's happened here? I don't believe it ... I simply cannot credit it ... It's monstrous. The copyright to books that have been out of print for years and that no one wanted to read when they were in print ... can you imagine a more worthless thing? It's deliberate. She's thought about this carefully. She's punishing my daughter from beyond the grave. It's a wicked thing to do! Quite wicked!'

And Lou watched as her mother, who almost never spoke her mind, who was terrified of making an exhibition of herself, burst into noisy tears and sank on to the sofa.

'Don't cry, Mum!' Lou ran to her side and put an arm around her shoulders. 'It doesn't matter.'

'But it does! It does matter. She's putting the knife

in from beyond the grave ... It's hateful and unkind. She's saying it loud and clear, Lou ... can't you hear? *You loved him while he was alive, didn't you? Well, here are his books and you're welcome to them. No one else wants them.*'

'Never mind, Mum. Honestly.' Lou stared at them, her family, all talking, all tut-tutting and shaking their heads. Suddenly, she had a longing to be somewhere else. To be with Poppy in the grotty flat. Anywhere but here, in Milthorpe House.

'I'm going home now, I think,' she told her mother. 'I'll see you soon.'

'Let me drive you to the station, darling.' Phyl wiped her eyes, and sat up straighter. She stood up and gave Lou her hand. For the first time that day, Lou felt as though she wanted to lie down and cry for ever. She nodded, unable to say a word.

'I thought you might need cheering up, that's all,' said Ellie, sitting down at the kitchen table. 'You stormed out of the drawing room looking like thunder. Anyone could see you were about to explode or something.'

Nessa went on washing up, taking care to rinse every single plate and cup and teaspoon in hot water. It never failed to amaze her how quickly the dishes mounted up whenever more than two people got together. Who'd used all this stuff? And when? She didn't bother to turn round to face her mother.

'I don't need cheering up. It's too late for anger.'

'Doesn't stop you from feeling like hell, though, does it?'

Nessa decided that how she felt was none of her mother's business. She'd forfeited the right to be involved when she'd handed over responsibility for her children to a husband she'd tired of almost before the honeymoon was over, and then later to his boring new wife. Nessa made an effort not to think along these particular lines now. It wasn't an appropriate time to go into every single grudge she held against Ellie. There were many of them and just at this moment Nessa was too furious with Constance to be able to attend properly to her mother's failings. And she could certainly do without this belated effort at cheering her up. She changed the subject, 'This is the only house I know which doesn't have a dishwasher. It's quite relaxing really, all these suds and hot water.'

'You don't look relaxed, darling. I can see the knots of tension in your neck from here.'

'It's Justin's neck you ought to worry about. I could strangle him.' Why am I saying this? Nessa asked herself. I don't want to sound off to Ellie. God, I wish Mickey was here. She ought to have come to the funeral with me instead of Gareth.

Michaela Crawford was her best friend. They'd met ten years ago when Mickey was working for the florist who dealt with Nessa and Gareth's wedding. In those days, Nessa worked part-time in a bank and was going mad with boredom. When Mickey confided her ambition to start a business selling artificial flowers, it was Nessa who suggested that she might be able to help with the business side of things. Together they set up a company called Paper Roses, which had been a bit of a struggle at first but was doing very well now. They provided artificial flowers of every variety for businesses, for town dwellers who didn't have a garden, and for anyone who loved flowers but didn't have the money to keep forking out for fresh ones. She was the business expert and Mickey the creative brain, and for the last five years Nessa had known that there was someone in her corner. Someone who'd support her whatever she did. Gareth was always, typically, mouthing off about Mickey's lesbianism, but Nessa couldn't have cared less about that. She'd never talked to Mickey about her sex life. Her friend never discussed it and Nessa would have died rather than ask about it. Mickey's lover, Dee, used to live with her in the small and pretty house outside Haywards Heath which was also the Paper Roses HQ, but Dee had gone off with a Jamaican bikini designer and, for a while, Mickey was heartbroken. Nessa consoled her as best she could, but privately thought she'd had a narrow escape. Dee had always struck her as frivolous and selfish, happy to live off Mickey without contributing too much to the relationship. It didn't surprise Nessa in the least to discover that Dee was unfaithful: she'd even flirted with her a couple of times, and she was married. Good riddance to her, Nessa had thought.

Ellie had fallen silent. She screwed a cigarette into a long, black holder and lit it. Was it worth telling her to go outside? Probably not. As Nessa thought of Gareth, a vision of his round pink face and chubby hands came into her mind and produced a wave of irritation. Even here in the kitchen, she thought, she could hear his voice booming away in the drawing room. What was the matter with her? What kind of wife was she? Gareth was cheerful. Pleasant. When they'd first met, she'd loved his jolliness, his bluff, ex-rugby player's easy manners. She had fancied him rotten then and he was good company: generous and outgoing. He worked for an insurance company, and although Nessa was never quite sure what it was he actually did, he was obviously quite successful at it. Now he was stockier and a lot less fun. She couldn't really pin down what it was that annoyed her lately whenever she looked at her husband, but she was painfully aware that her misgivings were making sex – okay, not awful, but a hell of a lot less enjoyable than it used to be. She simply didn't find him as attractive as she once had. Perhaps that was normal when you'd been married for ten years. And there was Tamsin. She would always be grateful to Gareth for their daughter, whom she loved more than anything else in the world. The way she felt about Tamsin from the moment she was born made it even harder for Nessa to understand Ellie's lackadaisical attitude to her and Justin.

She thought, blushing and hoping that her mother couldn't see her, of the fantasies she'd trained herself to conjure up the moment she felt Gareth's hand slide over to her side of the bed and rest on her thigh. Nowadays, when he touched her, she closed her eyes and summoned up stuff she tried hard to keep out of her head once daylight came. Things which ... Never mind. Just the memory of them made her shiver a little with remembered pleasure. Nessa shook herself to clear her head.

Concentrate on Justin, she told herself. That was what was making her angry. She said to Ellie, 'Why the hell didn't Constance sell the property and divide the proceeds? Why on earth should Justin get all this?' She waved a hand in the air to indicate Milthorpe House and everything that went with it.

'You heard that ginger lawyer. She thought, quite rightly, that you were taken care of already. You've got a husband who makes lots of money, a super house, a business which is doing better and better. What more could you possibly want? You'd never live here, would you? Count yourself lucky to be getting half the estate. It'll be a lot of money, you know. Much more than most people see in a lifetime.'

'That's beside the point!' Nessa was almost crying at the injustice of it. 'Just because Justin hasn't done anything with his life and is wasting his days show-ing people round grotty flats he gets rewarded with a property that must be worth over two million. Not fair. I hate things that aren't fair.'

'Oh, God, Nessa, you're always so hard done by!' Ellie laughed and leaned back in the kitchen chair.

'I *am* fucking hard done by—'

'Language, darling!'

'... and I always have been. First of all, my mother ups and dumps me with a husband she's obviously totally bored with – and then his wife. What on earth possessed you, Ellie? I can't even call you Mummy, can I? You've never been a mother. Not to me and not to Justin either. And just think: we always called Phyl and Matt by their names and not Mummy and Daddy. From the very beginning, because Matt felt we should remember our real parents, at least notionally. What that means is I've never had anyone I can call Mummy. Or Daddy.'

'Well, heavens, Nessa, I'm sorry really, but change the record, sweetheart. We've been through this before, haven't we? Don't you think it's time to let it drop? I wasn't cut out to be a mother, that's all. I don't *do* little kids – you're okay now of course. You've turned out very pretty and I'm proud of how well you've managed with Paper Roses and so on, but back then, well – I won't hide it from you, there's no point – I couldn't wait to leave. In spite of Constance loving me like a daughter, and in spite of Matt's devotion, before he realized my attention was fixed on something else. Paolo was a ticket out, that's all.'

'And Constance was there to pick up the pieces. D'you know, I think you were the only person she really, really loved. I've often wondered why that should be, but she was a law unto herself, right? Maybe she'd been disappointed in Matt for some reason, I don't know. But she saw her chance with us. I reckon she encouraged you to go off with Paolo because she wanted total control of me and Justin. She wanted *us* to be her children. Partly because we were yours and she loved you but partly because, well, she seemed to like us, in those days anyway. You were too old. She could start over with us.'

'She adored you and Justin. She told me so often. I was quite happy about leaving you because I knew, I just knew, that she'd look after you and make sure Phyl and Matt didn't squash the life out of you.'

Nessa said nothing. It was true that her grandmother had taken good care of them both, her and Justin. They'd never wanted for a single thing, but at nine years old, she'd felt unloved, and still did sometimes. Her mother had chosen to go and leave her behind, so it followed, didn't it (that was the way the young Nessa had explained it to herself), that she wasn't really lovable. Nothing anyone had said or done in the years since then had altered this view; not really, not deep down. Deep down she wasn't worth loving. She wasn't worth staying with, and she worried often about what would happen if her world were to be blown apart by something. She was aware, more than anyone she'd ever met, and much more than Justin, of the precariousness of everything; the fragility of so much that most people thought of as solid and fixed. She'd tried to discuss this with Gareth early in their relationship, but he was almost allergic to any kind of serious talk and had seemed so genuinely puzzled when she'd brought the subject up that she'd dropped it at once.

One day, when the business had started to do well, when things seemed to be on the up and up, she'd asked Mickey a question out of the blue. They'd been sitting at the twin desks that took up most of the space in Mickey's study and Nessa had suddenly said, 'What if we lose all this, Mickey? What if we fail?'

Mickey had looked up, surprised. 'We'll manage,' she said. 'We'll recoup what we can and think of something else to sell. Don't worry, folk are forever needing things, aren't they? We'll work out what and give it to them. Now, stop fretting and get on to Prague and see what they're doing about the silk orchids. Should have been here two weeks ago.'

'And do you think it's okay to call the business Paper Roses when so much of our stuff isn't made of paper at all?'

'It's fine – it's a song title, for goodness' sake – everyone knows that. And we're famous for the paper range anyway, aren't we? *Prettiest paper flowers in the world* ... Look, it says so, right here in this catalogue! Relax, why don't you? I know you find it hard.'

Nessa took a tea towel from the drawer and began drying the spoons and putting them away. She wondered what Mickey would say about this will and its implications.

'I'll talk to Justin,' said Ellie.

'It won't do any good. He won't let this slip out of his grasp. He's been after it for years. You've been abroad, you don't know how he's been sucking up to Constance in the last couple of years. He practically lived here. She had him running errands for her all over the place. And they were quite sickening together – darling this and sweetie that and forever kissing her and saying how beautiful she was still – that kind of thing. And, naturally, Constance saying he was beautiful too. It made me sick to my stomach listening to them sometimes.'

'Aaah!' Ellie stabbed the air with her cigarette. 'That's it. He knows how to talk to women. You have no idea, darling, how important it is to be told over and over again how beautiful one is. And you have to admit Justin *is* rather gorgeous. Though I'm probably not the one to be saying so, he takes after me.'

'And I take after the person who was your husband so long ago you've practically forgotten his name.'

Tears sprang into Nessa's eyes. Her father had never been around much even when he was married to Ellie, and his early death from a fever caught in Kenya on a business trip meant that he disappeared from his children's lives when they were both very young. No one ever asked children anything. No one consulted her and Justin about being adopted by Matt and Phyl. Even though they called their new parents by their first names, they had both taken on the Barrington surname. As it happened, Ellie's first husband's name had been Connor, which was okay but not something whose loss one would actually mourn. Unless it was yours, of course, Nessa thought, remembering how long it took her to get used to the change. Justin had loved Barrington from the very beginning. He said, 'It's long. Long names are better than short names, aren't they?' No one contradicted him.

'Pat Connor. You can thank him at least for your lovely colouring, dear. Black hair, white skin, green eyes. A proper Colleen.'

But not gorgeous, just about okay. A bit too thin, no tits to speak of, good hair. That's it. Justin, on the other hand, has people staring after him in the street and has done since childhood.

Ellie went on, 'You're a lot prettier than Louise, even though she's improved a great deal. She's a bit too big, isn't she? Not fat, not at all any longer ... but a bit too tall for a woman and well built.'

When Louise was born, Nessa had just celebrated her tenth birthday. She'd loved the baby, and her best memories of childhood were looking after Lou. That didn't last long. The moment Lou could walk, as soon as she began to speak, everything changed. She quite soon became a burden, trying to follow Nessa and her friends everywhere, wanting to join in with their games, and crying as though she were being murdered when she was denied anything. A bloody nuisance. And how many hours of unpaid babysitting did Phyl get out of me when I was a teenager? Nessa reflected. She couldn't help feeling she was owed something for those times when she'd had to stay home and take care of Lou and Justin while her friends were busy somewhere else, doing something a whole lot more interesting than gazing at the telly.

'You know your trouble, darling?'

'You're going to tell me, I'm quite sure.' Nessa sighed and sat down facing her mother.

'You often think other people are getting more than you are. That you're missing out somehow. You always have, whether there was reason to or not.'

'There usually was. I feel ...' She sighed again. Ellie wouldn't understand. Nessa felt that a lot of things were simply unfair. She believed that other people had things better than she did. She was aware of how child-ish this was, knew that if she confessed to this envy, told Gareth about it for instance, he'd look at her in astonishment, so she said nothing. Sometimes she felt guilty about her behaviour. She knew she ought to try to control herself; not give everyone such a hard time so frequently, but it was difficult to change habits like this when it came to members of her own family.

'You're a great deal better off than Louise,' Ellie said, standing up and moving to the door. 'Think of other people for a change.'

'Ellie?' Nessa called after her. Her mother turned round, looking a bit uncertain about whether she ought to come into the kitchen again or not.

'What is it?'

'I've just thought. Maybe you could speak to Matt? Prepare the ground for me? I want to ask him about the possibility of contesting the will.'

'He'll say you shouldn't. I promise you, that's what he'll say, even though he's angrier than you are, because of Lou being cut out like that. And why d'you think he'll listen to me?'

'I just think he would, that's all.' Nessa remembered the months after her mother's abrupt departure. It seemed to her then that her stepfather hadn't been very happy with what was going on, in spite of getting married to Phyl and even after a baby was on the way. He'd always, she reckoned, had a soft spot for her mother and probably still thought of her fondly. It wouldn't hurt for Ellie to sound him out.

'I think you owe it to me,' Nessa said.

'Oh, God, if you're going to be injured all over the place, I'll have a word with him. I'm not going to his office, though. Nor his house. He'll have to come and meet me.'

'Ask him, then. See what he says. Bet you he'll jump at the chance to escape the clutches of the NWS.'

'Which is?'

Nessa laughed. 'The Non-Wicked Stepmother. That's what Justin and I used to call her sometimes when we were kids. She went to such lengths to be nice to us, it was quite unnatural. And we never did think of her as a mother. Constance was more like a mother than she was, whatever she did.'

'Constance was always a hard act to follow, and I don't know whether I'd have been as tolerant as Phyl was with you.'

'You certainly wouldn't. But thanks, Ellie, I'd be so grateful. Honestly.'

'I'll fix up something.' She left the room again, leaving the door wide open behind her.

Nessa laughed aloud. What a nerve! If ever anyone had gone through life thinking about precisely no one but herself, it was Ellie. Still, she did say she'd speak to Matt and she was right about poor old Lou. What a slap in the face for her! Nessa decided to phone her sister and commiserate. And of course they could bitch about Justin. It was many years now since they'd lived under one roof and, while Lou wasn't her best buddy or anything, Nessa had given her more squished-up baby meals than she cared to count and sung her more lullabies than anyone else except Phyl – that had to mean something, even though they'd hardly seen one another in the last couple of years. Nessa had been too busy setting up Paper Roses to get involved in the family drama surrounding Ray the Abuser, which was how she thought of him, a bit like Vlad the Impaler. Naturally she'd heard all about it from Phyl, whose anguish for Louise and for Poppy, her beloved grandchild, was natural and commendable but meant she didn't have much time or energy left over to enthuse over Nessa's new business.

Nessa sighed. Fair enough, she told herself. And ultra-bad luck on poor Lou, falling for a bastard half-way through her second year at university. A waste of her brains, too, working part-time for that obscure film company for a pittance. Fleetingly, she wondered whether there might be a time when Lou might work for her. Not now, but when Paper Roses had expanded into more than a mail-order business and she took on a shop somewhere ... No, that was mad. Louise wouldn't see the point of the product she'd have to sell. She'll be on her way back to Phyl's now, Nessa thought. Or maybe back to London. Do I even have her mobile number? I don't think so. She stood up. I'm useless, she told herself. I'll go and ask Matt. I'll phone her.

Lou let herself into the flat, closed the door behind her and leaned against it. She'd lied when her mother urged her to stay the night with them, to take some days off work, even volunteering to go up to London the next day and bring Poppy back with her. Phyl would have done anything to keep her daughter near her at a time like this, needing to be cared for, looked after, cherished. As it was, Lou had to promise to go back the following weekend. Phyl announced that she was inviting everyone to dinner. They had to talk, they all had to *discuss* the will and its implications. Lou didn't see the point of that, but agreeing to come down to Haywards Heath very soon had allowed her to escape now, when she wanted so desperately to be alone. She'd put on a much braver face than she thought she was capable of and promised her mother that she'd go straight from the station to Margie's house. No way, she'd told her, will I be on my own. Promise.

She'd known she was lying even as she spoke. She had no intention of telling Margie where she was. Let her look after Poppy for the night as they'd arranged. Lou wanted the time to think about what had happened at Milthorpe House.

She went into the tiny kitchen – okay, kitchenette – switched on the kettle and stared out at the night. What she saw was other people's windows: some lit up, some in darkness, curtained and uncurtained, revealing, concealing, enticing. Lou loved the view, even though Mum shuddered every time she came here, which was as seldom as possible. It was thanks to Dad and Mum that this place now resembled something like a habitable space.

Lou insisted on thinking of it as 'the flat'. More like a shoe box, with its one bedsitting room, a teeny second room which was Poppy's bedroom, and a bathroom and kitchen that looked like something from a doll's house. The street wasn't up to much either. When Dad and Mum came to see it, there had been a mattress in the front garden of one of the houses across the street and she could feel her mother shuddering and making a noble effort to say nothing. The wallpaper was grim, there was no washing machine and nowhere to dry clothes.

'You can't live here with a small baby,' Mum had cried.

'Of course I can. Lots of people live in places that are far worse,' Lou said. 'I'll be fine.'

'You *will* be fine,' Dad announced, 'but only because we'll fix it up and make it okay. We'll get it painted, and put in a washing machine and hang some decent curtains and you'll be all right here, for a while anyway.'

In the end, she'd done all the decorating, with Margie's help, and money had done the rest. Lou sighed. Money. Mum and Dad had always helped her, so how real was the narrative she'd made for herself of how she was managing on her own, being independent, doing her own thing? How could she justify working three days a week and paying someone else to look after Poppy while she struggled along reading scripts for Cinnamon Hill Productions and reporting on them for £50 a throw? By allowing her parents to help her. They paid for all the extra things that she would never have been able to afford, most importantly, Poppy's nursery fees, but Lou paid the rent and bought the food. She glanced at the small pile of papers on the left-hand side of her desk and reflected that she could certainly get more money as a temp, but she liked her work, she liked being involved with movies, even down among the helots, and felt, maybe wrongly, that it gave her at least a tiny chance of making her dreams come true.

She'd told no one about these, though her parents, if they'd thought about it for ten seconds, would have realized that their daughter might have had ambitions to be something other than a part-time script reader for a small film company. Didn't they remember all those exercise books she'd filled with stories, poems, sketches and, above all, plays when she was a child? Didn't they know how much she'd always adored the movies? Had they forgotten how she and Grandad used to spend hours and hours on the sofa at Milthorpe House gazing at flickery black and white films in the afternoon? Evidently her parents hadn't put two and two together. What she wanted more than anything else was to write screenplays. She'd never told anyone but Grandad about this. He'd understood. He knew what it would be like to see her words spoken by actors, her ideas made visible on the screen, reaching out across the dark to everyone watching and lodging in their minds the way the films she'd seen as a kid were still within her, part of her mental furniture.

Constance's voice rang in her imagination: *You haven't got time for silly dreams. You shouldn't have had a child if you didn't intend to look after her. No one forced you to do that. You have a duty to look after your daughter and not farm her out to someone else. How do you know you won't scar her for life if you leave her with other people during her infancy?* Lou blinked and made an effort not to think about her grandmother, but that was impossible.

Earlier, she'd felt frozen. All the way back to London on the train, she couldn't get her head round what had happened at Milthorpe. Her thoughts seemed to come up against a wall of ice and fall away to nothing. Now, Lou noticed that she'd spilled a little tea on the table. She dipped her finger into the liquid and traced a pattern with her finger on the yellow Formica. That'll have to go soon, she thought, I can't live with that colour much longer. She took a deep breath and considered what Constance had done.

She's disinherited me, Lou thought, and the word with its echoes of Victorian novels frightened her a little. It was a final word, a harsh one. It meant – what did it mean? That Constance didn't just not get on with me, that she didn't just like or love me less than Nessa and Justin, but that she hated me. It wouldn't have been enough for her to give me less, she had to give me something which everyone could see she thought was rubbish and which would tell them that I was less than nothing in her eyes. Not even as much as Mum, whom she'd never liked and who'd got fobbed off with glass and china when Ellie had walked away with an armful of jewellery worth a fortune. She's punishing me, Lou decided.

What about Milthorpe House? Did she care about the house? Beyond its financial worth, what did it really mean to her? Apart from the insult, would not setting foot there ever again truly matter? Lou had never considered what would happen to the house when her grandparents were dead. You couldn't imagine Constance not being there, and now that she was gone Lou realized that the place she carried always in her mind was more important than the bricks and mortar; more important than the garden and the land surrounding the property.

The best days of her childhood were spent there, but all the best memories were of her grandfather and no spiteful bequests could take them away. Grandad was always in the hall to meet her when Dad drove her up there for the day, or to stay overnight. Fresh flowers everywhere meant that the hall was filled with fragrance. Constance saw to that, making sure that Alfie, the gardener, and his son, Derek, kept everything up to scratch so that she could fill the vases with whatever was in season. The roses were best of all: *your grandmother's pride and joy*, Grandad called them.

The best room in the house was Grandad's study.

'What on earth do you find to do up there?' Constance often asked, and Grandad would say, 'All sorts of things, darling. Isn't that right, Lou?'

She'd nodded, and once or twice she'd noticed Constance's lips tightening in disapproval. Sometimes she gave a not-quite-silent sigh. She was, Lou understood now, jealous. How astonishing! Grandad worshipped his wife. He was in awe of her. The story about how he was struck dumb by her beauty when he first saw her (*He just stood there staring at me with his eyes popping out of his head and blushing like a rose*) were common family currency. As was the tale of how Constance fell in love with him too, so completely that she didn't listen to anyone who advised her against this hasty match, but married him in spite of her family's disapproval. She told his part of the story now as though she'd made a mistake; as though her life would have been different and better if she'd heeded her parents' wishes.

By the time Lou knew Constance, she was the one who ruled the house and Grandad did exactly what she told him to in almost every department of their lives. She was the one who decided who to invite to dinner. She saw to the organization of everything in the house, even overseeing the post each day, making sure Grandad had given her all the letters he wanted to post and also going over anything that arrived at Milthorpe House. She used to sit at the table in the dining room before Grandad came down to breakfast and sort the mail into two piles: one for him and one

32

for herself. Then there were the things she tore up. Lou was shocked when she saw it happening for the first time.

'Why are you tearing those letters up, Granny?' she'd asked.

'Please call me Constance, dear ... I do hate *Granny*.'

'Sorry,' Lou apologized, not feeling a bit sorry. She'd overheard her own mother calling this hatred of any variation on Granny 'an affectation' and while she had no idea what one of those was, she thought it couldn't be very nice and so decided to agree with her mother. 'But why are you?'

'They're not proper letters,' Constance explained. 'They're – well, they're rubbish, really. You'd think people would have better things to do.'

Lou had believed Constance then, but realized now that the things she'd been destroying were most probably Grandad's. She'd never tear up a message addressed to herself. What could they have been? God, what a bloody cheek that woman had, she thought. How did she dare tear up someone else's letters?

Lou recalled the roll-top desk in Grandad's study. Constance got rid of that as soon as he died. I'd have liked that desk, Lou reflected, but no one consulted me. Briefly she wondered who had it now. The desk had pigeon-holes filled with pieces of paper, quite neatly arranged. Lou never saw her grandfather writing anything. He usually sat in the armchair under the window. This was covered in faded gold-coloured velvet, and even when he wasn't in it, the cushions held his shape. She used to sit on the big hard chair at his desk and they chatted about everything. She would moan to him about her parents, about Nessa and Justin, about school teachers and school friends – she told him everything. He gave her books to read: Hans

Andersen's fairy tales, *Alice in Wonderland*, *What Katy Did* ... all sorts of things. He introduced her to Shakespeare, helping her when they started reading *A Midsummer Night's Dream* at school, showing her how scary and terrific *Macbeth* was by acting out some of the best scenes with her. What fun it was being all three witches and Lady Macbeth as well! He read her bits and pieces that he thought might amuse her from the newspaper and, towards the end of his life when his eyesight had faded a little, she returned the favour and read him book reviews and leaders, and news stories which generally made him harrumph and sigh and close his eyes. Occasionally, she asked him things. He wasn't as voluble then. It was as though, Lou thought now, he was trying to forget about his childhood. He was, for instance, vague about his mother.

'Do you mean Rosemary,' he asked, 'or my real mother?'

Lou had never met her father's grandmother, Rosemary, but she'd seen pictures of her in the family albums: a stout, square woman with tightly permed white hair, wearing a twin-set and pearls.

'Wasn't Granny Rosemary your real mother?'

Grandad smiled. 'Well, she was. To all intents and purposes.'

'What does that mean?' Lou wanted to know.

'I was very young when my real mother died.'

'What was her name? Your real mother?'

This was a ritual they often went through. Lou knew what her grandfather's mother was called, but he smiled and answered her once more. 'She was called Louise. You're named after her. You know that very well.'

'But she died. What happened to you then, Grandad?'

34

'I was fortunate. Rosemary – well, she adopted me and brought me to England with her.'

'Didn't you have a dad?'

'He died. This was during the war, you know. The Second World War. An awful lot of people didn't survive. Rosemary's husband died too, and she married again after we arrived in England. A lawyer called Frederick Barrington. He was my stepfather and I went to work for him straight from school.'

'But what about your real mother? Can you really not remember her?'

'No, I do remember certain things about her, of course. She was French, though you'd never have known it, and she never spoke about her childhood, as I recall. We spoke English at home. If she had a foreign accent, I didn't notice it. She was very pretty. Her hair was like – well, like gold.'

Grandad must have had tears in his eyes, Lou thought. I didn't realize what they were because he took out a hankie and wiped his eyes and he did that a lot, for all sorts of reasons. I never asked him her surname, she thought. He must have changed the subject. Dad will know what happened to her; how she died and what her name was. I'll ask him. How awful if she were totally forgotten!

Lou found that she was crying and she wasn't sure who exactly the tears were for. Perhaps, she thought, they're for me, because I feel hurt at what Constance has done. I can see now how much she must have disliked me.

Stop crying, she told herself. Pull yourself together. She was a wicked old woman who never got over the fact that I loved Grandad and was rude to her as a child. She's never forgiven me for that night. Anyone else would have put it down as a childish tantrum, but not her, oh, no. Lou could see that this one occasion, more than fifteen years ago, had marked their relationship for ever and that Constance had made up her mind that night and never changed her opinion.

Nessa and Justin hadn't been at home. Nessa was at university in Bristol and Justin still at his expensive boarding school, paid for by Constance of course. Mum and Dad needed to be somewhere or other and Lou was sent to stay at Milthorpe House for a few days. She could still remember packing her little case; how happy she'd been to think that for once she'd be the one who was going to be fussed over. Justin was an attention-magnet and when he was there, Constance circled him as if he were a candle and she a dizzy moth. It didn't matter to Lou because Grandad was always happy to talk to her. Constance, on the other hand, usually reduced her to a sullen silence within minutes. She wasn't what Lou thought a granny should be. She was too well dressed, too pretty, even though she was quite old. You couldn't imagine cuddling her. She made Lou feel large and clumsy and hideous and tongue-tied.

On the first night of that visit, she waited in bed for Grandad to come and kiss her goodnight. When her grandmother came instead, Lou was astonished to see her. Constance sat down on the end of the bed and said, 'Are you ready to go to sleep, dear? I've come to tuck you up and kiss you goodnight.'

'I want Grandad,' Lou had said.

'Well, you've got me.' Constance smiled. 'So sorry.'

Lou recalled in every detail the ferocity of the tantrum that followed. She'd screamed and yelled and shouted that she wouldn't go to sleep ever, ever if Constance kissed her and why didn't she go away and never come back and she wanted her grandad and wouldn't go to sleep till he came – on and on, beating her pillow with her fists, and sobbing and ending up with the child's litany of *I hate you I hate you I hate you*.

Constance had left the room of course, but not before she'd stood up and looked down at Lou.

'The feeling,' she'd said, her voice full of contempt, her eyes freezing blue, 'is entirely mutual.'

Then she'd left the room and Lou had stopped crying in the end. Grandad never did come upstairs to see her that night. Next day, he'd advised Lou to apologise to her grandmother.

'She's good at bearing grudges, Lou,' he'd told her. 'Better all round to do what's needed to keep the peace. Go on, tell her you're sorry.'

Lou went. She never told Grandad what Constance had said the previous night. When she'd said it, Lou hadn't quite understood it, but she thought about it afterwards and realized that it was her grandmother's version of *and I hate you too, so there*, but put in a more grown-up way. I don't expect she really meant it, Lou told herself as she went to find Constance. No one hates their grandchild, do they?

She'd had to ask Miss Hardy, the housekeeper, where her grandmother was and she could tell by the way Miss Hardy's words came out of her mouth that she'd already been told all about last night. The housekeeper had pink cheeks and looked a little like a rabbit with sticky-out teeth and white hair. Even though she smiled a lot, her smile never reached her eyes, which were like small chips of ice: very pale blue and chilly.

'She's in the garden,' Miss Hardy said and this time her smile was absent.

Lou had gone out of the French windows and saw her grandmother sitting on a white wrought-iron chair, at a white wrought-iron table, wearing a big sunhat. She took a deep breath to give herself courage and walked towards her. The sunhat threw a shadow over Constance's face.

'I'm sorry for what I said,' Lou told her.

'Indeed,' Constance said, and Lou stared at the curly pattern of the table, like a vine or a plant of some kind. 'Well, I have to accept your apology, I suppose.'

'Then we're friends again?' Lou asked.

'We'll see,' Constance replied. 'It depends very much on you, I'd have thought.'

And that was that. Life went on, Lou reflected now, but she never did really accept my apology then and she's still punishing me now. She could see that I'd meant what I said, and that I didn't really take it back.

And did I hate her? Probably not, till now, maybe. I was scared of her, I didn't like her much. I thought she was bossy and domineering. I thought it was disgraceful that she loved Ellie better than her own son and took her side when she walked out on Dad. If anyone had asked her, Lou would have said she didn't get on with her grandmother. Nothing serious. Every family had strained relationships here and there – you couldn't love everyone equally – but hatred? She'd never felt that before. She wasn't even sure if what she was feeling now could be called *hatred*. How would she recognize such an emotion? It wasn't one she'd felt very often. She avoided anyone she didn't get on with and that was that. Hatred was close to love. You had to be a little obsessional to indulge in it. She hated and feared Ray, but that was only because she'd loved him so much to begin with. As she'd never loved Constance properly, she wasn't up to hating her exactly, even now.

What she felt was saddened, depressed, and also a little ashamed that her whole family would now understand something she'd tried to hide. Would Nessa and

Justin feel sorry for her? Think she'd brought it on herself? Offer to help her? No, that wouldn't happen. Justin didn't care enough and Nessa would be so pissed off that her brother had got the house and land that she wouldn't have the energy to think about Lou's problems too much. There was ten years between them, and Nessa had always been a little – what was the right word? Distant? Uninvolved? In any case, not interested. Dad was furious. She'd have to stop him trying to do anything about it. She couldn't think how to manage that, or how to keep Mum from swooping down and swallowing her and Poppy up and taking them back to Haywards Heath. She wanted, above all, not to have that happen. Not to become the daughter who couldn't cope, the one who'd been abandoned by her partner because even though there was talk of domestic violence *you had to see both sides and there was no smoke without fire*. That's what Constance would have said. The bitch. The vindictive old crone. Fuck her.

'Fuck you!' Lou shouted at the walls and felt only a tiny bit better afterwards. She rested her head on her hands and let the tears run through her fingers. Oh, God, she thought, I must stop. I can't do this. I won't be able to see tomorrow. Poppy – I have to be in a calmer state to look after Poppy.

Lou sniffed and tore off a piece of kitchen towel and blew her nose. It had only just occurred to her that her grandmother's bequest was a double whammy. She'd ensured that Lou got nothing, but to do that she had to proclaim to the whole family that she thought her late husband's work was worthless. Nothing. Nothing anyone would ever want. That dealt with his memory too, just in case there was anyone around who might still be inclined to admire him.

But I do, Lou thought. I always have and I always

will. As a child, she'd been impressed and awed by the books he'd shown her. She knew every one of the covers so well that she could have drawn any of them by heart. They came from a time when novels had dust-jackets showing repeating patterns, sort of lime green or pale orange or pale blue on white, with an oval shape left blank for the title and author's name to appear in an attractive font. The first of his five novels was *Blind Moon*, and that was the one he'd read out loud from to Lou – the one she remembered a little, though the details had disappeared from her mind entirely. As for Grandad's other four books, she'd never read them and knew very little about them. She went to the shelf where the Barrington books stood together, took out *Blind Moon* and read the first few words again:

> *Now he could tell the whole story. He could speak about what happened during their time in the camp; in the bamboo-gated prison overshadowed by the blue mountain, under the eye of a moon that looked at everything and saw nothing; like a blind, white eye gazing down at them all.*

Lou closed the book. At first, it had seemed quite different from how she remembered it. She couldn't find, at least in the first few pages, any passages she remembered. Grandad must have chosen particular bits to read aloud to a child and much of what she'd glanced at didn't look suitable. It would probably, she realized, be a harrowing tale. She would read it carefully now, from cover to cover.

She looked at the dust-jacket. The reddish-brown pattern of palm leaves showed that it was mainly set in foreign parts. The pages felt brittle and dry and the edges of each one had been stained yellowish-brown from years and years of the smoke from Grandad's cigarettes. She leaned closer to the book and breathed in the fragrance of ancient tobacco. Then she read the dedication (*To my mother*) and the blurb. There were several old cuttings from newspapers, carefully folded and placed in the back of the book. I'll read those in a minute, she thought. And I'll read this properly. That'll show Constance. Then I'll go on to his next and then the others. I'll read every word. They're mine now. I own them.

The thin shrilling of her mobile sounded very loud in the empty flat. Lou reached for her handbag and found the phone. She glanced at the number displayed on the little screen. It was Nessa, who scarcely ever rang her. What on earth could she want now, only hours after they'd been together in Milthorpe House?

'Hi, Nessa,' she said. 'What's up?'

2

Matt was driving to Brighton to meet Ellie. He'd been surprised to get a phone call from her in the office a couple of days after the funeral, asking whether she might discuss something with him. He could guess what that was, of course. Nessa had probably got to her and asked her about the will and whether there was any prospect of challenging it. It saddened him that Ellie's daughter hadn't wanted to come straight to him. He'd always felt like a real father to her, and whenever it suited her, Nessa took advantage of his devotion. He liked to think he'd helped her and Michaela a great deal when they set up their business, and Nessa was grateful for that, he knew. But there was something she always held in reserve, feelings that she would have lavished on a real father and which she kept from him. Still, for most of their childhood, hers and Justin's, he'd been the Good Cop to Phyl's Bad Cop. She had been the one to see to all the day-to-day things that seemed to cause an enormous amount of friction and argument. Phyl had stood firm while Nessa's rage at her own mother's defection crashed against her.

Phyl, poor thing, had also been second-best to Constance. Ellie's children adored their step-grandmother, and whenever things were difficult Nessa had even articulated this by saying: *I don't see why we can't be adopted by Granny Constance. She'd love to be our mother. Why can't she?* Phyl had explained that Granny Constance was too old to take care of children at her age. This story didn't cut much ice with Nessa and was contradicted by the fact that his mother so often had Nessa and Justin to stay at Milthorpe and devoted so much time and attention to them. She loved them both but Justin was always her pet.

Poor old Phyl. As he parked the car, the image of his wife, standing at the front window of their house and staring after him, came into his mind. She was so good, so kind, so eager to take care of anyone who needed taking care of that she'd never once complained about the burden of being a mother to Ellie's offspring. Maybe she resented it inwardly, but she'd never said a word to him and he'd tried hard to share the weight of responsibility even though she'd done most of the day-to-day work. I'm lucky to have Phyl, he thought, and feeling suddenly happier than he had for a while, he found himself looking forward to his meeting with Ellie.

There she was, standing by the iron railings on the front, and waving to him as he approached. She'd suggested Brighton. She'd always liked the place, with its overtones of dirty weekends and assignations. He kissed her cheek and smelled the perfume he'd not smelled since the days when she was his wife: Oscar de la Renta. How strange memory was! He would have sworn that he'd totally forgotten that name.

'It's good of you to see me, Matt.'

'A pleasure, I promise you,' he answered, and discovered that he meant it.

They began to walk along together. The sea, on his right, was flat and grey, reflecting a sky like gun-metal. It wasn't cold for March, but not really seaside weather either. Matt preferred seaside resorts out of season and winds, low temperatures and cloud masses that looked like mountains in the sky suited him better than heat. He glanced sideways at Ellie. She was wearing trousers today, and a jacket the colour of raspberry fool in some velvety fabric. Her hair, still dark, was twisted up on top of her head and held in place with a kind of metal pin thing that he supposed was ornamental, though to him it looked more like a twisted outsize paperclip. There was a silk scarf wound round her neck.

Perhaps they made an odd couple. Matt Barrington had never deluded himself. He prided himself on his honesty. He was aware that many people thought him, if not dull exactly, then unexciting. He could understand what had led them to such a conclusion and, while the fact that they were wrong about him could have annoyed him, it actually quite amused him. When people look at me, he thought, they see a provincial solicitor, tall, dark and greying at the temples. The very picture of respectability. The sort of person who blends into his surroundings; the very opposite of Ellie who stood out in bright colours against every background. He, for his part, regarded himself as a bit of a dreamer in some ways, the opposite of practical. Romantic, perhaps, wouldn't be too strong a word.

'You look quite well, Matt,' Ellie said, turning her head to look at him. 'I was just thinking at the funeral, you've hardly changed since the last time I was in England.'

'Five years ago. Well, a great deal's happened since then.'

'Tell me about it.'

'Really?' His father's death just over two years ago, and now his mother's, and all his fears for Lou. Her history with that ghastly Ray ... no, Matt had no

44

intention of going into any of that. 'You don't want to know about my life.'

'Why not? I'm very fond of you, you know. We were married once, even if it was only for about five minutes.'

'Indeed.' He was still shocked by the brevity of their marriage. From meeting Ellie at a cocktail party hosted by his mother to her leaving the country with that frightful Italian couldn't have been more than a couple of years. If he thought about it, he could transport himself to the night he'd met her. He'd never seen anyone like her before. If she was exotic now, in those days, more than twenty years ago, she'd lit up the room. She was twenty-nine then and he twenty-five, and the age difference had always been something that – well, there was no doubt it heightened the desire between them. Ellie liked younger men, and Matt wasn't too disgustingly youthful. Eyebrows would have been raised if she'd latched on to an eighteen-year-old, but those four years! They allowed her to be the teacher, the one who instructed, the one who took the lead in sexual matters, even though Matt had already had several lovers by the time they met. It suited her to think of him as almost virginal. It suited them both for *her* to be the one who seduced, who demanded, who set the tempo. And he'd never wanted anything in his life as much as he wanted to be wrapped around and swept away by her, absorbed into her.

The wind whipped Ellie's scarf into her eyes, and Matt had a sudden vision of the first time he'd seen her naked. He heard her voice in his head: *Come here, my sweet boy, come to me ...* and he had to stop for a moment and pretend that his shoelaces needed retying as a memory as sharp as a photograph came into his mind: Ellie holding out her arms to him, sighing as he came to her, opening her lips under his. He stood

45

up, trying to collect himself. This was not the sort of thought he was supposed to be having. If Phyl knew ... She'd looked a bit askance when he mentioned that he was going into Brighton to meet Ellie and had asked why she couldn't come to the house.

'It makes it obvious, doesn't it, that it's you she really wants to see,' she said just before he left the house this morning. She couldn't help an aggrieved note creeping into her voice, he noticed, even after so long.

'She might want to talk to me about some legal matter,' he'd told Phyl. 'In fact I'm sure she does, but there's nothing sinister about it, I promise. It's Nessa, more than likely. Getting at me through her mother. She'll be wanting to discuss the will.'

'She could have come into the office, couldn't she? If she didn't want to see me, particularly. Or you might have mentioned that I'd asked everyone here to discuss things ... She could even have come to dinner on Saturday, at a pinch.'

Matt sighed. 'I've got to go. I had the impression she didn't want to come to Haywards Heath.'

He'd left before Phyl could say another word, but now he wondered whether there might be something – well – something more personal in Ellie's invitation. He let his mind return to the past.

In those days, he seemed older than he was. Constance used to tease him about never having been a proper rebellious teenager. Born middle-aged, she'd say, laughing, to her friends. He knew she thought of him as a stick-in-the-mud and hadn't realized that this was a disguise, a protective colouration adopted at an early age to avoid trouble. Or maybe she had known. Maybe she'd *always* known that he was capable of passion. Maybe that was why she'd practically thrown him together with Ellie. Made the match ...

He answered, a little belatedly and as casually as he

could, the last remark his ex-wife had made.

'I didn't leave the marriage, you know,' he said. 'It was you, Ellie. Who knows – we might still be together, if it had been up to me.'

'Oh, Mattie darling, I was bored to sobs – not with you but with the life. I wanted to travel, and Paolo promised me so much. He wasn't a patch on you in bed, of course.'

She smiled and stopped, then turned to him. They were standing very close together. She took his face between both her hands and kissed him lightly on the mouth.

'Don't do that, Ellie. It makes me feel ...'

'Still? You surprise me. Aren't you a happily married man?'

'Of course I am. But let's change the subject, shall we?'

'Fine. I just wanted to ask you what might be done about the will.'

'There aren't any grounds for contesting it, but I do feel so bad for Lou—'

'I know, but I don't mean Lou, Matt. You must know that. It's Nessa. What about her? She's been done out of her share of the property, you know.'

'She's got her business, and a lovely house and Gareth is doing very well too, I believe. They're ... she's not short of anything as far as I can see.'

'She thinks Constance ought to have allowed Milthorpe to be sold and the proceeds divided ...'

Matt was impatient. 'She's not the only one who thought that. Those were the original provisions, that the property be sold and the proceeds divided equally between me and the children. You don't see me moaning on about being done out of my inheritance, do you? Nessa can't really complain, Ellie. She's in exactly the same position as I am and she's not even

47

a blood relation, though of course that sort of thing never worried Mother. But just look what she's done to Lou. She's gone and cut her out of the bloody will altogether. Everyone knows what she thought of Dad's novels. I feel dreadful. Lou had such an awful time with that man she took up with. My only consolation is she didn't marry him.'

'D'you want to tell me about it? About him?'

Matt shook his head. Where would he begin? Even thinking about Lou's time with Ray made him shiver.

'No, you tell me about yourself, Ellie. How long will you be staying? There's not much we're going to be able to do about the will, you know.'

'I'm buying a flat in town. A lovely conversion, two bedrooms, in Portland Place. Brighton Portland Place isn't like the London one, of course, but I couldn't resist the address. There, now you look more surprised than I've seen you look in your whole life. Why's that, d'you suppose?'

'Well, because. I don't know, Ellie. I thought you were committed to never living in England.'

'I've changed my mind. Abroad has come to be a bit ...' She paused, searching for the right word. 'A bit *tiresome*. Wearing, even. I feel – well, I've got a grandchild now, you know.'

Matt smiled. 'That wouldn't cut any ice with the Ellie I remember.'

'I've mellowed, perhaps. Is that out of the question?'

Yes, Matt wanted to say. *Quite out of the question. As likely as a tiger turning vegetarian.* He said instead, 'If there's anything I can do to help the sale along, just let me know, Ellie. It'll be nice to have you as a sort of neighbour.'

'Lovely, I know.' She touched his hand briefly. 'We'll see one another *so* much more, won't we?'

'Of course we will.' He was working out what he'd tell Phyl when Ellie spoke her name.

'How's Phyl?'

'She's fine. She likes being a granny. I like being a grandfather.'

Ellie smiled and Matt wondered what they could talk about now that they'd dealt with the will and also with Ellie's plans. They'd arrived at a Starbucks. There was no one much about at this time of day on a Wednesday and they took a table in the window. Matt went to get two cappuccinos and, while they were being prepared, he watched Ellie settling down and arranging her scarf and jacket over the back of the chair.

'I've got the hard part, you know,' he said, when he returned. 'After everyone's made noises about Lou and the disinheritance – God, if Constance were here, I'd strangle her – there are boxes and boxes of papers to go through. Mother hung on to everything, you know. Dad's stuff too. I did ask her to give those boxes to me when he died, but she wanted them at Milthorpe for some reason. Don't ask me why. Anyway, it's my job to go through the lot now, but I'm so short of time. I thought I might ask Lou to help me. What do you think?'

'Darling, why ask me? How do I know what's best? Does Lou like sorting through old bumph? It would kill me, I think. I can't imagine why anyone would keep ancient papers.'

Matt stirred the foam in his cup. 'I never knew Dad had hoarded so much. Things from his childhood, all brown and falling to bits.'

'Did he ever speak about his childhood?'

'Well, no. He didn't talk about anything much, to me. By the time I was born, he'd pretty much closed in on himself. What I remember is his black moods. The failure of his novels hit him hard, I think. Lou was the one he softened up for. Became a different man when she was born. Loved her more than anything.'

'I thought his books were supposed to be very good. That's what Constance told me.'

'Oh, God, Ellie, she never read them! Mother liked the idea of being married to a writer. She imagined Dad was going to be famous, but as soon as she saw that the odd good review was all it was – a few words in some of the stuffier papers and no money forthcoming – she gave up the idea of being a muse and moving in literary circles.'

'Shame. Constance would have run a very good salon, I think.'

Matt shook his head. 'She wasn't really interested in the books. Not as books, if you know what I mean. She was never much of a reader, as you know.'

'Well, neither are you, are you?'

Matt frowned. 'No, I'm not. Not of novels, anyway. I never could see the point of things that were made up – untrue. I don't mind a good biography. Or history. I like that.'

'Then you're just the person to go through your father's papers. Find out about the family history. But d'you think Louise will have the time to help you? Young children are so demanding.'

'Possibly not. She couldn't do it unless ...'

'Unless what?'

'Unless she and Poppy came home to live with me and Phyl for a while.'

'Both of them? A baby in the house, at your age? You'd have to do the looking after, I promise you. Lou won't want to stop work, will she?'

Matt sighed. 'It's not me, it's Phyl. She's got a bee in her bonnet. Lou's work is only reading scripts and writing reports about them. She could do that equally well here.' A vision of his daughter in London, sitting crouched over that too-small and rather rickety desk with his granddaughter in the little box room that was her nursery, made him sad and he shook his head to dispel the mood. 'I don't know what I think any longer.'

'Then don't. I've nearly finished my coffee. Let's get another and pretend we're young and foolish again.'

Was Ellie flirting with him? Matt went back to the counter, thinking about the implications of this, wondering how he ought to respond, and at the same time imagining what Phyl would say if she knew. She'd always been jealous of Ellie and when he left the house this morning, he would have pooh-poohed the possibility of anything at all happening between himself and Ellie. But now ... Pull yourself together, man, he told himself as he approached the table with the coffee. It's just the way Ellie is, and always has been. It doesn't mean a thing.

Cinnamon Hill Productions had its offices on two floors of a rather tall, thin house in one of the seedier streets behind Tottenham Court Road. Even so, Lou always started walking more quickly as she approached this rather unprepossessing place. She loved going to the office. She only did so when she had a script to discuss with Harry Lang, and wished she could go there every day to escape her four walls and sit in someone else's space. Going to the office meant more to her than to most other people, she realized. It was a sign of many things. It showed, for instance, that she was a grown-up. This was something she had trouble believing and, okay, part of it was her age. She was only twenty-three, for God's sake, which seemed to her not a bit grown-up and certainly far too young to be a mother.

She'd had fifteen months to get used to Poppy, but even now she felt a sickening plunge of pure fear when she reflected that she was in sole charge of a young child. From the moment her daughter was born, she'd been on a dizzying seesaw that moved between terror and elation. That had got a bit better, after the first few weeks. Nowadays, she knew how to bath, dress, feed and comfort her baby, but still, Poppy was often an enigma and Lou was constantly aware that she could spring surprises; that occasions could arise when she, Lou, would be at a complete loss and need to ask for help; when all the experts with their users' manuals for mothers were worse than useless and she was left feeling hysterical and more often than not in tears.

I'm always so relieved when I drop her off at nursery on the three days she goes there – that must mean something, she told herself. It must mean I'm glad to be without her. How unnatural is that? She'd discussed this rush of pleasure with Margie, who pronounced it perfectly normal and assured her that everything would get a whole lot easier and better when Poppy could talk. Lou hoped she was right.

Working at Cinnamon Hill Productions also gave her a link, however tenuous, to the film industry. She was a part of it, even if only a tiny one. Films were Lou's passion. It was difficult for her to go to the movies very often these days. The price of tickets and a babysitter was simply too much for her, but she hadn't been able to say no to her father's present of a DVD player and she would have gone without food in order to pay for her Amazon rentals.

The office was up a couple of flights of stairs that badly needed sweeping. The first thing you saw when you came in was a small, shared open-plan space where a couple of people worked at computers, sometimes getting up to use the photocopier. From time to time a phone would ring. Three small offices opened off this one. The Cinnamon Hill producers worked in a couple of these and the third belonged to the script development officer, which was Harry's job description and sounded very grand. Upstairs, in what must once have been the attic, was the conference room, which sounded more impressive than it was. That was where meetings were held on the rare occasions when they involved more than three people. Lou had discovered that Harry was only five years older than she was and he was one of those people who looked even younger than his real age. It was quite surprising that high-powered producers took any notice of him at all, but he was, from the little Lou had gathered from chat in the office, very well respected. She knocked at Harry's door and opened it a crack.

'Harry? Can I come in?'

'Hello, Lou! How's things? What have you got for me?'

'It's this *When the Deathbeast Awakens* thing.'

'Not one for us, you reckon?'

'Don't think it's one for anyone. Here's my report.'

'You look a bit – I don't know – a bit rough. Something wrong? Your baby okay?'

'She's fine. My grandmother died. I was at the funeral a couple of days ago ...'

'God, I'm sorry, Lou. Really. Were you close? Are you up to this? *Deathbeast* and so on?'

'I didn't love her. She was a bitch ... she ...' To her horror, Lou felt her lip trembling before she burst into tears. God, how could she be speaking like this of Constance, and to someone whom she hardly knew. Mortification at the very idea of breaking down at work made the tears come faster as she dug in the bottom of her bag for tissues. Harry jumped up and took a handkerchief out of his pocket. It was shiny white; the kind of white you saw only in ads. It was also ironed. Who had ironed hankies in their pocket? Didn't men do tissues?

'Take this, Lou. I'm so sorry. You shouldn't be here, really. D'you want to go home? I can call you a cab.'

'No!' That came out too loud and desperate. Lou took a few deep breaths and blew her nose. 'I'm okay. Truly. I don't know what ... and your hankie. Thanks so much. I'll wash it and give it back next time.'

'Bugger hankies,' Harry said, and opened the door. He spoke to Jeanette in the outer office. She doubled as a receptionist and did most of the photocopying and other menial work that cropped up around the office. Gofer should have been her job description, Lou thought. He was going to order coffee. Jeanette was chief coffee fetcher.

'Can you get us a couple of lattes, Jeanette?'

Jeanette smiled at Harry and stood up at once. He added, 'And pastries or croissants or something. Chelsea buns. Muffins. I don't care, but sweet and filling, okay? Ta.'

Harry shut the door and went to sit behind his desk again. Lou looked at him and thought, as she'd often thought before, that he looked very much like a small boy stretched out into a tall, slim adult. He had light brown hair that flopped over his forehead; his glasses, square and tortoiseshell-rimmed, made his brown eyes look larger than they really were. He favoured denim and T-shirts or checked shirts and wore Timberland shoes. He seemed to spend most of his time seeing writers, chivvying and encouraging them, or talking to producers, and consulting with Lou about anything she thought might be worth developing. Mostly, Lou and Harry between them gave scripts the thumbs-down. Then poor Jeanette or one of the others had to feed them through the shredder. Now that so much was online, the days of addressing Jiffy bags were almost over.

There was a tremendous amount of rubbish out there, Lou knew, and most of it seemed to be given to her to read and comment on. It was partly the knowledge that (given half a chance) she could produce something so much better than what she was reading for Harry that kept her own scriptwriting dreams alive. Ever since she'd realized that movies were written down first, like plays, she'd wanted to be the person who did work like that. She filled exercise book after exercise book all the way through her childhood, making up what she called film-words.

'I'm sorry, Harry. I didn't sleep well last night. You quite often don't, with a little kid in the house. And I've got to go down to my parents tomorrow. They're having a family gathering to discuss my grandmother's will.' Lou pushed the hankie into her handbag.

'Was she wealthy?'

Lou hesitated. Should she say anything? Wasn't stuff like this private? She hardly knew Harry, even though he was the one who'd hired her. They'd had long chats about work and got on well. He often made her laugh and had always been kind to her, but they'd never talked about anything personal. She didn't even know if he had a girlfriend. She'd never seen any sign of one, but why should she have?

'Yes, she was,' Lou began and before she could stop herself, she found the whole story pouring out of her, as though Harry had unplugged something. She could feel, as the words came out of her mouth in a rush, relief at being able to speak about everything: stuff she couldn't tell members of her family because they were too close. Thoughts she hadn't articulated properly before. And Harry was listening carefully. He wasn't letting it wash over him, he was paying attention. The brown gaze fell on her and remained fixed on her and she went on telling him more and more. Confessing her fears and her anger and the resentment and anguish that made her do things like burst into tears in the office, which was not grown-up behaviour by any stretch of the imagination.

Lou only stopped talking when Jeanette knocked and brought in the coffees. She was grateful for the thought, but the first mouthful she took of the Chelsea bun tasted like sweet cardboard in her mouth.

'So now what happens?' Harry seemed to be enjoying his bun.

'Well ...' Lou was coming to the end of the story. 'We'll all have to discuss it over a meal, I expect. My father will be a kind of chairman. My siblings will bicker. Nothing will get decided. In the end, Constance's will is perfectly valid and we've just got to live with it.'

'Bloody hell, Lou, that's tough. Wouldn't your sister and brother help you out? Or your dad?'

'He will. He'll try and give me his share and I'm not going to take it. He'll say, it's going to be mine and Poppy's when he dies and why shouldn't I have it now.'

'Why shouldn't you? If he and your mum are okay and you need the dosh?'

Lou shook her head. 'They do enough. Poppy's nursery – I couldn't afford that – and decorating, and everything in the flat. My TV. The washing machine. I rely on them.'

'Don't forget the royal fees we pay you.' Harry smiled.

'How could I possibly!'

'Your grandad's books. What are they like?'

'Old-fashioned. They look as if they might be good in a stodgy kind of way. He used to read bits of one of them out to me when I was about ten or so. Must read them all again. When I can stop being useless and crying at inconvenient moments.'

'You're allowed. Please feel free to come and borrow my hankie any time you like. Really.'

'Shouldn't we do *Deathbeast* now?'

'I've got to go. It can wait. It's not urgent.'

'God, I've held you up. I'm sorry, Harry. It won't happen again.'

'No worries. You coming too?'

He held the door open for her and followed her down the dirty staircase. Out on the street, the sun had come out and a brisk wind was whipping up litter that whirled around their ankles. Harry suddenly leaned forward and taking the two ends of her scarf in his hands, tied them tenderly into a knot around her neck and tucked the ends into her coat. Then he touched her briefly on the cheek.

'Take care, Lou,' he said, and waved at her as he walked away. Lou stood looking after him, feeling overwhelmed suddenly by how nice he was: how gentle and unscary. She liked the way he said her name.

Phyl was standing in the middle of her kitchen wondering what she ought to do first. Usually, the preparations for a full-scale family meal didn't faze her a bit. She loved entertaining and still clung to the belief that she was a good cook, even after overhearing a remark Nessa made to Gareth a few years ago: *Oh, Phyl's meals are fine, but they're hardly imaginative. Just Delia Smith, right?* Who says, she told herself now as she went through a kind of running order in her head for all she had to do, you have to be imaginative? What was wrong with tasty and delicious? And the recipes worked. Every single one did exactly what Delia said it ought to do and reading her books had been a comfort to Phyl since the day she married.

She took the chicken pieces out of the fridge, ready to put into the marinade. Does anyone else besides me, she wondered, look at their life and wonder how it came to be the way it is? She fell in love with Matthew the first time she saw him. He'd brought one of his mother's cats in for an inoculation at the vet's surgery where she worked as the receptionist, caring for the animals she had to deal with and growing friendly with their owners. Matthew she'd adored from afar in a low-key, rather hopeless way, not expecting anything to come of it. I knew him before Ellie did, she told herself. Then, one day, he'd asked her out to the cinema and she'd been so excited at the thought that she mixed up several appointments and nearly let Mrs Sanderson walk away with Mr Purdue's dog, who'd been in for a small operation and was dozing in his basket in the recovery area.

Phyl smiled and started on the potatoes. She had always found peeling them a relaxation. Potato Peeling Spa – there was a thought! Your hands in the warm water, the peeler running smoothly over the skin, the white vegetable emerging at the end of it. Matthew. She could remember exactly what she wore on their first date. He'd kissed her on the mouth as he said goodnight and she hadn't been able to sleep. Phyl sighed. They'd only been out a few more times after that before he got snatched. That was how she thought of it. Ellie came along and blinded him. His mother pushed the two of them together in a shameless and blatant way. Ellie practically lived at Milthorpe. There was one time when she brought in a cat that had hurt its paw. She'd leaned over the counter and said, 'I'm bringing this creature down as a favour to Constance. Matthew's away this week.'

I ought to have asked him point-blank, Phyl thought, remembering how helpless and hurt she'd felt. I should have said: *What do you feel for me? Do you feel anything?* I was a fool. I just let him slide away to marry her without uttering a squeak. Tears came into her eyes even now, after all this time, when she recalled that she'd practically made up her mind to sleep with Matthew just as the whole thing came to an abrupt end. She was a bit of a late starter when it came to sex. She, alone among her friends, was still a virgin and she hid this fact as though it were something to be ashamed of. She'd had boyfriends before Matt, but hadn't liked any of them enough to undress in front of them and sleep with them. Matt was different. She'd let him kiss and caress her, and he had touched her breasts and made it clear to her that he wanted her, but she'd hesitated. Would things have been different if she'd slept with him before he met Ellie? Somehow, Phyl doubted it. And as things turned out, when he did go off with Ellie, and then ended up marrying her, she felt vindicated.

Now she turned away from the sink and went to find a big saucepan for the potatoes. Aloud, she said, 'But I got him in the end, didn't I?' and immediately felt foolish. What would someone think if they heard her crowing like that? I don't care, she thought. I still *do* feel triumphant, even now, and in any case the house is empty. Matt's at work, Lou's in London. I'm alone. The vision she often had of Lou and Poppy coming down here to live with them drifted into her head and out again. Phyl would have been delighted by such an arrangement but Lou loved London and Matt, even though he adored his granddaughter, wouldn't welcome a baby in the house all day and every day.

Ellie had been the worst wife in the world and that was why Phyl set out, quite deliberately, to make herself the best stepmother and second wife in the whole history of second wives and stepmothers. She knew that something was up with the marriage when Matt started to come into the surgery to buy the special pet foods that you could only get there ... She realized at once this was an excuse to see her again. He needed her. She could see on his face that he was unhappy, and it didn't take long for her to get him to talk. In the surgery at first. That developed quite quickly into a coffee after work. And then it all came out: how miserable he was; how Ellie had been unfaithful to him almost from the very first day they were married. Yet how could he cope alone? What a fool he'd been to leave Phyl and marry Ellie – and on and on it went. One coffee, and then a drink in the pub and then lunch. And then dinner. And dinner again. Then one day, Ellie simply upped and left with Paolo and the divorce proceedings began. She and Matt had married six months after that came through.

Phyl went to find flour and sugar. It was time to start thinking about the cake, but maybe she could break off for a bit and have a coffee. She made a cup and took it into the conservatory. This was her favourite room in the house. She regarded it as hers because she'd planned it, and filled it with the plants she liked without consulting anyone else. Matt was happy to let her get on with it, but Nessa looked down her nose a bit whenever she was in here. She thinks I should cram the house with her artificial flowers, but why on earth should I when I can have this beautiful miniature jungle, right here in Sussex? She'd told Nessa, quite sincerely, that although her silk and paper flowers were glorious, she simply preferred growing things. Nessa had made her feel guilty even as she said it didn't matter a scrap. Also, she'd made sure that for the last couple of years, every present she ever gave her stepmother turned out to be something Paper Roses was selling. The breath-taking cheek of it made Phyl smile when she was in a good mood. When she was in a bad one, it struck her as deliberate cruelty on Nessa's part, as though she were saying: 'I know what you like, and you're not getting it from me. Not ever. Quite the reverse in fact. You're getting things you've told me you don't like.' She began to wonder whether the two Chinese vases from the Milthorpe House library would look good in the conservatory. Perhaps they'd be better in the hall. More people would see them there. Something to think about. Matt reckoned she'd been slighted in some way by that provision of Constance's will, but she found she was very happy at the thought of all the china and glass arriving in this house. The phone rang just as Phyl sat down. She looked longingly at her coffee and picked up the receiver.

'Nessa! How lovely! What time will you be getting here tomorrow? Oh, okay, if you're sure. And I'm really sorry you're not bringing Tamsin. You'll have to come with her another time. But yes, I suppose there *is* going to be a bit of ... No, it won't be a row. Surely? Have you spoken to Justin? He'll behave properly, won't he?'

Phyl finished the conversation and had a twinge of the same resentment she'd been harbouring for twenty-four years. For Matt's sake she had put a lid on the mixed feelings she'd had about being a mother to Ellie's kids and screwed it down so firmly that, for most of the time, she managed to convince even herself that what she felt for them was love. But if I'm honest, she thought, taking a sip of coffee and enjoying the sight of a particularly feathery fern in a pretty terra-cotta planter, they've always been able to irritate me and make me cross and, what's more, leave me feeling inadequate. Nessa never tried very hard to hide the way she felt. Even as a nine-year-old, she managed to show me over and over again that I was second best, a poor mother substitute. And not as pretty as her real mother. Not pretty enough. She made it quite obvious that she preferred staying at Milthorpe and her dear mother-in-law took advantage of that. Extra people coming to stay was never a problem for Constance, mainly because Miss Hardy was the one who did all the hard work in that house. Her stepchildren went to stay there so often that this house wasn't ever a proper home to them. Was it my fault for allowing them to go there? Could I have stopped them? Matthew used to say *my mother misses Ellie, you know. More than I do. It's only fair to let her have the children whenever she wants.* Which was almost all the time, Phyl reflected now. And one of the reasons I agreed was because I loved it when they weren't here, especially after Lou was born. I wanted to be with Lou every minute. I didn't want my time with her diluted in the least; I didn't want my attention deflected on to the problems of prickly and demanding stepchildren. She closed her eyes. She'd never breathed a word of this, either to Matt or to anyone else. She'd gone from day to day in a kind of trance of love for Lou, and the others had just had to fit in around that. She didn't know if she was dreading tomorrow or longing for it. A bit of both, probably. She closed her eyes. I'll make the cake in a minute, she thought, and slid into a doze with the chilly spring sunshine that came through the conservatory windows transformed by the glass into a warming light that fell on her.

When Poppy was behaving herself, this was the time of day Lou liked best. They'd walked back from nursery via the park and looked at the ducks, whom Poppy greeted with squeaks of joy each time she saw them. She leaned forward in her pushchair as though she wanted to join them in the water, waving her arms in the air and calling out, 'Wack, wack!' in a ringing voice that carried through the air and made Lou wonder what the other mothers, with quieter and less enthusiastic babies, thought of her exuberant child.

Tonight, Poppy had eaten up all her supper (squashed things of a vaguely green variety, made with the food processor that Mum had insisted was a necessity) with every appearance of pleasure. Then she'd been deliciously cute in the bath and had fallen asleep after only one story and a couple of songs. As Lou sang her way through 'Over the Rainbow' which was Poppy's favourite and watched her daughter's eyelids close, she was suddenly fearful. What if? The thought was so dreadful, so paralysing, that her whole body began to shake and she couldn't even begin to think it. It was just *there*, in the back of her mind, feeling like a wave that was about to break and engulf her: something bad happening to Poppy. She didn't dare even outline the terror, not wanting to give it either a shape or a name. She had to avoid, above all, tempting Fate, but every time she read or saw anything horrible happening to a small child anywhere, that fact, that awful thing that you didn't want to begin to imagine, somehow got added to the stock of horrors already there, building up in your head: your worst worst nightmare. Nothing must ever happen to Poppy. Lou wasn't religious, but she prayed for her child every night: Don't let anything bad happen to her. If you keep her safe, if you keep her healthy and happy, I won't want anything else. Nothing else at all ever in my life. Just that.

As soon as she left Poppy's room and went into the tiny kitchen to make herself something for supper, Lou began to feel more normal again. Of course that's nonsense, she thought. Of course I want other things, but Poppy's the most important. She sat down at the table, suddenly feeling weak. It's not love making me feeble, she thought. It's low blood sugar. I need to eat. It had been ages since she'd not eaten the Chelsea bun Harry had bought her. How kind he was! He was so unlike Ray that it was hard to think of them as being the same species. She shivered. How come she still thought about Ray, after all this time? Poppy was fifteen months old; Ray had thrown her out when she was six months pregnant. She hadn't heard from him for almost two years. But I still think of him, she told herself, because he still frightens me. I still dream about how it was, how it used to be when we were together.

Ray had come up to Lou in the Student Union bar, only two weeks into her second year at York University. She was very happy as a student, and it was hard to remember now how much she'd enjoyed her work, even though it was only a little over two years ago. She'd been doing her A levels just before Grandad died and he'd encouraged her. 'Go to university, Louise darling. It will be the making of you. You'll get away from all this' (and she'd known he meant Constance) 'and find your friends and your vocation. You'll read so many wonderful things. I'm envious, but you can tell me what your tutors are saying and we'll discuss the books together.'

That hadn't lasted. Ray had come up to her in the bar, and from the very first time she met him, she was hypnotized: not in control of herself, not the person she thought she was. He was tall and broad-shouldered and if you'd asked Lou what her ideal man was like, it was someone very different from Ray. She had always thought she liked small, dark men: the Johnny Depp type. The 'doomed poet' look was what she'd thought she favoured. Someone pale, with intense blue or dark brown eyes and long thin fingers, who appeared to be in the final stages of some wasting disease.

Ray was altogether too healthy-looking. He had grey eyes and short-cropped fair hair, like a male model for a particularly butch brand of aftershave. He was a handsomer version of Jonny Wilkinson. Ray had asked her what she wanted to drink and that was that. They went out together only twice before she went to bed with him, and by the time they'd arranged the third date, the one which ended with the two of them tearing the clothes off one another, Lou was in love. Being in love with Ray was like drowning. Everything else was blotted out and he filled every single part of her with his overwhelming presence. During the first weeks they were together, she couldn't think of one single other thing apart from him. Her family, her friends, her work, her books, her dreams, her whole life up to this point, just disappeared as though they'd never existed.

I was drunk, Lou thought as she beat up two eggs for an omelette. I allowed the sex to cover everything. To smother everything. I thought it would last, that drunkenness. When Ray suggested she drop the course she was doing to come and live with him in London, she hadn't hesitated for a moment. He'd graduated the year before and it was just her luck that he'd come into the bar that night, on a visit to some old friends. When she met him, he'd just taken a job as a courier. He moaned about the waste of his talents and his degree but he did like bombing around the streets on his motorbike. How he looked in leather and a shiny black helmet went with his image of himself. She blushed to remember how casually she'd said goodbye to everything: her tutors, who didn't understand and muttered about her returning to education later on;

her friends, who understood a little better but who still thought she was crazy; and, above all, her parents, who were heartbroken. Mum had pleaded with her to go on with the course. 'You can see Ray at weekends, darling. And holidays. There are such long holidays at university ... Surely that's enough?'

But it hadn't been. Ray told her he couldn't live even one day without her and she'd believed him. She smiled. It had been true, but she hadn't realized at the time that this love meant ownership. Almost as soon as she moved in with him, he changed. He became jealous. At first, she was flattered. She marvelled at her own power; at the way she could transform someone so big, so tough, so strong, into a kind of slave. She lay in bed and allowed him to caress her and love her and worship her – that was his word. *I worship you. I'd do anything for you. I can't get enough of you.* Those were the sentiments you thought you wanted to hear from your lover, but she soon discovered that when they were literally true, they became a threat.

The first inkling that anything was wrong came after they'd lived together for a month. One evening, she'd made a couple of friendly remarks about Venice to the waiter at the Italian restaurant where they were eating and he'd said something back: something ridiculous and meaningless about Venice being a beautiful city for a beautiful lady to visit. Ray, sitting across the table from her, had frowned and said at once, 'Come on, we're not staying here.'

She'd made some remark about being just about to order and Ray had turned to the waiter. 'You can go away. We've changed our minds. We're leaving.' He spoke violently, as though he intended every word to fall like a blow. Then he walked over to her side of the table and grabbed her by the arm and pulled her to her feet.

'Stop it! You're hurting me. What's the hell's going on with you?'

For an answer, he'd gone on pulling her. No way she could get free. He was too strong and too angry. His face was red now, puffed out of shape with rage. When they were safely out of the restaurant, he'd let her go and stomped off like a sulky child, up the road at a much faster pace than she could keep up with.

And I ran after him, Lou remembered, lifting the edges of her omelette with a fork. I should have run back into the restaurant. I should have taken off in the opposite direction. I should never have gone back into his house. But she did go back. She was crying and calling after him all down the road, like a pathetic creature. *Ray ... wait for me. Ray ... I'm coming. Please, please.*

He waited for her. He was in the hall as she came bursting in, and he caught hold of her by both wrists and yanked her up so that her feet were barely touching the floor and her face was on a level with his.

'Don't dare do that again,' he said, quietly, almost whispering.

'Do what?'

'Don't pretend you don't know. Whore.'

'Ray? What are you saying? WHORE? What's got into you? Are you drunk? It's me. Lou. I love you. How ... how can you speak to me like that?'

The injustice of everything: the pain in her arms, the shock of his behaviour, made her start crying. That was a mistake. He dropped her abruptly and slapped her across the face.

'Shut up! Shut up crying! That's what you do to make me feel bad. Fucking crying, for God's sake. What the fuck have you got to cry about? I'm the one who ought to be crying!'

'WHY! What have I done?'

'You tell me.'

'I haven't done anything.'

'You've fucked him.'

'Who? Who d'you mean?'

'That waiter ...'

'You're mad, Ray. Are you serious? I've never seen him before.'

'That's your story. I saw the way he looked at you. I just know. You've fucked him. Who else have you fucked? There must be others. Go on, tell me.'

Thank God, Lou thought, sliding her omelette on to a plate and taking it over to the sofa, that I had the sense not to marry him. Not that he ever asked me to. Sometimes, she woke up in the night terrified that Ray might come back and knock on her door; take it into his mind that he had rights to see Poppy. Dad had explained to her about injunctions and legal things you could do to keep someone away, but she still felt scared from time to time. He'd thrown her out six months into the pregnancy, cramming her clothes into the two suitcases she'd come with and actually hurling them out of the window on to the street, like someone in a movie. All he'd said was, 'Think you can tie me to you by getting yourself up the duff, do you? Well, forget about it. I don't intend to fork out for that bastard you're carrying, not a single penny. Only got your word for it that it's mine, right?'

Lou had been so happy to go that she didn't deny a thing. Let me just get out of here, she'd thought. She hadn't heard a word since. He'd vanished out of her life and that was something she never stopped being grateful for. She'd picked her suitcases off the pavement and hailed a taxi and gone straight to Victoria station, phoning her mother from the back of the cab to let her know what had happened. The first thing I have to do, she thought, is change the sim and get a different number on this phone. Make myself as out of reach as I can. But Ray could always find me through Dad's firm. When Mum opened the door, Lou remembered now, she was crying with relief and I started crying too. He never had got in touch with her, for which she was profoundly grateful.

Enough memories. She still had to pack for going down to Haywards Heath tomorrow, and not just for her, but for Poppy as well. There was less clobber to pack these days, because Phyl had duplicated practically everything to save her the trouble, but there were always the current favourite cuddlies and odds and ends. What did Dad think of having one of the spare rooms turned into a nursery at his time of life? He was almost as besotted as Mum with Poppy, so he probably loved the whole idea of storing a travel cot and baby wipes and extra nappies for whenever they came to visit.

Lou wasn't a bit sure that this meeting of the five of them to discuss the terms of Constance's will would do any good whatsoever, and the very idea of sitting round a table with Nessa and Justin and Mum and Dad would only remind her of when she was a little girl and the others all talked over her head about things she didn't understand. Once, she'd emptied a bowl of cereal into Nessa's lap because she wouldn't include her in the conversation. I can't do that now, she thought, even though there's bound to be something someone says that will irritate the hell out of me.

She finished her omelette. It was amazing how little appetite you had if you lived on your own and never had to cook for anyone. For a second, a scene of her making supper for Harry flitted into and out of her mind. Come on, she told herself, why would he want to eat with you, anyway? He's sure to have a girlfriend. Or even a boyfriend. You're being pathetic.

Harry, for goodness' sake! She put her plate into the sink and turned on the tap, making a mental note to try and find out about Harry's romantic situation from Jeanette or one of the others. There's nothing wrong, she told herself, with wanting to know stuff about your colleagues. It's natural curiosity.

She knew perfectly well that if Harry *were* to make a move, she'd probably run a mile. How long was it going to be before she could consider going out with another man? At the moment, the idea of sex terrified her. Something wrong with that, she told herself. You're in your early twenties – are you honestly going to be celibate for ever? In theory, she knew that one day she probably would want someone to touch her, to hold her and kiss her ... but whenever anyone tried to get close to her, the very thought of what it might lead to turned her hot and cold in turn and she made sure to avoid that person in the future.

She'd made up her mind to read some of her grandfather's first novel after supper. She'd meant to get reading straight after the funeral and somehow *Deathbeast* and other things had got in the way. The prospect of the novel didn't exactly fill her with glee, much as she'd loved her grandfather, but she wanted to be able to say how marvellous it was if Nessa or Justin asked her. She was going to say it was brilliant whatever she thought of it. It wouldn't be so bad. She'd get into bed and read there: just a few pages and then an early night. Poppy was waking up at dawn lately and tomorrow was going to be a long day.

Four hours later, at half past one in the morning, Lou turned out the light and closed her eyes. She was breathing fast, as though she'd been running. Which in a way, she thought, I have. When she'd settled herself in bed with the book, she'd begun at a section quite near the beginning of the novel:

Why, Peter wondered, couldn't he go with his father and the other men into their camp? There was something feeble, something disgraceful, about being put into the same category as the women and children. The camp wasn't what he expected. He looked around and what he saw was a collection of long huts, like the ones in Kampong Aya that he used to look at on his way to school: up on stilts, with leaves on the roof and no glass in the windows. No grass anywhere, only sand that got into his sandals and made his feet itch. The sun was high: a huge ball of white light that burned all colour from the sky. It must be lunchtime, but no one had eaten since they'd left Jesselton, hours ago. Sweat dripped down between his shoulder blades and the heat blurred the outlines of everything he looked at. The trees at the edge of the compound shimmered in the glare. The high fence topped with barbed wire had a guard post in each corner. The main gate, made of bamboo and wood, was as high as a house. No one could climb it, because it, too, was wrapped round in barbed wire. His mother and Dulcie stood in a line of women and didn't say a word, not to one another nor to anyone else. Some Japanese men were shouting. He looked at these men carefully ... the enemy. They didn't look very frightening, and he didn't know why he was stiff with terror. The men were short and skinny, and their voices sounded shrill and angry. Some children were crying. He wasn't. He wouldn't. He'd be brave. If Daddy can't be here to help Mummy, then I will, he thought. And Dulcie. I'll help her too. His mother was going to have a baby. Would

the baby be born here, in the camp? Did they have
doctors? He worried about that.

Poor boy! Lou imagined the heat, pressing down like
an iron, flattening everything. Sunlight so bright it
hurt you to stand in it, and being made to stand in it
or be punished in ways that the mind shied away from
because they were so horrible. Strange smells: brackish
water, salted fish, orchids with fleshy petals. Cries of
pain. A baby being born. The mother's agony. A child
crying and no one able to soothe it. Fever. Sweat.
Enemies everywhere. And hunger. Always, always, not
enough to eat or drink. Frantic longing for food and
water that could drive you to do desperate things. The
image of the moon, the blind moon of the title, was
important. Whenever anything happened in the camp,
whenever a particularly dreadful thing was described,
there it was, hanging in the sky. Peter and his friends
played a game in which they pretended the moon could
see what they were up to, but all through the book, the
moon was described as blind: blueish, pallid, glowing
in the dark and when full looking like an enormous
unseeing eye, peering at them all out of the black sky.
Most important of all, rising out of the pages breathing and alive, their words burning into her brain,
their deepest feelings entering Lou's bloodstream like
a transfusion, came the characters: Peter. His mother,
Annette. Her friend Dulcie. What Grandad had read to
her was, she now realized, a tiny fraction of the novel
and it was no wonder he left most of the story out. It
would have freaked her completely to hear about such
horrors when she was a child. He concentrated on the
boys' pranks and adventures and left out the tragedies.
No one tells children that this – these things – are what
can happen. You try to shelter the people you love.
You try not to show them the world when it's like

this. That's why Grandad hid most of the book from her.

Tears formed in the corners of Lou's eyes as she thought about John Barrington and the sadness of his not being here now when she needed to ask him about his book. About all his books, but this one most of all. She sat up suddenly, remembering something. Dad had spoken of two boxes full of Grandad's papers. She wanted them. She wanted to go through every scrap of what he'd left behind. There would, there *must* be clues of some kind. I'm going to find out everything I can about why Grandad wrote his books, and what they meant to him. There might be a diary or something in the boxes. I'll ask to bring them home with me. Dad and Mum won't mind. Dad'll be glad not to have to think about them and Mum'll just be pleased to have them out of the house. Lou knew Phyl would regard them as dust-gatherers. She began to look forward to the next day. The ordeal-by-family meal would be worth it after all.

3

Don't let anyone say it's just like old times, Nessa thought as she looked around the table. There was something about this house, something about Phyl, which set her teeth on edge, and now she came to think of it, had been doing exactly that since she was nine. She took a piece of chicken which looked (she had to admit it) quite tempting. Justin was already in charm overdrive. He couldn't help himself.

'Just like when we were kids, Phyl, isn't it? And I see you've made my favourite ... Sticky Chicken, I used to call it. Super.' He helped himself to three wings, and then to the vegetables and the sauté potatoes and attacked his plate with every appearance of pleasure, managing to smile at his stepmother even as he was eating. Today he was dressed in designer jeans and a black shirt. He looked terrific. Nessa had long ago stopped being jealous of her brother's beauty.

'Is Poppy asleep?' Phyl asked, and Dad chimed in before Lou had time to say yes or no, 'She's so pretty, isn't she, Nessa? Justin? Did you see her before Lou took her up?'

'Lovely,' said Nessa, trying to sound sincere. Well, the baby was sweet, and no one could deny that, but honestly, anyone would think there'd never been a baby born before. Clearly everyone had totally forgotten how cute Tamsin had been at that age. Still was, if it came to that. She'd turned out so lovely. Nessa caught herself looking at her daughter sometimes and finding her eyes filling with sentimental tears. Nessa was proud of her, and not just because Tamsin was slim and dark and a good dancer and athlete. She also couldn't help feeling slightly relieved that Tamsin took after her and not Gareth. Suddenly the idea of staying married to her husband into old age filled Nessa with weariness. There were times when he bored her even now, and how was that ever going to get better? It wouldn't. It'd get worse, for sure. She made an effort from time to time to recall how things used to be between them, but mostly she found she couldn't summon up the memories of how they were in the old days.

Nessa took a mouthful of Sticky Chicken and felt vaguely guilty at what she realized was a kind of disloyalty to her husband. There was one way of dispelling these thoughts and she decided to go for it. Time to take out the cat and set her down in the midst of what would doubtless be a lovely flock of pigeons.

'Delicious food, Phyl, as usual. You've gone to such trouble. But I really think we ought to get down to why we're here. We should discuss the will, don't you think?'

'Hang on a mo, Ness,' said Justin. 'We haven't all been together in this house as a family for such ages. Can't we enjoy the food and just chat for a bit?'

'Well, no, I don't think we can, if you want to know.' Nessa could feel a note creeping into her voice that was only there when she was with her family, and she struggled to sound like a detached adult and get out of whiny sibling mode. She took a deep breath. 'What d'you think, Lou?'

Lou looked up, clearly astonished to be consulted. She said, 'I agree with Nessa. I can't eat properly if I know there's going to be a *thing* coming up. It makes me feel nervous.'

'Nothing to be nervous about, darling,' said Matt. 'We're here to see what, if anything, can be done to even out the terms of my mother's will.' He helped himself to the carrots, cooked with honey, ginger, cumin and parsley, which were one of Phyl's specialities, then went on. 'She seems to have rather gone off the rails towards the end of her life.'

'Not necessarily,' said Justin. 'Perhaps she just knew her own mind and didn't dare tell you, Dad. She knew you'd argue with her and try and talk her round. Make her change it.'

'It ought to have been changed.' Nessa glared at her brother. 'How on earth do you justify her leaving Milthorpe House to you?'

'Well, she had to leave it to someone. You've got a house. So has Dad. I don't see anything wrong with her giving me one.'

'But Milthorpe isn't a *house*. It's a massive property which you couldn't possibly be intending to live in.'

'How much is it worth, d'you think?' Justin asked.

'I'm not altogether sure, of course, but somewhere between two and three million, I'd have thought,' Matt said.

Justin had the grace to look astonished, but he soon recovered his poise.

'But why shouldn't I live there?'

'You on your own? Unmarried and no children? It makes no sense.'

Justin glared at Nessa. 'I might marry and have *five* children. How can you, with your one daughter, say you've got more right than I have to inherit Milthorpe?'

'Nessa ... Justin ... don't start shouting at one another, please.' Matt was trying to look severely at the

76

two of them, Nessa thought, and was succeeding only in looking sad. He went on, 'I just thought we could consider perhaps ...' He paused. 'The thing is, there's no way I can contest this will through the courts. I had a long chat with Andrew Reynolds and he says that Mother was perfectly composed and sane when he saw her, and her nurses and the doctor haven't said a word about any – well, any change in how she normally was. So the thing is, it's up to you, Justin. To do what I reckon would be the right thing. Have you thought, for instance, about the possibility of selling the property and dividing up the proceeds? If everyone's honest, neither you nor Nessa actually wants to live in a huge old pile miles away from any of your businesses or work concerns. Isn't that true?'

'Well, no, as a matter of fact.' Justin pushed the hair out of his eyes and leaned back in his chair so that he was balanced on its back legs. Nessa wondered how long Phyl would last before she asked him to stop doing that. During their childhood it had been one of her more predictable exhortations and the ghost of *if you can't sit properly at the table, then please just leave and go to your room* was practically visible, floating over them all. Nessa caught her stepmother's eye and wondered if she could see it too. Obviously not, as she looked away at once and went on eating without much enthusiasm.

'I haven't thought about dividing it up. Of course not. D'you think I'm mad? I'm going to live there and I'm going to do great things, you see.' Justin was smiling now. 'I'm very sorry that Nessa is pissed off and it's bloody awful that Lou's been cut out altogether, but hey, that's none of my doing so I don't see why I'm the one that's got to be punished for it.'

'What about you, Nessa?' Matt looked at her.

'What about me? What have I got to do with

anything? It seems that Justin's made up his mind and if he won't listen to reason then we're stymied.'

'I get it.' Justin's face was going red. 'What you think, and what Dad thinks, is reason and what I think is crap. Is that it?' He never could argue calmly. He always lost it, Nessa thought, mentally patting herself on the back for at least staying cool during an argument.

'That's just typical,' he continued. 'It's what you've always done, Nessa, our whole life. You just sit there looking superior and as if you don't care and you do ... I know you do. It's eating you up, the fact that I've got the house and you haven't. And if you ask me, *that's* not fair. Anyone would think she'd cut you off without a farthing the way you're carrying on. You always do carry on, though, don't you? Nothing's ever good enough.'

'For heaven's sake, Justin. You're acting like a child. In fact, that's your problem.' Nessa leaned towards her brother to make her point more forcefully. 'You've never grown up!'

'Enough of that!' Phyl spoke for the first time since the beginning of the meal, sounding exactly as she used to long ago when she was settling stupid disputes between the two of them. 'Both of you are behaving like kids, and you aren't the ones who are hard done by, either of you. Why isn't Lou making a fuss? She's the one with grounds for complaint, I'd have thought.'

'Sorry, Phyl,' said Nessa.

'Yeah, sorry ...' said Justin, and his sister heard him putting a smile into his voice and saw the effort it took to transfer the smile to his face. Still, you had to hand it to him, he was good at pretending. Everyone else, Nessa felt sure, would be thinking sweetness and light had been restored, but she could tell that Justin was still fuming and, what's more, longing to be out of there. Well, welcome to the club, little brother, she told herself. I can't wait to get home either.

'That's okay,' said Phyl to both of them. She put her knife and fork down neatly on her plate. With a smile that Nessa recognized, the one that said *this is my loving and motherly smile but you're not deceived, are you?* she said: 'But Justin does have a point, Nessa. Constance left you a very large sum of money from shares and so forth, I think it's a little — well, I don't think Justin's the only one who should consider dividing his inheritance more equally between the three of you. Gareth and you both earn good money and I'm sure Lou's needs—'

'I haven't got any needs, Mum,' said Lou, interrupting Phyl just in time. If she hadn't spoken, Nessa was all ready to let rip. How dare Phyl? How dare her stepmother suggest that she divide her money when Justin was sitting on something that was worth so very much more?

'I don't see why either of us should make amends for Lou not getting on with Constance,' she said, feeling faintly guilty because part of her recognized that what Phyl said was sort of true. Matt had brought the pudding to the table and served it while Phyl was speaking. Nessa now took a big bite of apple cake in a manner she hoped looked nonchalant. She spoke again, trying to sound a little more conciliatory, 'It's not really our business.'

Lou glared at her. 'No it isn't. You're right, Nessa. I'm quite capable of looking after myself and I'd rather starve than take a penny from either of you, ta very much. Constance didn't like me, and I think I know why, though that doesn't matter now. In any case, you can both relax. I'm very grateful for your help, Mum and Dad, and I couldn't have managed without you this last year or so, but it's not always going to be like that. I can earn a living and I will, too. And till I do,

I'll manage, even if I'm not exactly rolling in it just at the moment. I don't care. I'm not accepting charity from Nessa and Justin.'

'Good on you, Lou!' said Justin. 'And I bet you *will* make a huge success of your life, too! I have faith – every faith – in your talent and character.'

'Yes, me too,' said Nessa, wondering whether the others had heard the relief in Justin's voice. Yet she rather doubted that Lou was ever going to have a brilliant career, poor thing. She hadn't even finished her course at uni and now, with a small child, there was little chance of that. Still, you had to admire her bravery. Nessa smiled at Lou and said, 'I think you're being really noble, Lou, honestly, and I hope it all works out. You do know, don't you, that you can always rely on me for help? You must come down and stay with us any time. Whenever – *whenever* – you feel you need to get away from London. I mean it. Truly.'

'Ta, Ness,' Lou said. 'When my hovel gets to be too much for me, you mean. That's kind of you. I might take you up on it.'

Nessa smiled and privately hoped it wouldn't be too soon or too often. She didn't think Lou would be rushing down to see them much, if at all, but she'd made the gesture so honour was restored. Justin, she reflected, hadn't made any such remark. Matt still looked pissed off. He obviously had no intention of leaving things where they were. There'd be letters going back and forth, emails, phone calls, and nothing would make any difference. Everyone would remain in exactly the same position as they were before. This meal had turned out to be precisely what Nessa had predicted: a total waste of time. She'd driven for half an hour to get here and now she'd have to drive half an hour to get home. Pointless and stupid.

She looked across at her brother and wanted, as she

so often did, to smack him across his smug face. He was helping himself to the cream Phyl had provided to go with the apple cake and looking as though he'd like to jump into the jug and swim about in it. Bathing in cream would be, Nessa felt sure, no more than he thought he deserved. Well, I've not finished with him. She decided to talk to Justin on his own very soon. He probably wouldn't change his tune but she wasn't quite ready to give up just yet.

'I could have done the night shift,' Phyl said. She'd come into Poppy's room while Lou was changing her daughter's nappy. It was two o'clock in the morning. Nessa and Justin had both driven off after the meal and the house seemed to settle into a kind of peace as soon as they'd gone. Phyl went on, 'In fact, if Poppy wakes up again, I'll do it. You go to bed now and sleep in in the morning, too – you don't have to rush off first thing, do you?'

'That's nice of you, Mum,' said Lou, fastening the sticky tapes of the nappy across Poppy's stomach and replacing her feet in the baby sleeping bag. 'I'll take you up on that offer. Ta.'

'D'you want to go off to bed now and let me take over?'

'No, that's okay. Next time'll do fine.' She picked Poppy up and held her close. 'She usually sleeps much better than this. It's the strange cot. She's not used to it.' The fragrance of clean baby skin and Johnson's baby wipes that filled her nostrils made her weak with a mixture of love and fear ... the old fear that somehow she wasn't going to be up to it, wouldn't be able to do everything she was supposed to do in the way it was meant to be done and then ... what then? Poppy would suffer.

'You know ...' Mum sounded tentative. She was whispering so quietly because of Poppy that Lou could hardly hear her.

'What?'

'We could look after her for a bit – just for a few weeks. To give you a break. I'd love it, Lou, honestly. I'm sure your dad would too. We'd take such good care of her. You wouldn't have to worry about her for a single second. And you could come and see her every weekend. Think about it, please, Lou. Think carefully. You look washed out, darling. I hope you don't mind me saying so, but it's true. This – this row about Constance and the will is the last straw, right? After – well, after everything else.'

Lou rocked backwards and forwards in a motion that she hoped very much would lull Poppy back into a deep sleep. She thought: I can just give her to Mum. I can leave Poppy here. I don't have to get up in the night. I don't have to take her to nursery. I can save some money. I don't have to have her in the flat. For a second, an image of how peaceful everything would be without a baby around swam in front of Lou's eyes and she found herself longing for it – longing for silence and freedom from worry and the permission to be completely selfish that vanished the minute you had a child. Mum was offering her a kind of salvation and she opened her mouth to say *yes, of course. Take her. I'll see her when she's five ...* and was then overcome by a wave of guilt so strong that tears sprang into her eyes. How could she think like that? What kind of monster mother was she? Anyone would think she didn't love Poppy. But I do. God, I do. I can't. I can't let her be here when I'm in London. I'd be thinking about her all the time. It's not as though I've got a proper job that takes me out of the house or that I need to be doing. I can't be reading things for Cinnamon Hill more than a couple of days a week.

'I will think about it, Mum,' she said, and Phyl nodded and slipped out of the room. Lou held her breath as she leaned forward to put Poppy back into the cot, doing the mental crossing of fingers, praying that the transition from warm arms to cool, flat sheets wouldn't wake her daughter. It sometimes did, but tonight Lou was lucky and tiptoed out of the room and along the corridor to her own bedroom. Mum was right to call this the night shift – that was just what she felt like – a worker coming off shift, light-hearted and carefree. Mum would be dealing with anything else that Poppy did tonight, and early tomorrow. Bliss ...

Lou closed her bedroom door and sat on the edge of her bed, knowing it would take her ages to get back to sleep. It always did when she had to get up for Poppy. At least tonight there was something to look at. Dad had put two big boxes of Grandad's papers on the desk for her to take back with her tomorrow. She was eager to see whether John Barrington had made notes or kept a diary. Boxes of papers – there was probably nothing important or interesting among them, but just the phrase made Lou feel interested and excited. And she wanted to know more about how he came to write *Blind Moon* and what he might have thought about it, and the kind of reception it had when it was published. Perhaps she was on the point of finding out something amazing and even if she didn't, simply knowing what was there would bring him closer to her. His handwriting – small, beautiful, carefully formed, right-sloping letters, always in black ink – would be a powerful reminder of him, and his words would make him alive for her again for a little while. There might also be letters from other people. What she'd probably find was bank statements and lists and boring stuff of every imaginable kind, but as long as the papers remained unread, they were full of possibilities.

When Lou had volunteered to take the boxes back to London, her father was obviously very relieved. In answer to her mother's queries about where on earth she was going to store them, she'd said there was lots of space, which was a lie. The boxes would end up under her bed. But Dad was going to drive her home. If Poppy stays here, Lou thought, then the car won't be full of all her stuff and the boxes could sit on the back seat all by themselves. Does that mean I've decided about leaving Poppy? It must do, but I haven't even thought about it yet.

Lou listened to the silence. Poppy's asleep, she thought. She must be by now, or she'd have called out, cried, or shouted for me to come back. Okay, so what about Mum's offer? She sighed and wondered whether she could really walk out of this house tomorrow and leave Poppy behind. Of course I can, she thought. Mum would be so happy. But maybe I'm deluding myself. It's not true that I'm only doing it because Mum wants it so much – a favour to her, giving her something she's longed for ever since Poppy was born. I'm doing it for me too. So that I can be on my own, doing what I want to do and nothing else. How selfish is that? Am I really such a terrible mother? No, she decided. There really is a good reason for it and it would make Mum so happy. Surely that had to outweigh the feelings of guilt that she found so hard to shake off.

Lou went to the window and looked out at the back lawn, shadowy in the dark but with the dim light of a half-moon outlining the tips of the shrubs with silver and making mysterious her mother's neat but rather uninspired garden. The prospect of empty days and days ahead of her ... she found it hard to imagine. She took a deep breath. Grandad's book might be a film, she thought. As soon as this occurred to her, she felt a little dizzy, as though she'd come to the edge of a high cliff and looked over into a kind of void. But she couldn't stop thinking about what a great film *Blind Moon* would make, if only someone wrote it who knew what they were doing.

The longer she worked at Cinnamon Hill, the more strongly she believed that the script was the single most important component of a movie. You could cover up for a weak one with any number of special effects, or photographic dazzle; you could employ the very best actors and directors, but when push came to shove, what made the difference between the flashy and mediocre and the lasting and good was the story and the way it was told. Harry ... he could do it. Or Martyn Westord, who'd written the most moving script Lou had read since she'd started working as a reader. Any number of other people came into her mind who might be ready and willing to take on Grandad's book and make something of it. And I could sell them the rights, she thought. I could make some money from it and that'd be one in the eye for Constance.

Then she sat down on the bed again, knocked back by a thought so startling that she had to catch her breath and think it over to herself a couple more times, testing it for madness, recklessness and general lunacy. No, the more she repeated it, the better it seemed to her. It was crazy perhaps, but when she thought it, she could feel excitement rising in her. She spoke the thought aloud, to test it in the air, to see whether it sounded like the ravings of a woman who was suffering from too little sleep.

'I'll do it myself,' she said. She said it again, slightly differently this time: 'I'm going to write the screenplay for *Blind Moon*.' Silently, she vowed not to tell a single soul. Because what if she couldn't do it after all? What if she failed? She knew she wouldn't be able to bear it if Mum and Dad and Nessa, and maybe Harry and other people at Cinnamon Hill, were all hanging on to see how she was progressing. Asking questions, or deliberately not asking questions. For the first time since Ray threw her out, Lou felt unalloyed happiness; a pure elation unmixed with any other emotion that you don't usually get to enjoy after you've stopped being a kid. Everything was going to work out. It was pure accident that Mum had offered to take Poppy on the same night that she herself had made such a momentous decision, but somehow Lou couldn't help feeling everything was being *organized*: being arranged so that she could do what she wanted to do, for the first time in a long time.

And Grandad's boxes would now be research. I'll only have a quick look, she told herself, just to see what's there and then I'll go to sleep. She picked out a notebook that was right on top and opened it.

Matt looked across the kitchen at his wife, who was sitting next to the high chair and spooning beige puddingy goo into Poppy's open mouth. This high chair lived normally in the box room on the attic floor. It had been used for Tamsin and now he brought it down every time Poppy came to visit. It was wooden and well made, and they'd bought it when Lou was born. Matt was concentrating on the chair in an attempt to calm down. He knew that if he began to argue now, while Poppy was being fed, Phyl would refuse to answer. It was one of her iron rules: no fighting in front of children. He wasn't altogether sure about how he felt at the prospect of Poppy's stay. He had no idea of how long she'd be with them, but it was sure to be a few weeks at least. Matt thought the world of

Poppy and was happy to have her to stay for a bit, but he also felt a little miffed that this had been decided without so much as a word of consultation with him. He listened to the babble of grandmotherly noise and chat that was coming out of Phyl's mouth in an unending stream. Was it going to be like this every day? And at night – and in the middle of the night? He liked to think of himself as a good grandfather, but that didn't mean that he was willing to relinquish his rights to a bit of peace and quiet altogether.

'I can see you're cross,' said Phyl, over her shoulder at him, with a smile that he knew was meant to disarm him. 'You don't have to try and hide it. I'm sorry. I *am* sorry, really, not to have asked you what you think, but I knew you'd agree. We both know how hard things are for Lou. She's trying to make a go of her career and she finds it difficult. Mothering, I mean. Not everyone's cut out for it and you don't know till you have a child what kind of parent you're going to be, do you? You should have seen her last night. She looked half dead. Pale and with shadows under her eyes. I hate seeing her like that.'

'I'd hate to see you like that,' Matt said, spreading marmalade on his toast. 'And that's how you're going to be, Phyl. What about *your* work? What about that? And our lives? Our sleep? Have you given any thought to how the house will have to be reorganized?'

'I have. It's not so much, when you think about it. We'll childproof it in the way we used to for Tamsin. I've got stair gates, a cot, a high chair, and Poppy's as good as gold. Aren't you, pet? As good as gold?'

Poppy leaned out of her high chair and hit her grandmother on the wrist with a plastic spoon covered in goo. Phyl wiped it off nonchalantly and Matt winced.

'This . . .' He waved a hand to take in the high chair,

Phyl still in her dressing gown, the baby now babbling more and more enthusiastically '... is how it's going to be from now on, is it? Are you absolutely sure, Phyl? How are you going to like being stuck at home with a baby every single day?'

'I'll love it. So will you, whatever you say. And of course I can't go back on what I said to Lou. She's counting on us, Matt. It's only to give her a short break. How can we fail her?'

'Fail her?' He couldn't help his voice rising and Phyl frowned at him. 'Sorry, I didn't mean to shout, but honestly. I would never fail her. I'm happy to help her in any way I can. You know that. Financially and otherwise. Neither of us would do anything else and for as long as it's necessary, obviously. Also, it's not as though we're not willing to lend a hand from time to time, but to take up the full-time care of a baby! That's a bit different, Phyl, you have to admit. I think you've been a bit hasty, that's all.'

'Your mother did it. She looked after Nessa and Justin lots of the time. They were forever going up there and staying for weekends, and half the holidays as well. And Lou, too ... she had the benefit of a grandmother.'

'It was easier for my mother. She had a housekeeper. Miss Hardy had a whole squad of young women coming in to help with the housework. And as it turns out,' Matt said, 'her grandmother turned out to be a bit of liability, wouldn't you say? Lou went up there for my father, not for Constance.'

'But you know what I mean. I don't want Poppy being – being distant from us. In the way that Tamsin is, for instance. We hardly ever see that child.'

'No, well, you know Nessa. I think she'd bring her more often but she does have that business which takes up her time, it seems. I don't see Lou keeping Poppy away from us ... but this is a bit much, Phyl. Don't you think it is? And' – Matt felt quite proud of himself for thinking of this argument – 'it's surely not good for a young child to be away from her mother.'

'Obviously it's bad if you deprive a baby of love and care, put her in an institution or something. But a grandmother – and grandfather – are fine substitutes for a short while. Poppy won't suffer. In fact, she'll thrive. I'll get her into a routine and she'll have much more attention from me than she gets in that nursery, I'm quite sure. And it's not just Poppy I'm thinking of, either. Having children means doing what you can for them when they need it, and Lou needs it. She needs the time to grow into motherhood. She has to get used to it slowly. Only a few months and then everything will be different.'

'A few months? *A few months?*'

'Keep your voice down, for heaven's sake, Matt. You'll scare the baby.'

'On the contrary, she's scaring me. But no ...' He stood up. 'I've got to go. If you're thinking of handing in your notice then one of us has got to earn a living.'

'What do you mean ... but no?'

'I mean, not *months*, Phyl. No way. One month at most. I really don't mean to be unkind, and you know how much I adore Poppy, but we do have our lives to lead as well, don't we? Say goodbye to Lou from me. I'll phone her from work. She's already sleeping in, I see.'

'We had a disturbed night,' Phyl said.

'And it's not going to be the last, is it? God, Phyl, is this wise?'

'As it'll be me that's getting up to see to Poppy at night and doing most of the childcare,' she replied in a chilly voice, 'I don't see that you've got any reason to object.'

89

Nothing to say to that, Matt thought, so he said nothing. The number of reasons to object was growing all the time. You thought you could do what you wanted when you wanted to: go off to Paris for the weekend, have friends over to stay, lie around on Sunday doing nothing more taxing than reading the papers, and then out of the blue you had to take someone else into consideration, and someone, moreover, who needed looking after twenty-four hours a day.

But. Being a lawyer, he was used to weighing up both sides of an argument. *But* – this was a baby you loved and cherished, and she was the daughter of your child whom you loved and cherished even more. And all that stuff about giving in notice and earning a living was nonsense. Phyl did enjoy working at the vet's. She'd been there for years and liked Dr Hargreaves and the contact with the animals and their owners, but of course they had quite enough money to employ help if they needed it and there was the extra money he'd receive from his mother's estate. He sighed. He'd have to put up with it, make the best of it, put a brave face on things, but he was a little pissed off. Annoyed. Phyl thought she knew what he felt about it but he could never tell her how he dreaded the coming weeks. And he couldn't say anything or Lou would hear of it and he didn't want that. There it was: the bottom line. He didn't want to hurt Lou. Not ever, not in any way.

He stood up, leaned over to kiss the top of Phyl's head and left the room before she could say anything else. He heard her calling after him: 'I'm not giving notice. Leave of absence. I'll take leave of absence. They'll have me back at work, I'm sure.'

In the car on the way to work, Matt thought about what Phyl had said. Could you take leave of absence from a vet's receptionist's job? Probably not, but it was true that there were always young women eager to come and work near animals, so it wouldn't be a problem to replace her for a bit.

He parked the car and leaned over to the back seat to pick up his briefcase. A kind of weariness overcame him and he shut his eyes. It wasn't just Poppy. It was everything. He genuinely loved his grandchild and he wasn't even the kind of person who disliked babies in general. So why was he resisting this invasion? *Because it will mean a loss of freedom*, he told himself. *And that's why Lou needs us to do it.* Her freedom was as important as theirs, he knew, but that meant also that his freedom – his and Phyl's – was as important as Lou's. *Round and round* ...

He turned his mind very deliberately to other things. He needed to stop thinking about his family in order to get through a day's work.

'Have you remembered, Mum?' Tamsin clutched her lunchbox to her chest as she got out of the car. She peered back into the window and Gareth took the opportunity to kiss his daughter. She accepted the kiss and returned it absent-mindedly. Nessa was pleased that their daughter never kissed her in that offhand manner and felt the warm glow that always came over her at the knowledge that she was the best-loved parent. Tamsin went on, 'I'm going home with Bryony today.'

'Yes, sweetie, I do remember. I'll pick you up from Bryony's about seven, okay?'

'Yes, fine. Bye, Dad, bye, Mum.' She was into the school gates without so much as a glance back at the car and Nessa felt proud for a moment, both of her independent daughter, who'd always been good at mixing and getting on with other children, and of herself. *I was the one*, she told herself, *who made sure she* was exposed to kids and other adults from a very early age. Tamsin was so pretty. Nessa prided herself on not being one of those mothers you met sometimes who believed blindly that their child was the most beautiful, the cleverest and the best, but still, she couldn't help feeling that Tamsin was outstanding in every possible way: a gifted gymnast and dancer and thoroughly delightful company. It wasn't just her being a devoted mother either. Everyone agreed.

Nessa always made a point of driving in a calm state of mind. It was hard sometimes, when there was so much in daily life that irritated her, and some things that made her seethe. Did anyone else seethe? She'd never asked her friends. They all grumbled in a mild way about their spouses and the strange things these flawed creatures had said and done but no one, she felt sure, wanted to take the AA roadmap and hit the person sitting next to them in the car about the ears as hard as possible. She turned to Gareth, whose own car was in for servicing and to whom she was giving a lift as far as the station. A couple of days had gone by since the meal at her parents' house and Justin was going to be hard to shift. She'd arranged to have lunch with him in Brighton next week, but she didn't hold out much hope of any change of mind on his part.

'What did you say?' This was part of Nessa's 'being calm' routine. Maybe what she'd just heard wouldn't strike her as so stupid the second time round.

'I said I thought Matt has a point. Justin too, come to that. We've got everything we want, haven't we?'

Nessa bit her lip hard to stop the expletive she'd have liked to utter. No, the remark was just as bad now she'd heard it twice. How to begin to answer? She recalled a newspaper article she'd read about a woman who managed to change her husband's behaviour using methods employed by animal trainers.

Worth a try. She decided to ignore Gareth's remark and change the subject. That way, she'd keep her cool and he'd realize that what he'd just said was not what she wanted to hear. Apparently dolphins, baboons and other creatures knew that if you didn't react you were not best pleased, but Nessa wasn't convinced that her husband's mental subtlety came anywhere near that of a dolphin. You also had to reward them for good behaviour, apparently, and that, when Nessa came to think of it, was what she'd been doing with Gareth and sex – for the last couple of years, certainly. She never felt in the mood unless he'd done something that pleased her, and that seemed to be happening less and less. She said, 'You'll be back in time for supper, right?'

'Yup.' They were at the station.

'Cheerio, then,' Nessa said. 'I may be quite late. Lots of spring weddings coming up and fortunately our flowers seem to be the thing everyone wants. But I'll pick up Tamsin.'

Gareth leaned back into the car and kissed the side of her head in a perfunctory manner before banging the passenger door shut. She watched him striding towards the ticket office: grey suit, mousy hair, very thick and sticking up a bit at the crown, and legs just that tiny bit too short – it wasn't a package that made her heart beat faster. Ah, well …

Her husband had blown it this morning, she thought, turning on to the main road that led to Mickey's house and the Paper Roses office. He'd been trying to mollify her, cheer her up. Telling her nice things she ought to have been happy to hear, about how he was glad to be able to keep them both very nicely, thank you, even without Constance's money and how there was even a prospect of promotion at work. And of course he was quite right. She knew it was greedy and unworthy to be so envious of Justin. The money from Constance's estate would probably come to nearly £200,000. She had no right at all to be grumbling and she was well aware of that, but somehow couldn't seem to help feeling a bit resentful.

Gareth went off every day to a shiny glass and silver building in London to slave away in a high-powered insurance firm. Nessa knew very little about his work, but he did keep on telling her how well thought of he was and how terrifically they were doing and, especially, how much better they'd be doing in the future. They really didn't, he'd announced as they were getting ready to leave, need a white elephant like Milthorpe House.

It wasn't the house, or the money – though both would have been nice and she'd have ditched their rather boring post-war detached with bog-standard garden for this particular white elephant any time – but the principle of the thing. It wasn't fair and, if he thought she was going to take it lying down, he was wrong. How she'd longed for Gareth to say *it's monstrous. I'll help you. We'll fight Justin together.* But such combative words weren't in his repertoire. He was someone who really would do anything for a quiet life. She just couldn't get her head round it. Never mind, there'd be a cup of coffee waiting for her at the office, and she could moan all she liked. Mickey was so good at listening. Gareth – they hadn't made love now for more than three weeks. Was he picking up some kind of signal from her? She sighed. Maybe she ought to make an effort, but as soon as this thought came into her mind, it was followed by another: *Why the hell should I be the one to make the effort? Why shouldn't he?* Oh, God, when did I become so dissatisfied? she asked herself. What'll it take to make me feel happy again?

Just as she was getting out of the car, her mobile phone rang. She fished around for it in her bag and flipped the lid open.

'Hi, Gareth. What's up?'

'I think I left my mobile in your car. I'm calling from a phone box. Can you check? Maybe between our seats? Are you at your desk?'

Sighing, Nessa peered into the space between the front seats.

'No, you're okay. I was just getting out. And it's here.'

'Thank the Lord. D'you – I mean, will you put it straight in your handbag, darling? Don't want it going astray again, okay? And turn it off, right? Doesn't need to be on if it's not with me. I'll take it back tonight, right?'

'Fine. Gotta go.'

'Thanks. Bye.'

Nessa was just about to turn off Gareth's phone and put it into her bag together with her own when it pinged. That, she thought, must be someone texting Gareth. For a second, she wondered whether to leave it, but she was too curious to do that. She clicked on the 'read' button and the name Melanie appeared in the middle of the lit-up blue square. Who the hell was Melanie? Nessa didn't know anyone called that. It took her no time at all to decide to read the message. How dare Gareth get messages from women she didn't know?

After she'd read it, Nessa sat for a moment and wondered what she was feeling. Was it normal to react like this? I've just, she thought, found out that my husband may be unfaithful to me. I think that's what this means. Perhaps it's only a silly office flirtation – but perhaps not. I ought to feel sad. Or enraged. Or threatened – what if he decides he wants to divorce me? Or something … what's the matter with me? She took a deep breath. The message had said *fone me cant wait to see you again keep thinking about us xxx.*

Melanie's texting skills obviously didn't run to spelling, capital letters or punctuation. She was probably young. Nessa closed her eyes. Should she confront Gareth, tell him he'd been found out? Should she leave him? She had no intention of doing anything of the kind. If she'd inherited Milthorpe House, there might have been a slim possibility of her jettisoning all interest in her present home; but as things stood with Justin being so amazingly stubborn, she was damned if she was going to hasten her own impoverishment by cutting loose from Gareth. He had many faults, but being able to keep her in a way she considered no more than her due wasn't one of them. Of course, with the money from Constance's estate, she would be even better off than she was now, but much better to have more than less. She closed her husband's phone and put it in her handbag. Then she shut the car door with rather more force than she normally used and made her way up the path to Mickey's front door.

'Hello, Nessa,' said Mickey. 'How's things? Any word from Justin?'

'I'm having lunch with him. See if he'll listen to reason. He won't, but I can yell at him when it's just the two of us. We had to be all sweetness and light *chez* Dad and Phyl, of course.'

'I'll make you a coffee.'

'Thanks, Mickey. I'm gasping.'

Nessa sat at her desk, listening to Mickey running the tap, filling the kettle, getting the mugs ready. She felt light, as though part of her was floating somewhere near the ceiling. Disembodied. I've had a shock, she thought. Gareth and another woman … what did she feel about that? What would she do? Should she say something to Mickey? No, she thought. I won't say anything for the moment. Not to anyone. I'll keep this knowledge to myself. The phrase *knowledge is power* popped into her mind, flashing there like a neon sign. She stared down at her hands, resting on some files, and realized two things. First, she wasn't surprised. Was that because she had a low opinion of men, or because she knew her husband? The latter, she felt. Gareth wouldn't know how to resist some woman who'd decided to seduce him, but she had to admit not many men would. He was a very long way from irresistible, but she remembered fancying him rotten once upon a time, and a part of her could still see the attraction for Melanie. The second thing she had become aware of was more shocking. She wasn't particularly hurt or upset and that was bad enough. No, it was worse than that. She felt relieved, as though she'd been given a 'get out of jail free' card. This Melanie, whoever she was (and Nessa made up her mind to go through the inbox on Gareth's phone later and work her way through his desk at home to find out more if she could), was a kind of permit allowing Nessa to do whatever she wanted. If Gareth objected to anything, anything at all, she could say *you've got no room to talk ... you don't love me. You've been unfaithful.* It's not, Nessa thought, as though I've got anything planned, but it's good to know there's something I can hold in reserve. She felt powerful, in control, and strangely excited. I'm not like other people, she thought, not for the first time. Anyone else would be in pieces and I'm ... what? Quite looking forward to seeing what's going to happen next.

'Here you go.' Mickey put the coffee cup down on the desk and then pulled up her own chair so that it was facing Nessa. She sat back and smiled, and Nessa admired the way she managed to be so stylish, even in casual clothes. Mickey's hair was somewhere between red and blonde and she wore it in a kind of long crew-cut which made her features look delicate and fragile, rather than tough and masculine. She wore jeans which cost more than most people's weekly grocery bill, and white shirts or T-shirts which were similarly expensive. One of her mottos was *nothing but the best* and she applied this rule to everything she possessed. She didn't have very many things, but those she did own were always perfect examples of their kind. It was this perfectionism which Nessa valued when it came to business, and to find it in someone who was also friendly and funny and kind she regarded as a real blessing.

'Is anything wrong?' Mickey said, frowning and peering more closely at Nessa's face.

'No – nothing really. I had a bit of a quarrel with Gareth in the car before I dropped him at the station.' She had better say something. Mickey knew her too well to be fobbed off. This might keep her happy for a bit. Part of Nessa was longing to tell the whole Melanie story, but she restrained herself and smiled. 'I'll be okay. Honestly. We have to get on to those Italians about that pink silk today. D'you want me to do it?'

'No, you're okay.' Mickey stood up and started to go to her own desk, which was on the other side of the room. She turned before she reached it and said, 'You do know, don't you, that you can tell me anything?'

'I do know. And I'm grateful – truly.' Nessa felt something like happiness creeping through her. It was comforting to know Mickey was on her side. I don't care what Gareth decides to throw at me, she told herself.

98

Lou stared at the piles of paper laid out on the table in her flat. She'd decided that until she'd read every single thing in the two boxes her father had helped her bring back to London, they had to stay out in the open: visible and available. And because Poppy wasn't here, anything she arranged on the table stayed in the same spot till she moved it. Lou was trying hard not to feel guilty about her daughter. There were moments, especially in the middle of the night, but also at what used to be bathtime, or bedtime, when she would be overcome with anguish, missing Poppy so much that she came close on several occasions to picking up the phone and ringing Mum to tell her this wasn't working and she wanted her daughter back here, where she belonged.

But she wasn't going to kid herself. Everything was working out okay. It was like being on a short holiday and though Lou felt guilty sometimes, she was also profoundly grateful to her parents. She phoned her mother every night and reports of Poppy's happiness and good behaviour were comforting. She's fine, Lou told herself. It's got to be good for her to relate to grandparents who love her, and she doesn't seem to miss me. Not a bit. This thought worried her a little, but she did now have hours and hours to spend on thinking, on reading, on trying to remember everything she could from her childhood and put it together with what she'd found in the boxes. This time was a precious gift and she was grateful for it.

The boxes had turned out to be a mixed bag of stuff. There were letters from publishers, mostly boring, but which would have to be read through again. A few fan letters from the months just after the publication of each book, an envelope full of newspaper clippings, and heaps of receipts, bank statements, and miscellaneous bits of bumph. None of this looked as though it would yield any useful information, though Lou didn't have a clear idea of what she was looking for. There were three notebooks, which she'd hoped would turn out to be diaries, but which were more like sketchbooks. Clearly, the things written in them related to events and times and places, but Lou wasn't sure if they were about the characters in the novels or about Grandad himself. Some of them were no more than ramblings. For instance, what was one supposed to make of a passage like this:

Not being who you are, or who you say you are, or the person you've been told you are has an effect on everything. Rosemary says I'm better off like this, and maybe that's true but my problem is I'm not sure who I'd have been if I hadn't been brought back here, to England. But of course I would have been someone else. C says who I am is what I've got and I shouldn't waste time worrying about things that are in the past and can't be changed however much I fret about it. I can't help fretting. Maybe that's all the book is: a kind of permitted fretting. Trying to see it clearer. But it's hard work.

Lou read the words again. Certain things weren't in doubt. C must be Constance, surely? And Grandad had been brought back to England from North Borneo. She'd known since childhood that her grandfather had lived there during the Second World War, and now that she'd read *Blind Moon*, she could see that he'd used that time as a basis for the novel.

She remembered one particular day when they'd been together in his study and he'd shown her something: a little ornament in the shape of a horse, painted turquoise, with a flying mane. He'd said that came from North Borneo. It looked Chinese. Had he talked to her then, about his childhood? If he had, she'd forgotten what he'd said. He hardly ever spoke about himself. What she did remember was an argument between her grandparents. They often argued, or rather, Constance was nasty to Grandad and he answered her mildly or not at all. Sometimes he managed to get through one of these sessions without saying a single word.

On this day, the one she remembered, Grandad had been late for lunch. Constance said, 'Punctuality is the politeness of princes.'

'We're not princes,' Lou told her, 'so maybe we don't have to be punctual.'

Constance lowered her head and looked at Lou over the top of her silver-framed spectacles. 'Nonsense, dear,' she said. 'It's simply a saying, that's all. Everyone should be as punctual as a prince. That's what it means.'

Lou opened her mouth to object, to argue and then Grandad walked in.

'So sorry I'm late, dear,' he said and then slid into his seat and began to help himself to the mint sauce. I'd forgotten about the mint sauce, Lou thought … We must have been having roast lamb that day, so it must have been Sunday. I was the only other person there.

'I was working, and quite forgot the time,' Grandad continued. 'It's going quite well, I think.'

'Well, I'm not surprised you think your scribbling is more important than luncheon. You've always put yourself first.'

Grandad said nothing for a while. Lou looked at each of them in turn. She burst out, unable to stop herself, 'It's not scribbling! He's writing a story.'

'Don't contradict me, Louise,' said Constance. 'What on earth do you know about it, anyway? Don't speak till you're spoken to.'

Grandad said, 'She's trying to be kind to me,

Constance. You should be a little more understanding.'

'I understand perfectly, John. And I think I must be allowed to discipline my own granddaughter.'

Grandad fell silent and the scrape and clatter of silver on china had sounded as loud as an orchestra in the room. Constance continued, 'Oh, I don't imagine it's a real story. Not what I'd expect to find in a novel anyway.'

Grandad put down his knife and fork. 'How do you know what I'm writing about, Constance? You've never shown the least interest in it.'

'Because I know you and I know what you're capable of. The sort of thing you're used to writing doesn't seem to me to be the kind of book that anyone sensible would want to read. I'd have thought you'd have realized by now that no one is interested in the sort of thing you write any longer. It has been a good many years since anything of yours was published.'

Grandad said nothing in reply, Lou recalled. She remembered feeling embarrassed for him. Wanting to cry. She could remember how the room smelled, of furniture polish and gravy. She had a memory of Constance talking to herself for the rest of the meal, chattering away about golf and bridge and coffee mornings and the last letter she'd had from Justin, written from his school. She could still see her grandfather's stiffness as he sat in the chair at the top of the table. He finished what was on his plate and then stood up.

'Please excuse me,' he muttered, and walked quickly out of the room.

Constance had nodded her head and turned to Lou. She said, 'I expect he tells you all kinds of lies, doesn't he? What he never mentions is that until he met me, he was nothing but a boring provincial solicitor. His mother, Rosemary, was a social climber and she practically forced him on to me. There were plenty of other young men I could have married and perhaps if I'd known then what I know now, I would have done.'

Lou had stared at her grandmother and wondered whether she was expected to ask what that was: what had she found out? Was there something about Grandad that she, Lou, wasn't being told? She said, tentatively, 'What do you know now?'

'You're too young to be told such things. Go and play, dear.'

Lou went away wishing she hadn't asked. Now, she thought how many more wonderful novels might he have written if he'd been married to someone other than a grudging old bat like Constance. Someone who might have encouraged him – loved his work, understood it. Someone who'd loved him. Lou knew that *that* was the reason Grandad had loved her so much. He realized not only that she loved him, but that she was perhaps the only person who did, really and truly, unquestioningly, and without reference to whatever he had done in the past or was still doing. The bonfire, Lou reflected, happened only a very short time after this. I was seven years old, and what I was watching, though I didn't think of it like that at the time, was Constance murdering Grandad's dreams and ambitions over the roast potatoes.

The bonfire. Lou sat down in the armchair and stared at the black face of the TV. She'd scarcely turned it on since she'd come back here without Poppy. Instead of television, she'd been absorbed in memories. She'd never realized how it worked, this remembering business. You thought of one thing, one conversation, and when that came back to you, it attached itself to another and soon you had a whole string of them and then that string led on to something else and so it went. The problem was, was what you remembered accurate? Had it really happened like that? Lou knew that anyone else who'd been around at the time would have a totally different recollection. Almost every conversation she'd had with Nessa and Justin since they'd grown up revealed that their memories tallied scarcely at all with hers. They didn't match up. And each of them would have sworn that theirs was *the one*, the truth, the definitive account of how it was.

Okay, so what she could recall of that day was probably not exactly what happened. She closed her eyes and leaned back in the armchair. Perhaps the bonfire was on the following Sunday. Did she only go up to Milthorpe House at the weekends? That was likely, if it was during term time, but it might just as easily have been during the holidays. Thinking back, Lou was almost sure it was. The day was a hot one. She could remember sitting in the rough grass at the back of the house and picking a couple of long-stemmed poppies, whose petals became disappointingly floppy and sad after they'd been pulled out of the ground. She'd thrown them away in the end.

She'd come out with Grandad. He must have been building the bonfire for days. It wasn't, Lou thought, as big as the one he always made for me and Nessa and Justin every Guy Fawkes Night, but it was quite big.

'What're you going to burn, Grandad?'

'Oh, rubbish. Just rubbish. Should have done it years ago.'

Next to his feet, there was a cardboard box overflowing with notebooks that had red cardboard covers. Dad sometimes used to bring them old ledgers from his work to scribble in and Grandad's notebooks looked a bit the same.

'What's in them?'

'Nothing anyone would want any longer. They're just gathering dust. That's what your grandmother says, and she's right.'

He lit the fire then, Lou reflected. I went and stood next to him to watch the flames catching the wood and rags, to see how they spread along the branches and gathered the whole pile into their scarlet and gold brightness. It was hot, too, and I took a step away. Grandad began throwing one notebook after another into the heart of the bonfire.

'Are you crying, Grandad?' I'm sure, she thought now, that his cheeks were wet. He must have been weeping, but in those days no man would have admitted to that. Certainly not someone of Grandad's generation. Men never cried.

'No, no,' he'd answered. 'The fire's making my eyes water, that's all.'

How many notebooks did he burn? Lou couldn't remember. The next thing that happened was that he took her by the hand and they went to sit on the bench that went all the way round the apple tree near the back gate which led out to the Downs.

'When I was a little boy,' he began, 'I was in a prisoner-of-war camp. D'you know what a camp like that is like?'

'No, not really,' Lou said, hoping for a story.

'You're too young to know about such things, but they teach you – being there teaches you something important.'

He'd sat silent for ages after that, staring into the distance till Lou prompted him. 'What does it teach you?'

'Not to get attached to anything. Or anyone. That's it. Don't ever get attached to anyone, because they can be taken away.'

She hadn't known what he meant. She sat staring at the flames she could still see burning at the other end of the garden, not sure of what she might say, and Grandad went on, 'It doesn't matter, it's complicated. You'll read my books, I hope, when you're a bit older. I've written about those years. Maybe I'll read some of the stories to you, one of these days.'

And now, she had read about those days in *Blind Moon* herself, and understood something of what her grandfather had gone through. She looked down at one of the passages she'd marked with a Post-it note stuck to the edge of the page:

Nigel, who'd had the next bed, and was only six, had died two days ago from a fever which turned his skin clammy and greenish and made him talk nonsense and his noises and babbling kept everyone in the hut awake all night long. Peter hadn't liked Nigel, but he wouldn't have wished his death. It was horrible in the children's hut and as soon as breakfast was over he went to find his mother and Dulcie and the baby. The baby was too small. He'd heard someone say that: one of the women. He didn't like looking at her, even though she was his sister. She was like a skinned animal ... perhaps a rabbit or a piglet. Mummy called her Mary but that was a name for a person and didn't suit her. You couldn't imagine her turning into a real child. Have you had breakfast? Dulcie used to ask every day. What a joke! It was a joke. He didn't know why Dulcie said it. There wasn't anything funny about a few grains of sticky rice in a small wooden bowl. Sometimes there were insects scattered through the grains, looking like sprinklings of pepper. But every day he ate it hungrily anyway. Peter thought of food all the time. Birthday cake and jelly and

meat but what he wanted more than anything was
lemonade. The water in the camp was cloudy and
tasted slightly salty. It was always warm. Ice cubes.
He dreamed of lemonade and ice cubes.

That, Lou thought, sounded awful. I'll find out about
that time. I'll go on the internet and read about the
camps in North Borneo. I'll speak to people who were
there if I can. But what had been in those notebooks?
More details perhaps, or earlier drafts of the novels
which would have been useful now. And why had
Grandad decided to throw them on to the fire? Lou
had been assuming that Constance had nagged him till
he couldn't bear it any longer and that he'd burned
them because she'd made him do it. Now another
reason occurred to her: perhaps there were things in
them he didn't want her to see. Didn't want anyone to
see. That was an intriguing possibility.

The phone rang and Lou sprang up to answer it,
feeling as though she'd been woken out of a deep sleep.
She shook her head as she picked up the receiver.

'Hello? Is that Lou?'

'Yes, speaking. Harry?'

'Yeah – hope you don't mind me phoning you at
home.'

'No, that's fine, really.' Where had he got the
number? Lou wondered, before realizing it must be in
her file in the Cinnamon Hill offices.

'The thing is, I wondered if we could get together
before your next visit to the office ... I need to find
something to show George Fuertes from Disney who's
coming over next week. There're a couple of things I
put in the almost pile I'd like to talk to you about, if
that's okay?'

'Absolutely.' This was not the moment to say she'd
quite forgotten what they'd decided ought to go in

the almost pile. 'I'll come in tomorrow, shall I? What time's good for you?'

'I thought it'd be good to do it over a meal. Are you busy Thursday night? There's a nice place in Camden Town – that's quite near you, isn't it?'

'Yes. Yes, it is. Thanks, Harry, that'd be great.'

'No probs. I'll pick you up at your place at seven-thirty, okay?'

'Yes, that'll be fine.'

A silence fell and Lou wondered what she ought to say next. 'I'm looking forward to it.'

'Me too. Bye.'

He was gone. She sat down at the table and opened her laptop. As she went through the moves that got her into her screenplay file, Lou kept returning to what she'd said; what Harry had said. He'd asked her out. He thought it would be 'good' to do this over a meal. That meant he wanted to have a meal with her, right? Not necessarily. It could be that he wanted to do this work and didn't have time at the office. This was just convenient. He'd said he was looking forward to it. But that was only in response to her saying she was ... Oh, God, did I come across, Lou thought, as too eager?

She'd wanted to do some more work and speaking to Harry had disturbed her. She felt ... she had no idea what she felt. Churned up. Worried. What on earth was there to worry about? She took a deep breath. She was worried that Harry might really like her. What if he meant this to be a date? A first step in trying to get closer to her. Was that possible? And if it was, what was she going to do? I like Harry, she thought. He's kind and good-looking and so why does the thought of him touching me, of *anyone* touching me, scare me stiff? She dreaded the thought that this, the way she was now, was how she was always going to be.

Surely not – she'd get over it in the end, of course she would. She knew that not all men were like Ray, but that knowledge didn't seem to make any difference whatsoever. Since he left her, she'd been out with a couple of men who seemed really nice and gentle and unthreatening. She was no longer attracted to bastards, and had developed a kind of radar that allowed her to spot the obvious ones a mile off. Still, the moment any relationship moved towards the physical, she'd been unable to cope and had pushed – sometimes literally – whoever it happened to be as far away as possible. I must, she thought, hold a kind of record for pushing blokes away. Tears came into her eyes as she stared at the screen and wondered how long it would be until she was normal again. How would she feel about Harry kissing her? She had no idea. She was drawn to him. She liked the idea of him, but wondered whether she would be able to relax enough to allow him to come that close to her.

She clicked open her computer file and tried to turn her mind to her work. This was all crap. Harry probably had no plans to do anything other than eat a meal with her and discuss movie scripts. Conceited as well as stupid, she chided herself. Who'd want to kiss you? Grow up. Do some work and take your mind off Harry Lang.

4

'I'm not complaining,' Matt said, aware of the complaining note in his voice and conscious that complaining was precisely what he was doing. 'It's just that ...'

She was gone. *It's just that I thought that tonight we might, you know ... it's been a while since we ...* Who was he kidding? He lay in the double bed. That was the thing with babies. You couldn't ask them to wait. No one ever did. Many years ago, when Lou was tiny, Matt found himself saying sometimes, 'Leave her crying for a bit. She may change her mind and go back to sleep again ...' But then as now, Phyl was out of bed and in her dressing gown and on the landing almost before he'd spoken. And in those days, he hadn't minded. Every one of Lou's babyish cries went right through him, and he'd have done the same as Phyl in all probability and rushed off to tend to her if she hadn't beaten him to it. His grumbles usually came when they were interrupted during sex, which happened, it seemed to him, almost every time he took his wife into his arms. It was as though the tiny Lou knew what was going on and wanted to put a stop to it. Phyl always claimed that she was the best baby in the whole world. The best behaved, the best sleeper. Simply the best. Lying, Matt had realized then, was part of being a parent. Phyl didn't even notice she was doing it and, moreover, that she'd now returned to doing it again.

Poppy was lovely, you couldn't argue with that. He loved her to bits, and had almost grown accustomed to having his house turned upside down. Phyl did her best, but babies seemed to come with a whole barrowload of *stuff*: baby wipes, nappies, fragranced nappy sacks (that was what Phyl called them) which turned out to be little plastic bags that smelled almost as unpleasant as the contents they were designed to contain. And what kind of a word was 'fragranced' for heaven's sake? Then there were cuddly toys on every chair, bricks underfoot, the fridge crowded with miniature pots of mush and the television permanently tuned to CBeebies. He even knew the signature tune for *Balamory* ... that was how bad it had become. Even when the child was out of the way, in bed, there were the endless telephone calls between Lou and Phyl during which every detail of Poppy's day had to be recounted in mind-numbing detail. He was drowning in a tide of babyness and Poppy had only been in the house a week.

When the children left home, Matt had thought that perhaps their sex life would improve. He wasn't the sort of man to confide in his friends and he would have been horrified and embarrassed to hear any confessions from them, but he had the idea that what went on between him and Phyl was pretty normal. They'd settled into a pattern early in their marriage which worked out, he reckoned (though he never really did calculate it ... that would have seemed too scientific), at about three or four times a month. Well, they were busy. And, he told himself, we weren't like a young married couple at all, even when we first got together. They started married life with Nessa and Justin to think of, and then Phyl became pregnant with Lou. The baby often interrupted them, that was true, but even worse was the knowledge that Ellie's children were just *there*, across the landing. That was the true inhibiting factor. At all events, he felt inhibited, even if Phyl didn't.

Phyl. Matt turned over in bed and looked out at the triangle of light on the carpet. Perhaps it was her fault. She wasn't ... he searched for the right word ... passionate? Abandoned? Reckless? He wasn't quite sure, but perhaps a combination of all three. His marriage to Ellie, however short-lived it had been, was full of specific occasions which he could still recall. Nessa and Justin were still very young in those days, and Ellie made sure they attended good nurseries so that she could have more time for herself. She didn't work, and seemed to spend most days visiting Constance and going to a bewildering array of coffee mornings, bridge afternoons and cocktail parties. But Ellie quite often summoned him home at lunchtime and once or twice they'd fucked on the stairs, unable to control themselves long enough to make it to the bedroom. They'd fucked in an armchair in the conservatory; standing up in the kitchen against the back door; and once, memorably, in his study late one night when Ellie, fed up with waiting for him to come to bed, just sat naked on his lap with her breasts in his face, forcing him to leave the papers he was working on. They were lucky that night. Ellie might easily have woken the children with the cries and the constant throaty moans and sighs that he loved to hear.

He was becoming aroused just thinking about it. Stop that at once, he told himself ... He turned his mind to Phyl. It was impossible to think of making love to her anywhere other than in their double bed. She'd regard it as a kind of showing-off – unnecessary and flashy, even pornographic. Phyl with her skirt pushed up and bending over the kitchen table – unthinkable!

Matt smiled at the idea. It didn't turn him on. She'd regard it as a kind of vandalizing of the kitchen which she kept so clean and pretty.

He'd had a vague notion of starting afresh: getting to know Phyl again, and being together in a way that hadn't been possible with three children growing up around them. And now look at us, he thought, taking care of Poppy for no very persuasive reason that he could see. The fact was, Phyl was besotted and wanted the baby near her. It was as simple as that.

He began thinking about his mother. The first sorrow that he'd felt after her death had been dissipated by fury at the provisions of her will. It was only now, after a few weeks had gone by, that he allowed himself to miss her a little. She had irritated him beyond measure more often than not, and his visits to Milthorpe House had become shorter and shorter because she always found a way to annoy him; to say exactly the thing that would rub him up the wrong way. It was like a game with her. She'd toss little hand-grenades into the conversation, and watch them explode. A criticism of Lou here, a catty remark about Phyl's clothes there, a comparison (always unfavourable) between the way he ran the firm and what used to happen in his father's day.

Matt smiled. Her technique was amazing. She'd say something that you'd rush to deny, but there was always just enough truth in the accusation or observation to get under your skin. For instance, about Lou, she'd once announced: 'I'd have thought you'd show such a young man the door, Matthew, instead of going along with Lou's childish infatuation.'

He couldn't, of course. You didn't, as Constance put it, show the door to the man your daughter said she loved – too Victorian and Heavy Father for words – and yet, Matt still felt guilty about allowing Lou to suffer for so long without intervening. She'd have called it interference and she'd have been right, but still. It was something he regretted. As for him, and the way he ran the business, Matt could remember very similar conversations at table when he was a boy, when Constance (who had forbidden him to call her Mum or Mother – why was that?) nagged his father ceaselessly. John Barrington had been a patient man, but there had been one or two scenes during Matt's childhood which he could still remember in detail. His father smashing a wine glass down on the table so hard that shards of glass flew into the air and fell glittering and sharp on to the carpet. Constance watching her husband leave the room and ringing the small brass bell that stood beside her plate to summon Miss Hardy, and smiling a particularly acid smile at Matt, transfixed in his chair, unable to move.

'Your father,' she'd said, 'is not himself.'

How old he was then Matt could no longer remember. Eight or ten, perhaps. Now, looking back, it occurred to him that smashing wine glasses maybe *was* Father's real self and the quiet, polite, self-effacing man, who spent a great deal of time shut up in the study and very little with his son, was the disguise. He couldn't remember what Constance had said that day. It must have been something to do with Father's books – that was what always got to him. The books were a bone of contention. His mother wouldn't have valued them unless they'd made money, which they never did. It was no good talking to her about their literary merit, she wasn't a reader. The books in the library were Father's and Constance put up with them because someone had once told her that they made a room look rather splendid, that they indicated culture and discernment on the part of their owners. They were a useful decorative fixture, no more.

Where was Phyl? This was ridiculous. Should he go down to the kitchen and get a cup of tea? He listened to the silence. Poppy wasn't crying. She must surely come back soon ... Yes, here she was.

'You awake? I'm so sorry, darling,' she whispered, hanging her gown on the back of the door and getting into bed next to him.

'It's okay. I was just wondering whether to go down and get a cup of tea.'

'I'll go, if you like. I'll get us both one.'

He leaned over and kissed the warm flesh of her upper arm. That was the thing about Phyl. She was kind: genuinely kind and loving and he felt retrospectively guilty about comparing her sexual prowess with Ellie's, who, if fucking were an Olympic sport, would have brought home the Gold.

'You're a darling,' he said. 'Thanks.'

Phyl got out of bed and put on her gown again. Matt settled himself against the pillows and turned on his bedside light. Why had his father stood it for so long? Why hadn't he simply left her? It might have been the money, which was hers and not his. It was his grandfather who'd started the law practice and Father joined it very young. And he was still very young when he married Constance. Matt wondered whether marrying people who were older than you ran in families. Milthorpe House, the business – they must have represented security for John after a very shaky start to life, out there in North Borneo, in a prison camp, no less. Perhaps he didn't want to lose that comfort.

Why didn't I ask Father about his childhood, ever? Why didn't we speak more? Matt treasured the fact that he and Lou had always been able to talk about anything, and frequently did, but the conversations – proper conversations – he'd had with his father were so few and far between that he could remember most of them quite clearly. Once, he'd asked about aunts and uncles. Did Father never have any brothers or sisters? He was sitting on the grass in the front garden of Milthorpe House and Father was on a deckchair with a book in his hand. Perhaps I'd just come back from school, Matt thought. Constance wasn't around. Neither was Miss Hardy. Father had put his book down on his lap and said, 'I did have a sister. She died when she was still a very small baby.'

'What was her name?'

'I don't know. She was too young to be named, I think. She died in the prison camp.'

'How horrible. Was it horrible in the camp?'

'Oh, yes. No food. Terrible heat, and if you didn't do what you were told at once, you got punished.'

'What sort of punishments?'

'We were made to stand in the sun.'

That didn't sound too bad to Matt, but it must have been very hot, he supposed. Like being in the field at cricket, when it was sunny. Father went on, 'We weren't allowed to move.'

'What happened if you did move?'

'We got – well, never mind. It didn't happen often, I'm glad to say.'

What would it be like to be in a place like that? He felt sick thinking about it. But Father hadn't seemed upset. He seemed quite normal, so he must have got over it.

Something occurred to Matt. Other boys he knew had aunts and uncles and cousins as well as brothers and sisters, but he had practically no relations. It wasn't fair. He said, 'Didn't you have any aunts and uncles or anything?'

'Not that I knew of. Everything got, well, complicated after the war. My real mother died, you know, and Grandmother Rosemary adopted me. She thought it best for us to make a fresh start when we came to England. I'm sure she was right. I didn't know anything about my mother's relations. She was born in France ...'

'Really?' Matt thought about this for a moment. That made him a quarter French. Was he pleased about this? He didn't know, but he could mention it at school tomorrow and see how his friends reacted to the news. 'Can you speak French, then?'

'Not really. And only the French I learned at school. My father was English, so that was what we spoke when I was a little boy. I've never – well, I've never felt in the least French, to tell you the truth.'

Constance had come out then, and called them both in to tea. Father had stood up and taken her by the hand. Perhaps – this thought was a new one and had never occurred to Matt before – perhaps he loved her passionately. You'd never have been able to tell. His father was the most buttoned-up person he'd ever known. Maybe Constance, like Ellie, to whom she'd been completely devoted, was extraordinary in bed and his father was entranced by her. It seemed very unlikely but you never knew.

Phyl came back carrying a tray which she put down on the small table that stood under the window. She handed him a mug and picked up her own.

'I'll regret this in the morning,' she said. 'It's after two. Bags under my eyes. And you've got to go to work. Can you lie in a bit? They'll be okay without you for a bit, won't they?'

'Yes, it's not a problem – but Phyl, tell me honestly. D'you really think it's a good idea, this looking after Poppy? I know it's only been a week, but ...'

'We've been through this, Matt. I'm not going to discuss it in the middle of the night, so don't think I am. I'm exhausted.'

'My point exactly.' Matt tried another tack. 'And what about *us*, Phyl? Wouldn't you like more freedom? More time together, just the two of us?'

She was looking at him strangely. 'We do have time together. All the time, when you're not at work.'

'I didn't mean that ... I meant ... well, tonight, for example, I felt like making love to you.' That wasn't exactly true, but he was making a point.

Phyl smiled. 'That's good to know. We can make love whenever you fancy, you know that ... only not now, because I'm finished, wiped out. Really.' She stood up and went to hug Matt, putting an arm around his shoulders and kissing the top of his head.

'That's what I've just been arguing. You've been tired this past week. Think about it, Phyl. We're not as young as we used to be. Let's ring Lou and tell her it's too much.'

'I can't. I promised her some time ... a week isn't time. Let's wait a little while, okay?'

He wasn't going to persuade her tonight. He said, 'Right. I'll leave it for now. Let's go to sleep or we'll be half dead tomorrow.'

'This is nice.' Nessa tried not to sound grudging. She'd been invited to have lunch in Justin's new flat in Brighton. He'd moved in here just before Constance's death. Would he move out soon and into Milthorpe House? It was one of the things she wanted to find out.

'You're the first person to see it. Haven't asked any of the others yet.'

'That figures.' It would be months before Matt and Phyl would be asked round and as for Lou ... well, she was up in London, wasn't she? In spite of Justin's remarks about filling Milthorpe House with a wife and children, Nessa didn't think that was terribly likely, or not in the very near future. Her dear brother gave a whole new dimension to the term 'commitment phobic'. All through their teenage years the house had been overrun with girls longing to attract his attention, and some of them did briefly, but no one lasted long and that pattern had continued without much change or interruption as far as she could see. There was a time when she thought Justin might be gay, but he wasn't. That wasn't, of course, to say he hadn't slept with men – she couldn't imagine him turning down a sexual treat, whatever the gender, but then, as she told herself, I'm only his sister, so what do I know? He'd never confided in her and she gleaned what information she had from the odd hint here and there. In any case, he certainly wasn't about to get married and start producing kids.

Nessa looked at the parquet floor, which was like a slab of shiny toffee, catching the light which poured in through the floor-to-ceiling window. There were two enormous, shaggy white rugs carefully positioned near the white sofa and a hideous but eye-catching painting took up most of one wall. It resembled a blow-up of the reds page from a Dulux colour chart, arranged in fuzzy stripes – Rothko Lite. Justin had obviously been watching homemaking programmes on TV. His flat was ridiculously clean and up-to-the-minute. It lacked soul, but then so did Justin, so no shock there. She wondered how he'd managed to afford such a place and said, 'Your bank manager must be very obliging. How did you manage to sweet-talk him into a mortgage? This place must have cost a bob or two.'

'He's putty in my hands,' said Justin.

'Not literally, I hope.'

'No,' said Justin, smiling, 'though that probably wouldn't be out of the question, if I fancied it. Which

I don't. Still, he's even keener now he's aware of my good fortune. Can't do enough for me. It's amazing how kind everyone becomes the minute they suss that you've got serious money.'

'Mmm,' said Nessa and went on, 'I reckon this place could do with some flowers. Shall I email you my catalogue?'

'No offence, Ness, but fresh flowers I think, don't you?'

'Surely you don't expect me to say yes, do you? Put myself out of business. No, I think you're my ideal customer. You want low-maintenance beauty, don't you?' The phrase struck her as rather good and she made a mental note to ask Mickey what she thought of it. Maybe they might incorporate it in one of their ads.

'Put like that – oh, well, if you like. It'd do no harm to send it, I suppose. Fancy a coffee or a drink, or shall we eat?'

'Eat, if you don't mind. I have to pick Tamsin up today.'

'Follow me, then.'

They went into the kitchen, and Justin produced some M&S tarts from the oven. Gruyère and onion, with some salad in a very pretty green glass bowl and ice-cold mineral water. Very nice too. M&S food was one of the things to which Nessa was unreservedly devoted. She'd already admired the entirely silver and white kitchen. How easy it was to keep a place tidy with no kids! No Sugar Puffs or Mr Men yoghurts and no omega-3-enriched bread in the bread-bin. Not that the pared-down, surgically gleaming space-age stuff was to her taste, even without childish things in it. And in any case, she thought, it's worth having a cluttered kitchen if Tamsin was the reason for it. Still, it had come as a surprise to her when she realized, seeing Mickey's kitchen in the cottage, that that was where she felt comfortable and relaxed: in a room with a dresser hung with beautiful china, an oak table, rag rugs on the slate floor and a new Aga against one wall. And, of course (Justin was quite right about this!), fresh flowers in the jug on the window sill, changing with the seasons.

'Have you thought any more about Milthorpe House?' she asked, taking a sip of the water. Nice heavy glasses, too, she noted.

'Mmm,' Justin answered, chewing rather longer than was necessary so as not to have to answer in any detail. Nessa was used to her brother. She waited till he'd finished and prompted him at once. 'Tell me. You can't avoid it, you know. I'll keep nagging.'

'Know you will ...' He loaded another forkful and conveyed it to his mouth. He smiled at her when he'd finished, and Nessa sighed. Having Justin smile at you was like being blinded by too many flashbulbs. She found herself, against her will, dazzled by his beauty.

'I have been having some thoughts, as it happens,' he said. 'Don't know if I want anyone to know anything about them yet, though. Early days, you know.'

Two could play the charm game. Nessa smiled a pretty smile of her own and leaned forward to touch Justin on the wrist. 'It's me, Justin,' she said. 'Big sister, remember? Do you remember? We were quite close when we were kids, weren't we? I can't imagine why we're not any longer but I think we ought to – well – don't start being all grown-up and distant on me now, please.'

'I'm not. Not at all. Of course, you'll be the first person – probably the only person – I'll tell.'

'You've got something up your sleeve, though, haven't you? No point denying it. I can always tell when you're fibbing.'

'I might have. I don't want to tell you now, though.

It really is too early to announce anything. Besides, it contradicts what I told Matt and Phyl. I don't want them to know at this stage. Or Lou either come to that. Matt'd try and stop me somehow. Not that he can. God, I'm grateful to Constance for making sure no one can pick holes in her will! But I'd rather present everyone with a *fait accompli*.'

'Oh, go on, Justin! Please?' She found her voice acquiring a sugar coating, the kind she used to use to get Gareth's attention in the days when she'd still fancied him. 'I won't tell a soul,' she added, knowing that was a lie. She would most probably share the details of this lunch with Mickey.

'I've been in discussions with Eremount.'

'Who's Eremount?'

'Property developers. You must have seen their hoardings. All over the south coast, those purple and green ones.'

'Oh, them. Hideous colours. Yes, I know who you mean.' Nessa felt a little uncomfortable. What was he about to tell her?

'They're interested, that's all. Nothing's firmed up yet.'

'Interested?'

'Yup. In Milthorpe House.' Justin went to a white cupboard and took out some water biscuits. The cheeses were already on a marble cheeseboard on the work surface and he brought this to the table too and set it in front of Nessa. 'They're dead keen, actually.'

She gazed at the cheeses and every trace of appetite left her. What was he saying? She took a deep breath. 'Let me get this right. You're thinking of selling Milthorpe House?'

'That's right. For a ton of money – and not only that, I'd have some shares in it.'

'In what?'

'Didn't I say?'

'No, Justin, you did not. You've got to tell me the whole thing now. It's not fair to let me know some of it and not the rest. Go on, cough it up.'

'God, what an elegant turn of phrase. Okay. Eremount want to buy it and turn it into a health club and spa.'

Nessa felt as though a rug had been pulled from beneath her and it was all she could do to stop herself from gasping in astonishment, but she didn't want Justin to think he'd taken her so completely unawares. She raised an eyebrow – that amount of surprise was okay – and kept her voice level when she answered.

'Well, that'll please some people. But a spa?'

'Why not? Spas are where it's at.'

Nessa positioned a square of Brie on a cream cracker and bit into it. She thought about what Justin had just told her. Careful, she told herself. Don't get his back up.

'Tell me more.' She let him witter on while she thought. She liked the idea. She could just imagine what Milthorpe House would be like, turned into a spa. It would be fantastic – a real money-spinner, she was sure of it. Suddenly, any thoughts she may have had about keeping the house in the family seemed unimportant. Justin was droning on about turnover ... returns for investments ... jewel of the area ... fashionable ... nothing but the best ... etc, etc. He fell silent eventually and when she said nothing, he added, 'What do you think?'

'Well,' Nessa said, helping herself from the cafetière Justin had brought to the table. 'I'd have to see more, of course, more detailed plans, and so forth, but it seems quite a good idea. A lot more realistic than you swanning about up there all on your own.'

'Thank God!' He looked relieved. 'So you won't say

anything to anyone, will you? Promise? I don't need the grief from Matt.'

'Well, I will keep quiet. But it'll cost you.'

'Cost me? What do you mean?'

'I want shares in the spa, too. I want you to cut me in. Thirty-five per cent, say?'

'You're mad! Totally bonkers. Why would I do that? Milthorpe's mine now and so are the profits from it. You can't stop me.'

'Well, I can't, of course, but I could tell Matt and you've just told me you don't want him to know yet. He'll hassle you, you know. He'll go ballistic, actually. I also don't think it's very brotherly of you to want to push me away. We could be partners, Justin. You have to see that Constance's will wasn't fair. Don't you see that?'

'Well, okay, maybe, but I don't see why I should feel sorry for you. You're not exactly poverty-stricken, are you?'

She couldn't really answer that. It was quite true, and every time she fretted at the unfairness of things she had to admit that she was very well off and that Constance's money was a treat and a bonus. She felt ashamed sometimes at not being more grateful for her good fortune.

'Of course I'm not poverty-stricken,' she said now, 'but I could help you. With the spa. I've got an awful lot of business experience, which is more than you have.' There was something about that sentence that sounded strange to her. It was like a lot of the things she'd said to Justin during their childhood when sibling rivalry was the order of the day.

'That's true, I suppose,' he said. 'But I'm pretty sure Eremount didn't get to be who they are by taking advice from small-business people like you, Nessa. No offence.'

'Well, actually no, not no offence. I *am* offended. But I'm not going to fight with you, Justin. Why can't we reach some other kind of arrangement? Talk to Eremount and persuade them to let me buy some shares in the spa at a favourable rate, or something. That wouldn't be any skin off your nose, would it? You'd still have your precious millions.'

'It's early days, Nessa. The probate on the will hasn't finally gone through. I'll think about it. I'll speak to my contacts at Eremount.'

'Just one thing I forgot to ask.' Her hand was on the doorknob and she turned to look at Justin. 'How much are they offering for Milthorpe House?'

'Nearly three million.'

The mere idea of so much money made Nessa feel a little light-headed. Fleetingly, she wondered if she ought to suggest to Justin that he gave Lou a few shares in the spa as well, but the moment passed and on her way downstairs to the street, every shred of an impulse to generosity had left her. This was nothing to do with Lou. Lou was, if you came right down to it, no real relation of hers or Justin's. They only knew her by accident, really, and though Nessa had nothing against her, she couldn't honestly say she felt a sisterly love for her. Constance had clearly, also, known something about Lou that others didn't, otherwise why on earth had she deliberately left her nothing at all? The copyright in those books was an insult. After all, Lou was the real grandchild. Justin and I, Nessa thought, weren't even distantly related to Constance. Which only went to show that, contrary to what the clever clogs of the world thought, blood wasn't thicker than water at all. What mattered in the end was how much someone loved you. For whatever reason. And Constance hadn't loved Lou.

As she turned into the traffic on the main road,

Nessa recalled a day when she was at Milthorpe House without Justin. Why was that? She couldn't remember the reason, but there she was. She must have been about eleven or twelve, sitting on the little stool by the window in Constance's bedroom. For as long as Nessa had known them, John Barrington and his wife had separate rooms. Grandad's bedroom was across the landing. It never occurred to her when she was a child that there was anything strange about this, but now, as an adult, she realized that the two people she called her grandparents can't have loved one another very much. Or, at least by the time she met them, they'd decided that sex was not an important part of their lives. I wonder why not, she thought now, waiting at a set of traffic lights. I'll never know, but Grandad was terminally quiet and sort of sulky and Constance loved a bit of fun. A party animal, caged in that huge house with a dull husband. Nessa felt a retrospective sympathy for her. There was always, also, an outside chance that they got their kicks from visiting one another's rooms as though this were some kind of clandestine treat. Nessa could imagine such a scenario with the right person being a real turn-on – you got the sex without the snoring, so to speak – but somehow she didn't think that this was how her grandparents' marriage worked.

On this day, the one she was recalling, she was conscious for the very first time of being spoken to as though she were a grown-up. Constance was telling her things. Nessa felt privileged.

'You're too young for all this,' Constance had said, but it hadn't stopped her. Nessa had no clue about why she was preoccupied just then with her mother-in-law, but she was. Granny Rosemary, as Matt used to call her, had been dead for some time, but Constance still seemed vaguely cross with her husband's mother.

'She didn't have much money, really. There was the law firm, which her husband set up – my father-in-law, you know – but that was it. Whereas I, well, I was sweeping suitors off the doormat, my father used to say. Milthorpe House and Daddy's money – let's just say it was a big step up for your grandfather when he married me. And the firm acquired a kind of glamour by association with our family, you know. People like lawyers to be well connected. Rosemary knew she was lucky. She couldn't have imagined in her wildest dreams that someone like me would come along and marry John. I fell in love with him, you see. That was my mistake. You shouldn't marry someone you're in love with, Nessa. It clouds the judgement. You can't make proper decisions when you're besotted. And I *was* besotted, believe me. At least for a while. Well, he was so handsome. He's lost his looks rather in later life, hasn't he? Some people do, though not me, I'm happy to say.'

How beautifully, totally, completely self-absorbed and conceited Constance had been! Nessa smiled. Such self-love was admirable, in her opinion. She, too, believed firmly that she was always right, and her faith in her own wisdom was so overwhelming that she mostly carried everyone else along with her and they did what she said without questioning her judgement. That was certainly why Matt and Constance got on so well ... he just followed instructions. Perhaps he'd even married Ellie because his mother told him to. How pathetic was that!

Nessa went back to thinking about that day in Constance's room. That was when she learned a little about John Barrington.

'My mother-in-law,' Constance said, 'wasn't even John's real mother. She adopted him after the war, you know. They came back here from that ghastly prison camp or whatever it was and she put him into boarding school and brainwashed him into forgetting his real mother. She was quite capable of brainwashing, believe me. A very determined woman. She became obsessed with things, you know. She used to set her mind on something and then there was no budging her. She told me once – I remember the very afternoon – that when she realized she couldn't have a child of her own, she'd thought her life was over. Then she said, "Until John came along. That was fortunate for me." And his real mother was supposed to be her best friend! Imagine! John's mother was French, you know. Rosemary told me that. John's never spoken about her. Never once. Or not to me. It doesn't worry me, but it's rather peculiar, if you ask me. Well, he's an unusual man. I think' (she'd leaned towards Nessa at this point, shaking a finger quite near her face) 'I think a great deal of him went into those silly books of his. Much good did they do him! There's only a sort of shell of him left, you know, even though it's years since he wrote anything. The books used him up, in a way. He doesn't really speak to me any longer. Not about anything sensible. He doesn't know how to gossip. I can't bear that. I do miss your mother, you know. She's a wonderful gossip. I wish she lived in this country. I expect you do, too, poor little thing. Never mind, I'm a kind of mother to you, aren't I? To you and Justin.'

I knew even then, Nessa thought, that Constance wanted me to say something along the lines of *yes, you're just as good as our real mother and much better than Phyl* and I didn't. In those days, I was more conscious of having to be good and what I was supposed to say and do and I knew Matt would be upset if I slagged off his new wife. I wanted an easy life.

Was she going to be in time to pick Tamsin up? She'd left it a bit late, but she probably would make it. If not, she could ring one of the other mothers and leave Tamsin with them till she got there. Her mind went back to Milthorpe House. What would she feel if it became a spa? Could she pretend that she was attached to it as a childhood home? Not really. She'd loved Constance. She liked going there, but if Constance wasn't around, would she really prefer to live there than in her own home? The answer to that was probably no. Now that she'd had time to adjust to Justin's news, she found herself rather more annoyed than she was at first. Okay, there was no real reason why her brother should share his wealth, but there was so much of it that surely he ought to have given some thought to his sister? No, of course he wouldn't. Why on earth should he? There was nothing in her financial position which might have persuaded him she needed help. And I wouldn't give him any money if our situations were reversed, she admitted to herself. Briefly, she thought of Lou – living on a pittance, apparently. Would Justin think of offering her any shares? Doubtful, as she didn't have anything to spare to buy into this kind of financial lottery. Besides, Justin and Lou never saw one another. She'd practically disappeared out of his life when Justin had moved out of Matt and Phyl's house.

'Damn and blast Constance!' she muttered to herself, as a sudden wave of anger overcame her. And shame that she was being a bit unfair. Just plain envious. After all, she'd been well provided for, but the idea of Justin in possession of three million pounds – it was too much. A spa in Milthorpe House. How would Matt and Phyl react if they knew? Mostly they'd be pissed off that none of the money, not one penny as far as they could see, would be ending up in the bank account of the number one daughter, Lou.

Harry would be arriving in ten minutes or so, and Lou was as ready as she was ever going to be, as well as completely exhausted. It had been over a year since she'd spent more than ten minutes deciding what to wear. Since Poppy's birth, all she strove for every day was something clean. It didn't even have to be properly ironed. Everything would get Poppyfied: spittled on, food-spattered, sometimes even vomited over. She hadn't even had to think about her clothes for Constance's funeral, because there wasn't a choice to be made. She had one decent suit and she'd worn it, thanking her lucky stars that it was black. She'd also put on make-up that day, but since then she'd lived in jeans and a selection of T-shirts and sweatshirts.

This date with Harry was a bit of a problem. If she dressed up too much, she'd be signalling that this was 'a date'. So, easy on the lip-gloss, no red nails suddenly after weeks and weeks of colourless varnish, and probably no dresses of a 'take me out to a smart bar' variety. As she didn't own such a garment anyway, it was lucky that she didn't want to wear it. By the time every single item in her wardrobe was lying across her bed, she was out of breath and time was short. In the end, she opted for a dark red skirt with a swirly hem, a nice leather belt and a blouse that didn't have that much going for it apart from the fact that it was new and clean. If you were being kind, you could call it classic. Otherwise, boring just about summed it up. Shoes were okay. She'd bought a pair of fabulous black suede boots in a sale last Christmas and they were still the smartest thing in her wardrobe. Or were the heels too high? For a panicked second, she wondered whether she should change into flats, but then there wasn't time and in the end she was glad of the way the boots made her look – far more in control than she felt.

The front-door buzzer sounded at precisely seven-thirty.

'Hello, Harry!' she said, as she opened the door. He stood on the landing, dressed in the same kind of clothes he always wore.

'Hello, Lou. You look nice,' he said. 'I've never seen you in a skirt.' Then he frowned. 'I'm sorry – is that too personal? I'm never sure if it's okay to say someone looks good.'

'It's fine. Thanks ... I like getting compliments.'

'It's a shame I'm not going to meet Poppy.'

Lou felt awkward. 'I know, she's staying with my mum. I left her there for a bit to give me a chance ...' She stopped suddenly, aware that she'd nearly told him about the screenplay she was writing. She took a deep breath. 'Well, a chance to get myself together. You know ...' Her voice faded. Was this going to be hard work? She went on, 'Actually, I think my mum is the one who wants it more than anyone. She adores Poppy.'

Harry perched on the sofa and waited for her to get her jacket and pick up her handbag. How, Lou wondered, did you do this? Everything she thought of saying sounded too hearty and jolly. In the end, she just went to the door, hanging on to the strap of her handbag for dear life, and looking at Harry for some kind of lead. He jumped up.

'Sorry ... you're ready. Let's go, I'm starving.'

'Me too.'

They stepped out and Lou locked the flat door behind her.

'It's not far,' Harry said as they walked down the road. 'D'you like Indian?'

'Love it. It's my favourite.'

'You okay with the Tube?'

Lou laughed. She couldn't help it. 'Sorry ... only

no one's ever asked me that before. Yes, the Tube's fine.'

'I do have a car,' Harry said. 'It's just not very reliable. Feeling its age. And it's pointless driving in London. I just keep it for going away at weekends.'

'Where d'you go?' Lou regretted the question as soon as it was out of her mouth. Would he think she was being too nosy?

'All over. I like Cornwall, and I've got friends who live in the Lake District near Kendal … Norfolk's nice too. My parents live there.'

They sat next to one another on the Tube, and talked about nothing very much. The train was quite crowded and noisy with tourists speaking in several languages, so Lou was able to gaze at Harry's reflection in the window and think all over again how nice-looking he was, even if no one could call him properly handsome. She was beginning to enjoy herself.

I needn't have worried about the talk drying up, Lou thought. Harry was deep into a discussion of the three screenplays he'd fished out of the almost pile by the time the poppadoms arrived, and by the end of the meal, they'd discussed them from every possible angle and arrived at a consensus.

'Okay … that's that,' Harry said, pushing the bits of paper that had taken over a corner of the table into his briefcase. 'I'm glad you agree with me. We'll go for *Hearts on a Merry-Go-Round*. Fuentes is going to love it. Not a lot of people are doing this kind of La Ronde-type thing – I like it. It's funny and touching and there aren't enough love stories around, I reckon.'

'Me too. I thought men didn't go for that kind of movie, though. A chick flick. A date movie – d'you really like them?'

'If they're good. I like anything if it's good. Chicklit, westerns, dramas, comedies, SF, thrillers. Not mad about broken-glass films.' Harry smiled at her. 'That's my name for the kind of movie that has cars bursting through plate-glass windows, or else spaceships exploding all over the screen. Anything, really, with a lot of crashes and bangs and broken stuff about. Boys' flicks, I suppose you'd call them, but I expect you could even do those well if you put your mind to it. A good script makes the difference.'

Lou nodded, and nibbled absently at a piece of naan bread. There hadn't been any of the silences she'd dreaded during the meal, but that was because it was an extension of work. And what's wrong with that? I don't want him making a pass at me, do I? But I do like him. Maybe ... Thinking about Harry kissing her confused her suddenly because she didn't know how she felt. Scared. Excited. Both together. What would she do if he tried to ... He was speaking. She said, 'Sorry, Harry. What were you saying?'

'Nothing important. You were miles away. What were you thinking about?'

Lou cast about for a convincing lie and said the first thing that came into her head. 'Families.'

'Ah. Okay.'

That wasn't good enough. Lou added, 'I was wondering about your family, actually.'

'Oh, right.' Harry didn't seem fazed. 'Well, I've got a mum and dad in the aforementioned cottage in Norfolk. They're retired now. My dad was a doctor, a GP, and Mum was a school secretary. I've got two much older brothers. One's also a doctor. He's in Scotland, near Aberdeen. That's Martin. He's married to Jeannie and they have two kids ... great kids. Teenagers. They think I'm cool because I get them into movie premières from time to time. Sally and Tom, they're called. My other brother lives in Cardiff. He's an architect and single at the moment. He's gay, which is a bit of a problem with my parents, though of course they don't say so. They'd never say so and they make a big deal about it not mattering a bit, but that's not how Jack sees it. That's his name. Jack.'

'And you get on better with him than with Martin. Is that right?'

'It is, as it happens. For one thing, he's nearer my own age. How did you guess?'

'Just lucky, I suppose.' There had been a warmth in his voice when he'd spoken about Jack. She wondered whether she could divert him on to himself. He was the one she was interested in. Could she ask him ...? Why not? Nothing ventured.

'What about you, Harry?'

'Me?'

'Yes, you.' Had she gone too far?

'I was married, but I'm not any longer. No children, I'm glad to say. Well, not glad to say. I really like kids, but it was easier to divorce without that to take into account. We married too young, that's all. Nothing wrong with Maggie, but we were like two cats in a bag after a bit. I know people say they've had an amicable divorce, but we actually did. Well, okay, not amicable exactly but not as adversarial as it might have been. We were just both relieved to be out of the marriage. No one else was involved. We just ... we annoyed one another. We didn't get on. I felt as if I was in a game that had got out of hand, and the lawyers were like parents who come along and say, okay, we're going home now. This game is over. I felt rescued. You know how it is.'

Lou nodded and Harry added, 'I'm sorry. Maybe you don't know how it is, only – well, I knew you were single and I know you've got a baby, so I assumed that something must have gone a bit pear-shaped somewhere – and you don't have to say anything, you know. I'm not prying.'

'It's okay. I don't mind.' Lou found she didn't. 'I wasn't even married, but I know exactly what you mean. In my case, I felt as if I was in a permanent thunderstorm with lightning flashing around my head every day, threatening to strike me, and then it just blew away over the horizon and that was that. I felt relieved. I still do. Sometimes I worry that the storm might come back but I don't think it will. He's disappeared entirely. Actually, I don't think he loved me … I'm sure he's moved on to someone else, but my dad's ready with injunctions and every other legal weapon at his disposal in case Ray – that was his name – does pitch up suddenly.'

'Is Poppy his daughter?'

'Yes. But he never believed that. He was … he was pathologically jealous. He thought I was involved with every man I saw. Waiters, postmen, the milkman – it didn't matter who. Any man I spoke to was a suspect. It was, well, it was unbearable.'

'Did he – was he – violent?'

'Sometimes. That wasn't the worst thing. It was the constant vile – what do they call it in the tabloids? – verbal abuse. That sounds kind of sanitized and almost respectable, doesn't it? He just – he said such foul things to me all the time. I was …' Lou found to her horror that her eyes were filling with tears. Oh, God, I must pull myself together, she thought. He'll think I'm feeble. He'll think I can't cope. She made a supreme effort to sound light-hearted. 'He was a bona fide, straight down the line, copper-bottomed bastard and I don't want to spoil this evening by talking about him any more, okay?'

'Okay,' Harry said, and summoned the waiter over.

'Let's have a coffee, shall we? And a pudding if you'd like one?'

'No, I'm so full, but a coffee would be good.'

Harry smiled at her. 'How long is Poppy going to stay with your mum? Are you happy about that, or do you miss her?'

Did he really want to know the answer to these questions, or was he hoping to cheer her up by mentioning something he could be fairly certain she'd enjoy telling him about? Just as she was about to answer, he took her hand across the table and squeezed it. It was a friendly and not a romantic squeeze but it made her feel good. He said, 'You're wondering if I'm really interested in Poppy or if I'm just trying to cheer you up, aren't you?'

'How did you know?'

'I'm a mind reader. But I *am* interested. Have you got photos?'

'At home. I don't carry them around with me. Except on my phone ...'

'Let's have a look, then.'

'Seriously?'

'Absolutely. Hand over.'

Lou did as she was told and Harry flicked her phone open and grinned at her. 'You ought to get one which does videos.'

'Oh, God, a phone freak ...'

''Fraid so.'

She watched Harry looking at each shot with every appearance of total absorption. He'd told her about his divorce, but not whether he was involved with anyone at the moment. It was none of her business, but she found herself wanting to know. Just not at this moment. Next time, she'd ask him straight out.

'Would you like another coffee, or a drink perhaps?' Lou turned to Harry and asked this question, hoping very much that the doubts she was feeling about asking it weren't obvious to him. The whole way home on the Tube, all the way up the hill to her flat, she'd inwardly rehearsed how to say it: lightly, as though she were used to asking men up for a drink and not as though she had no idea what she was feeling. She didn't even know whether she wanted him to say yes or no. Her mouth was dry as she spoke.

'I'd better not,' said Harry, sounding completely normal and casual. 'Very early start tomorrow and got to get back on the Underground.'

Immediately, Lou felt guilty. 'God, I'm sorry. I could have come home on my own, I always do. Really, I feel bad about this, Harry, taking you so far out of your way.'

'Sssh ...' He put a finger out and touched her on the lips. 'I wouldn't dream of letting you come home by yourself. And it's fine, honestly. We'll do coffee another time, right?'

'Right. Thanks, Harry. I enjoyed the meal so much.'

'Me too. We must do it again. Night, Lou.'

'Night, Harry. Thanks.'

Was he going to kiss her? Shake her hand? She felt a fool just standing there, not certain what her cue was for moving up the stairs and into the house. He put his hands on her shoulders and, leaning forward, kissed her hair, not quite on the top of her head, but almost. 'Bye,' he said. 'I'll see you next week at work, right?'

'I'll come in on Tuesday.'

He walked away down the hill and Lou waved at him until he was out of sight. He turned round twice to wave back. She let herself into the flat and locked the door behind her, feeling happier than she had in a long time.

The next day, Lou went to the library to work. Concentrating at home was becoming more and more difficult and the space and quiet she'd loved so much when Poppy first went to stay with her grandparents was now a bit – a bit what? She didn't want to admit it at first, but it was lonely. Once you had a baby, it was much harder to keep up with your friends. She was beginning to feel cut off, isolated, sitting all day in the flat without her baby and she was spending far too much time missing her, going into her room and staring at the mobiles she'd hung from the ceiling. The sight of the empty cot made her want to cry if she looked at it late at night. It was the left-behind soft toys (always called cuddlies) that did it, the rejected ones who hadn't made the cut when it came to accompanying Poppy to Haywards Heath. They had been propped up against the sides of the cot, but most had flopped over and lay limply face down on the sheet. They look, Lou thought, like I feel.

She'd taken to going to the library more frequently simply to get out of the flat for a while. She'd discovered this branch, hidden away in a square near Poppy's nursery, just after Christmas last year, and she had a favourite place there which she privately thought of as hers: at a table near the huge plate-glass window, with a view of the small garden provided by the council for the benefit of library users and others. Someone had had the imagination to plant an apple tree very near the window and all through the winter, Lou had been looking forward to what it would look like in the spring.

Now, even though there was a storm of blossom blowing about on the other side of the glass, she was unaware of it. She'd come in to look something up about the prison camps in North Borneo during the Second World War but, with the book in front of her on the table, she drifted into thinking about last night's meal with Harry and wondering why she was disappointed. What had she been expecting? She went over everything they'd said to one another; the smiles, the laughter, the finger on her lips, the kiss on the hair, the words *we must do it again. We'll do coffee another time*. What they meant; what weight she was supposed to attach to anything.

I wanted more, she thought gloomily. I wanted him to be more ... more interested. Did I want him to make a pass at me? This was at the same time the most hopeful and the most despair-making thought of all, because if it was true that she was wanting Harry to go for it, then that meant she could be in the process of getting over her terror at the very idea of a physical relationship with a man. The despair came with the realization that he was probably just not interested. Okay, he liked her, he thought she was fun to go and have a curry with from time to time, but that was it. There was no evidence whatsoever for any other dream scenario she might have been concocting in her head. She stared at the page, not really seeing the words, not interested in them; outside the window the clouds of blossom blew about and she didn't even turn to look at them.

'Mummy's coming tomorrow, sweetie pie,' said Phyl, beaming at Poppy who was sitting in her playpen in the living room, looking as though she might be about to become bored with the entertainment (soft bricks, board books, chunky little cars with brightly coloured wheels) her granny had provided for her. She pulled herself up on the bars of the pen and said, 'Ummy.'

'That's right. It's the weekend. Won't it be lovely to see her?'

'Teddy ...' said Poppy, noticing the one cuddly toy missing from the plastic compound.

'He's sleeping upstairs,' said Phyl. 'He's having a nap. D'you want to go for a nap? Let's get a bottle and go and find Teddy in the cot,' she said, murmuring the words into the sweet-smelling skin of Poppy's neck, loving the feel of her, the weight in her arms.

Poppy clutched the bottle and the muslin cloth (called Muzzly) that had to accompany it as part of the feeding ritual and submitted to having her nappy changed. As Phyl did up the poppers on the baby-gro, she wondered whether there'd be time to unpack some of Constance's stuff before Lou arrived. She'd already worked out where the main pieces would go. The two huge vases probably in the hall, or maybe in the conservatory, and some of the best china on the dresser. The pretty rose-sprinkled, gold-edged teacups deserved to be displayed. I can get rid of some of our mugs and ancient plates to Oxfam or somewhere. So many of them were chipped and stained. She left the room, smiling. Chip and Stain, she thought. A whole new way of paying for things. She listened for a moment outside the closed door and went downstairs to start on the china.

She began with the pair of Chinese vases which had so impressed her on her first visit to Milthorpe House. She still loved them. They stood as high as her waist – what was that – three feet or so, she thought. They seemed to her slender and elegant in spite of their size, because the porcelain was almost thin enough to be translucent. Not too fat round the middle, with narrow necks and patterns of dragons and leaves and butterflies scattered over them in colours that were at the same time piercingly bright – turquoise and blue and red and gold and startling black – and so delicately applied that you could see the white of the porcelain through every stroke of the paintbrush. In the hall, one on each side of the door leading to the dining room – that would look good, she thought.

Then suddenly, in her head, she could hear Rosemary's voice. Phyl hadn't seen much of John Barrington's mother, who was quite old by the time she and Matt were married, but there was one day when they'd been standing in the hall in Milthorpe House and Rosemary had spoken quite firmly and also quite loudly. She always spoke, Phyl remembered, as though there was substance to what she had to say, even when the subject was trivial. She assumed that everything coming out of her mouth was of the utmost import-ance and interest to everyone, and now she declared: 'If you'd been a prisoner of the Japanese, you'd think twice before giving house room to anything quite so *Oriental*.' She made the word ring with contempt.

'But, Granny.' Matt came to his mother's defence. 'These aren't Japanese. They're from China, and they're over a hundred years old.'

'Nevertheless,' said Rosemary, stalking off in the direction of the library, and that was her last word on the subject.

Phyl smiled. Then she fetched a damp cloth and began wiping the beautiful curves of the vase. Conflicted, that's what Rosemary was about her experiences during the war. It was from Matt that Phyl gathered most of the story. John Barrington had spent time in a prisoner-of-war camp as a child. One of his books, too, had that setting. Perhaps she'd ask Lou to bring it with her this weekend. Maybe she should have read it before, but somehow it had never appealed to her. The trouble with me, Phyl thought, is that I don't dwell on the past. Mostly, she knew, she forgot things almost as soon as they'd happened, and though she never said so to anyone, she reckoned sometimes that this was the reason for her general contentment. I don't keep going over stuff that's gone by, she told herself. I don't fret.

Almost immediately, she realized that *some* things, a few particular times, or events, did stick. She remembered the day of Matt and Ellie's wedding, for instance, because she'd been ill. She'd spent most of the night before vomiting and wanting to die. That's my problem, she thought. I get sick when things get too bad. I'm allergic to unhappiness. The idea made her smile.

Constance had hardly ever talked to her. She made it quite clear that she was very unhappy when Ellie left and what's more (how she managed this, Phyl didn't know) that the situation was possibly temporary and that her beloved first daughter-in-law might just decide to come back and take up with Matt where she'd left off. She never actually said this, but Phyl was given to understand that it wasn't out of the question. The love and devotion she lavished on Nessa and Justin; the barely disguised dislike of Lou – that was all part of it. Constance was asserting her conviction that Ellie was better: more important, more suitable, more everything. Especially, Ellie was sexier.

Phyl hated the modern fashion for exchanging details of your sexual life with everyone you met. She never spoke about her own and was uncomfortable when other people gave her blow-by-blow accounts of what went on in theirs. She never expected any kind of revelation from Constance and that was why this particular conversation stuck in her mind. She'd been heavily pregnant at the time. Why were they in Constance's bedroom? That detail had gone, but she'd been sitting, she remembered, in a chair with no arms, upholstered in velvet, and Constance was lying on the bed, dressed in what she called 'a house coat', but which was in fact made of some brocadey fabric and looked like something you'd wear to a fancy-dress party if you were going as a Chinese empress or similar. Now, with the benefit of hindsight, Phyl wondered whether Constance didn't rather overdo the Oriental stuff purely to irritate her mother-in-law. Out of the blue, then, came the first remark.

'I shouldn't think you're in a position to satisfy Matt sexually these days, dear, are you? In your condition ...'

Phyl had blushed to the roots of her hair, and had not a clue what she was going to answer. Her first, her overriding feeling was of pure embarrassment, quickly followed by indignation. How could Constance be so ... so *rude*? It was none of her business, but Phyl would not have dared to say that. Constance hadn't paused for an answer, but had just gone on speaking as though Phyl were an audience rather than a conversational partner.

'Men get funny when their wives are pregnant, you know. If you're a love object, it reminds them that you're very soon going to be a mother and somehow that does take the gilt off the gingerbread for some. The sucking of breasts ...' (had she winked as she said this? Phyl could no longer remember) '... becomes functional rather than erotic. Or maybe you don't like that? I love it – I used to love it, but alas, I married the wrong person for that kind of thing.'

She'd sat up suddenly then, and swung her legs round so that she was sitting on the edge of the bed. She'd glared at Phyl and said, 'He's useless. John. Quite, quite useless. And it's not his fault, I know, but it's difficult to keep on blaming his mother. Though I do. I blame Rosemary. She sent him to that ghastly school and they – they repressed whatever sexual feelings he might have had almost to extinction.'

She laughed. 'I revived them, when we met. For a while. I taught him. It was like rubbing life into a statue at first, I can tell you. I spent hours and hours on him and he did – he thawed out a little, but it was never ... Well, I wanted more. I needed more, do you understand what I'm saying, dear?'

Phyl thought she ought to say something, but didn't know what. What was the appropriate remark when your mother-in-law told you your father-in-law had not come up to scratch in the bedroom? It's none of my business, she told herself. I wish I could leave. I wish I could just get up and leave. Instead she said, 'Why did you stay with him?'

'God, darling, you are naïve! I stayed with him because he was handsome, presentable, someone respected by other people I cared about and because ...' Here she'd grinned at Phyl. 'He couldn't complain if I took lovers. Which I did. Many. I was discreet about it, but he knew. He must have done. So we were both happy. I'm an old woman now, but in the early days, oh, there was no stopping me. I was – well, I was a bit like Ellie. No stopping her either, was there?'

This was especially cruel. Constance enjoyed that, Phyl realized. She was very good at the tiny little remarks which, if you challenged her, she could say were not meant in the way you thought they were ... *Oh, I was only mentioning Ellie because she was so like me ... nothing to do with you at all.*

Not half, Phyl thought now. Constance had been comparing Ellie with what she'd been presented with after the divorce and Phyl had clearly been found wanting. She hadn't been prepared to sit there and chat about Ellie. No way. She'd decided to make some excuse and leave. She was just wondering what she could say when Constance had gone off on another tack.

'At least,' she said, swinging her feet up on to the bed again and leaning back against a pile of about four pillows, each one edged with a frill of ornate lace, 'John got it up long enough to father Matt! All his energies went into his books after that effort!'

This was supposed to be a jokey remark, but Phyl felt sick.

'I've got to go, Constance,' she managed to mutter. 'Matt'll be waiting for me.'

She'd staggered downstairs, and there was Matt, in the hall.

'Anything wrong, darling?'

'No, I'm fine. Just want to go home. I'm a bit tired.'

In the car, he'd glanced across at her and said, 'Was Mother being nasty to you, Phyl? Don't take any notice. She can't help it sometimes. She doesn't really mean it.'

'No, she wasn't nasty, I'm just tired. I told you.' She knew that Matt would have supported her if she'd complained about Constance's behaviour, but she also knew he avoided trouble when he could and particularly didn't enjoy fighting with his mother, so she decided not to speak to him about it. She couldn't have repeated what Constance had told her in any case.

She'd made a decision then to put what Constance had said out of her head and forget about it. But I haven't, she thought now. I've never forgotten it. When Lou was born, things got even worse, because who would have thought that John Barrington, famously quiet and undemonstrative and devoid of passion, would lose his heart to a baby? But he had, and Constance, Phyl could see now, had never forgiven Lou for that.

The phone rang and Phyl flew to answer it. She

145

didn't want Poppy woken up before she'd had time to do a bit more unpacking.

'Matt? Hi ...'

'Hi, Phyl. What are you and Poppy up to?'

'She's napping and I'm unpacking.'

'Right.' Matt was silent for a second and then said: 'Shan't be back for lunch today, darling. Just wanted you to know. Hope you haven't made anything?'

'No, don't worry, no problem at all. I'll keep the soup for the weekend. Put it in the freezer. Anything exciting?'

'Ellie's just phoned and said she's coming in. Wants to talk about Justin and the house, Nessa – that kind of stuff. Easier to go to lunch than bring her home, right? Over more quickly.'

'I don't mind at all, if you'd both like to come here. It'd be fine.'

'Well, no, it's okay. There's Poppy and – well, it's easier just to go out somewhere. You don't mind, do you?'

'Good Lord, no,' said Phyl, sounding too hearty, even to herself. I do mind, though, she thought as she put the phone down. I'm still jealous of bloody Ellie. I can't help it. Matt wouldn't do anything, would he? Of course not. He was too – what was the word for it? Too upright. But she'd been thinking about Constance and John and their sex lives – how long had it been for her and Matt? She blushed as she realized she couldn't remember. I have to do something about that, she thought. I can't blame everything on Poppy not sleeping well. Am I undersexed? Is something wrong with me? Matt and I get on so well in every way that we could easily fall into something that's more like friendship. I'd hate that to happen.

She opened another box and started to take out the second Chinese vase. I don't want to think about this, she told herself. I won't. Not now. Later. She couldn't shake the feeling that something like a shadow had fallen over the morning.

Matt put the phone down with a sigh and a feeling that he'd been let off the hook. I haven't got anything to reproach myself with, he thought, so why do I feel guilty? He'd almost wished that Phyl had kicked up a fuss, been outraged and jealous, forbidden him to see Ellie at all, much less go out to lunch with her, but (typically of her) she didn't, so here he was, waiting for his ex-wife to arrive and pretending to himself, his secretary, the other partners in the firm that there was still stuff to talk about relating to his mother's will. This was not true. Constance had tied everything up extremely neatly in just the way she should have done and all he had to do was see that it was executed according to her wishes. Ellie had no more to say on the subject and neither had he, so what was this lunch about?

She'd phoned him a couple of days ago and Matt was ashamed to admit that since then he'd turned the thought of Ellie over and over in his mind, imagining different scenarios, most of which morphed quite quickly into a sexual fantasy of one kind or another. He laughed out loud, hoping very much that no one was near enough to his open door to hear him. He was amused at the thought of any kind of shenanigans taking place at the Belle Hélène, which was where he'd decided they would go. He liked the food there and it was near enough to the office for them to walk.

Phyl hadn't noticed how carefully he'd dressed this morning. She didn't notice much that wasn't related to Poppy and it occurred to Matt that the way to get the child back with her mother was to throw himself on Lou's mercy and confess that the presence of this beloved baby was having some unforeseen side effects – e.g. a non-existent sex life. She'd take her back at once if he did that, but he was too embarrassed to utter such a thing, and besides, he didn't want to put pressure on Lou, who was evidently doing some kind of intensive work she wasn't prepared to tell them about. All she'd said was, 'It's amazing to be able to work uninterrupted. I'm so grateful to you and Mum.'

So – nothing was going to change any time soon, and because he loved his granddaughter he didn't mind the disruption as much as he might have done. He stood up from his desk and went to the partners' lavatory, where the mirror had been hung near the window. He peered into it and was quite happy with what he saw. All my own hair and teeth, at least, he told himself. And not too much grey, either. While they were married, Ellie had taken charge of his wardrobe and bought all his shirts, and she'd once told him that blue was his colour. He'd believed her. Today he was wearing a grey suit with a pale blue shirt and a tie he hoped went with both. He wasn't going to improve his image by staring at it, so he washed his hands and left the room.

Ellie was waiting in the comfortable chair in his office when he returned.

'Ellie, hello. So sorry I wasn't here to welcome you ...'

'No problem, darling. I've been reading the letters on your desk. Oh, God, Matt, I'm joking! I wouldn't, honestly. All your secrets are safe with me.'

'Ellie, you don't change. Are you ready to eat? I've reserved the table for one o'clock.'

'Let's go then,' said Ellie, leading the way out of the room.

They walked down the road in the spring sunshine.

'Lovely weather,' Matt said and Ellie made a sound between a laugh and a snort.

'Oh, come on, Matt,' she said. 'Do say we're not going to talk about the weather.'

'I was just remarking on what a nice day it was.' Matt knew he sounded huffy and didn't care. Why did Ellie think *she* could decide what was and wasn't to be spoken about? This attitude was something she shared with Constance. It was only one of many things they saw eye to eye about. His mother used to do it all the time: tell him that some topic he'd initiated was boring or stupid or just nothing to do with her.

'Oh, Matt darling,' she'd say, 'don't let's talk about that ...' Or, 'Please, Matt, not ...' and then you could insert about a thousand topics in which she had no interest whatsoever. These included him, his wife, his daughter, his work, politics, sport, movies, TV. What on earth *did* we talk about? he wondered. He knew the answer: they'd talked about her, about Constance. And about Rosemary, his grandmother. Relations between the two women were strained, to say the least.

La Belle Hélène was a small and pleasant restaurant which tried to look like a provincial French bistro and almost succeeded. The tablecloths were gingham; there was a straw basket on each table overflowing with chunks of good French bread. The house red was more than drinkable and the unpretentious menu appealed to Matt. He couldn't bear food which needed three lines of purple prose to describe it and particularly hated the term 'enrobed' which menu writers used when talking about thick sauces. Phyl had never eaten here, as far as he knew, which was part of the reason he'd chosen it today. He could never get her to understand why anyone would choose to eat out when there was perfectly good food at home. Restaurants in other towns was one thing, but a place just down the road from where she lived struck Phyl as silly.

As soon as they'd sat down, Matt noticed that Mrs Blandford and a friend of hers whose name escaped him – Mrs Whitsomething ... Whitford, wife of a local councillor – were at a table on the other side of the room. He turned quickly to the menu, but not before Mrs B had caught his eye and given him a flirtatious wave. He waved back, and smiled broadly, as if to say *I'm not doing anything underhand or hole in corner. All perfectly respectable.*

'Who're you waving at?' Ellie wanted to know.

'A silly old trout called Mrs Blandford who knows me from the time her husband left her. I handled the sale of her house after the divorce. Years ago.'

'Mmm,' Ellie said, who was already bored by the subject and considering what to order. Matt was relieved when the waiter arrived and they could turn their attention to the food. He wondered whether Mrs B knew Phyl and decided she probably did. Many people knew her from the vet's and he could just imagine a pack of Pekinese dogs snapping at the rather thick Blandford ankles. He decided to put all thought of the ladies in the corner and what they might be saying to one another about him and Ellie totally out of his mind. Phyl knew he was having this lunch. He wasn't doing anything wrong. He poured a glass of white wine for Ellie and one for himself and said, 'I've been thinking about the family lately. You met Grandmother Rosemary, didn't you?'

'God, yes,' Ellie said. 'John's mother. Scary woman.'

'Was she?'

'Mmm, she was a control freak, I thought. Quiet and demure-looking on the surface but steely underneath. I was never fooled by the twin-set and pearls façade. I wouldn't have crossed her in a hurry. She made your dad what he was, didn't she?'

The waiter arrived with their food, and as he served the vegetables, and the potatoes, Matt thought about Ellie's remarks. He said, 'What do you mean, made him what he was ...?'

'She never let him forget,' Ellie said calmly, 'that he was second-best. She wanted a girl.'

'How d'you know that? Is it true? My father never said anything to me.'

'I know because she told me.'

Matt stared at her with a forkful of mashed potato halfway to his mouth. 'D'you mean to say my grand-mother told you this and didn't tell me? Why, for goodness' sake?'

'Because you weren't interested, I suppose. And I was. I – I drew her out. I asked the right questions. She was bitter, Matt. A bitter woman, because she couldn't have children of her own. That poisoned her, I think, and turned her into who she became.'

'What did she actually say? I mean, *really* – not things you deduced or inferred from what she did ...'

'You never stop being a lawyer, do you, Matt? Well, she told me that when she went into the prison camp, she wanted to die. She'd just found out her husband had been killed in some hideous battle or other. This on top of years and years of trying for a baby and not succeeding. It was the last straw. They'd been very much in love, she told me, and finding another husband was the last thing on her mind. But she had to take care of John. He was her friend's son, after all. Don't you think you'd have done something similar?'

'No, I don't think I would have,' Matt said. 'I'd have tried to find the mother's relations. Or something. I'd have made an effort.'

'But this was wartime. People were dying and

disappearing all over the place. It must have been a nightmare keeping track of paperwork. She persuaded the authorities that John was *her* son.'

Matt thought about this for a moment. 'Why didn't my father say anything? He was old enough to remember exactly what happened to his real mother, wasn't he?'

Ellie put her knife and fork down tidily on the plate. 'He didn't say anything because he was terrified. Rosemary told him that if he said one word about her not being his real mother, they – whoever they were – would take him away and put him in an orphanage. And by the time they got to England and she'd remarried and she and Frederick Barrington had adopted John and he'd gone off to school (which he hated, by the way), he'd almost persuaded himself that he *was* Rosemary's birth child. It was easier that way, I suppose.'

Matt looked down at his plate. He finished what was left on it silently, trying to analyse his feelings. Part of him was interested in what Ellie was saying about his father. Why had she not mentioned it before? Perhaps she assumed he'd known all along, and didn't take into account his father's habitual silence and Constance's lack of interest in anything that concerned her husband. Another part of him (and he felt ashamed admitting this to himself) was growing more and more irritated that this lunch had turned out to be more serious than the flirtatious and pleasant occasion he'd imagined. A voice in his head said *did you truly expect her to initiate anything – anything romantic – at lunch? At La Belle Hélène, of all places? If so, you're a bloody fool. She's probably not interested. She's probably only after free legal advice of some kind.*

'You're not saying anything,' Ellie chided him.

'Sorry. I was thinking. I didn't mean the whole meal to be devoted to my family history.'

'Then,' Ellie smiled at him, 'let's talk about something jollier.'

'Jollier? You haven't come to ask advice? Or talk about the will?'

'No, whatever gave you that idea? I just fancied the idea of seeing you. Justin's saying nothing and Nessa's stopped moaning quite as much. What about Lou?'

'She's not said anything lately. I'm the one who's still angry. The money, the property – either of those would have made such a difference to her situation.'

'How are you liking life with a baby?'

'It's bloody hard work,' Matt said, and at once felt disloyal. He added, 'Though of course, we love having Poppy. She's a sweetie, really.'

'But your nights are interrupted and Phyl smells of baby vomit.'

'You don't mince your words, do you, Ellie? No, it's fine, really.'

'You always were,' Ellie said, putting her hand gently over his and gazing into his eyes, 'a useless liar. You're hating it and wishing it was over and Lou would take her kid back. You can't fool me.'

Matt felt himself blushing. 'You're a witch, Ellie. You see right through me. I can't help it. I adore Poppy, but I think I'm a bit old for babies, that's all. But Phyl's happy. She loves it. Thrives on it.'

He felt her fingers caressing the skin of his wrist. 'I think,' she whispered, 'that you might deserve a bit of a treat.'

'What are you suggesting, Ellie?'

'Nothing, really. Just the occasional lunch. We might do a movie or a play up in town?'

'And what would I tell Phyl?'

'You'd work something out.'

'Get thee behind me, woman,' he laughed, but his heart was pounding and he felt for the first time in a long time the excitement that came with the contemplation of a deliciously forbidden possibility. It could happen. Ellie was willing to sleep with him, he knew, but he wasn't – he couldn't! What would it do to Phyl if she found out? *She needn't find out. No one need ever know.* He couldn't do it. He wasn't cut out to be an adulterer. As Ellie said, he was a rotten liar. He sighed and said, 'Though I wouldn't rule out another lunch.'

'Soon,' Ellie said. 'Can it be soon? It's such a treat to see you, Matt. Sometimes I wonder why I ever left you.'

Out of the corner of his eye, he saw that Mrs Blandford and Mrs Whitford were no longer at their table. When had they left? He'd been too preoccupied to notice. Would that become part of the anecdote the two ladies would spread around town? *My dear, he was so absorbed in this woman that he didn't even look up when we passed their table.*

Ellie signalled the waiter and asked for the dessert menu. The tables were small at this restaurant. He was aware that her knees were almost touching his under the hanging whiteness of the tablecloth. He could put a hand on her knee. She was wearing a shortish skirt ... he could move his fingers gently under the hem and ... He shook his head to clear it of the knowledge that Ellie always wore stockings and not tights. He closed his eyes briefly, remembering, so vividly remembering, how soft the white skin was at the top of her thighs ...

'Are you having a pudding?' Ellie's voice brought him back to the real world, where he was a respectable lawyer married to another woman, having a perfectly decent lunch with someone he was supposed to have got over two decades ago.

'No ... no, thanks. Just a strong black coffee, that's all.'

He hoped devoutly that the caffeine would knock some sense into him. He felt inflamed, feverish, and found himself trying to answer two completely contradictory questions. The first was *where can I get Ellie on her own and how soon?* and the second, *how do I run away from this ghastly temptation and avoid wrecking my life with Phyl?* There was no way he knew to reconcile these conflicting desires but he was certain of one thing: whatever Ellie wanted from him and was willing to give him, it wasn't any kind of permanent relationship. I don't care, he thought. I want her. I wish – I wish I could take her back to the office, to the comfortable chair she was sitting in an hour ago. I'd push her skirt up above her knees and ...

'Your coffee, sir,' said the waiter.

5

We apologize for the delay, which has been caused by a signal failure ...

The tinny voice burbled on for a while, explaining, and saying sorry in every tinny way it knew, but the bottom line was a delay. Damn and blast and bloody hell, Lou thought, staring out of the window at a bank of more than usual boringness. Just grass, and those purple flowering plants she didn't know the name of but which weren't buddleia and which grew in profusion by every railway line in the country, or so it seemed. She took out her mobile and phoned Haywards Heath to tell them she was going to be late.

'It's okay,' said her mother. 'Just phone when you're nearly here and Poppy and I will come and fetch you in the car.'

Poppy. She'd only been away from home for a couple of weeks but even so, when it got to this stage, when she was actually on her way to see her daughter, she could hardly wait. I'm going to tell Mum, she told herself. I'm going to tell her that I'm taking Poppy back as soon as I've finished this screenplay. Lou had come to the conclusion that in spite of the convenience of solitude; in spite of the fact that she could do exactly what she wanted when she wanted; in spite of the hours and hours of work she'd managed to put in while Poppy wasn't there, she wanted her back. She wanted her there in the next room. Her voice. Her silly words, her cries, her smell, and the smile that she produced every day when Lou went in to pick her up out of her cot: shining, pure, totally loving – and all for her. The little arms stretched out, the pink and white striped fleecy bag that she slept in twisted up around her feet, hobbling her – I miss all that, Lou acknowledged. And I'm jealous of Mum and worried that if I leave Poppy there, she'll get to love Mum better than she loves me. It's not enough that she loves me. Lou recognized that these feelings were stupid and petty but still, it was true. She needed Poppy to love her best. *I love you all there is* – that's what her own mother used to say to her when she was a child and Lou had always remembered it. Now Phyl was saying it to Poppy. Do I mind that? Am I jealous of my own daughter? That is beyond stupid. It's ridiculous. I'm going to stop thinking such nonsense right now.

The train remained at a standstill. Passengers were becoming restless, getting up and going to the loo, peering out of the windows, and there was a lot of sighing from the overweight woman opposite her, who looked as though she might be on the point of starting a conversation. No way, Lou thought, and scrabbled round in her bag for *Blind Moon*, which she took everywhere with her. She'd covered it, primary school style, with an offcut of wallpaper to preserve the original dust-jacket. The book fell open at a passage which Lou had read so often that she knew it almost by heart:

There were always screams at night and he often slept through them, so he didn't know why these screams were different. Why they'd woken him up. Peter lay in the darkness, and the sound went through him, making his skin crawl. He sat up. Everyone in the hut was lying quite still and he thought: some of them might be dead and we won't know till the morning. Probably, though, they were just sleeping. It was easy to think bad thoughts in the night. That's what Dulcie called them, bad thoughts. Things that came into your mind at night which made you cry, or frightened you. Things you remembered when you lay down which you didn't have time to remember when the sun was shining. Like what they'd done to Mrs Atkins. They made her stand in the sun and didn't allow anyone to come near her. For hours. She fell over in the end and he hadn't seen her since. She was dead, most likely. She'd tried to escape and they didn't like that. There were lots of things they didn't like but the worst punishments were for trying to get away, over the barbed wire looped in thorny curls over the top of the fence.

The screams had got a bit quieter now. Suddenly, he knew. He knew who was screaming. When you scream, you don't really have a voice and yet he recognized the sounds. His mother was making them. She was screaming.

'What's the matter? Why're you sitting up?' That was Derek, who slept in the next bed. Derek was a mummy's boy and Peter didn't like him much, but he said, 'It's my mother. Can you hear the screams? It's her. I know it is. I'm going to the women's hut.'

'You can't. They'll find out.'

'Shut up and go to sleep. Don't say a word or you'll be sorry.'

Peter made his way from shadow to shadow across the compound. A thin moon in the sky made small patches of light on the earth and he followed the screams to the women's hut and crept up the steps. He paused on the second one, because he could see in from there, right across the floor to where his mother was lying. He could see the women, gathered round the dirty mattress on the floor. Peter didn't know what to do. The screams were getting worse now. Mummy must be ill, he thought. Why don't the guards come? They should bring a doctor – there must be someone who could help. And then quite suddenly, Peter realized what was happening and wondered why it had taken him so long. He was as stupid and babyish as Derek. She was having a baby. The baby was coming. If he said something, would they send him away? He decided to keep quite silent and tiptoed into a shadow in a corner of the hut where no one would see him. No one noticed. They were all, all the women, paying attention to nothing but his mother's pain.

Later, Peter wished that he'd run back to the children's hut before he'd seen what happened. His mother was being torn apart; that was what it looked like. There was so much blood. His mother's legs were streaked with it; it pooled in a dark puddle on the floor. And the screams had stopped and she was sobbing and then there was another sound, coming from a thing that looked like a skinned animal. A rabbit or something very small. How could such a small thing open up a scarlet gash in his mother's body and leave her splashed with sticky blood? The skinned creature was screaming very small screams. It was lying on his mother and she had her bosoms out and Peter felt embarrassed and wanted to run away and cry and never see a thing like that again. It was horrible. His mother was broken. Split open. Horrible horrible horrible.

By the time she looked up, the train was moving again and the woman opposite had given her up as a bad job and gone to sleep. It wouldn't be long till she was there, with Poppy, with her parents. Her thoughts turned to her screenplay ... this scene was very vivid in her mind. She could see the darkness, hear the voices, those screams. And no words. Or not many. She'd decided on a voice-over for some parts of the story. Voice-overs weren't fashionable but she didn't care. This story needed one. So much of it was Peter's own thoughts, and it would be a shame to lose too many of his words.

When the train stopped, Lou was the first to leave the carriage. She almost ran to the car park, where she knew Phyl would be waiting. She saw her at once, standing by the car with Poppy in her arms.

'Baby! Darling Poppykins baby ...' She took the child from Phyl and clasped her close, aware of her solidity, her plump pink cheeks, the chubby little hands patting and patting her as if Poppy were making sure that yes, this was Mummy. There were tears in Lou's eyes as she felt herself overwhelmed with a tangle of feelings: pleasure that her baby hadn't forgotten who she was since last week; guilt that she'd been away from her for so many hours and gratitude for her health; for the fact that she wasn't the baby in Grandad's book – the skinned creature, the rabbit, the newborn who was so thin and tiny that there wasn't ever a chance of her surviving ... 'Come along, Pumpkin,' she said, 'get back into your car seat. Granny's going to drive us to her house and then we'll all have tea and cake, won't we, Granny?'

'You certainly will. Poppy helped me to stir it, didn't you, darling?'

'Ummy!' Poppy pronounced and started to wriggle as Phyl strapped her into the seat. 'Ummy yap!'

'You can sit on Mummy's lap when we get home,' Phyl said. 'Now you've got to sit in your car seat like a good girl.'

'I'll sit next to you,' said Lou, and slid into the seat next to Poppy, suddenly remembering the night she was born. The pain – had she screamed? Maybe she had, but her screams had been sanitized, made safe in the white and silver hi-tech labour ward of the hospital. Then they'd given her an anaesthetic and taken her in for a C-section. Poppy had been beautiful right from the start, staring into Lou's eyes with a gaze that everyone said was quite unusual. Most babies, they said, don't focus for ages but, in the words of one of the midwives, 'This one's been here before.' This baby's skin had been pale and unwrinkled from the moment she first drew breath and she'd managed, unusually, to look like neither Winston Churchill nor Queen Victoria.

'What's the news, darling? Had a good week?' said Phyl, over her shoulder.

'I went out to dinner with Harry on Thursday.'

'Really?'

'Oh, God, Mum, stop it. It's not like that. We were discussing a work thing, and he took me for a curry, that's all.'

'Is it? Is it all?'

Lou recognized the yearning in her mother's voice. She was always on the lookout for romance in her daughter's life. She'd have adored putting a big wedding together.

'Yup. Forget it, Mum. No wedding alert yet.'

Phyl sighed. 'I live in hope.'

'Iven ope, iven ope, iven ope,' sang Poppy, now gurgling away in her car seat.

'She's really getting the hang of this speaking lark,' said Lou. 'But let's sing a song now, okay?'

She began to sing 'This Old Man', which was near the top of Poppy's hit parade. By the time they'd reached 'He plays five' the baby's eyes were closed, and her mouth was half open. Lou wanted to kiss her but also didn't want to wake her up. A spasm of love so strong that it was almost like a pain in her heart took hold of her and she, too, closed her eyes, willing herself not to cry.

Gareth was nuzzling her neck, murmuring endearments, moving on top of her in a way that Nessa had come to know so well that she could respond without really engaging her brain. But on this occasion it occurred to her to wonder, with a spasm of disgust, how long it had been since he'd been doing exactly this with Melanie. She tried to think of something far removed from sex: the deal Justin was going to strike with the spa people; how that might benefit her, and Paper Roses; how Tamsin needed new gym shoes and new T-shirts and knickers, too. She seemed to be growing very fast lately and Nessa mentally went through her diary for the next few days wondering when they could fit in a visit to M&S. Gareth was nearly done. She could tell from the way he sounded, his breathing working up to its usual rather gurgly gasping shout. She made a few noises herself to show willing, and sure enough, a few seconds later it was all over. Her husband lay beside her, panting after his exertions.

'Mmm,' said Nessa. 'Lovely, darling.' It was what she always said. Gareth usually answered with something along the lines of, 'Yes, darling – lovely,' and by then the snoring was only seconds away. She got out of bed to go to the bathroom. He'd be fast asleep by the time she got back.

'Darling?' When she got back, he wasn't snoring. He

was propped up against his pillows and he'd turned his bedside light on and was looking at her oddly. Nessa frowned. 'What's the matter, Gareth? D'you want a cup of tea or something?'

'No, it's okay. I just wanted ... Well, I wanted to talk to you.'

'Fine,' Nessa said. She was uncertain where to put herself. She wasn't quite sure what was going on but didn't feel like sliding between the sheets to lie next to her husband. He was looking uncharacteristically serious. If there was one quality about Gareth that she liked it was his carefree unconcern about most things, and the shambling, rather sweet way he bumbled through life, not fretting, not going into dark moods, not sulking for the most part. She had to admit that he was easy-going, and there was a lot to be said for being married to someone like that, especially if you were exactly the opposite. Because Nessa took everything so seriously and privately admitted that she was very quick to take offence and stalk off in a huff, she found it restful to be with someone who was even-tempered most of the time. He was going to confess about Melanie, she felt sure.

'Go on, then,' she said, standing up again. She walked round to the chaise longue, which was pushed up next to the wall on his side and sat down facing him. She couldn't, even on the edge of what looked like being a confession of adultery, stop herself from stroking the fabric in which she'd upholstered this piece of furniture: a luscious, apricot velvet. Gorgeous. The right decision, she told herself. It looked so good with the bronze silk curtains. She felt a small flutter of self-satisfaction.

'I don't know how to say it, Nessa. I'm not good at stuff like this.'

Nessa tried to look concerned but she wasn't going

to rescue him with helpful questioning. He'd get there in the end.

'I ... this ...' Gareth heaved a huge sigh and ran a hand through his hair, which made it stick up comically. He had his ridiculously traditional pyjama top on: blue, piped with dark brown and for all she knew he'd put the bottoms on again too while she was in the bathroom. They hadn't, as a couple, ever slept naked. From the beginning, Gareth always put his pyjamas on straight after they made love; Nessa did the same, but she never wore a nightdress when she slept alone. The mere touch of cool linen on her bare skin made her feel deliciously sexy. She'd suggested it to Gareth once when they were on their honeymoon and he'd looked panic-stricken so that was that.

'I want a divorce, Vanessa.'

Don't speak, she told herself. He never called her *Vanessa*. Her heart was thumping rather loudly and quickly and she blinked. Here we go. Should she pretend ignorance? Or admit that she knew all about Melanie? Divorce! What was he talking about? Did he really want to break up the marriage? A terrifying thought came into her mind: this house. Buggered if she was leaving. Gareth's money. How would it work out for her? What about Tamsin? Custody arrangements, tears – a trauma for their daughter, whom she loved beyond everything and who must not on any account suffer because of her father's stupidity. What should she do? She said, more to buy time than because she hadn't heard or understood, 'What did you say?'

'I'm asking you for a divorce. I'm in love with someone else. I want to be with her. I'm so sorry, Nessa. Truly. I didn't mean it ...'

'Mean what? What are you talking about? You're not making sense.'

'Well, I thought it was just an office flirtation. You know how it is ...'

'Do I?' Nessa's voice was icy now. 'You mean you've done this office flirtation thing before? Before this?'

'Well, it was nothing serious before. Not really ...'

'How dare you say that? How *dare* you? Are you really saying you've been unfaithful to me *often*?'

'It didn't mean anything, honestly. And it was only once or twice. That's all.'

'ALL?' Nessa was screaming now. 'ALL? I can't believe it. And this suddenly, this new thing that you want to divorce me over – that's different, is it? That *does* mean something, right?'

He nodded, blushing. 'She's ... I love her. And – well, she's pregnant.'

Nessa put her head in her hands. She hadn't been expecting that, and found that the thought scared her. Then she looked at Gareth and spat out the words.

'Pregnant! I see. So this new baby suddenly takes precedence over our baby. Our Tamsin. Suddenly, you don't give a shit about her, do you? She means nothing to you. You're about to get a new model. How convenient!'

'Stop it, Nessa. You're mad. Of course this baby won't take Tamsin's place. You know she'll always be my darling daughter.' A look of terror crossed Gareth's face quite suddenly as a thought occurred to him. 'You're not going to stop me seeing her, are you? I'd fight it in court. You can't do that, you really can't.'

'I wouldn't dream of it,' said Nessa, scrambling for the moral high ground even though for a split second the idea of giving Gareth full custody, simply because she knew he wouldn't want that, shimmered before her like a mirage. She smiled sweetly as she went on, 'No, you can have more than your fair share of childcare, never fear. I'll make sure of that. Let's see how Melanie manages with a new baby and a possibly quite traumatized eight-year-old. She'll have her hands full. Probably won't fancy fucking you quite so much as she did in the office. It does take it out of you, having a baby. You're never quite the same again, your priorities get rearranged.'

'How d'you know her name? I've never told you. Go on, tell me how you found out.'

'I read an illiterate text from someone called Melanie. On your phone, when you left it in the car, remember? You're an incompetent adulterer, as well as being a total bastard.'

Gareth was ashamed of himself. Nessa could tell from the way he looked down at his feet and chewed on his bottom lip. But he pulled himself together and tried to convey a kind of bravado.

'Have you ever thought that you're part of the problem, Nessa? Have you any idea what it's like to be married to someone as cold and selfish as you?'

'Oh, so it's my fault, the fact that you can't keep your hands off the secretaries, is it?' She stood up and went to the door and held it open. She said, 'I've had enough of this discussion for now, thanks. You can leave. Leave this house and don't come back. I'm getting in touch with our lawyer first thing on Monday and filing for divorce. Mental cruelty, infidelity, you name it. I'm going to screw you for every single penny I can, I'm warning you. You can go and live with Melanie. You deserve one another.'

Another thought occurred to her and she added, 'Does Melanie know *we're* still screwing? Not ten minutes ago, you were huffing and puffing all over me. Does she know that? I might text her to tell her what a fabulous lover you are, I *don't* think! Well, you're not answering. Does Melanie know you're still making totally inadequate love to me?'

Gareth had the grace to hang his head. 'No – no, she doesn't. And what do you mean, totally inadequate? You've never complained. You always seemed – well, quite satisfied.'

'I'm a good actress, you bloody fool. You're about as sexy as cold rice pudding. I bet you told her I was a cold fish and didn't let you come anywhere near me.' From his silence, she knew she'd guessed correctly.

'I knew it. You're *disgusting*. Just go and sleep somewhere else. I don't really care where – the sofa, the spare room. Somewhere where I can't see you. Go on. Go now.'

'But—'

'Don't say another word, okay? I swear, if you say one more thing I'm going to pick up this lamp and hit you with it.'

'I'm going, I'm going ...' He looked silly with his pyjama bottoms clutched in his hand and Nessa almost laughed as he left the room. When he'd gone, she sat without moving for a long time. I'm not getting into that bed again, she thought. It'll be a symbolic gesture. I've let him make love to me in it knowing he had someone else. I'll buy a new one in the morning. I'll ring up a moving firm and give this one to charity. She leaned forward, pulled the duvet off (that would go as well – all this linen – she wasn't going to use it any more *ever*. This was going to be a clean sweep) and, wrapping herself up in it, lay down on the chaise longue. She was further from sleep than she'd ever been in her life and intended to use the rest of the night to work out what she had to do next. Talk to Matt. Talk to Ellie. Talk to Justin. It had suddenly become more important than ever to get a slice of the deal he was cooking up. Tears came to her eyes. Mickey. If only Mickey were here. For a second or two, Nessa wondered whether she could drive through the night and wake up her friend for a comforting chat. Mickey wouldn't mind but she'd wait till morning. She'd go and see Matt and then her mother and get that part over with. Then she'd drive to Mickey's cottage. Should she warn her or just turn up? Tomorrow, she thought. I'll decide tomorrow.

'Coffee, Ness?' Lou looked across to where Nessa was sitting at the kitchen table, with Mum and Dad on either side of her, leaning towards her in a supportive manner. If it looks like a crisis and sounds like a crisis, Lou thought, then it is a crisis and yes, your sister coming in first thing on Sunday morning announcing that she was about to be divorced does count as something dramatic. If anyone had asked Lou what was the least likely thing to happen, ever, it was this: Gareth going off with a secretary from work. The cliché of clichés was being re-enacted right here in the kitchen, and Lou couldn't help being interested on a purely gossipy level, while at the same time being unable to squash completely a feeling of low-level resentment. Nessa's stuff, Nessa's concerns, always seemed to trump her own. But you've got nothing important to divulge, she told herself, trying to be kind. Nessa's whole life is ... is what? Her sister didn't look as though she'd missed out on sleep. Lou searched most particularly for signs of late-night weeping, and there wasn't a red-rimmed eye to be seen. But what a surprising thing this was! Lou had always thought Gareth was completely devoted and under Nessa's thumb. He did everything she suggested and seemed to have no opinions of his own, but perhaps this was the result. Maybe he'd found a person who liked doing what *he* thought he'd like to do. Maybe he hadn't been devoted so much as henpecked. Being married to Nessa had to be totally exhausting. Her sister liked describing herself as having high standards but to Lou it often looked as though she was simply more bossy and pernickety about most things than other people.

'No, thanks, Lou. I'm in danger of caffeine overload. Green tea of some kind?'

'I've got all sorts.' Mum jumped up and went to the cupboard, taking out a wooden box neatly subdivided into little sections: green tea with jasmine, with orange, with lemon, with Uncle Tom Cobbleigh and all – you could take your pick.

'Oh, God, anything,' said Nessa, sighing. Lou took the teabag from her mother and poured boiling water over it. Nessa hadn't been too distressed to care about what she was going to drink from. 'I can't bear those thick mugs,' she always said, and Mum had got into the habit of using the delicate china teacups when Nessa was around. Today, even though she'd come to the house in what was supposed to be a terrible state about the ending of her marriage, she'd made a point of repeating her 'no mugs' mantra when a drink was proposed.

'I can't understand him,' Mum said. 'Such a lovely house and child and a wife like you, Nessa. It's madness. Don't you think if you hold your ground, he might think better of throwing everything away? Come back to you in the end?'

Lou wanted to smile but stopped herself. In her mother's world, husbands always came back and that was always the best thing, the desirable option.

'I wouldn't have him if he did,' Nessa said, stirring her tea. 'He can go and see what life with Melanie is like. He'll have to pay maintenance for Tamsin till she's eighteen and I'm certainly keeping the house. I can, can't I, Matt?'

'Of course – you're the injured party. In any case,

the house is in both your names, isn't it?'

Nessa nodded. 'I made sure of that,' she said. 'God, it's such a drag. This whole thing. I don't need it now. There's a lot going on at Paper Roses and the thing with the will – too ghastly. I didn't sleep a wink last night. Not a wink.'

Through the kitchen door, Lou could see Poppy crawling about in the hall. She'd been in the kitchen, milling about under the table where they were all sitting, and even Mum, whose attention was usually fixed on the child during her every waking moment, had been distracted by Nessa's sudden arrival and what she had to say. Now Poppy was playing quite quietly with a set of Dinky cars that used to belong to Justin. Dad must have brought them down from the attic. Lou wondered whether she ought to go and pick her up and take her for a little walk in the buggy while this was going on – how long was Nessa staying? For lunch? All afternoon?

She listened to her sister going on and on, looking very far from desperate. Up all night? Either Nessa was lying or her make-up was spectacularly good. She looked as pulled together and smart as ever. The fact that she'd got up this morning and done her face so perfectly said everything really. This divorce was obviously a logistical problem; a financial one especially, but Nessa's heart wasn't broken. No way. It occurred to Lou to wonder whether part of her wasn't quietly happy. If she hadn't been properly in love with Gareth (and Lou didn't have the sort of relationship with her sister which meant that she could ask her outright) then this might be a kind of relief, even though it was a drag and a nuisance in all sorts of ways at this stage.

The unmistakable splintering noise of something shattering – glass? A window? – cut across the conversation.

'Poppy!' Lou shouted, and ran out of the room. Poppy was shrieking. 'Oh, darling Poppy … are you hurt? What's the matter?'

As she scooped her daughter up into her arms, Lou was dimly aware of her parents just behind her; of Nessa standing by the kitchen door and of the hall floor covered in thousands of pieces of porcelain, like a scattering of sharp-edged white leaves. She buried her face in Poppy's neck, murmuring over and over again, 'It's okay, baby, it's okay. You're fine, darling. Nothing's hurt. Nothing's wrong.'

After a few moments, Poppy began to calm down enough to sniff and ask for a bottle. Mum, Dad and Nessa had gathered in the doorway to the kitchen. Mum looked heartbroken, as though a living person had been accidentally harmed.

'God,' said Nessa, 'aren't little kids amazing. All those tears, and when they stop they're not a bit blotchy or revolting. Fantastic powers of recovery.'

'Give her to me,' Phyl said, putting on a brave face. 'I'll get her bottle. I think I'll put her down for a nap. Come to Granny, precious, come on.'

Lou handed her daughter over and felt a bewildering mixture of emotions. She wanted to say *no, it's me, I'm her mother. I should do it*, but Phyl was already scooping her up. She was obviously sad about the vase, but Lou wondered why she'd put it in the hall after all her efforts to make the house child-proof. Maybe she thought it was too big and heavy to come to any harm.

'God, Mum, it's your lovely Chinese vase. I'll clear it up,' she said. 'I know how much you love it – how on earth did Poppy manage to smash such a huge thing?'

'It doesn't matter,' said Matt, presenting Lou with the dustpan and brush he'd already fetched out of the cupboard under the stairs. 'Those vases are fragile. God knows, Mother used to say that to me often enough. Turns out she was right. Doesn't matter about the vase, Lou, really. But Poppy could have been seriously hurt. I dread to think ...'

'But she wasn't, Dad,' Lou said. 'She's fine. I think she pushed one of those cars too hard and it must have crashed against the china. There's no carpet just there. Or maybe she pushed it over and it was falling on the wooden bit of the floor that made it break. I'm so sorry, Dad. I know Mum loved that vase.'

'It doesn't matter, Lou. As long as Poppy's all right ...'

'She's fine, Dad.'

'Unlike me, Matt,' said Nessa. 'Can I have a word? I've got to go soon, and I want to know how to proceed.'

'D'you mind, Lou?' Her father looked bewildered.

'No, go on, Dad, you go and talk to Nessa. I'll clear this up. Then poor Mum won't have to see it in bits. I'm fine, honestly.'

Left alone in the hall, Lou began sweeping china into the dustpan. There was a folded piece of paper lying in the midst of the white fragments. What's that doing? she wondered. Someone must have dropped it in there by mistake. It was the sort of thing a child would do, but it certainly wasn't Poppy. This was a whole sheet, neatly folded and curling up a little at the edges as though it had been there for some time. Curious, she put the brush and dustpan down and unfolded the paper. A letter, handwritten in a spidery, obviously foreign hand. Fleetingly, she wondered why it was that Continental handwriting was so different from British. It must have to do with the way children were taught to write – what was this? She peered at the paper.

The date was 27 July, 1985. This letter was over twenty years old:

Dear Mr Barrington,

You will please forgive this bad English I write. Many years I do not write in this language. I find a copy of your romance, *Blind Moon*, in the shop of second-hand books and now I read it, I must ask you questions. I think the woman you write of may be my younger sister though you have changed her name. She left us to go to North Borneo and married an Englishman. They are different times then. My family do not speak to her again. I do not write to her. I am shamed of this. But maybe you make everything up. If not, if you are indeed son of Louise, my sister, then please answer me soon. I am sixty-five years old. Louise is sixty-seven if she has lived. My family never speak of her, but we think she died in North Borneo, perhaps in a camp like you have written. Your book I read with horror, because I am so sad. Please reply to this address: 4, Rue du Treixel, Paris 14ième, France. I am obliged to you.

With true regards,
Manon Franchard.

Lou sat back on her heels and read the letter three times. What did it mean? And why was it in the vase? Constance must have thrown it in there. Frowning, Lou tried to reconstruct what might have happened. Her grandmother was trying to keep a bit of fan mail away from her husband but why had she not simply torn up this letter? Dad had told her that Constance always dealt with the post and didn't show Grandad everything. She was jealous of any publishing success he had and for sure she kept things hidden from him when it suited her. This letter was particularly one that she wouldn't want him to see. She'd have justified this. Lou could almost hear Constance's voice, definite and confident, speaking to her from the past: *I'm not having him going off on a wild goose chase to find his aunt in France, which is full of confidence tricksters anyway. She's probably a wily woman chancing her arm, claiming a relationship with a writer just to profit from it in some way. She doubtless thinks he's making pots of money. He's not seeing this and that's flat.*

Well, okay, that was fine but this person knew that Grandad's mother was called Louise. Would a confidence trickster know such a fact? And why had the letter been posted into the vase? It was a mystery – perhaps someone had come into the room and she'd panicked, stuck it down there thinking to retrieve it later and then forgotten about it. She'd have thought of it as trivial, nothing to occupy her mind for very long. Once she'd dismissed the writer as a nutcase and a foreign one at that, she'd have lost interest in the letter and in everything it contained.

Rue du Treixel, Paris. Perhaps it wasn't a trick. What if this Mme Franchard *was* who she said she was? There was no one around who would even know whether Franchard was the correct name. Grandad's aunt. Dad's great-aunt. If she'd been sixty-five in 1985, she might easily be dead. I could write to her, Lou thought, and wondered whether she ought to tell Mum and Dad. Part of her longed to keep this small mystery to herself, but that wasn't fair. Dad was more closely related to this Mme Franchard than she was. She couldn't not tell him, not show him the letter. But Nessa was there in the study, monopolizing him, when he wasn't even her father. Lou smiled. Didn't matter how old you were, you still had the same old childish jealousies lurking somewhere in your head. But honestly, she thought, why hadn't Nessa gone to pour out her heart to her mother? Now that Ellie no longer lived abroad, she was just as available as Dad – but of course he was a solicitor. Nothing like getting free legal advice, and a good dollop of sympathy into the bargain. Briefly, she wondered what Gareth's girlfriend was like. She imagined a restful type, the exact opposite of Nessa.

Lou folded the letter carefully and put it into her jeans pocket. I'll show it to Dad and Mum later on, she thought, and went on clearing up. Many of the pieces she was collecting to throw into the bin outside were painted with such pretty things: butterflies, flowers, leaves, tiny birds. It seemed a shame to get rid of them but there was nothing else to be done with them. Lucky that there was another vase just like this one, waiting to be unpacked. Perhaps Mum ought to consider keeping it wrapped up for a few years and taking it out only when Poppy was a bit older. Lou emptied the pieces from the dustpan into several thicknesses of newspaper and wrapped those in a carrier bag to take outside.

Just as she opened the lid of the wheelie bin, something struck her. Paris was easy to get to by train. You were there in two hours or so by Eurostar. I could go and come back the same day. I could go and see her. Obviously, it would be more sensible to write ahead and save herself the expense of a trip if Mme Franchard was no longer alive. But I don't want to, she told herself. I want to go to Paris. A day trip – a treat. Dad might come with me. I'll ask him. She didn't see how talking to Mme Franchard would help her with the screenplay, but you never knew – she could call it research and that would make her feel a little better about the expense. The screenplay was going okay, she thought, but how could she be sure? How do you ever know if work is going well? Maybe all the words she reckoned were powerful, evocative and moving were in fact pathetic and didn't work. She wanted to ask

Harry but she wasn't ready to tell him what she was doing. A sudden longing to get back to the work, open her laptop and immerse herself in the terrible world John Barrington had created came over her. She'd been all ready to ask Mum whether she could take Poppy back to London, but perhaps now she should wait at least until she'd been to Paris. She'd make sure instead that Mum and Dad were okay with holding on to Poppy for just a little while longer.

Lou leaned against the wall by the kitchen door in the spring sunshine and tested herself for the presence of guilt. She did still feel bad about leaving Poppy with her parents, but her daughter was loving every minute and being well looked after, and that made Lou feel better. But I'm still her mother, she told herself, resolving to take her to the park as soon as she woke up. I'll spend every minute with her while I'm here, at least.

Her thoughts went back to the letter in her pocket. An old Frenchwoman (Lou imagined her like an ancient version of Isabelle Huppert, but that was just silly. Most people weren't in the least beautiful ...) might at this very moment be sitting in Paris, waiting to greet her with a warm embrace, after having yearned for such a moment for over twenty years. Or perhaps not. Perhaps she'd forgotten all about the letter by now.

Matt turned the piece of paper over in his hands. The words jumped about a bit in front of his eyes and he wondered whether he might need bifocals, after all. Old age getting to him. This woman, this Mme Franchard, if she was real and who she claimed to be, would be in her mid-eighties. There was something thrilling about the thought that he might have a relative still living, but perhaps he'd better not raise his own expectations in case nothing came of it in the end.

The silence was broken only by the rhythmic sound of Phyl's knife moving on the chopping board. She was standing at the work surface near the cooker, getting the vegetables ready for tonight's supper. He could tell that Lou, sitting on the other side of the kitchen table, was holding her breath, waiting to see what his reaction would be.

'If this is real—' he began, and Lou interrupted him.

'What do you mean? Why wouldn't it be? What are you saying, Dad?'

'Nothing, nothing, only – it might be a trick of some kind. Someone writing to a person she says is related to her, out of the blue, like that. Perhaps she thought an English author would be rich. That there might be some advantage to her in claiming a relationship.'

Lou looked so let down that Matt was almost sorry he'd spoken. He went on: 'There's no need to look upset, Lou. I'm as excited as you are in a way, but perhaps you're setting yourself up to be disappointed, you know. She's very old by now, if she's still alive. Maybe she's lost her marbles – maybe anything.'

'But if she *is* your great-aunt, Dad,' Lou said, 'don't you want to meet her? Find out about her? See what your own dad's aunt is like? She might know stuff about your real grandmother you'd want to know.'

'I suppose so.' Matt sighed. How could he tell Lou that alongside his excitement there was also a kind of nervousness about making new discoveries? He was wary about resurrecting stuff which might turn out to be anything: distressing, unfortunate, life-changing even. Matt wasn't keen on the whole 'life-changing' thing. His life was fine, thank you very much. Most people must be dissatisfied, he supposed, constantly wanting their existences to be altered, made different. He said, 'You've fallen for it as well, haven't you, Lou?

This craze for finding out about your ancestors on the internet and so forth. You could try Googling this Mme Franchard and see what you get, I suppose.'

'I don't want to Google her. I want to visit her. Paris is so close, Dad, I could do it in one day on Eurostar.'

'Really? You actually want to go and see her?'

'Yes, I do. Why not? I can't imagine why you don't, or don't seem to. You could come with me. Aren't you curious?'

'How about a letter? We could explain everything in writing before we go traipsing over the Channel on a whim.'

'I want to traipse. I'd love to go to Paris. I've never been.'

'Sorry, darling,' Matt said. 'I never thought of that – a bit of a treat for you, I suppose. D'you really want me tagging along?'

'Why not? It'd be fun.'

'Work,' Matt frowned. 'What about that?'

'No one'd mind. You're the boss, after all. And Mum, you'd be all right, wouldn't you? On your own with Poppy for a whole day?'

'I usually am alone with her for a whole day,' Phyl said, turning on the tap to rinse the vegetables. 'And I love it. Can't imagine why you're not keener, Matt. A trip to Paris and a possible relation. Would you lay the table, you two? Ta.'

Lou went to the dresser drawer to get the knives and forks out.

'I'll think about it,' Matt said, and took the wine glasses out and put them out on the table. He had a sudden vision of himself and Ellie strolling along beside the Seine and shook his head as though that would dispel it. If only – no, he had to stop such thoughts at once. He said, 'When d'you want to go? I would pay for your ticket, it goes without saying.'

'Really? Thanks, Dad. That's great. Really kind of you. Soon. This coming week. Any day you like except Tuesday, when I'm in the office.'

'Right, we'll go,' Matt said, looking in the cupboard for the salt and pepper. 'We haven't had a day out together for ages. It'll be fun.' He felt bad about wishing he could go with Ellie. What was the matter with him, for God's sake! Lou was so keen, and Matt wondered why he wasn't feeling more excited than he was. Perhaps there was something wrong with him – didn't he want to know about his own family? If Lou hadn't found the letter, his life wouldn't be worse in any way that he could see. How would having an ancient French great-aunt make any difference unless she turned out to be a nuisance ... a scenario of Mme Franchard being in some unexpected way a burden flashed into his mind – he'd become responsible for her welfare. She would be impoverished and suffering from Alzheimer's and incontinence and he'd find himself having to take care of her ... No, that was nonsense. Why was he being so negative about everything? I'm not going to worry about something before I really have to, he told himself. It'd be wonderful to go to Paris with Lou, and he was looking forward to it already. Whatever they found there, it would be good fun travelling with her. They used to go on excursions and outings and adventures when she was a girl and this was just a grown-up version of that. Thinking about it this way made Matt realize how much he missed those occasions. Let us hope, he thought, that we find Mme Franchard in the best of health. It would be quite something to find a great-aunt and he would welcome her into the family.

Why did the bloody phone always ring when you were right in the middle of something? Lou stopped typing and reached down for her bag. There was too much in it. Maybe she ought to get rid of the printed duffel bag thing that had carried her rubbish about for ages and invest in a proper handbag like the ones she saw featured in *Grazia*, where her mobile would never become lost among the rest of her belongings.

'Hello! Sorry – my mobile was hiding.'

'Hello, Lou. It's Harry. I'm just ringing on the off chance you're in.'

'Yup.' What was this?

'I could come up to your flat for a coffee if you like. Or you could meet me down here.'

'Where are you?' Did that sound inhospitable? Yes, it did. She tried to sound enthusiastic as he told her.

'Then come here – I could do with a break, but Harry ...'

'Yes?'

'There's nothing in the flat. I've just finished the last gingernut.'

'Disaster,' said Harry. 'Don't worry, I'll bring something. See you soon.'

Lou put the mobile down next to the computer and went back to staring at the screen. She was very careful to save the work she'd done this morning before she closed the machine, but once she'd put the laptop away in its place under the sofa, she began to move a little more quickly. What was more important: that she should look respectable, or that the flat should be tidy? She pushed cushions into shape, took her empty coffee cup from breakfast into the kitchen and rinsed it quickly under the hot tap. Then she ran a cloth over the work surfaces and once she was in the bedroom on her way to the mirror, she straightened the duvet on the bed. No time to change. Jeans – they were okay.

She was wearing a white shirt – clean, so okay. She ran a brush through her hair and slicked some lip-gloss on. Perfume? No. That would seem as though she was trying too hard. Trying too hard to what? To make herself attractive for Harry. No, of course not, she told herself, but then what was all the duvet-straightening, cup-rinsing and hair-brushing about? To say nothing about the lip-gloss. No, all it meant was she was trying to make a good impression on someone who was, after all, her boss. She wanted to look competent and 'together'.

The doorbell rang. As Lou went to answer it, she noticed that she was still wearing slippers: the ridiculous, fluffy pink ones in the shape of bunny rabbits. Oh shit shit shit. How fashionable were skinny jeans if they had bloody Flopsy and Mopsy poking their noses out from under the hems?

'Hi, Harry, come in,' she said.

'Thanks, Lou. Hope you didn't mind me ringing up like that. Only, as I said, I was here in the area. I was seeing Ciaran Donnelly, who lives right round the corner from you, so I thought ...'

'Glad you did. I was just about to make myself a coffee when you rang. I was working.'

'Really?' He glanced around at the flat which suddenly looked to Lou rather too tidy. Perhaps she ought to have scattered a few scripts about to give the impression that she was hard at it, reading stuff for Cinnamon Hill Productions.

'Not reading,' she said. 'I was on the computer. I put it away when you rang.'

'You writing something?'

'No, no – just fiddling about. Sit down, Harry. I'll put the kettle on.'

'Here.' He held out a plastic bag. 'I got some goodies at the deli. Hope they're okay.'

'That's lovely. A treat. Thanks so much.'

Lou went through to the kitchen and Harry sat down on the sofa. She prepared the cafetière, put the delicious-looking slices of cake out on her best plate and got the cups and saucers ready on a tray, wishing she'd taken up Phyl's offer of nicer crockery when she'd first moved in here. She was aware that Harry could see her moving about from where he was sitting. Ought she to take her slippers off? She was just considering this when he called out: 'Love those crazy rabbit slippers!'

'Oh, God, don't,' she said. Lou put the tray down on the table, and began pouring the coffee. 'My mum thought it was a good idea for Poppy to give them to me last year as a Christmas present. They're embarrassing, aren't they? But Poppy likes it when I wear them. They make her laugh.'

'Fair enough. They make me laugh, too.'

He grinned at her, and Lou found that she was giggling. He's got such a gorgeous smile, she told herself. And he's made me appreciate my slippers.

'Milk?' she asked.

'Yes, please. And a bit of cake. What did I get? Walnut? Carrot? I'll have walnut. Smashing.'

Lou left her cake on the plate and took a sip of coffee. 'Who's Ciaran Donnelly? I've heard of him, I think.'

'Yeah, he's a producer. American but lives here half the time. Ensley Gardens, number forty-two. You ought to see it. It's like a Tardis. Nothing much from outside, just a semi like all the others in the road, but once you're in, well, you know at once where you are. He invited me to discuss the Ratcliffe script but most of the time he was interrupting our conversation to take calls from this or that director. Steve, Martin ... you know.'

'Spielberg? Scorsese? Not seriously?'

'Oh, yeah. That's the kind of company Donnelly keeps. I was amazed he even called me. Not surprised he's put me off. Par for the course, when you're not a player.'

'Aren't you a player, Harry?'

He shook his head. 'Not really. Small independent British production company? Long way down the totem pole, I promise you, for people like Ciaran. But he's a good guy, made all the right noises. Don't let's talk about him, though. Tell me what you've been doing. Are you missing Poppy? She's been away for ages, hasn't she? A few weeks.'

'Yes, and I do miss her, but ...'

'You can do what you like when she's not here, right?'

Lou nodded. 'I feel guilty when I think of it, but Poppy's so happy and settled and it's all working out so well. My mum loves having her there.'

'I'm sure you're a smashing mum. Why are you being so hard on yourself, Lou?'

'I'm not. Not really. It's just that I know my limitations. Let's talk about something else. I'm going to Paris with my dad soon. That'll be good.'

'Really? How come?'

Lou took a deep breath and began to tell Harry about Mme Franchard's letter. When she'd finished speaking, he said, 'Wow – that's amazing. What a story. You must tell me what happens. Promise? Ring me after you get back and we'll have another curry, okay?'

'Yes, of course. I'd love that.'

'Or it doesn't have to be a curry. It could be Chinese, if you fancy a change.'

'I'm not fussy, it's something to look forward to.' As soon as the words were out of her mouth, Lou regretted saying them. Too eager, but the invitation had made her feel excited, like a kid who'd been asked to a party. Not a bit frightened. She liked having him in her flat, liked having coffee with him, liked talking to him.

He stood up. 'Got to go, Lou. That was a great cup of coffee. Ta. You haven't touched your cake, though.'

'I'll have it when you've gone, Harry. I was talking too much.'

They were standing by the door and Lou opened it.

'You're on your own too much, you know. I think you ought to get out more. Preferably with me. We should do a movie.'

Lou was just about to say *yes, I'd love to. Let's go to the movies, whenever you like* when Harry put his hands on her shoulders, pulled her gently towards him and said, 'Bye, Lou, I'll phone you, okay?' and kissed her swiftly on the lips. He was waving at her from halfway down the stairs before she pulled herself together. Then his voice came to her, shouting out from the floor below hers: 'Bye, Fiver. Bye, Hazel!'

It took her several seconds to work it out. Fiver ... Hazel. They were characters from *Watership Down*. Harry seemed so friendly and affectionate. A little shaken, she went back into the flat and sat where Harry had been sitting, and let herself fall into the kind of daydream she'd been indulging in since childhood. Herself and Harry ... No. I won't do that, not yet. I'll think of something else. Ciaran Donnelly. Just round the corner. Top producer. Forty-two Ensley Gardens. She knew exactly where that was. She had a vision of herself walking into the house with the script of *Blind Moon*. Would she have the nerve to do that? Probably not, but it was a piece of luck that Harry had mentioned his name. Maybe it was a kind of omen.

Oh, grow up, she told herself, you're not in a Meg Ryan movie now. She picked up the slice of cake from the plate in front of her and addressed her slippers: 'Carrot cake, Fiver and Hazel. Eat your bunny hearts out!'

'It's almost warm enough to sit outside,' Mickey said, opening the door of her study, which led out to the terrace, which wasn't really a terrace but which, as Mickey said, 'will be called a patio over my dead body.' The small space was beautiful: greyish-beige flagstones, and two or three blue glazed pots with ferny things growing in them. Nessa wasn't sure of their names but loved the soothing effect they produced.

'No, I'm okay,' she said. In truth, she was nearly asleep. Mickey had made tea, drunk it with her, listened to the details of last night's revelations and then said, 'Okay, Nessa, we can talk about this later – let's just relax now, there's plenty of time for everything. What about Tamsin, though? Have you told her?'

Nessa sighed. 'I don't want to think about it. Gareth says we have to tell her straight away, but I don't see why, really. I'd rather wait till everything's sorted out and the legal side taken care of. I'm dreading it, if you want to know.'

'Do you know what you're going to say?'

'My ma, with her enormous expertise in leaving off-spring high and dry, told me exactly what was needed: *We still love you ... this won't change the way we feel about you ... we still like each other lots and lots but just can't live together, that's all.* God, it's too Trisha Goddard for words, Mickey! And it's not even true. I can't stand him at the moment, if you want to know.'

'Still, she's right. I'd add – tell her it isn't her fault. Tell her it's got nothing to do with her.'

What was going on? Nessa felt tears coming into her eyes, her throat filled up with what felt like a lump of something or other – was there such a thing as a lump of misery? – and before she quite knew what was happening, she was weeping. 'I'm sorry, Mickey,' she sobbed. 'It was that – what you said – I remember thinking that. Exactly. I remember saying to Justin, trying to shift the blame, really, a bit, *it's your fault. Our fault. We're naughty and horrible and that's why she's gone.* How ghastly I was, even then, but now I can feel it. How it used to be. How sad I was for ages when she went, in spite of Matt and Phyl doing their best. Oh, God, what will I look like if I can't stop crying?'

'It's okay, you're allowed to cry.' Mickey came and knelt next to Nessa's chair and began to stroke her knee, very gently, as though she were an animal to be calmed down.

Nessa said, 'I need a tissue, Mickey. My nose is bubbling in a totally ghastly way.'

'Here you go. Kleenex on demand.'

'Thanks. What would I do without you?'

'You don't have to. Do without me, I mean. I am, as they say, here for you. You can come and stay for a few days if you like. If that'd help.'

'No, thanks, love. I'm not moving out of that house. For all I know Gareth would move in and change the locks.' She giggled. 'No he wouldn't, of course he wouldn't. It wouldn't occur to him. I'm sorry, I'm hysterical. Can we go for a walk or something? I feel – restless.'

'Sure. I've got to go down to the village and pick up something for supper. We'll go the long way, through the wood. Okay?'

'Lovely. Can I borrow some old trainers or something? I can't walk in these.' Nessa stuck her feet out.

'No,' Mickey said, smiling up at Nessa. She'd gone back to sitting on the floor. 'They're not used to Manolos at the village shop.'

'Manolos! I wish – these are Russell and Bromley.'

'Lovely, though.' And then Mickey put out a hand and ran her fingers quite slowly up the back of Nessa's leg, and then down again. Then she withdrew her hand and stood up and Nessa did too. She could still feel an echo of the tickly, shivery feeling of Mickey's touch on the silky fabric of her tights. She'd never had a woman caress her like that before. It was a caress. There was no mistaking it. It was strange in a way she couldn't have described. She followed Mickey out to the hall, a little trembly. Well, it was natural to feel like this after all the crying she'd been doing. That must be it. She wasn't used to emotional upheavals. Was this what people meant when they talked of someone feeling vulnerable? Yes, she told herself. It must be. That's what I am. *Vulnerable*. Like a snail out of its shell.

'It's lucky we're here this month and not last.' Matt gazed out of the window of the Eurostar train at the housing estates on the outskirts of Paris, which looked to Lou just like estates on the English side of the Channel. Perhaps a little cleaner on the face of it, but rushing past at high speed wasn't the best way to get to know somewhere.

'Why, Dad?'

'Because it's April now and we can sing "April in Paris".'

'You can sing it, I'm not going to.' Lou stood up and pulled her jacket from the overhead rack. 'I love this train – why can't all trains be like this?'

That morning, getting ready to go and meet her

father at Waterloo, Lou felt the kind of excitement that she associated with school trips. When she arrived at the Eurostar terminal, Matt had been waiting for her. Of course he had. Her father always arrived so early at railway stations that he frequently managed to catch the train before the one he was going for. Lou had admired the airport-style departure lounge with its cafés and shops full of touristy things that you'd never buy anywhere else – biscuit tins with the Union Jack on them, for heaven's sake. Why would you want one of those?

'We can't turn up empty-handed,' Matt said, as they walked through the Gare du Nord. 'Let's get her some *marrons glacés*. If she's popped her clogs, we'll enjoy them.'

'Honestly, Dad, what a way to talk about your great-aunt.'

'Alleged great-aunt. Possibly deceased. I'll be more respectful if she's who she says she is. And let's get a cab.'

They came out of the station. Matt said, 'Paris is doing its Paris in the spring thing, you see.'

'Dad! Stop it with the Paris clichés. You're driving me mad!'

But the clichés were hard to avoid, because Paris was, from the view Lou had of it out of the taxi's window, living up to all of them. A cloudless blue sky, sunshine, trees wearing misty veils of green and the buildings just as clean and elegant as she'd imagined. It was strange coming to a city you'd never visited before but whose 'look' you knew so well from a hundred posters and movies. What she hadn't been prepared for was the beauty of the real thing.

'Isn't it fabulous, Dad?' she said. 'And ta for the taxi. I'd never have taken one if I'd been on my own.'

'If we're only here for a few hours, we ought to

avoid spending some of that time down a hole.'

Matt leaned back against the leather headrest. 'D'you mind if I ask you a personal question, darling?'

'No ... not at all. You sound very serious.'

'I don't mean to. I'm just nosy, really, about what you're up to. Are you writing a novel?'

'What makes you think that?'

'It's occurred to me as a possibility, that's all. Are you?'

'No, Dad. It's not a novel. And I'll tell you soon, promise, only I want to keep it to myself for now. D'you mind?'

'Of course not. As long as it's going okay. How you want it to go, I mean.'

'I think it is. I'll tell you soon, I promise.'

'Okay.' Matt smiled at her. 'Back to tourist mode again. Look, there's the river.'

A *bateau mouche* was passing under the bridge just as they drove across it and on their left, Lou caught sight of the unmistakable façade of the cathedral of Nôtre Dame.

'Not a word, Dad. Don't say it.'

'Say what?'

'Possibly *the bells*! *The bells!*'

'Charles Laughton in *The Hunchback of Nôtre Dame*? Never seen it, though I know the cliché, of course!'

They laughed as the taxi made its way at alarming speed through streets that were suddenly narrower and far less grand than the main avenues. The people were normal: not tourists, not movie stars, but men and women going about their business. The butchers' shops, the pâtisseries, the flower stalls, the cafés with their striped awnings, still looked as though they were part of a stage set, but at least there were fat old women and shabby men walking about, some of them carrying black string bags and others, gratifyingly, wearing berets.

The taxi left them standing outside a door with the number '4' on a blue plaque screwed on to it. Suddenly, Lou felt nervous. She'd managed not to think from the moment she left home this morning right up until this second. There had been so much to look at that pushing thoughts of Mme Franchard out of her mind hadn't been too difficult. After all, she'd sat up late on Tuesday night, thinking of questions to ask and things to say. Now, here they were. Perhaps she didn't live here any more. Quite probably she was dead, as Dad had kept suggesting.

'We should ring this bell, I think,' Matt said and pressed it firmly. Nothing happened.

'You were right, Dad. She's not here. She must, as you said, have popped her clogs. Let's go. We can get some coffee or something.'

'Nonsense, not giving up yet. She's old. Perhaps it takes her a long time to get here from wherever she is.'

'*Oui?*' Lou was startled to see the door opening. A woman peered out at them. She wasn't young, but she was nowhere near eighty. Not Mme Franchard, then.

'Er ...' Lou's French, such as it was, had run away to a very distant corner of her brain. Where were the words when you needed them? '*Nous cherchons pour ...*' No, wrong. Wrong. Chercher *means to look for* so you don't need 'for' as well. The voice of Miss O'Callaghan, her French teacher at school, came back to her briefly and Lou pulled herself together. '*Nous cherchons Mme Franchard. Je suis ...* (no!) *je pense que je suis la grande-nièce* (was that right? Too bad if not) *de Mme Franchard. Nous sommes de la même famille.*'

Lou smiled, quite pleased with her effort, and the woman still holding the door smiled back.

'*Ah, c'est vrai? C'est tout à fait étonnant. Elle m'a toujours dit ...*' Lou listened to a long speech of which she understood very little, but managed to work out that Mme Franchard had told this woman that she had no family – that was the astonishing thing. So who was this woman? Lou took a deep breath and wished her father could help her, but no, he was standing by, looking pleasant and respectable and that was it. She'd have to do it.

'*Est-ce que c'est possible de parler avec Mme Franchard? Est-ce qu'elle est ici? Dans cette maison?*'

Not exactly Voltaire but she'd made it clear that she wanted to talk to Mme Franchard and asked whether she was here. Lou didn't want to get into dying. She knew the word for 'death' *(la mort)* and the infinitive *(mourir*: to die) but didn't fancy tackling stuff like tenses. Was it the Japanese who only had a present tense? Amazingly sensible.

Out of the stream that emerged in reply to her question, Lou grasped two things. The first was that this person was a concierge, a kind of caretaker. Her name was Solange Richoux and yes, Mme Franchard did indeed live here. Solange held the door wide open with an air of triumph and led them across a kind of inner courtyard to another door which had a small brass card-holder next to it and on the card, in faded brown ink, Lou read the name: *Madame Manon Franchard*. Solange had taken a bunch of keys out of her overall pocket and was about to open the door when she turned suddenly and said, in broken English for some reason – maybe what she had to tell them was so important she couldn't leave anything to chance – 'She is antique, Mme Franchard. She has more than eighty years. I go in first. I tell. She does not hear so good.'

'Oh, yes,' said Lou. 'That's a very good idea. *Bonne idée!*'

'Don't look so worried, Lou,' Matt said.

'But she's here, she's alive. We're going to see her. Oh, God, I'm so nervous. What if she's—'

'You come now.' Solange was back, and beckoning them with her finger, looking for all the world like someone out of a fairy tale. And the apartment they stepped into could also have come straight out of a spooky story. Lou and Matt followed Solange down a dark and narrow corridor and into a room that opened off to the right. At first, Lou couldn't see properly, but behind her Solange was switching on a light, which didn't help much, but which was something. The whole room was full of books. As well as shelves-full on the walls, there were piles of them on the floor, and a kind of path between these tottering mountains of mostly hardbacked volumes led from the door to an armchair in which a small, thin, wizened old lady sat surrounded by newspapers. She was dressed in black and was skeletally thin. Her skin was almost translucent and seemed stretched over the bones of her face. A strong, beaky nose and a gaze which was still quite sharp and must once have been piercing gave her the look of a bird. She wore two pairs of glasses on gold chains round her neck, and – was that a cat? Yes, there was definitely a cat curled up on the table next to the armchair. Ginger by the look of it, and quite oblivious to all the goings on. Only an ear pricking at the sound of their footsteps and a snore every so often convinced Lou that the creature wasn't an ornament. She wouldn't have been a bit surprised to have found a stuffed pet in a room like this.

'I'll do this, Lou,' said her father and she was grateful. 'I'm good at old ladies, though I've not seen anything like this in my life. Surely so many books must be a fire hazard?'

'Go on, Dad, she's waiting,' Lou whispered, as Solange said, '*Approchez, approchez*. Mme Franchard wish to see you. Speak.'

A thin, clear voice, quite at odds with the Dickensian setting, came from the corner.

'Please forgive my indisposition. I am too old to rise to greet you, but please speak now.'

'Thank you, Madame. You're very kind,' Matt said.

'I go to make the *thé*,' Solange announced, picking her way back through the books to the door. 'I return soon.' She disappeared and they were left alone with Mme Franchard.

Lou listened as her father explained what had brought them to Paris. He told Mme Franchard who he was, how he was perhaps related to Madame's sister and how very interested he was in finding out everything he could about his great-aunt, because his own father was dead. Lou thought it was no wonder that the old ladies of Haywards Heath and beyond wanted her father to draw up their wills. He was so comforting. He had such a pleasant manner and such a lovely voice. And she could sense his emotions as he spoke. He was clearly quite moved by the occasion. He was quite handsome, too, she realized. You never think of your parents as handsome or pretty – they're just your father and mother, but Dad was rather gorgeous in a middle-aged sort of way. Lou felt quite proud of him. Now he was talking about her. Lou blushed when he described her as her grandfather's favourite but she stepped forward when she was beckoned to come closer.

Mme Franchard peered up at her. Then she swapped the glasses she was wearing for another pair that were lying on the table and once she'd put them on, she stared at Lou for what seemed like ages.

'*En effet ...*' Mme Franchard breathed and took a hankie from a pocket in the depths of the knitted garment that was draped over her shoulders. 'You are Louise? The same name, the same face. *C'est incroyable ... Tiens ...* you bring that photograph over there ... the big one.' She pointed to a dim corner of the room and Lou saw two or three silver frames peeping out from behind a pile of old letters, and pages torn from newspapers and magazines. This flimsy paper wall almost hid them from view but she went over and picked up the largest of them, which was about the size of a postcard. It showed two young women sitting in a garden under a tree which could have been the twin of the one she liked looking at in the library in London – an apple tree in full bloom. One of the girls was thin and dark and even in the bad light and even after the passage of what was practically a whole lifetime, Lou could recognize Mme Franchard.

'This is you,' she said, putting the photograph into the old lady's hands.

'*Oui*, and this is my Louise. You see how she is. So resembling you. *Incroyable*. I feel ... I feel *bouleversée*. How do you say? Turned up and down?'

'Upside down,' Matt said and leaned over to see the photograph. 'My goodness, Lou, it's quite striking. This Louise *does* look like you. Really. It's not just ...'

'Let me see.' Lou took the frame from Mme Franchard and gazed more closely at the photo. This Louise is prettier than I am, she thought. Better dressed. Her hair's not a mess tied up in a ponytail. She wore it in a way that reminded Lou of the Duchess of Windsor: parted in the middle and with a kind of roll all round the head. You did that by pinning the hair on to a sausage-shaped thing, which Lou knew because she'd been in a school production of *An Inspector Calls*. But it's true, she thought. She does look like me. How odd, how worrying and fascinating and strange, that such things could happen: that a random collection of cells and enzymes and whatever else made up a person could arrange itself *twice* into a person, who was in some ways the same and in others completely different, separated by years and years. Lou shivered.

'Yes,' she said. 'I do look like her. I can see that.'

'And you are named like her.'

Lou nodded. She knew of that connection, and had always been proud of it.

Solange came in at that moment and performed the walk through the books, which must have been even more hazardous when you were carrying a tea tray, but she was clearly used to doing it. She also poured the tea and handed it round before leaving the room again.

'You must be alone,' she announced from the door. 'You have much to speak.'

'Tell us, Madame,' Matt said. 'Tell us about your sister, Louise.'

6

'It's so lovely,' said Ellie, 'to have the chance for a proper chat. Such ages since we last met. I've been meaning to get in touch since the funeral. Such a palaver, getting settled into the new flat and so forth.'

'Yes, it must have been,' said Phyl. 'Have another scone, Ellie.' She had no intention of taking up that particular baton. She didn't want to hear Ellie's moving-in stories.

'I won't, thanks, though they are delicious. I'm sure you must have baked them yourself. You're such a wonderful homemaker.'

Phyl smiled. 'I'll just put the kettle on again. I could do with another cup – how about you?'

'Lovely, thank you.'

Phyl plugged in the kettle, her back to Ellie, and tried to work out how she felt about her husband's ex-wife sitting at her kitchen table. She'd invited her – couldn't not have invited her once she'd phoned and said she was 'in the area' – and now here she was. Did they have anything to say to one another? Nessa. They could talk about the impending divorce, Phyl supposed. Poppy had been a distraction for a while, with Ellie exclaiming and making the kind of noises you were supposed to make when you met a small child, but Phyl could tell from Ellie's body language that she was less than comfortable with such an unpredictable and possibly destructive creature as a baby. She shrank away even while she was hugging the child, and that amused Phyl. She'd seen the same sort of physical recoil at the surgery in people who weren't entirely happy about being near animals. Poppy was now on the other side of the room, happily engaged in some elaborate game with two dolls, a spoon and a couple of empty yoghurt pots and her mutterings and gurglings interspersed with the odd word here and there were a comfort to Phyl.

'You've missed Matt, I'm afraid,' she said. 'He's in Paris today.'

'Paris! Goodness,' said Ellie. 'What on earth is he doing there?'

'He and Lou went for the day to see someone – well, it's a long story really. But we found a letter last weekend. From a Frenchwoman who claimed to be John Barrington's aunt.'

'Really? How thrilling! Are we about to have revelations? I've always thought there was a mystery about John. He was far too quiet, don't you think?'

'It's not something I've given much thought to, if I'm honest. He was Matt's dad and didn't say much to me, not really, but I never worried about it, or thought he was hiding anything. I just assumed he was a silent sort of man.'

'Hmm. Well, I always,' Ellie leaned forward confidingly, 'had the impression that there were lots and lots of things he could have told us if he'd wanted to.'

'Maybe he put them into his books. Lou says *Blind Moon* is very good.'

Ellie wrinkled her nose. 'I did read it once, ages ago when Matt and I first met. You know how it is – you try to immerse yourself in everything to do with

197

the beloved, don't you? If you're in love with a chess player, say, you learn all about the game and maybe start playing it yourself, even though it's not your thing at all. That's what I've found. Well, I thought that reading his father's books would somehow get me closer to Matt.' She laughed. 'How wrong I was!'

Phyl said nothing. She didn't like the way Ellie called Matt her 'beloved'. Of course, she'd say she was clearly referring to a time that was past, but still, it made her feel ... feel what? Disconcerted, you could call it. Not pleased. Ellie talked on and on. It wasn't easy to stop her once she got into her stride.

'I can't remember all that much about *Blind Moon* between you and me. Not my kind of thing either. This boy, in a country I couldn't get a handle on somehow. North Borneo? Well, I knew that was the Far East and I also know they suffered dreadfully there during the war and in those Japanese camps, like the one in *Empire of the Sun*, but honestly, the adventures and thoughts of an eight-year-old boy ... I think there's something a bit weird asking adults to read a book which is written from the point of view of a child.'

'It's supposed to be very powerful,' Phyl murmured. 'Very moving. Sad.'

'Well, yes, exactly. It was, but really, why would you want to read a book that made you feel miserable? Mad, I call it.'

'It ends hopefully, I'm told. The child – the boy gets to go to England with his mother's friend. She adopts him.'

'Whatever John did,' Ellie leaned forward confidingly, 'it wasn't a huge success, was it? Constance always said that the books didn't make a penny piece.'

'Money's not the only measure of success,' she said. 'No, but it's one of them.'

'Well,' Phyl said, 'John clearly felt he had to write

them. I expect it gave him an interest. Something to take him out of himself.' She searched for a way to change the subject. She didn't know much about literature – certainly not enough to be able to discuss it with Ellie. She was also not about to give her the satisfaction of agreeing, but she, too, had found *Blind Moon* not exactly to her taste, and hadn't finished it. That was one reason why she'd been so upset when Constance had left Lou the copyrights as her part of the inheritance. It seemed to Phyl like something that wasn't really worth having, though she never said so. Ellie had changed tack. She was back to Paris.

'So tell me – this Frenchwoman – what is she claiming? Is she for real?'

'Matt'll find out, I suppose. She claims to be the sister of John's real mother.'

'Thrilling! I'll make sure to get Matt to tell me what she said.'

So, a phone call to Matt would follow shortly. Phyl wondered how abruptly she could move on to something else. Nothing ventured. She took a deep breath and said, 'How's Nessa? That was a bit unexpected, wasn't it?'

'Well ...' Ellie took a sip of tea, refuelling, Phyl thought, for another stream of words. She was wearing a pale blue cashmere cardigan over a cream blouse that had to be silk. Her shoes looked as though they'd never done anything as vulgar as stepping on an actual floor. Her make-up was immaculate and as for her nails ... Phyl's own hands with their plain, square-cut nails hadn't changed much since she was a schoolgirl, except for the fact that now the odd brown spot had appeared on the skin, and they were sorely in need of what Ellie would doubtless call 'pampering'. She moved them to her lap where they were out of sight, safely under the table. Briefly she wished she'd changed after Ellie's phone call this morning, but Poppy had been demanding her breakfast and then there was a nappy to change and she'd had to make a choice: scones, home-baked and fresh out of the oven, or half an hour spent trying to beautify herself. The scones were wonderful and she was never going to come anywhere near Ellie's style so Phyl now reckoned she'd made the right decision. She tuned in to what Ellie was saying. Nessa was still the topic, so she can't have missed too much.

'Of course it's hard to begin with, but she'll get used to it. And I'm sure it won't be long before she marries again, don't you think? They'll share custody. Just between you and me, I think she'll resent every moment Gareth has with Tamsin. You know how besotted with the child she is. I was quite surprised, to tell you the truth, that Nessa turned out to be so maternal.'

Phyl said, 'Well, we're not all the same, are we?' when what she really wanted to say was *no wonder you were surprised. She doesn't take after you in that, anyway.*

Ellie laughed. 'I'm a fine one to talk, though, aren't I? Not a maternal bone in my body, so she's quite different in that respect.'

'And she's got the firm, of course. To keep her busy, I mean, and take her mind off her problems.'

'And to make money, I hope. Gareth will pay maintenance for Tamsin but it's very fortunate that Constance left Nessa the money she did. Although,' she went on, 'as you've no doubt discovered, it's not nearly as much as one thought it might be. Most of the wealth is that house and Justin is sitting firmly on that.'

'You could sell some of your jewellery,' Phyl said innocently. 'If you wanted to help Nessa financially.'

'No need for that, I'm happy to say. Though I might get rid of some of the less stylish pieces and pay off a little of my mortgage. You must come and see the flat, Phyl. You and Matt. It's what they call *bijou*, which basically means small, as you know, but it's quite enough for me, now that I'm on my own.'

'One bedroom?' Phyl asked.

'No, two. One doesn't want to be entirely unable to put someone up for the night.'

'And there's Tamsin, of course, isn't there?' Phyl couldn't help it. The temptation to say something that would take the wind out of Ellie's sails a little was overwhelming. As she'd been speaking, Phyl found herself growing more and more irritated. It was a bit of a cheek, she thought, Ellie moaning about poor old Nessa's financial difficulties, which appeared to be entirely imaginary, when she must have known that Lou was struggling along on next to nothing. Perhaps she thinks that we help her. Well, we do of course, but Lou very often won't let herself be helped. Phyl knew that her daughter needed to be independent but still she wondered about very basic things like whether she ate enough. She'd never economize on Poppy's food, but it was more than likely that Lou herself sometimes went without. When it came to a choice between going to the movies or having a meal, the movies won every time. And every time she did go out, she had to pay a babysitter and would never accept any money for that. And here was Ellie, nattering on about bloody Nessa. She said, quietly, 'How lovely for you that your grand-daughter can stay over now! I used to love sleeping at my granny's house.'

Bingo! You could see that this idea filled Ellie with dread. She'd gone quite white and had to gather herself together before she answered: 'Yes, well, I'm often away, of course.' She stood up. 'Must dash, Phyl. Thanks so much for the divine scones – you must give me the recipe sometime.'

'Mmm,' Phyl said. Poppy had crawled under the kitchen table and was now holding out her arms and saying, 'Up! Up!'

They made their way to the front door and Phyl caught a whiff of Ellie's perfume as she kissed her goodbye. Once the car had gone off down the drive, she turned to Poppy and said, 'Why d'you think people say that, Poppy? *You must give me the recipe sometime.* Ellie's as likely to bake scones as I am to dance with the Royal Ballet. It's bobbins.'

'Bobobobobob!' Poppy cried and Phyl laughed. She put the baby into her high chair and gave her half a scone to eat or crumble into the tray as she saw fit. Then she began to gather up the toys scattered over the kitchen floor. It suddenly occurred to her to wonder why Ellie had really phoned here. She couldn't simply have wanted to upset me, could she? By rubbing in how successful Nessa was? Well, maybe she could, but it was more likely that she'd wanted to speak to Matt. All that stuff about not having seen me since the funeral was simply Ellie thinking on her feet. I needn't have invited her when she rang, Phyl thought, but that would have seemed very inhospitable and as though I didn't want to see her. She sighed. That would have been mostly true. There was something about Ellie that made Phyl feel churned up, less than relaxed, not herself, and she was relieved to be alone with her granddaughter.

'Why,' she said, addressing herself to Poppy, who was exploring her scone with impressive thoroughness, 'didn't I think to ask her what she wanted from him? She'll have to ring him again now, won't she?'

Poppy gurgled and muttered something through a mouth full of crumbs. Phyl laughed. 'You're the best kind of person to have a chat with. You answer in your own way and you listen, and you don't say a single thing I disagree with. Perfect.'

'Puff ...' Poppy said. 'Puff.'

'You'll get it right soon, chicken,' Phyl smiled. 'Puff's fine for now.'

They did the paperwork first. Mme Franchard instructed Matt on the mysteries of how to find her sister's birth certificate, directing him to the right pile of paper and making him burrow in it until the document came to light. Lou wasn't a bit surprised to find that her methodical father had brought with him Grandad's birth certificate, which had miraculously survived the war and all the upheavals he'd gone through during his childhood. The names tallied. The dates of birth tallied. Mother's name: Louise Martin née Franchard. Father's name: William Martin. How long had it taken Grandad to get used to being called Barrington? Millions of women got used to their husband's name but did they ever lose sight of the name they'd been born with? Lou made a note to ask Phyl about it. She certainly had no intention of changing her own name when she got married. *If* I get married, she corrected herself.

Mme Franchard took her time getting started because, before she did, a space had to be cleared for them to sit on. The sofa had been literally buried under drifts of books and papers and Mme Franchard oversaw its excavation with great aplomb.

'You put that please here – and those papers down on the floor ...' None of this was quickly done, but eventually, there was enough faded red velvet to accommodate Lou and her father, even though they did have to sit very close together.

When Mme Franchard was satisfied that they were both settled and comfortable, she reached down to a bag that looked like an old-fashioned doctor's bag:

black leather, with a brass clasp at the top. Was it a Gladstone bag? Lou made a mental note to herself to look it up on Google. Mme Franchard hauled the bag on to her lap and opened it. Inside, more paper ... Sometimes, Lou thought, you really do feel as though you've fallen into some surreal movie. David Lynch's *Eraserhead* came to mind, and Orson Welles's *The Trial*. So much paper wasn't natural. There would have been something distinctly spooky about it were it not for the matter-of-fact manner and very reasonable-sounding voice of the old woman, apologizing for her bad English.

'I speak good English once,' she said. It was like listening to an old machine cranking into life. 'But you forget, if you do not use. Like a metal thing. You grow – how do you say – rusting.'

'Rusty,' Matt spoke gently.

'*C'est ça*. Rusty. I am rusty for the English. But it is good to tell a story I want to tell since very many years. I look for your father for many years.'

Lou said, 'My grandmother – John Barrington's wife – never showed him the letters. She hid them from him. I found this one by accident. It's the only one I found. Did you write more than one letter?'

'I write many, many letters.' Mme Franchard shrugged her shoulders and Lou almost giggled because it was such a stereotypical French gesture. Constance must have destroyed all the others – what a bloody nerve! '*N'importe*. You are here now, and this is luck. I am unhappy not to see my nephew but you are his son' (she leaned forward and patted Matt on the knee) 'and your daughter is like my sister and this is good for me.'

She thrust her face into the opening of the bag, looking for something, turning over the papers inside it and moving things – documents, letters, who knew what they all were – from the depths to the surface. At last she found what she'd been searching for, a flat, black leather wallet, about the size of an A5 envelope. She took a sheet of paper out of it which had been folded and unfolded so often that the creases were practically worn through. The whole thing nearly fell to pieces as she opened it.

'This is the only letter from my sister I have. She writes from North Borneo. The date is in 1942 just before she go in the camp with her son. She is waiting too for another child.'

Matt took the letter and Lou peered over to read it as well. The paper was thinned by age and the ink was so faded that she could barely make out the words, but of course the message was written in French.

'I tell you what she say,' Mme Franchard said. 'I know this by heart, you understand. She say: everything is hard because they go to the camp soon. She tells that she is sad that many years have gone and she is not writing to me. She say she will write to me now very much and tell me all her thinkings. All her feeling. She say she is sad for what she does to me. She say her son is a beautiful boy and she wish I could see him and he could see me. She wish to visit our father's grave.'

Mme Franchard sighed and wiped her eyes with her hankie. 'I can still cry. It should not have been so. My father, he does not forgive. Never. And I, I too do not forgive. I am angry for so many years. But I miss her very much. In the end, I write and write to her but she does not answer.'

Lou noticed that her father was sitting up straighter. He wanted to interrupt and was waiting for a chance to say something. As soon as there was a tiny gap in the story, he spoke, slowly, to make sure Mme Franchard took in what he was saying.

'Madame, there are things I don't quite understand.

Would you mind starting at the very beginning? Why were your father and your sister estranged? And you and your sister, too. I mean, not speaking to one another?'

'Ah! It is because of me. We live in the house in Brittany then. The big house – before we move to the smaller house close to Penmarc'h. My father is a good shopkeeper. *Épicier* – grocer. A very nice shop in the town. We are prosperous. My mother is dead since we are children. He pays a Englishman to teach us, me and my sister. He wishes us to speak good English and this he can afford. My sister is older than me. I have a passion for our tutor. He is handsome. Tall, and with dark hair and brown eyes so deep – *c'est un prince, en effet*. I tell Louise, but I do not tell any other person. Even William – that is his name, William Martin – does not know this. I love him but I do not speak of it. Louise is more pretty than me. Also a little older. And she is charming and speaks with smiles and I find it hard to speak anything then. I am shy then.'

Mme Franchard was silent for a long moment and let her head fall forward on to her chest. Talking so much must have been an effort for someone in such a frail condition. The only sound in the room now was the breathing of the still-sleeping cat and the ticking of a clock on the wall. Lou gave her father a questioning look, wondering whether they ought to say something.

'I am not stopping,' Mme Franchard said, lifting her head again. 'My father finds Louise and William in the bed together and throws him out of the house. Louise cry and cry and say she loves him and my father say to her, no, you do not stay in this house like my daughter if you see him, and Louise, she is stubborn and she goes. Pouf! Just so – she packs her *valise* and runs from the house. I beg her, do not go. Stay. I am torn in

206

two – how does she do this to me when she has known since a long time how I love William? I ask her, I say: you know I love him. How do you go to the bed with him when you know my heart will break?'

The clock ticked and ticked. Lou could imagine it: the sisters, facing one another, weeping – was Louise weeping too or just Manon? Where had this scene taken place? In one of the bedrooms? Outside, in a garden? Perhaps, as it was Brittany, they'd gone out for a walk and were on a cliff ... Lou caught herself short. What was she doing? This wasn't a film script she was writing, it was true. It had happened to this woman, who was still, even after more than sixty years, suffering because of it.

'She hold me, she kiss my hair and she say I cannot help it. I love him too and he loves me. We are going to be married now. Forgive me. Please forgive me, I cannot help. But you see that I do not forgive because I am broken in the heart. I scream at her. I say go and do not come back and never, never write to me because I don't want to hear of you anything. So she goes and I am stiff and young and stupid and I do not forgive. I find out from a friend of Louise what happen to her. The friend tells me she goes to North Borneo – it is so far. My father is sad and he also die very soon after this. A big attack of the heart. He also does not write to Louise. Her friend from when we were in school is the one who write to tell her about our father's funeral, but she does not come. And that is how it was. We do not find one another again.'

'And then,' Matt said, 'you read my father's novel, *Blind Moon*.'

'I find it by accident. Many years after the war. You see how I collect the books. I think: this is like Louise. It is something like her story, perhaps. So I write. It is a chance, *n'est-ce pas*?'

'I know the parts of the book that made you think that,' said Lou. 'You were right to try and get in touch.' She moved to kneel in front of Mme Franchard and took her hand. 'It's such a dreadfully sad story. I'm so sorry. So sorry that you never found your sister again. That you never found your nephew. It's awful. Awful.'

'But you are here! Both of you – this is good. I am happy now. You will speak to me about John Barrington, please. I am anxious to hear.'

As her father spoke, Lou lost herself in a kind of trance. The mother in Grandad's novel was a shadowy character and Lou had decided when she started writing the screenplay to omit any mention of her back story. She wanted everything here and now and happening in front of the eyes of the audience, focusing their minds on a single storyline with no flashbacks. But, she thought, now that I know some of the story of Grandad's real mother, I'll read the novel with new eyes. How closely had John Barrington based the character of Annette on his real mother? Will knowing something of this background make a difference to what I think about the character?

'Tamsin, darling, sit down for a moment, will you?'

Tamsin paused by the door and looked sulky. She was still in her school uniform. 'But I want to go up and change, Mummy. Can't I come down a bit later?'

Nessa said, 'No, because Daddy won't be here later and we want to speak to you about something. We both do.' She did her best to sound both upbeat and serious and that was harder than it looked. She glanced at Gareth and made a sour face that meant *you say something, you bastard. This is all your doing, so bloody well pull your weight.*

'Come and sit by me, sweetheart,' said Gareth from the sofa, holding out an arm, ready to embrace her. She sidled over and sat next to him and he hugged her close. 'How's my little Tamsy?' he said. Nessa felt ill. All this cutesy stuff wasn't going to cut any ice when he broke the news. This meeting followed negotiations as intricate as those attending a Middle East Peace Summit or something, and one thing they'd decided was that Gareth was the one who was going to do the talking. Nessa enjoyed seeing how uncomfortable he was with this. He took his arm away from around his daughter's shoulders and stood up and faced her. Yes, that was probably a good idea. It was almost impossible to say something to someone tightly clamped to your right flank.

'Tamsy, have you noticed that I've not been at home a lot lately?'

'Mmm,' said Tamsin. 'Mummy said you were working extra hard and had to go to your office more.'

'Have you missed me, darling?'

Nessa sat up straighter and frowned at Gareth. This was below the belt, this appeal to the emotions. Hadn't they decided to be cool? To keep emotions out of it as much as possible?

'Yeah.'

'Well ... Mummy and I wanted to speak to you tonight, because we think you're a big enough girl to be told what's happening.'

'What is happening?' Tamsin was starting to look a little alarmed. Get on with it, for heaven's sake, Nessa thought. Get it over with.

'Nothing. Well, not nothing. Something *is* happening. Of course it is ...'

Witter, witter, thought Nessa.

'Ahem – well, this is the thing, darling. I'm not going to be living here any longer.'

'Where will you be living?' Tamsin wanted to know. 'And why not, anyway? Are you getting a divorce?'

'Well, yes, we are. How did you guess?'

'Doh!' Tamsin was scornful. 'It wasn't very hard. Lots of people get divorced. I know what it means. Chloe's mum and dad are divorced and so are Brett's. And Freddy's.'

'One thing it doesn't mean,' said Gareth, 'is that we feel any differently towards you. We both love you to bits and want you to be happy, and none of this is anything to do with you. It is not your fault that we've decided we have to part.'

Nessa felt herself relaxing a little. At least he'd managed to get that out. But it needed reinforcement, so she added, 'Dad's right, Tamsin. Absolutely right. We do both love you and we're going to do our very, very best to see that you're happy and agree with any arrangements we make, okay?'

Tamsin nodded, slowly taking in what this news meant. Gareth sat back down on the sofa and started hugging her again. This had the effect not of cheering her up but of seemingly making her feel worse. Her face began to crumple up in a way that indicated tears weren't far off. Nessa hurried to offer reassurance.

'There's no need to be sad, darling, really. We'll still see lots and lots of Dad. He'll have you to stay often, won't you, Gareth?'

'Of course I will,' said Gareth. 'I'm in the process of getting a lovely little house nearer to your school. And you can spend all the time you want with me, promise. You'll have two bedrooms instead of one – that's got to be good, right?'

'I wish,' said Tamsin, 'we could just stay as we are. Why can't we?'

'Your father has stopped loving me in the way that he did,' Nessa put in. Let the child be told the truth. Why did they have to sweeten this particular pill? 'Sometimes grown-ups can't help it. They meet someone and fall in love with them. That's what's happened. Your father has fallen in love with someone else. Her name is Melanie.'

'Oh,' said Tamsin, absorbing this information and picking at the hem of her school skirt with rather grubby fingers. 'Is she nice?'

'I'm sure you'll like her,' Gareth said quickly. He glanced at Nessa as though expecting her to challenge his remark, but she said nothing.

'When can I meet her?' Tamsin asked, with what appeared to Nessa a rather indecent haste. Already, her daughter seemed to be less upset. She'd taken it on the chin, and they were going to get through this conversation without the tears and wailing that Nessa had been half-expecting. She'd read enough magazines and newspapers to know that the scars from divorce could often run deep and wounds could express themselves in all sorts of ways. Let's hope I can escape without too much difficulty for Tamsin, she thought.

I can't bear to think of her being sad. Surely if Gareth and I are civilized about it, we can avoid too much trauma for Tamsin. Part of her would have enjoyed the cutting-up-your-husband's-suits scenario, the screaming revenge and virago-like bad behaviour, but if she was honest with herself, she'd never really loved Gareth enough to justify a sudden onset of wild, thwarted passion at this stage.

'We'll go out for a meal soon, how about that?' Gareth was beaming now, relieved that the worst was over.

'McDonald's?' Tamsin was looking more cheerful already.

'No, somewhere much, much nicer than that,' he replied, with a big grin on his face. Poor fool. He didn't realize that in Tamsin's opinion, McDonald's was the nicest place in the world. Never mind, he'd soon learn a whole lot of stuff he had no idea about at the moment. Nessa intended to let him have full access. She wondered what Melanie would think about having her and Gareth's daughter as part of her new family. She'd certainly have her hands full with a tiny baby. Nessa smiled at the prospect, while at the same time not being able to help feeling somewhat sorry for poor Melanie. She was about to find herself a lot busier than she'd ever been in the office. Gareth would have a full-time job soothing ruffled feathers. What a delightful thought that was!

Lou sat at the table in her flat with her copy of *Blind Moon* open in front of her. She'd just finished her supper (a toasted pitta bread with hummus, a tomato and a few olives. One of these days she ought to try some cookery) and taken the dirty plate and knife to the sink in the kitchen. This was the time of day when she felt most alone. This was when she longed for Poppy. Her mother would be bathing her and putting her to bed and singing her songs and holding that small body close and smelling her lovely baby smell and her clean hair. Stop it! Lou told herself. She made herself a cup of coffee and took it back to the table. I have to finish this script first, she thought. It's what I want to do and it's good. It's really good. This realization came to her in one of those flashes of confidence that seemed to arrive in her head from time to time … moments when remembering the words as she'd put them down filled her with a kind of glow. This didn't happen often. Mostly, she found herself waking up in the night and going over what she'd done that day and then it was as though her heart was plummeting down and down, leaving her awash with low-level misery.

She turned the pages till she found the passage she was looking for. When she'd first read the novel, she was unsure about this bit. She wondered what Grandad had intended by this – what could you call it? – this interlude. It came just before everything moved from the merely distressing to the truly ghastly, an interval of peace and cool in the prevailing noise and heat. Peter finds he can tell stories to the other boys in the camp. He sees the effect this has; the way he can soothe and comfort and, best of all, provide a way of leaving the confines of the bamboo prison they are all shut up in and move to another place. A better one.

The stories they liked best were about the sea. There were two girls, he told them, who lived by the sea and Derek and Nigel said, 'Why do they have to be girls? Couldn't they be boys?' And Peter said: 'No, they can't be boys because they're girls in the story. My mother tells it like that and I am too.' He sat up on his mat, and stared at the bodies of all the children in the hut. Outside in the compound the trees were black and the sky was black too but you could see the shapes of the trees even so. Everyone was quiet. They were quiet listening to him. No one cried while he was speaking.

Peter said: 'This story is about two girls who lived by the sea. The sea was dark blue with white foam on the waves and the waves got very high in winter. One day the girls went for a walk by the sea. They climbed over rocks and picked seaweed out of pools and watched crabs scrabbling on the sand, running away from the water. The sisters lived in a small white house with a red roof and blue shutters. Their mother was dead. They were happy, but there was something they didn't know. They didn't know their father was a wizard who'd put a spell on them.'

'What spell? What was the spell?' That's what they always wanted to know and Peter said, 'They couldn't leave this place, this house with the red roof on a cliff above the beach. If they did, they would die.'

'But the house is nice and the beach is nice,' someone said. 'Why would they want to leave it?' Peter had no answer. He had asked his mother once and she'd said, 'No, you're right. There's no good reason to want to leave.'

Lou imagined Mme Franchard reading this passage. It must be them: Louise and Manon, running on the beach and climbing over the rocks ... perhaps their house had a red roof and blue shutters. Next time I'm in Paris I'll ask. Thinking about Mme Franchard made Lou feel happy. She and Dad had spoken on the way home about this surprising development: a new member of the family – how would they deal with it? Could Mme Franchard come over and visit Milthorpe? Would she want to? They'd decided that Lou ought to go over again soon and she'd hinted that she had a friend she'd like to take with her. Dad didn't seem to hear that bit ... he sometimes didn't listen as carefully as he should. He sometimes drifted off into his own head and what you said didn't reach him. But Lou wanted to ask Harry whether he'd come with her. She wondered whether she would have the nerve to invite him and what he would think. Was it too much? She smiled. Maybe I want him to know how much I like him. Of course, he might not come. That was a possibility, but she didn't want to think about it too hard because that would stop her from enjoying the daydreams she'd started to have every time she did think about it.

Matt was sitting in his office, thinking about Mme Franchard, when the phone in his pocket vibrated and rang at the same time. He was still a little nervous of his mobile. He'd avoided owning one for years, telling everyone how unnecessary he thought they were; what an infestation on public transport (not that he was on public transport very often), and most of all, how very unhealthy they must be. He could, he told people, envisage horrible waves of blueish radiation beaming into thousands of ears every day, rendering their owners surely a little less themselves with every phone call. No, he wasn't about to buy one. Never.

He'd changed his mind when Ray started treating Lou badly. Overnight, the necessity of being constantly available at every hour of the day and night and wherever he was became imperative. He wanted to know that his beloved daughter could get hold of him and summon him to her side. She never had, which Matt put down to her determination and bravery. It never occurred to him that Lou might have felt embarrassed or ashamed to call him to help her. Phyl, who watched her husband going through agonies all through that relationship, used to say, 'If you're so worried, you could phone her, you know,' but he knew he wasn't very good on the phone – not himself – and so he tried to avoid this as much as possible. Phyl and Lou used to chat for ages, and then she'd hand him the phone and he'd speak to Lou for a few minutes. The mere fact, Matt reflected, that Phyl thought of them as 'chats' showed him what a different attitude his wife had to telephone communications. He regarded them as a way of conveying information and making arrangements to meet. They were not a substitute, in his opinion, for conversation.

For a long time, he'd used his mobile gingerly. He phoned someone. He received calls from some people, those few to whom he'd given his number. That was it. He knew about text messaging – you could hardly avoid knowing about something so ubiquitous – but would no more have dreamed of sending a text than diving off the end of Beachy Head.

Ellie had changed that. She had taken to texting and to mobiles in general and her handset, fully equipped with what she referred to as 'all the available whistles and bells', was an elegant and very expensive silver rectangle with an unnaturally blue screen and a ringtone which drew far too much attention to itself. An electronic version of Handel's *Water Music* – why would anyone need that blaring out every few minutes? It would have driven him bananas. His ringtone was as near to that of a normal phone as he could manage. When he first got a text from Ellie, he nearly jumped out of his skin. It happened during a meeting and amid profuse apologies he'd simply turned off the handset, vowing to return to it later.

There was no one he could ask. Phyl would have shown him how to read and answer his messages in a moment, but he certainly didn't want her to know Ellie was texting him. Perhaps it was the novelty, but he found this way of sending messages rather erotic: not a thought he could express to his wife. As it was, he was forced to consult the booklet that had come with his phone. It took him some hours but he worked it out in the end. For weeks now, he'd been laboriously tapping out little groups of two and three words but on the train back from Paris, Lou had introduced him to predictive text and that had changed everything.

Now he was getting – well, you couldn't call it speedy – but certainly comfortable.

Lou had also shown him the vibrate thing – amazing! He opened the handset and read the message. He'd known as soon as he got it that it must be from Ellie because she was the only person who ever texted him. Briefly, he wondered how the mobile phone had altered adulterous habits of men and women. He deleted every message he received the moment he'd answered it, and just the other day, realized he had also to delete his sent messages folder, or someone could look at his phone and read every single word. Not that he was an adulterer and not that he had sent anything incriminating, but still.

dying 2 hear paris news fone me lunch next week xxx

Ellie didn't go in for punctuation and Matt assumed that there was supposed to be a question mark at the end of the message. And that '2' was an affectation. With predictive text it was only a matter of moments to write the whole word. He sighed and tapped in his answer.

Will phone tomorrow. Matt.

The triple x at the end of every text Ellie sent thrilled him, though she probably put kisses after every message she wrote. And maybe it was something everyone did. Certainly his messages to Phyl and hers to him always had kisses added. Did they mean anything? Maybe they did and maybe not. He'd ring Ellie back, but could they really keep on having lunches? And what could he tell her about Paris? He'd come back from the trip feeling unsettled. Meeting his great-aunt had revived feelings in him he thought he'd forgotten years ago. It made him feel sad for his father in a way he'd never managed when John Barrington was alive. How hideous of Constance to do that: keep his letters away from him, for God's sake. He wasn't quite sure but it was probably against the law. She was tampering with Her Majesty's mail. I'll never forgive her for that, Matt reflected. The more he thought about it, the more unkind an act it seemed to him. My mother was a bitch, he told himself and even thinking such a thing shocked him, but it was true. What she'd done to Lou had started off his process of disillusionment with his mother and this just confirmed that he'd been right.

Mme Franchard was frail. He'd spoken to Lou about the possibility of having her to stay, taking her to see Milthorpe House, and so forth, but in truth he didn't think that would ever be possible. She appeared to be soldered to the chair she sat on and you felt that if you moved her, she would dissolve into grey dust. Her mind was sharp enough, but he'd noticed how close to her eyes she'd held the letter and Solange had told him that she ate 'not enough to fill a tooth'. Matt had wanted to ask what the financial situation was, and whether perhaps he might contribute something towards his ancient new relative's upkeep, but didn't feel it would be tactful on a first visit. Lou said she was going to go over to Paris again soon, but he'd have to see Mme Franchard as well. There might be ways in which he could make her life easier and he felt a duty to try and do that, at least.

His father hadn't been a great one for family. Whenever Matt had asked him about it as a child, John had deflected the questions, retreating into his 'I'm a writer and can't be disturbed' persona, which now Matt suspected he put on like a cloak of invisibility whenever he wanted to avoid a subject. And I'm not much better, he told himself. He'd been surprised to see how shaken he was by the discovery of a great-aunt he'd never known about. Part of him was intrigued, amazed – and irritated that this new relation couldn't tell him anything about John's mother to add to what he already knew, apart from filling in her background as a girl in France. For the most part, however, he was worried. Now that Mme Franchard was part of his family willy-nilly, he couldn't help feeling responsible. I'll have to go back, he thought. I could take Phyl for a weekend break, if it weren't for Poppy. Passing across the back of his mind like a shadow yet again was an image of himself and Ellie walking along the banks of the Seine and he tried hard to concentrate on Phyl. Me and Phyl walking along the banks of the Seine. Matt sighed. Why didn't his wife fit into the romantic cliché as well as Ellie did? Because I've not had a chance, he told himself, to get close to Phyl since Poppy arrived. Of course it was important for Lou to do this thing, whatever it was, that she was engaged in. He had a good idea of what it might be, because ever since her early childhood she'd been scribbling away in note-books. She was no doubt writing a novel, and from everything he remembered about his father, this was a long and difficult process. What if she took a year over it? Two years? He squared his shoulders and decided to discuss the matter with Phyl that evening.

He glanced at his watch. It was nearly lunchtime. He'd go out soon and get something at the pub down the road. And I'll phone Ellie from the call box there and tell her about Mme Franchard. What must it be like for her, spending almost the whole of her adult life first separated from her sister and then only guessing at what must have happened to her? He'd often wondered what it would be like to have a sibling. Quite unbidden, he had a flash of memory – a day he'd forgotten came back to him in detail. They'd gone out together, Matt and his father, on a fishing trip. Neither of us liked fishing, he thought now, so why did we do it? He had no idea. Maybe it was a way of getting out of the house. In any case, there they were, sitting on the riverbank in the sun. I had a hat, he recalled. A blue cotton hat and blue and white shorts which I hated wearing because I thought they looked girlish. How old was I? Six? Maybe seven – it was hard to remember. But he did recall most of the conversation. He'd asked his father, 'Why haven't I got any brothers or sisters?'

'Some people just don't. You're an only child. That's not a bad thing to be.'

'Isn't it? It's a bit lonely, though. We could play together all the time, if I had a brother.'

'I haven't got any brothers or sisters either.'

The silence that fell then lasted for what seemed to Matt like a very long time. Then his father sighed and said, 'Well, I used to have a sister, but she died. Remember? I told you about it. We were all in a prisoner-of-war camp. During the war.'

Even at that age, Matt had heard of the war. He knew how horrible it must be to have a dead sister, but he was still quite sorry that he had never had a sister. He thought his father wasn't going to say anything else about it but then he spoke again.

'Everyone said it couldn't be helped, my sister dying, but I felt ... well, I did feel it was my fault, a bit, that she died.'

'Why? Why was it your fault?'

'It's complicated. You don't need to understand, really, and I don't think I could explain. I just felt – sometimes I thought I ought to have died instead of her. That's what happens sometimes when you're very sad. It changes what you feel about things.'

Thinking about that day, Matt wondered how much of what he was remembering was how it was, and how much he was inventing things that might have been said – no, it was reasonably accurate. He remembered feeling sorry for his father, sorry about the dead sister. He'd never asked him about it again, not from lack of curiosity but because he sensed that John Barrington was more comfortable not discussing it. He hadn't thought about that day for years, but when he was younger – probably before he met Ellie – the memory of it came to him from time to time, which was why he could see it all so clearly now. He wondered, briefly, what his father had meant. Probably he was experiencing a kind of survivor's guilt, which he knew was common: the feeling that you had no right to be alive when someone you loved very much was lying dead.

'These are beautiful,' Nessa said, touching one of the handmade silk flowers that lay in one of the lined drawers of what looked like the kind of filing cabinet you saw in the offices of architects: lots of wide, flat compartments, about twenty of them. She and Mickey had travelled down to Dorset together to visit someone called Clarrie Armitage (must be short for Clarissa, Nessa thought, or possibly Clarice) whose handiwork Mickey had spotted in a back number of *Country Life* at the dentist's. Clarrie turned out to be a middle-aged lady of the sort who'd always call herself that: lady, not woman. She lived in a small, semi-detached cottage in a pretty village. She wore her iron-grey hair in a bun, and her rather peasanty skirt in burgundy wool had flowers embroidered all round the hem in bright shades of purple and pale pink. A fisherman's smock-type top in pink cord didn't do much for her bust, which was just that bit too big for it. A V-neck would be so much better, Nessa reflected, as Clarrie led them into her studio where flowers at every stage of their creation lay on an enormous table which almost filled the entire room. The filing cabinet took up most of one wall and they'd been looking at its contents for the last hour. Clarrie might not know what was what in the flattering tops department, but her flowers were miraculously beautiful, every petal perfect, exact, and yet somehow not quite like the natural flower ... lifted into the realm of art by some tiny detail: a whisper of glitter here, an edging of velvet there. The colours, too, were natural shades, slightly enhanced or modified, and because these flowers were made of silk, there was no limit to the palette Clarrie could use – and did. A black rose, silk trimmed with velvet, caught Nessa's eye. We can charge a fortune for something like that, she thought, and there'd be women flocking to buy it. In fact, Nessa was convinced that the more expensive a thing was, the more everyone would want to own it.

While Clarrie was in the kitchen making them a cup of tea, Nessa and Mickey discussed in whispers the possibility of stocking the flowers. They were nothing like the rest of the Paper Roses stock but that wasn't necessarily a bad thing.

'She's the only one making them,' said Mickey. 'We can't carry more than a very limited stock.'

'Doesn't matter. Even if we have very few – *especially* if we have very few – they'll just fly out of the catalogue. Wait and see. We emphasize the handiwork. Maybe even a picture of Clarrie, making them. Exclusive. No two flowers exactly alike. You know the sort of thing.'

'How much can we charge?'

'Clarrie's price is £20 per flower. That's peanuts. I'd have thought £40 was reasonable.' Nessa frowned. 'Even £50 is possible. Maybe we can persuade her to be exclusive to us, not to sell these flowers anywhere else. What do you think? D'you reckon she'd agree?'

'She might. How many can she sell in a year? If we guarantee to take as many as she makes, and give her a better price for them than she's getting by going round craft fairs, then why should she refuse?'

Nessa sat down at the table. 'She might not like the pressure that supplying us will put on her. She might not be able to fulfil orders.'

'We've got to emphasize, then, that there's no pressure at all. She can please herself, make as many or as few as she wants to, and we'll sell them. She'll clean up. We're going to give her a lot more per flower than she'd get anywhere else.'

Nessa was already foreseeing a problem. 'What if she gets fed up? Stops making them? Gets arthritis in the fingers ...'

'Then we'll have to stop selling them. That's the point about them. They aren't going to be on sale for ever. Clarrie isn't young. If we have a picture of her, anyone who wants to buy will get that message, subliminally.'

'I'm not quite sure,' Nessa said, 'that I believe in subliminal. I like upfront and loud and clear. D'you think she'll agree?'

'We'll ask her. I do think they're stunning.' Mickey picked up the black rose and held it against Nessa's face, her fingers just touching the skin. 'You look beautiful,' she said. 'I'm going to buy this for you as a present – a cheering-you-up present. Clarrie will be pleased.'

At that moment, their hostess came into the room, carrying a tray laden with tea things. Mickey went to take it from her, and Clarrie carefully moved the flowers she'd been displaying to one side to clear a space.

'Clarrie,' Nessa said, 'we want to make you an offer.'

'Getting a deal like that gives me a real kick,' Mickey said, as she drove through the village. The sun was setting. The sky was streaked with apricot and mauve, and puffy clouds were arranged along the horizon in a pleasingly symmetrical way. 'I feel like celebrating. Do you feel like celebrating?'

'How? We're on our way back. Gareth's mother's got Tamsin, but I do have stuff to do tomorrow in the office. Helmut's phoning in the morning.'

'Helmut is a business associate. If he finds we're out, he'll try later. He'll think we're out on a work-related thing, which we are in a way.'

'What d'you want to do? Have a nice meal somewhere?'

Mickey's smile, Nessa thought, altered her rather sharp features and made her look almost pretty. Because of her boyish, slim figure, and her short, very fair hair, pretty wasn't exactly how Nessa would have described her, but now the light from the sunset streaming in through the car windows made an aureole of radiance around her head. 'You look like an angel,' Nessa said aloud and blushed. That had been the thought in her mind and she'd spoken without thinking.

'Let's spend the night in a gorgeous hotel,' Mickey said. 'We could do with a treat. You could do with a treat.'

Nessa imagined it: a delicious dinner. A long bath. A soft bed and nothing anywhere to remind her of her home, or her silly bloody fool of a husband, or her greedy brother, or the rest of her family. She would even forget about her beloved Tamsin for a while. It could be just her. Her and Mickey.

'We haven't got any spare clothes – no toothbrush even.'

'We can buy some toothbrushes. Sleep naked.'

Nessa didn't say a word. Thinking about sleeping

naked in a hotel with no one knowing exactly where she was made her feel a little giddy.

'Why not?' she said. 'Let's go for it. What if there's no nice hotel anywhere near here?'

'Oh, there is. I looked it up when I knew we were coming down this way.'

'You,' Nessa laughed, 'are a sneaky devil.'

'I was an angel a moment ago.'

'You're both.' Nessa was aware of a weird sensation, like something being flipped over under her ribcage.

'You're being quite unfair. Unreasonable,' Phyl said, then aware that she'd spoken far more sharply than she'd intended, she added, 'I know it's hard for you, Matt. I realize that, but don't you think we owe it to Lou to make life easy for her? You found out in Paris that she was writing something, and when I spoke to her the other day, I did ask her whether she wanted Poppy back. And of course there are many, many ways in which she does, but on the other hand, it's much easier for her to work at whatever this thing is without Poppy to worry about.'

'It's her bloody job to worry about Poppy. It's not ours, Phyl.'

'I know, but still.' She went on picking up the toys from the carpet and putting them into the box she'd moved into the lounge to make life easier.

'Come here, Phyl,' he said, suddenly speaking in a quite different tone of voice. 'I want to talk to you. Seriously.'

'Gosh.' She went to sit beside him on the sofa. 'That sounds a bit ominous.'

'No. Not really. Only, well – I don't know how to say this, Phyl. We've never – I mean, we talk about everything else under the sun but we don't talk about these things, do we? We never have ...'

'What things?' She had a good idea what he was referring to. Was he really going to ...?

'Sex,' he said, after a slight pause. 'We haven't – I mean, it's been several weeks since we ...'

'I know, I know. I'm so sorry, darling Matt. It's ... it's not that I don't want to, you know that.'

'I do know that but it's hard for me. I feel ... I feel unloved.'

'You're *not* unloved. How can you say that? I love you more than anything.' Phyl felt as though a stone were dropping through her body. How peculiar! *Her heart sank*. That was exactly right. 'I'm sorry, you're right of course. We have made love a lot less often since Poppy's been here, but how can I just tell Lou she must have her back?'

'I'll do it if you like – and I've got an excuse. We're going to Paris. Wouldn't you like to go to Paris? I'll need to see Mme Franchard again reasonably soon. We didn't have time to discuss the things we ought to have done. I want to make sure she's all right ... her financial position, for instance. I want to do my bit. It's not often you find a long-lost relative. You want to meet her, don't you?'

Phyl nodded. It would be marvellous to go to Paris. And Matt was right – they couldn't go on like this, with every night interrupted by the baby. It was tiring. She knew that her own energy levels during the day were lower than usual because her sleep had been disturbed.

'Okay,' she said. 'You tell her. And then I'll speak after you ...'

'Should I do it now?'

'No point putting it off, I suppose.'

As Matt dialled the number, she couldn't help feeling sad. It didn't matter how many arguments her husband put forward, or that it might be better for Poppy to be reunited with her mother. She, Phyl, would be bereft. She would miss the constant company, the gurgling smiles and (she'd never have admitted this to anyone), most of all, she would miss those precious minutes during the night, when Poppy was sleepy and warm and lay against her shoulder as she took her out of the cot to give her a drink and change her nappy. She'd miss singing the bedtime songs in a darkened room, and watching her granddaughter as she fell asleep at last, clutching her favourite cuddly polar bear. In return, she and Matt would make love much more often. Well, that would be nice, but Phyl had to admit to herself that the thought didn't thrill her as much as it ought to have done and she immediately felt guilty. Then there was the morning smile, like a beam of warmth and light, with which Poppy greeted her every day – she wouldn't have that any longer either. And worst of all, she wouldn't be able to watch the child growing and changing. At this age, babies changed almost overnight. By the time she saw Poppy again, she'd be a different child. She tuned in to what Matt was saying to Lou.

'Not that we're not devoted to Poppy, darling. You know we are, but – yes, of course. Of course – you must both come down every possible weekend you can. I'll let you know when Mum and I are off to Paris.' He paused, and listened for a while to what Lou was saying. She seemed to be talking for a very long time with Matt hanging on to the receiver and nodding from time to time. Then he said, 'All right. That's perfect. Come down on Friday. We'll expect you at about six, is that right? Fine, fine. Give me a ring when you leave Victoria and I'll come and pick you up at the station. Yes ... yes, thanks, darling. I knew you'd understand.'

Phyl waved a hand at him, and pointed at the phone and then at herself. He said, 'Hang on a mo, darling. Your mum wants a word. Yes, yes, I will. Goodnight, sweetheart.'

He gave the receiver to Phyl, then got off the sofa and left the room.

'Hello, Lou darling. Your dad's just leaving the room ... hang on.'

'God, Mum, I'm so, so sorry. Has it been ghastly for you?' Lou sounded very far away and Phyl hoped the mobile connection didn't suddenly go wonky, as it sometimes did.

'Ghastly? No, of course not. The very opposite, honestly. I'll miss her like mad, you know I will. It's your father. It's not that he doesn't love Poppy, he really does, but he needs things round the house to be calm and peaceful and he says, well, he says he doesn't see as much of me as he'd like to. He says I'm always taken up with Poppy.' Phyl laughed. 'He's right really. I *am* taken up with her. Also, he tells me he's going to take me to Paris to meet Mme Franchard. That'll be nice.'

'I want to go and see her again as well. I'll go one weekend when you're free to look after Poppy again. You could come and stay here while I'm there. I could go for the day, but it would be nice to have a weekend and do something touristy. I could take a friend, or something.'

What was it in Lou's voice that alerted Phyl? A warmth in the words as she spoke of a 'friend'. Did she, could she mean a man? Ought she to ask? She decided to risk it.

'A girlfriend?'

'Not necessarily.'

'Have you ... Do you ...'

'Don't be coy, Mum. You're asking if I have a

boyfriend and the answer is very much no – but I might take a male friend.'

'Oh,' said Phyl, trying to keep the disappointment out of her voice.

'You sound disappointed.'

'Not at all, really.' Phyl started to ask Lou about her work but was interrupted.

'Gotta go, Mum, sorry. I'm going out for a meal.'

'With the same person who isn't a boyfriend?'

'Don't be so nosy!' Lou was laughing.

'Okay, bye,' said Phyl, suddenly feeling quite optimistic. Lou sounded really upbeat. That had to be a good thing.

Plastic air. That's what hotels had circulating through them, Nessa thought, lying in her single bed in a room that, even though it hadn't lived up to Mickey's dream of an idyllic country retreat, didn't seem all that bad from the outside. It wasn't bad on the inside either, not really, but somehow most of the expenditure seemed to have been directed at the public rooms and the bedrooms had missed out. For a moment, Nessa followed a daydream of the kind of place she'd have if she owned a hotel. She'd make sure that the rooms were both luxurious and simple. Lots of white. Pale grey and apricot perhaps for the curtains. Printed velvet, chenille ... something that you wanted to touch. Lots and lots of Paper Roses flowers everywhere. It could be a feature of the place: unreal blooms in every room. Could you get away with something like that? She sighed and sat up, turning on the bedside light to reveal the beige and scarlet décor, the flouncy pelmets, the too-fiddly lampshades, and wondered whether it was worth getting out of bed to make a cup of tea. She was finding it hard to fall asleep. Being naked might have something to do with it. She was restless. She'd been to the loo only a moment ago and got into bed again, but now she was wondering whether a drink might help.

Mickey was in the room next door. The hotel was suspiciously empty when they'd checked in, even taking into account the fact that it was midweek and this was the depths of the countryside. No one said anything about them having no luggage. Dinner was lovely. Just being able to sit quietly and talk to someone who wasn't on her case was restful. Mickey was funny and asked all the right questions. They'd talked about everything: the divorce, Tamsin, Justin, and Ellie, too. Maybe, Nessa thought, Mickey's still awake like me. Perhaps I'll text her – that might wake her up if she's asleep. But she usually goes to sleep late.

She was still debating what to do when her own mobile, which she was holding in her hand, trilled into life. She dropped it at once, and it fell on the floor near the bed. For a moment, she felt a chill of fear. Had something happened to Tamsin? Who on earth could be texting her in the middle of the night? She read the message: *U awake? M.* Mickey, thank heavens. She texted back *Can't sleep and bored. Do come and visit. N.*

Soon, there was a knock on her door. Nessa wrapped herself in the flowery bedspread and went to open it. Mickey stood in the corridor, bearing a bottle of wine and a tube of Pringles. She was wearing her coat, a sort of trenchcoat-style mac, and she was, Nessa realized, completely naked under it, just as she was under her bedspread.

'Midnight feast,' Mickey whispered, and Nessa opened the door wide to let her in.

'Where did you get that bottle?'

'I went down to the bar and sweet-talked the barman.'

'Seriously?'

'Yup.'

'Before or after you undressed?' Nessa giggled.

'Oh, after, of course – gave him a flash of my boobs as a reward.'

'I'm full of admiration. And a bit shocked too. It would never occur to me to do that. Thanks so much. Just what I need. I can't sleep.'

'No, nor can I,' Mickey said. 'Can I get on the bed?'

'Yes, of course.'

'I'll pour the wine first.' She went into the ensuite bathroom and brought back the glass. 'We'll have to share, I'm afraid.'

'Doesn't matter,' Nessa said. She was already in bed, suddenly very conscious of her body, feeling the sheets on every inch of her bare skin.

Mickey handed her the glass and said, 'You first.'

She went round to the other side of the bed and stretched out next to Nessa.

They lay there for a while, not saying anything, but passing the glass between them, and drinking the wine rather too quickly.

'Pringle?'

'No, thanks,' Nessa spoke quietly.

'Are you feeling sleepy?'

'Not really. I'm a bit pissed, I think, what with the wine at dinner and now this ... Mickey?'

'Mmm?'

'Are you stroking my hair?'

'D'you mind?'

Mickey's hand felt wonderful on her hair. She's caressing me, Nessa thought, and closed her eyes. She is. I haven't been caressed for years. Had Gareth ever touched her hair like that? Her mind was becoming more and more fuzzy, but she couldn't remember an occasion when he had ... Oh, it felt good, so good.

'Should I stop?' Mickey whispered. She's turned over on her side, Nessa told herself. I can feel her breath on my cheek. She shook her head.

'No, don't stop.'

Nessa didn't dare to open her eyes, in case the whole of the scene vanished like a dream: she and Mickey on the bed, Mickey stroking her hair, the wine warming her, the bedclothes lying on her body. Mickey's fingers seemed to be moving over her face now, tracing her profile and lingering on her lips, and down over her chin until they reached the bedclothes. What now? Would she – would she go on? What do I do if she asks me? What if she says something now? How will I answer? Nessa found herself shuddering into goose-flesh ... Oh, please don't stop, she said soundlessly. Go on. Touch me there ... and Mickey did. Oh, God, she's touching my breast ... oh ...

'Nessa.' Mickey's mouth on her ear. Nessa thought she would faint. 'I want to touch you all over. Can I? Can I touch you all over?'

Nessa couldn't speak; didn't want to say anything. Saying something would be dangerous. She'd have to admit how this was making her feel: as though she were melting. Her body like a lit candle, parts of her liquefying, on fire, singing at the touch of Mickey's fingers. The fingers – they were hard and soft at the same time – how could that be? How did she do that? The hands touched and touched till Nessa's whole body was inflamed, and throbbing and then Mickey peeled back the covers and went to crouch between Nessa's legs and all at once there was a sound erupting from her throat that was a shout and a sob and she was electric all over, struck by lightning, and then limp and wet and crying properly now, clinging to Mickey, who lay with her head on Nessa's shoulder, her naked body intertwined with hers.

'Nessa?'

'Mmm.' Nessa had no idea what she ought to say. No clue what she was supposed to do now. She didn't even want to open her eyes because she didn't know where to look, so she lay with her them firmly closed.

'Look at me, Nessa.'

'Must I?'

'Don't you want to?'

Nessa said, 'I don't know what ... I'm not sure ...'

'You should look at me. Speak to me.'

Nessa opened her eyes. 'Oh, Mickey ...' she said.

Mickey brought her mouth close to Nessa's ear and whispered, 'Are you embarrassed?'

Nessa nodded. 'A bit. I've never – I didn't know ...'

'You're going to say you've always been straight, never been attracted to a woman before, don't know what came over you, it was the wine talking. Stuff like that, right?'

'I *have* always been straight but ...'

'But what?'

'Oh, Mickey that was so good. I felt – I don't think I've ever felt – and you, you're so dear to me, Mickey. You're my very best friend, you've been that for ages. It's so confusing. I'm confused. I don't know what to think or what I feel, but it was so lovely, Mickey. I thought I was going to die of bliss.'

'Don't think too much, Nessa. Not now. It's late – time to go to sleep.'

'You're not going back to your room, are you?' Suddenly Nessa found she was dreading the thought of being all alone in bed again.

'D'you want me to?'

Nessa shook her head.

'I love you, Nessa,' Mickey whispered.

'Don't say that, Mickey. Please don't say that!'

'Why not? It's true – I do. I'm not afraid to admit

it. I fell in love with you the very first time I saw you. But you were married and straight and I wasn't about to ... Well, we were good friends and I've had to let that be enough. But tonight – I couldn't help it, Nessa. I've been wanting you so much for so long. It's been awful.'

'You should have said.' Nessa turned so that she was lying alongside Mickey, staring into her blue, blue eyes.

'You'd have run a mile. I bet you still think there's something disgraceful about being with a woman. Admit it.'

'I do, a bit. I feel as though I'm being extra specially wicked – it makes it more exciting, though, in a funny way. It's like having butterflies, a bit. In my stomach.'

'I'm going to kiss you now, Nessa. Have you ever kissed a woman before?'

'No,' Nessa breathed. Their mouths were very close together. She could feel the breath coming from between Mickey's lips, fluttering on her own skin. She closed her eyes and felt a hand on her neck, pulling her gently till their two mouths were touching, softly. Nessa opened her lips, and let herself be absorbed into the kiss. She could taste Mickey. Feel her. It was nothing, *nothing* like being kissed by a man. Mickey smelled of herself: a combination of skin and soap and the perfume she always wore: Vivienne Westwood's Boudoir. Her flesh was soft, and her slim body smooth and her hair was silky when Nessa touched it. That's what I'm doing, she thought. I'm touching her hair. I am. She was hugging Mickey tightly, wanting to fuse their two bodies, wanting to be swallowed up herself and then suddenly wanting, oh, wanting overwhelmingly, *so, so* much, to be the one who touched; the one who did the caressing. Nessa moved her mouth to Mickey's breast and began to lick it, and it was Mickey's turn to moan and sigh and Nessa felt powerful and loving and went on touching and touching and stroking and caressing till Mickey shivered into her own orgasm and lay back against the sheet, smiling.

'Now,' Nessa whispered, leaning over to kiss Mickey lightly on the mouth. 'Now's when I could murder some Pringles. And there's still a bit of wine left, too.'

7

The blossoms on the tree outside the library window had fallen from the branches and for a while had lain on the ground below like a scattering of confetti. Lou was trying to concentrate on the book in front of her, making an effort not to look at the pale green mist of leaves pressing against the glass. She blinked. It didn't matter how many times you read about it, or saw it in movies and TV series as different as *Empire of the Sun* and *Tenko*, the realities of Japanese prisoner-of-war camps were so horrendous that it was hard to take them in. As if the crushing heat, the lack of food and water, the unhygienic sanitary arrangements, the insects, the inadequate shelter and bedding, the dirt and mud when it rained were not enough, on top of all that, there were the guards. The pleasanter ones were rigid, stubborn and unreasonable. The worst ones were horrifically cruel. The commanders of some camps gloried in the humiliation of their charges, giving out the most sadistic of punishments for tiny little infringements of the rules. Everyone knew about this on some level and Lou, though she wanted to make sure that the background details were exact, was quite certain she didn't want her screenplay to be simply another catalogue of atrocities.

It's about Peter, she said to herself. His life there, his

problems, the people he's dealing with. It's a human story. That's what I'm interested in and that's what the movie's about. People. There would be some extras needed, of course, but Lou had limited her main cast list to nine people: Peter, Annette, Dulcie, Derek and Nigel, two more boys with speaking parts, and two other women in the camp, called Marjorie and Shirley. All the names were from Grandad's book, which solved one problem for Lou.

The smaller the cast, she knew, the cheaper it would be to make. It would only need one set: the camp, and that, she imagined, could be reconstructed almost anywhere. For a while, she'd seriously considered flashbacks, both to the colony in the days before they were 'in the bag' as they used to say: imprisoned. Or perhaps to France, now that she knew more about where Grandad's real mother came from. She'd decided against it in the end, not only for economic reasons (more than one set, possible location shooting) but also because she was going to be using some voice-over and having both wouldn't be a good idea. She sighed and closed the book and looked at her watch. Only another half-hour and she'd have to go and pick up Poppy from nursery.

Lou had gone to fetch her from her parents' house the weekend before their proposed visit to Paris, but that hadn't happened in the end because Dad had to do something urgent at work. They still hadn't been to see Mme Franchard and neither had she, but they all still intended to go, she knew. Poppy had now been with her for three weeks, and Lou had to admit that in so many ways it was lovely to have her home. Who am I kidding? Lou thought, and felt guilty at once. Of course she'd been thrilled to have her daughter safe in her cot at night, and there all the time to cuddle and chat to and take care of, but it was all so – so relentless.

So unending. So every-day-with-no-time-off-for-good-behaviour. She wasn't cut out for motherhood. That, at any rate, was what she thought when she had to get up in the middle of the night. Bathtimes, mealtimes, cuddling times were fine and fun and there was, thank heaven, the three-hour space every morning when Lou's time was her own.

That was how she'd managed to finish the screen-play. She'd done it. Typing in THE END was fantastic. She'd felt out of breath, elated, and wanted to go out into the corridor and yell the news at the closed doors of the other flats. Because she'd kept the writing so secret, there was now no one she could phone. Not one of her friends knew about it, nor did her family. She told Poppy in the end.

'I've finished, finished, finished,' she sang, blowing raspberries into her baby's soft stomach while she was dressing her. 'I'm a screenwriter, I am. A proper writer. I've finished, finished, finished.'

Poppy, caught up in the excitement, started saying: 'Fish, fish, fish ...' which was quite close, considering how young she was.

The elation lasted one whole day and then that night, when Lou opened up the laptop, dread washed over her for no good reason she could see. What if it's awful? What if I only *think* it's good and it isn't? Everyone will say it's mawkish. Sensational. Plain old bad. She took a deep breath and started reading it. She'd gone through it about ten times since that night and now she was almost as convinced it was good as she had been on the day she'd finished it.

There came a time when you had to stop re-reading. She'd now done the final, final edit, making it as good as it could be, she'd taken it to be printed out, and had re-read it on paper, where somehow it looked differ-ent. Next week, she was going to do something which made her feel faint with fear whenever she thought about it: she'd decided to take it round to Ciaran Donnelly's house and pretend that Harry had sent it in for the great man to look at. She'd been wondering for ages what to do with the screenplay once it was written. She wanted a sympathetic reader, but not one who knew her and whose opinion might be swayed by their opinion of her. Harry was the obvious person to show it to, but she worked for him, apart from anything else. Having him assess her screenplay was a no-no. She wasn't about to put him on the spot.

Taking it round to Ciaran Donnelly had occurred to her in the middle of the night, but there were problems with that, too. If he hated it, he'd get back to Harry and say *hey, how come you took the trouble to send me over such a crappy screenplay?* and Harry would say *what screenplay?* Her deception would be uncovered. What would the consequences be? What if Harry never forgave her for not going to him first? For not trusting him with her secret? For not allowing that he might be in a position to vet what she'd written before she went thrusting it under the nose of a top Hollywood producer? She'd have to plead girly foolishness, not thinking properly, etc., etc., but she'd be so contrite that he'd forgive her, she was sure. He wasn't the kind of person to be angry for a long time and upsetting him was a risk she was prepared to take.

Why had Harry chosen this particular time to go off to the States for a month just when things had started to go so well? Never mind, he'd be back soon and meanwhile there were the emails. They wrote to one another every couple of days. Lou's instinct was to answer his messages by return, but she'd forced herself not to. It wasn't exactly like *You've Got Mail* (a ridiculously soppy and romantic movie which she'd never have admitted she liked), but sort of the same, because for the last couple of weeks she looked forward to opening her laptop every single morning. Harry's messages were typical of him: short, quite funny, and with no hint of the sort of vibes she'd been getting from him the last couple of times she'd seen him, when he seemed to her to be working up to the point of actually making it clear he was interested in her in a more than just friendly way.

Lou had almost asked him to go to Paris with her, but her nerve failed her at the last moment and then he'd flown off to what he called, Hollywood-style, 'the coast'. That had allowed her to invite him by email and she'd spent almost as long on composing that message as she had on writing certain parts of *Blind Moon*. She knew it by heart:

I'm thinking of going to visit Mme Franchard in Paris soon – would you like to come with me?

Lou smiled when she thought of the variations on those few words she'd worked through before she was ready to press 'send'. So many of them contained words that could be *double entendres*: 'come', 'coming', 'fancy', even 'being with you'. It was exhausting and reminded her of being a schoolgirl again. In those days, she used to spend hours analysing every single note, phone call, word, that some boy she liked had said to her, or sent her. Nothing had changed. She rejected: *How about you come with me? What about making a weekend of it? How'd you fancy coming? It'll be so much more fun if you're there. Fancy coming with me? I fancy you ...* She'd actually written that at one point and then stared at it for ages before deleting it. Even after it had disappeared for ever, it hung around in her head. Do I fancy him? she asked herself and came to the conclusion that yes, she did, and if he fancied her, she wasn't going to put up a struggle. Harry would never hurt her, she was sure he wouldn't, and since she'd started working at Cinnamon Hill, she found herself thinking about Ray less and less. Sometimes, in the dark hours, when she was trying hard to get to sleep because she was going to have to get up properly in a couple of hours and it was really, really important not to stay awake, nasty little ideas popped into her mind. Ray was lovely to begin with. He was lovely for a long time. He only became violent and horrible later. Harry might be like that. No, he's not, he's not. He's really gentle. No one says a bad word about him in the office.

She'd sent the message in the end, and he'd replied. What he'd written in the Subject line of the email made her laugh, because it was so typical and so sweet: *We'll always have Paris*. Harry and herself: Bogart and Bergman in *Casablanca* – nothing to choose between them! She'd printed out the message and pinned it to the noticeboard in the kitchen where it made her feel happy every day: *Sure thing, kid. Anytime. Can't wait. Harry x*.

That had been the first 'x' and since then, she'd added the letter to her signature and it had appeared after his, every time he wrote to her. It was her inner schoolgirl thinking but she attached an enormous weight to that 'x'. Was she mad? She knew lots of people (e.g. Nessa, when she wrote, once in a blue moon) who added an 'x' to their name automatically and to whom it meant nothing and less than nothing. What if Harry was one of those? I don't care, she thought. I mean my 'x' to be a kiss and I'm going to imagine he does too, until I know he doesn't.

Nearly time to fetch Poppy. Lou closed the library book she'd stopped reading ages ago and went to put it back on the shelf. After lunch, she told herself, we'll go to the park. We'll feed the ducks and I'll work out what I'm going to say to Harry in my next email. I'll write one tonight. Then tomorrow, I'll take the screen-play to Ciaran Donnelly. If I dare.

Matt read the letter twice. The message had been clear enough the first time, but better to make sure. His secretary had opened it and brought it straight in, before processing the rest of the morning's post. She must have been attracted to the thick cream paper of the envelope and the fact that it looked like a proper letter and not a circular of some kind.

'I think you'll want to see this,' she said, putting it down in front of him. 'It looks interesting to me.'

The letterhead was as impressive as the paper it was printed on. GOLDEN INK, it read, and there was a little logo of an inkpot with a pen sitting beside it. The implication was that the words GOLDEN INK had just that minute been written in ... wait for it ... golden ink. As puns went (and Matt was fond of puns) it wasn't bad. The letter was from someone called Jake Golden. The address was somewhere in Bloomsbury.

Dear Matthew Barrington,

I very much hope that you are the person I think you are. I am on the trail of the son of the late John Barrington, who wrote a novel called *Blind Moon* (as well as several others) in the 1960s.

I came across a copy of *Blind Moon* in a second-hand bookshop some time ago and learned from the author biography that John Barrington was a solicitor in Haywards Heath. The internet did the rest and now I'm writing to ask whether you are, as I assume, John Barrington's son.

If you are, I would very much like to meet you to discuss the possible reissue of your father's fine book. We are a small firm, but I think I can say we've made our mark, in a world increasingly dominated by the search for the next bestseller, as being a company more interested in the quality of the text than the dazzling effect of the bottom line.

I'd be happy to speak to you at any time, and my numbers are …

Matt frowned and allowed himself a moment of something like glee. If he'd understood it correctly, this chap – this Golden chap – was offering (or might be offering) to republish his father's book. There would be money in this for Lou if that happened, and he found himself ridiculously happy at that prospect. He took out his mobile to talk to her. He wasn't going to go through the office switchboard, even though there wasn't anything secret about this. His reason for keeping it to himself was superstitious. He didn't want to jinx what was perhaps about to happen.

'Lou? Hello, darling,' he said when she answered. 'I want to read you a letter. Can you talk now? Good, so listen to this.'

He read the letter, then listened to his daughter's questions.

'Yes, yes, I know. I'll check up on the firm, don't worry. But may I give this Jake chap your number? I'll tell him that the copyright belongs to you and then we'll see. He'll no doubt be in touch. Okay? Fine. Got to go, darling. I'm going to see Justin – no, no, nothing much. Going to see his new flat, that's all. Right. Take care. I'll phone Jake Golden right now.'

He rang the number for the mobile given on the letterhead and waited for Mr Golden to answer with a rising sense of excitement. He wasn't about to let himself get carried away, though. Many a slip …

Lou arrived early at the nursery, and sat on the wall outside, trying to take in what had just happened. Perhaps she'd been dreaming. No, it was true. Dad's number was still on her mobile. From what she could make out, this person called Mr Golden wanted – or maybe wanted – to reissue Grandad's book and Dad was going to give him her number. She had no idea of how the timing would go. She didn't know how long it took to get a book published, nor what it entailed, but for a few moments, she allowed herself to day-dream. Imagine if the book and a movie made from her screenplay came out at the same time! No, that wouldn't happen. Movies took ages. She had so many hurdles to leap that just thinking about them depressed her. Even if Ciaran Donnelly liked it, and that was a big if, it wouldn't necessarily get made. An option was the best she could hope for. But, of course, very few screenplays were optioned so why should hers be? Then even if you did get your work optioned, that was often the end of the story. So few optioned screenplays got made into movies that the possibility was only a little more likely than a win on the Lottery.

She didn't know much about publishing, but was aware of various initiatives to get out-of-print books back into the shops. She'd bought several gorgeous silver-jacketed Persephone books, which came with their own bookmarks, and this Golden Ink – that must be a pun on Golden Inc., surely – was probably a bit like that. Grandad's book was easily as good as the Persephone reissues, so the idea of it being avail-able again, on the bookshelves once more after years of neglect, didn't strike her as particularly unlikely. *I* ought to have thought of it, she told herself. If I hadn't been so taken up with writing the screenplay, I could have approached publishers myself. I could have made it my business to find out who might have been interested in it. Her mobile started ringing and she scrabbled for it in her handbag.

'Hello? Yes, this is Louise Barrington. Who? Oh, I'm sorry ...'

The phone almost slipped from her hand. It was Jake Golden. Amazing. Dad had only phoned her just an hour or so ago. Jake Golden was American. That was a surprise. He sounded like Clint Eastwood: a quiet voice.

'Miss Barrington, I've just spoken to your father and he tells me that you're John Barrington's grand-daughter and the owner of his copyrights?'

'Yes, that's right.'

'Then I'm honoured to talk to you. I'm a great admirer of your grandfather's books and I'd very much like to meet with you to discuss them.'

'Umm ... yes, of course. That'd be – I mean, I'd love to.'

'Great. I don't mean just a literary discussion, you understand. Much as I'd enjoy that – they're such unusual books – no, I mean I'd like to talk about the possibility of reissuing *Blind Moon*. I'm going to be in the States for the next while, but may I phone again when I get back? We could have lunch one day. How would that be?'

A publisher wanted to take her to lunch! Lou tried to sound nonchalant, as though this were something that happened to her all the time.

'Sure,' she said. The Clint Eastwood thing was catching. 'That's fine.' Another thought occurred to her. She added, 'Is your company based in America?'

'No, it's based here,' Jake Golden replied, laughing. He had a lovely laugh. 'But I'm wanting to open an office in New York. I do have international ambitions, but I've lived in London for ten years and I love it.'

They said goodbye and he promised again to be in

touch. Lou put her phone back into her bag, not quite able to believe what she'd heard. She couldn't wait to tell Harry about it on email. Possible publication! She wondered what Jake Golden looked like. She imagined someone a bit like Leo McGarry in *The West Wing*. Wishful thinking, probably. But he'd be about Dad's age, for sure.

She looked at her watch. Time to go and fetch Poppy. A couple of other mothers were already going through the glass doors.

'Say something, for God's sake. Bloody hell, Matt, this is hard enough without you clamming up like that. Why don't you say anything?' Justin was fidgeting. He was standing by the window, almost hopping from foot to foot, running his right hand through his hair over and over again.

Matt continued staring at his stepson and kept his mouth shut. Serve the bastard right, he thought. I'm not speaking till I know what I'm going to say. Let him sweat. He felt winded, as though someone had aimed a kick at his stomach. He'd stopped breathing for a moment but now he was gazing at the lines of golden parquet in Justin's flat, and they stretched away to the window, the chevrons in which they were arranged growing and shrinking in an optical illusion in front of Matt's eyes, the way a sheet of netting sometimes did. He'd rung Justin earlier in the morning, asking whether he could come round and see him. The matter of Justin had been on his mind for the last couple of days, ever since someone at the bridge club had said, in passing, 'Goodness me, Matt, you didn't waste much time. I see Milthorpe House has been sold.'

It had taken all Matt's training as a poker-faced lawyer to remain calm, to stop himself from asking for further details. He'd muttered something non-committal and moved away quickly. He phoned Justin the minute he got home and now here he was and the story, which he'd tried to persuade himself was mere rumour, had been confirmed. Matt was good at saying nothing. He could keep it up for a long time. He'd been trained for it from his very earliest childhood. Constance didn't do tantrums. She simply wasn't prepared to tolerate them, and Matt learned quickly. There hadn't been more than two or three occasions when he'd lost it. How old could he have been? Four? Five? Very young anyway. He'd screamed and wailed and drummed his heels on the floor and couldn't for the life of him now recall why. What was still vivid in his mind was his mother's reaction. She'd taken him by the arm, not roughly, but firmly and had led him to the back staircase, the one that led from Miss Hardy's room down to the kitchen. The whole staircase was dark, even when the dim light was turned on. In fact, it was even worse then. The bulb made shadows gather in the corners and these seemed to Matt deeper, more full of monsters and other unthinkable things than any shadows he'd ever seen before. Constance had pushed him down on the first step and said, in a chilly sort of voice: 'You're to stay here, Matthew, till you realize that screaming and shouting are not the way to attract my attention. I'll return for you in a little while and from now on, we'll talk in a grown-up way *without raising our voices*, d'you understand? Without tears, especially. Boys do not cry. I'm sure you'll understand my point of view in a little while.'

She'd gone and there he was, sitting on the lino-leum shivering with fear at the dark and the silence and filled with rage at his mother and guilt at feeling the rage, and tears welled up in his eyes and rolled down his cheeks, and what was he supposed to do?

He couldn't help crying but his mother said *boys do not cry*. He wiped his eyes and nose on his sleeve and sniffed and sat there and sat there, his arms and legs so cold he could scarcely feel them. No one came near him. Where was Miss Hardy? For a moment or two he wondered if his father might rescue him but he knew that wasn't going to happen. Dad worked in his study in the morning and no one was allowed to disturb him. No one at all.

The time had gone by in the end and after what seemed like hours, Constance came back to release him from his punishment.

'No more tantrums, Matthew. Do we understand one another?'

He nodded. He'd already made up his mind never to make his mother cross again. If he wanted things to go smoothly, if he wanted his mother's approval, he'd have to become quiet. He'd made up his mind on that day never to scream, never to yell, never to cry unless it was for a broken arm or something, and he never had, not even today.

He looked up at Justin. After what he'd just been told, he reckoned a bit of shouting wouldn't be in the least out of order. He glanced at his hands. He wasn't, had never been, a violent person, but a wave of fury swept over him and he clenched his fists. *Hitting Justin won't help. It won't make any difference* was one thought that kept running through his mind. *But it would make me feel better* was another. No, of course it wouldn't. Matt closed his eyes. Could he risk speaking? He said, 'Justin, I'd like you to tell me the facts of the matter again, please. I've had time to take in what you said, but I want the details. Facts, figures. That sort of thing.'

'I'm useless at that stuff, Matt. You know that. Why don't I just get my accountant, or better still,

Eremount's accountants, to get in touch with you? Explain the deal.'

'Later. I'll speak to them later, of course.'

Justin gazed down at his own feet. He can't meet my eyes, Matt thought. He's a coward as well as a fool. He went on, 'For the moment I'd like to hear from you why you thought it was a good idea to get rid of our family home.'

'I didn't get rid of it, I sold it. To Eremount. I've explained all this, Matt. They're going to turn it into a very high-end health club and spa.'

'High end? God, Justin, speak English why don't you?'

'It means posh. Superior. High class.'

'I know what it bloody means.' Matt could feel himself getting even angrier, could hear the volume rising when he spoke. He swallowed. 'Okay, high-end spa. I get it, completely. Why did you want to turn Milthorpe House into a health club? What was the matter with it as a house? A home, even.'

'Matt, it's not that I didn't love Milthorpe House …'

Of course not, Matt said to himself. You couldn't wait to part with the place. Fat lot of love that shows. Justin went on, '… but they made me an offer I couldn't refuse.'

'Spare me *The Godfather* clichés, please. You could refuse. You should have refused. You should at the very, very least have *consulted me.*'

'Don't shout at me, Matt.'

'I'm not shouting.'

'That's what it feels like to me.'

Matt sighed. 'If I'd been shouting at you, Justin … if I let you have even a tiny percentage of what I'm feeling, you'd be on the floor and unable to pick yourself up for a week.'

'Is that a threat?'

'No, no ... what good would a threat be? You've done it now, without telling a soul. In fact, if I hadn't heard rumours at the bridge club and asked you about it, I dare say you'd not have come clean even now.'

'I would have told you in the end.'

'Exactly. In the end. You just didn't have the courage to let this matter be discussed in the family. You sold the family home. I still can't take it in. *My* family home. The place I grew up in. How much did they give you for it?'

'I don't have to tell you that. A considerable amount of money. And it's not yours, Matt. After Constance died, it became mine. To do with as I thought best. And don't give me that family home shit. You've never shown the slightest interest in Milthorpe House.'

'Because I thought the place was safe, you fool. I don't believe what I'm hearing. It nearly killed me when Constance left it to you if you must know ...'

'Oh, I do know. Believe me, we both know. Me and Nessa just didn't count when stacked up against your precious Lou. That was obvious. Well, too bloody bad, Matt. Constance left the house to *me*. No one else. Just me. And I didn't need the hassle of taxes and so on, did I? I didn't have to consult you and I didn't have to get your permission and I'm glad I went ahead and sold because now, instead of sitting there like a stonking white elephant that everyone gets all sentimental over but no one actually wants to live in, it's going to be a jewel in the crown of the Eremount empire and I'm going to be almost three million quid richer and I don't give a flying fuck what you think.'

He sank down on to the sofa, exhausted by this outburst. Matt stood up. He'd long ago decided, not because of anything Constance had done in his childhood, but after years of dealing with hysterical and sometimes abusive clients, that it was quite pointless to go on trying to discuss something with a person who'd become foul-mouthed.

'Goodbye, Justin. I'll see myself out.'

'You're running away because you haven't got a leg to stand on,' Justin was shouting himself now. 'You're not going to admit there's even a tiny bit of justice on my side.'

Matt forced himself to smile pleasantly. It took some doing but it was worth it. He was well aware that nothing would infuriate Justin more than him walking out right now, without saying another word, so that was what he did. As he went down to the ground floor, the sound of the flat door being slammed echoed round the stairwell, which made Matt feel marginally better, but not for long. Once he got outside, he started walking quickly along the street. Justin will be looking at me from up there, he thought. I won't give him the satisfaction of appearing anything except brisk and upright. Once he turned the corner, he leaned against the wall, closing his eyes and breathing in and out in an effort to calm himself. What now? Where to go? He didn't feel like going back to the office. He took out his mobile phone and stared at it. Ellie's flat was quite close by. Portland Place. Would she be in? Was he mad to try and see her? No, he wasn't. Justin was her son after all. Maybe she'd be able to talk some sense into him. Worth trying, Matt thought. He flipped his phone open and punched in Ellie's number.

I'm having withdrawal symptoms, Phyl thought, as she sat behind the counter in the surgery waiting for the last animals of the day to leave with their owners. She'd just shown Montpelier Tango, a Borzoi with a spoiled and arrogant mistress, into Doc Hargreaves's room, and since there weren't any new animals to process she went through to the back where the cats and dogs who'd had surgery that day were lined up in their boxes, waiting for their anaesthetic to wear off.

'You'll be going home soon,' she whispered to Mimi, one of her favourite cats, who'd been coming to get her boosters here for the last ten years or so. Mimi was an affectionate creature. She'd been in for a minor operation and had now recovered enough to purr a little as Phyl stroked her head and spoke to her. 'I wish I could take you home with me. Actually, I wish I weren't here at all, if you really want to know. I wish I still had Poppy to look after.'

When Lou came to take the baby back to London, Phyl had made all the right noises. I didn't show how much I was going to miss her, she thought now, how empty my days would suddenly become. I rattled on about how Doc Hargreaves would be pleased to have me back; how much I missed the animals, and if Lou didn't believe me, then she pretended to.

To be fair, Lou did seem to be coping a lot better with Poppy nowadays. Perhaps she was growing into motherhood at last. Or maybe (and this was a possibility that Phyl favoured) there was somebody in her life who was making her happy.

'A boyfriend, Mimi,' she told the cat. 'That'd be good, right? A possible dad for Poppy.'

As soon as she said those words, a chill came over her. I've read too many tabloid newspapers, that's my problem, she thought, and urged herself not to be so stupid. Not all stepfathers were either cruel or sexually predatory to their stepchildren, and it was a very long way from being that kind of relationship, wasn't it? If indeed there was a relationship at all. Lou hadn't said so. She hadn't said anything. It was more a feeling that Phyl had picked up. I won't think about it, she said to herself. She sighed. As soon as she stopped fretting

252

about Lou, there was Matt to worry about. He hadn't been himself in the last couple of days. She'd asked him about it, and he'd denied there was anything wrong. He was obviously lying, but they'd never been the kind of couple who probed and prodded one another, digging after innermost thoughts. He'd tell her when he was ready.

The talk about Paris, which was what had made her agree to giving Poppy back in the first place, hadn't come to anything yet, and they were already well into May. When the Poppy business came up, Phyl had the impression that a trip to France was imminent, but then some things had happened at work which Matt needed to attend to, and they'd put it off 'till another time'. Those were his very words. 'Sometime soon,' he'd gone on, to dispel her disappointment.

And she'd cheered up. She wasn't a sulker. Paris would happen when it did and meanwhile it was something to look forward to. And with Poppy gone, they'd started making love again. She had to admit that it was lovely to be gathered into Matt's arms, caressed, kissed, fondled. She was conscious of the fact, though she'd have died rather than tell a soul about it, that perhaps she wasn't getting the full – what could you call it – value? That sounded funny. The full *glory* – yes, that was better – out of sex that other people did. She wasn't one of those women who'd never experienced an orgasm, but she was aware, from the pages of the fiction she read, that others were obviously much more highly sexed than she was. Or something. Some writers created heroines who went off like a rocket the moment a man came within inches of an erogenous zone. Were they lying or just exaggerating? Or maybe some people truly were like that and it was seen as something for more run-of-the-mill readers to aspire to ... Her thoughts flew to Ellie. Phyl had always assumed she was very highly sexed. She'd be one of those rocket-women for sure. Then another thing occurred to her: maybe the sexual exploders were pretending, at least for some of the time. She herself didn't have the amorous sophistication to know how to pretend and would have felt a fool groaning and moaning and arching her back if she didn't mean it.

The mobile in her handbag was ringing. She went through quickly to the reception area and found her bag under the counter. By the time she got there, the phone was silent. She flipped it open and listened to Matt on the voicemail.

'Er, it's me, darling ... I'm going to be a bit late, I'm afraid ... Something's come up. I'll tell you all about it when I get back. Don't wait supper for me. I'll be ... well, see you when I see you, all right? Sorry, Phyl.'

She listened to the message again, feeling worried. That was silly. It couldn't be anything to do with Lou or the baby or Matt would have said. So what was it? He'd tell her later, so nothing private, but he sounded – how had he sounded? He was never quite himself on the phone anyway and he hated leaving messages. She decided to phone him back. When he picked up and said, 'Hello?' she thought she could detect a note of something like panic in his voice. Why did he sound like that? She said quickly, 'It's only me, Matt. I was a bit worried by your message, that's all.'

'Oh. Oh, no need to worry, love. I'm fine. Really.'

'Has something happened?'

'No ... no, nothing's happened. It's just ...'

'Tell me, Matt. Or I'll worry. Please.'

'No need to worry. And I'd rather tell you later. I've just been to see Justin, that's all.'

'Is he all right?'

Matt gave a laugh, though it was clear he didn't think anything was in the least funny. 'He's more than all right, believe me. I'll tell you all about it when I get home.'

'Why can't you come now? Where are you?'

'Oh.' He paused and Phyl wondered why he wasn't answering at once. He must know the answers to both her questions. She was just about to prompt him when he said, 'I'm in Brighton. I ran into Neil Freeman, remember him? We're going to have a quick meal together before he goes back to London. Okay?'

'Fine. That's fine. I'll see you later then.'

'Yes. Of course – shan't be long. Bye.'

Phyl dropped the phone into her bag and went back to sit with Mimi, who had now fallen asleep.

'You're not much company,' she whispered and sat staring into space, not really thinking, but aware of a sense of unease. Something wasn't right. Matt sounded as though someone else was listening in on the conversation. Well, they probably were. He wouldn't have been able to speak freely if Neil Freeman could overhear what he was saying.

The room where Poppy's cot took up most of the space was dimly lit and she could see her baby, sweetly asleep among the cuddly creatures she adored. She'd dropped off almost as soon as Lou had put her down and now she lay with her plump cheek making a lovely smooth curve and her hand on top of the blanket, the fingers spread out. It looked like a small pink flower. Poppy's hair fell into ringlets, and spun gold described it exactly. Bloody hell, what's brought on all this poetic nonsense? Lou left the room feeling rather silly, but unable to stop herself feeling a pleasant glow of satisfaction and happiness, most of which had to do with the prospect of the nice glass of wine she'd promised herself. But some of it was pleasure at having her daughter there in the next room, fast asleep. Perhaps she was getting the hang of motherhood at last. She'd have a drink and then just look at the screenplay once more before taking it round to Ciaran Donnelly's house in the morning.

She sat down and took a long sip of her wine. Grandad's novel lay on the table, and she picked it up, handling it carefully, as she always did. She couldn't stop thinking of it as a living part of her grandfather, though no one else would see it like that. An out-of-print book which wasn't exactly a bestseller even when it first came out. Now though, there was some hope of it being reissued and then other people would be able to read it. What would they think of it? Even if that did happen, which was far from certain, it didn't affect the work she'd done on the screenplay.

I wonder if I've got it right? she thought. What will it be like as a movie? Some things were so difficult to write, like the scene where Peter's baby sister dies. She knew exactly where it came in the book:

Dulcie said it wasn't his fault but it was. She didn't know. He'd hated the baby. He wasn't a wicked person usually but he'd done it. He'd killed her. Dulcie came to tell him. 'You must be a brave boy, darling,' she said to him. 'Your poor little sister's dead.'

'I know,' he whispered. 'I killed her.'

'You didn't! What on earth would make you say a thing like that? You're a naughty boy, you know. This isn't to do with you. It's poor little Mary ... yet you're trying to turn attention to yourself. That's not ... that's not helpful. We're very sad, you know. Your poor mother ...'

'I'm not sad. I hated her.'

Peter didn't say that aloud. You couldn't say

things like that, not ever. But you could think them.
The creature (he couldn't call her by her name)
was horrible. Her skin was grey and clammy and
her fingers were just a collection of tiny bones.
Her head was huge – too big for her skinny body.
When she breathed, you could practically see her
heart bursting out of the skin. And he'd killed
her. He used to lie in the dark and imagine it: you
wouldn't have to do anything much. Just hold a
bit of cloth or a pillow over her face for a bit and
then she'd stop breathing and that would be that.
Peter wouldn't have to look at her any more and he
wouldn't have to think about her. He could imagine
she'd never been born. He could forget his mother's
legs covered in blood. The way she screamed. He
wouldn't have to listen to the baby crying which
was a sound that sliced his heart when he heard it,
sliced it into pieces so that he could feel the bits of it
in his body, hurting. His mother was sick now. She
was getting thinner and thinner and she didn't have
any strength left to speak to him. Tomorrow, he'd
go and sit with her and try and talk to her. The last
time, she'd hardly looked at him. Not really. She
didn't want to speak to him. The baby – that's what
she was interested in and he wished more fervently
than he'd ever wished anything that she'd die. Die,
die, he said to himself. I want you to. I want you not
to be there, next to Mummy. In her arms. Sucking
at her breasts. There was no milk in his mother's
breasts, so the baby died. That was the reason. It
didn't have anything to do with him, not really, but
Peter felt as though it did. He felt as if he'd made
it happen. I've killed her. My own sister. He closed
his eyes and all he could see was his hand, growing
and stretching, reaching out through the darkness
like a monstrous claw, over the sleeping bodies of

*the other children in his hut and snaking over the
compound and past the latrines and up into his
mother's hut and into her bed and over the nose
and mouth of little Mary, the bony, skeletal baby
who didn't want to live, who was halfway to being
a skeleton already. Killing her. It could be true. If
you wished something often enough, it might come
true. No one knew, not for certain.*

Lou took a sip of wine. First this scene, and then,
later, the death of the boy's mother. How had her
grandfather, her gentle, mild, rather strict and solemn
grandad, thought up a scene like that? It wasn't a bit
like him in real life. Well, she supposed that this was
what made a good novelist: the ability to inhabit different people. Writers had to imagine themselves in the
same position as their characters. Had to put themselves in the same situations however horrible those
were. It would have been a bit easier for Grandad than
for some others because after all, he'd spent time in a
Japanese prisoner-of-war camp. He'd have had to do
less research than most, but the force of the scene was
striking. Perhaps Constance resented the fact that he
lived so much inside his own head. Maybe that was
one of the things that led to the difficult relationship
he had with her. Maybe if he'd been able to talk to his
wife about how awful things had been in the camp, he
wouldn't have needed to write the novel. Lou smiled
when she imagined how Constance would have greeted
a description of life as it was lived in the camp:

*Oh, darling, how absolutely ghastly! But for good-
ness' sake, do we really have to dwell on such hideous
things? That was all a very long time ago, I'm happy
to say, and there's nothing about our lives now which
could possibly be reminding you of all this. I think
you ought to go and play golf or something. It doesn't*

do to wallow in such things, does it? I've got nothing against you writing a book, darling, but who's going to want to read about horrors like that? Why don't you try a nice comedy? Or a detective story? People love detective stories, don't they?

She'd have tried to put him off, and when he persisted she'd have lost interest in the whole writing thing and that would have been that. Another thought occurred to Lou. He'd read parts of the book out to her when she was very young, as though he knew she'd be the one who'd appreciate it. He'd never read aloud to Matt. Lou knew that because her father had told her so.

'You're honoured,' he'd told her. 'Maybe he knows that you're the one person who'd enjoy *Blind Moon*.'

And she knew she was privileged. She was called after John Barrington's mother and it was clear from *Blind Moon*, even though it was a novel, that the love Peter has for his mother was something John himself must have felt. You couldn't invent such a thing. Grandad had loved his mother. That much was clear.

She got up from the sofa and went to fetch her screenplay. Annette's death, the moment when Peter sees Dulcie for what she really is, the moment when he understands everything: that was the scene that had to be right. That had to work.

'This is jolly nice,' Matt said, allowing himself to relax against the cushions. Ellie's small basement flat was decorated in a style he thought of as Bohemian: lots of cushions, covered in satin and velvet, too many pictures on the walls for his taste, not terribly clean and more than a little untidy, but welcoming. Piles of magazines, a few books, not too many ornaments and a rather splendid set of brocade curtains which had seen better days but still managed to make a good impression. Vaguely orange, he thought, making a mental note of the colour to tell Phyl and then wondered in almost the same moment whether he'd been right not to tell her the truth about where he was. Whatever the case, it was too late now. He'd already given her that Neil Freeman story. He'd have to work out something to say about their meeting – *to lend verisimilitude to an otherwise bald and unconvincing narrative*. The words from *The Mikado*, which he loved, came unbidden into his mind.

There was no real reason why he shouldn't have told Phyl that he'd come here. Justin was Ellie's son. He wanted to complain, let off steam, etc., so what more natural than to go and visit the chap's mother? He knew, though, that however he spun it, Phyl would be jealous. She'd always tried to hide them but her sentiments about his ex-wife emerged in all kinds of ways. Like the small, pursing movement of her mouth whenever Ellie's name was mentioned. She had no idea she was doing it, but Matt understood what it meant

'Lots of my stuff is still in storage, darling,' said Ellie from the kitchen where she was making tea. The thing about ex-wives was odd, he thought and wondered whether other men shared his feelings. Perhaps it was a little like what happened to ducklings. Didn't they get imprinted with the first adult they saw? Bond with that particular duck and all march behind her in a line to the pond or wherever else she decided to lead them? Didn't babies fix on their mother in the same way? That's what must have happened to me, too, when it came to Ellie. I loved her so much that it's been hard to wipe away the ... what could you call them? ... the leftovers of that love. One of which was the desire he felt for her. He'd never stopped wanting her. She left me too soon, he thought. We hadn't been married long enough for me to tire of her in bed. He smiled. Would one ever tire of Ellie in bed? Ever get used to her? Take her for granted? All he knew was, after she left him, his whole body remembered her for years and it had taken some effort of will to blot her out of his mind while he was making love to Phyl, and he didn't always succeed either. This was a shameful secret and for a long time he'd felt terrible about it, but over the years the memories of Ellie had grown more and more faint and it was only from time to time that he recalled what things used to be like. And then she'd appeared at Constance's funeral and he'd started remembering all over again.

'Here you are, darling. Now,' Ellie began pouring the tea, 'tell me all the gossip about Justin.' She was wearing a sort of kimono affair, which looked silky and was printed all over with bright pink flowers against dark green foliage. As she handed him the cup, she leaned towards him and the front of the robe gaped a little, allowing him a glimpse of cream lace that edged a bra which seemed to be having trouble containing her breasts. She sat up again, decorum restored. She said, 'What's he done now?'

Matt told her about Eremount and the spa and the enormous amount of money and Ellie listened in silence, giving him her full attention. When he'd finished, he took a sip of his tea, which had grown quite lukewarm while he'd been talking and waited for her to sympathize.

'I think,' she said finally, 'that you're making a bit of a mountain out of a molehill.'

'What?' Matt could scarcely believe it. 'D'you mean you're on his side? I'm ... I'm amazed at you, Ellie. Surely you must see—'

'Calm down, darling. It's you who's having trouble seeing, you know. This is none of your business. Justin owns the house and okay, it was a shock when we heard what Constance had decided to do with her property, but we've all got over that now, haven't we? Come to terms with it.'

'But that was my home, dammit.'

'Don't be so ridiculous, Matt. It hasn't been your home for years. What do you care if middle-aged ladies want to lie all over it and immerse themselves in five kinds of warm water on the premises? Put it out of your mind.'

'It's not fair!' As soon as the words were out of his mouth, he realized how childish he sounded. Ellie laughed. She said, 'Never mind. Come here ...' She patted the sofa and Matt went to sit beside her. It would have looked ungallant to do otherwise. As soon as he was within reach, Ellie put an arm around him and pulled him closer.

'I'll cheer you up, darling,' she said, and before he knew it, before he could move away and do something to prevent it – did he want to prevent it? Not really, oh, God, no, he didn't, he wanted it, yes, it was something he'd been thinking of, obsessing about for days. Weeks – she had her mouth on his and his lips were opening under hers and it was like a tune you thought you'd forgotten but then realized you remembered ... every note of it. He groaned and started to pull away but Ellie had one hand in his hair, holding his head so that he couldn't move. She stopped kissing him briefly and said, 'Come to bed with me. Now.'

'I can't, Ellie, it's mad. We've got to stop this. Now. Stop it at once.'

'We don't have to stop at all. Think about it, Matt. You want to. I can tell you do.'

'I've got to go, Ellie ...' he murmured.

'Don't go. Stay with me. For a bit. Please.'

'I can't. You know I can't.'

'But you want to. Say you do. You do, don't you?'

He sat up, suddenly afraid, the erection that he'd been trying to hide disappearing in a moment. Fear of discovery, of Phyl learning about this, had suddenly put all desire to flight. 'No, I don't, Ellie … I can't, don't you understand? I can't do this to Phyl.'

'Seems to me,' she said, 'that you're halfway to doing it already.'

'I'm not, Ellie. It must be … I was feeling … well, it was a weak moment. I just …'

'Okay, darling. I won't rock the boat. But you'll be back. I know you will. You'll remember and you won't be able to stay away.' She laughed. 'I might blackmail you into coming back. I might say: come back or I'll tell Phyl.'

'What will you tell her? Nothing's happened.'

Ellie shrugged. 'I think I've got enough to make you uncomfortable. You came here rather than going straight home when you were feeling upset. That's something.'

'No, it's not. Justin is your son. That's why I came to see you. You needed to know what he was up to.'

'You could have told me that in a phone call, couldn't you?'

'Well, yes, but …'

Ellie smiled. 'You were looking for comfort. From me. Not from her.'

'Oh, for God's sake, Ellie, stop it. It was a kiss. Nothing more. Let's forget about it. Okay?'

'If you say so.'

'I do say so. And I'm late now, so I ought to go.'

They stood up and walked together to the front door. 'Kiss me goodbye at least,' Ellie said, leaning towards him. She brought her lips together into a pout that was meant to be seductive. Matt kissed her as briefly as possible and stepped out of the flat, closing the door behind him, slightly queasy with a mixture of relief and regret.

Once he was safely in the car, he looked up and caught sight of himself in the mirror. What had he done? Nothing. Not really. Just a kiss. A sudden closeness to Ellie after years and years of being with Phyl. The stirring in his flesh could be put down to a sudden rediscovery of someone who'd been imprinted upon him, duckling-fashion, years and years ago. It didn't really mean anything. But those breasts, creamy under the silk folds of the kimono … He shook his head. Not going to think about that. He turned his mind deliberately to Justin in an effort to replace a vague sense of yearning and desire with the irritation he'd been feeling when he arrived at Portland Place.

'Dyke. Lezzer. That kind of thing.' Nessa was sitting at her dressing table, smoothing moisturizer over her face. Mickey was lying on the chaise longue, already dressed and ready for the day's work. 'If I don't make a secret of our relationship, that's what he'll say. Those are the terms he thinks of you in, Mickey, and this isn't going to make things better. It'll make them worse. So really, I'd rather not make any – well, I'd rather …'

'You'd rather keep it a secret is what you mean. You like what we do in bed well enough but you're not brave enough to confess it. Having your cake and eating it is a speciality with you, Nessa, you know that?'

'I'm not having my cake and eating it, I'm simply protecting Tamsin and making sure that her father doesn't start a whole lot of nonsense about custody. I know you think of Gareth as easily led and a bit thick, but he's got strong views about this, funnily enough. He'd say I wasn't a fit mother. Something. And I simply couldn't bear to lose Tamsin.'

'And a divorce judge would take his side? Who on earth could look at you and say you were an unfit mother?'

'Honestly, Mickey, don't be naïve. A judge who shared Gareth's prejudices, and I promise you there are plenty of those about. Gareth'd make out that we were constantly having orgies, that Tamsin would be in mortal danger of turning into a lesbian herself. Shared custody would go out of the window. I might even lose the house. I'm not prepared to do it, Mickey, and if you loved me, you'd understand.'

'I do understand. I just don't like it, that's all. Bottom line is: you're ashamed. You must be.'

Nessa went on applying her make-up. She leaned into the mirror and widened her eyes, ready for mascara. They'd spent the night together in Nessa's house because Tamsin was with her father, and everything would have been perfect were it not for this bloody row they'd managed to begin having almost before they'd got out of bed. She didn't say anything and after a while, Mickey got up.

'I'm going down to make some breakfast. I'll see you down there. We'd better get a move on if we're going into work today.'

She didn't quite slam the door behind her, but she almost did. Nessa felt the waves of her annoyance in the air, like an invisible vibration. She closed her eyes and took a deep breath. Mickey was right. Nessa could admit it to herself, though she wouldn't ever say it to anyone else. There was a part of her (okay, not a very big part, but still) which *did* think there was something strange about the whole affair. A smidgen of shame was lodged somewhere deep in her brain and she was struggling to rid herself of it, because she loved Mickey so much and because the sex was amazing.

Even the thought of it made her blush. How many

gatherings of women had she been to where the subject of discussion had been so-and-so running off with another woman, my dear. No lesbian tendencies ever before as far as anyone knew and now look at her! Running off and leaving her husband and young children for another woman! Well! We'd never be able to do a thing like that – unthinkable. Unimaginable. We've never had the slightest desire to kiss a woman, much less get up to all the sorts of things they did get up to … What *did* they get up to? Did anyone have any experience? And oddly enough, no one did, ever. Not a single woman of Nessa's acquaintance had ever piped up with stories of her lesbian past, much less details of 'what went on'. There were rumours about dildos and appliances and sexual aids but no one knew anything for sure. Or said they didn't. Perhaps there were others like her in those groups: in love with a woman and not brave enough to say anything.

I'll be brave, she thought. I'm not embarrassed about Mickey. She imagined a scenario where everyone was gathered round Matt and Phyl's table together, with her female lover there instead of Gareth. Phyl wouldn't mind. She'd always been tolerant. Too tolerant, in Nessa's opinion, never putting her foot down over anything. Being wishy-washily kind all over the place, which had nearly driven Nessa mad when she was a teenager. There was nothing to kick out against with Phyl and she'd always been able to make you feel like a swine for throwing even a tiny tantrum. *I'm being kind and reasonable so why can't you?* was the message she was conveying and it had made the young Nessa grind her teeth and want to hit her. She'd be just the same now.

Matt was a different matter. His attitude to gay people was reasonably modern and enlightened but it hadn't been tested. It was one thing not to have prejudices when you were reading articles in a newspaper, or laughing at things on the TV, and quite another to welcome a lesbian couple into his house, particularly when one of them was his stepdaughter. No, he'd be all right. Whatever he felt, he'd not make a fuss, but underneath, she was sure, he'd be disapproving and if asked he'd mutter something about Tamsin: her welfare. Quite bad enough, he'd be thinking, to be the child of divorced parents without also being the daughter of someone gay.

I could tell Ellie. She'd just laugh and want to know what she'd undoubtedly refer to as 'the gory details'. In fact, Nessa thought, it wouldn't surprise me a bit if she hadn't been there, done that and got the T-shirt. Ahead of the curve in matters sexual, that was Ellie. The thought of confiding in her would have been comforting. It would have given Nessa someone with whom she could discuss Mickey, but she didn't trust Ellie not to give away a secret. Discretion wasn't her thing. No, far better to keep the whole thing under wraps. In fact, she told herself as she went downstairs to try and make it up with Mickey, I love the idea of knowing something, doing something, that no one else knows about. The truth was, she liked the secrecy. She got a kick out of people not realizing who she was: assuming she was one kind of person when in truth she was someone quite different. And it was years since she'd felt this overwhelming longing, this wanting to be with someone all the time, wanting to say her name to everyone, wanting wanting wanting. I love her. I'm in love with her, she thought. I'm in love with a woman. Nessa shook her head. It was true, and yet she hung back, didn't want to tell anyone, still felt as though – as though this relationship was a kind of dizzyingly beautiful holiday from real life; not who she really was.

8

'Could I possibly have a word with Ciaran Donnelly?'

The woman who'd opened the door to Lou looked as though she'd been artificially stretched: she was only a couple of inches taller than the average but so thin that she seemed to Lou, as she stood in the porch of the Donnelly house, to be looming and swaying over her. Lou had left Poppy's pushchair at the nursery with Poppy, just this once, with special permission from Mrs Warren, who looked as though she were giving temporary shelter to a Chieftain tank. Lou had put a skirt on for the occasion and it felt strange after months of living in trousers. Her shoes, quite high-heeled for her, made her long for her trainers.

It had taken her ages to screw up her courage sufficiently to walk up the drive and knock on the door, but she'd done it at last and was a bit disappointed not to see the man himself, but that was ridiculous. Of course a top Hollywood producer would have a staff: a secretary, a PA, or even a housekeeper. Why had she thought he'd be living like an ordinary person who opened his own door?

'I'm afraid Mr Donnelly is rather busy this morning. May I help you?' Help was what her mouth was offering, but her body language, the way she was standing in the hall, suggested she was ready to fight to the death anyone seeking to cross the threshold.

'Harry Lang has sent me over. I work for Cinnamon Hill Productions and ...'

'Who's that, Monique? What's happened to coffee?' A short, fat man who looked like Santa Claus out of uniform stuck his head round the door of one of the rooms opening off the hall. 'Did I hear Harry Lang's name mentioned?'

'Yes, I mentioned him,' Lou said, leaning to the right a little so that this man – it must be Ciaran Donnelly himself – could see her. She smiled at him, trying to appear nonchalant and as if she spent every day delivering screenplays by hand.

Monique had the grace to step aside as Mr Donnelly said, 'Come in, come in ... Monique, coffee, please. D'you drink coffee?'

'Yes, thank you.' Lou stepped into the house. 'But I don't want to disturb you.'

'You're not, I swear. I'm bored beyond words. Nothing but phone calls asking for money. Don't you just hate that?'

He sounded American, though Lou could still detect the Irish accent in his voice. She said, 'No one's ever asked me for money and I wouldn't have any to give them if they did.'

Ciaran Donnelly laughed uproariously, much more than her remark deserved and went to sit behind a desk heaped with CDs, books, papers, newspapers, magazines. She couldn't see him properly till he'd cleared a few of them away. He did this by picking up a handful of stuff and chucking it haphazardly on to a chair that was already quite full to begin with.

'So, Harry Lang sent you. Why was that?'

'There's a screenplay he wants you to look at.' Lou was beginning to feel hot with guilt. Ciaran Donnelly was being so friendly, so nice to her, and she was deceiving him. And deceiving Harry too.

'He's in the States, right?'

'He emailed me ...' Lou started to say and then couldn't bear it any longer. She stood up. 'I'm sorry, Mr Donnelly. I've done something awful. I've got to go ... it's ... I'll see myself out. Really. I didn't mean to disturb you ...' To her complete amazement and horror, there were tears in her eyes and she wanted more than she'd ever wanted anything in her life to be somewhere else. Anywhere else. She turned and began to cover what seemed like a mile of carpet that lay between her and the door.

'Wait a minute, please. I don't even know your name, but please – come back here and sit down for a moment. You seem ... you're upset. Just sit down and take a deep breath.'

She couldn't, she just couldn't. Where would she find the courage to turn round and face him? As she was wondering whether to make a run for it, try for the front door, she found herself gripped quite firmly by the arm and led like an invalid to the leather chair in front of the desk and gently pushed into it.

'I'm sorry,' she said again. 'I must go. Really. You ...'

'Please stop apologizing, Miss ... do you mind telling me what to call you?'

'I'm Lou. Louise Barrington.' Lou sniffed. She was trying very hard not to start howling with embarrassment. What in the world had she been thinking? How had she reckoned she could get away with this madness? Stupid. Stupid and reckless, and if Harry found out he'd never want to talk to her ever again, nor read one of her reports, much less get into any kind of romantic relationship. Oh, God, she thought, let me just escape from this whole thing and I'll never, ever again do anything so ridiculous and mad.

'Nice to meet you, Louise. Now.' He beamed at her across the desk. 'Please tell me why you're so distressed. I'm curious. Really. What I have so far doesn't make much sense. Harry Lang sent a screenplay over and you're having some kind of conniption.'

'Harry doesn't know I'm here. I came off my own bat. I wanted to – well, I wanted you to read my screenplay and I thought this was a clever way of getting you to do that. It's mad, stupid and unprofessional and if Harry knew about it, he'd kill me. Please don't tell him I came. Can you not tell him?'

'I *could* not tell him and I'm intrigued, I must say. Why haven't you shown this screenplay to Harry?'

'I thought – I think he might not be able to tell me what he really thinks of it. Because he knows me. He might not want to hurt my feelings, so he wouldn't be completely honest. I need a completely honest opinion.'

'You say you work for Harry? What d'you do?'

'It's nothing very much. I read stuff that's sent into Cinnamon Hill and write reports on what I think might be worth pursuing.'

'Don't tell me. You read so much rubbish that you thought you'd have a go yourself? Is that it?'

Lou shook her head. 'No, that's not why I wrote it – this screenplay, I mean.' She took a deep breath. 'What I mean is, yes, I've always wanted to write for the movies, but this – well, it's a personal thing. An adaptation of a novel by my grandfather. The novel's called *Blind Moon*.'

'Your grandfather wrote a novel? Okay, Louise Barrington. This is what's going to happen. I'm intrigued, I confess. I'll read your screenplay, then I'll get in touch with you and tell you what I think. We won't, either of us, say a word to Harry. Deal?'

'Really? You'd do that? I don't know what to say.

It's … it's so kind of you. I'm … I'm speechless. Sorry, that's stupid of me, but I can't …'

Stop talking, Lou said to herself, before you start to sound like a drivelling idiot and he changes his mind. She smiled and handed him the file which she'd been clutching to her bosom. He took it and placed it on top of a tottering paper mountain. Lou glanced round the room. She could see at least a dozen files that looked exactly like hers. There must be others hidden under something which she couldn't see. These probably also contained screenplays. For a split second she wondered whether this was going to be the end of everything. The other files probably contained scripts which were much better than hers; more commercial, more artistic, more everything. She didn't have a chance, she was sure of it. But still, here was Ciaran Donnelly willing to read what she'd written.

'Thank you so much,' she said, getting to her feet. 'It's very kind of you.'

'Not at all, not at all,' he said, coming out from behind his desk and escorting her to the front door. 'Not a word to Harry, right?'

'Yes. And I'm very grateful.'

'My pleasure, Louise,' Ciaran Donnelly said. 'I'm looking forward to reading what you've written. I'll be in touch …'

Lou felt as though she were floating down the drive. She wished she'd had the gumption to ask Ciaran Donnelly why – why he was willing to read a screenplay handed over to him by someone who'd simply walked up and knocked on his door. Willing, also, not to tell Harry about it. Never mind, he'd taken it, and now she had to wait. She had no idea how long it would be before she heard from him, but she was willing to wait however long it took. Just don't let him forget about it and then lose it under someone else's file, she thought. It wasn't till she was on the Tube to Poppy's nursery that she realized Monique hadn't brought in the coffee Ciaran Donnelly had asked for. Perhaps she was protesting at the way her boss had taken over and allowed Lou to walk in off the street.

'I have done this before, you know, Lou,' Phyl said. 'Poppy's stayed with us for several weeks, remember?'

'You haven't done it in London. It's different. You're not used to the Tube ... the pushchair might be a bit of a problem.' Lou was prowling round the flat, going over to the small suitcase that had been standing packed and ready by the door when Phyl arrived. There was a list of foods, the doctor's telephone number and the numbers of three taxi firms pinned up over the table in the kitchen. The cupboards were groaning with all the stuff Lou had considered necessary for Poppy's welfare in the next forty-eight hours.

'I'll be fine with the pushchair,' Phyl said, 'and you've got enough food in to last us a month. Considering you're going to be back tomorrow night, I think we're going to manage.'

'And you'll leave plenty of time for going to fetch her, won't you? There are sometimes hold-ups on the Tube.'

'Stop! Just stop, Lou. You're driving me mad. You're like – I don't know what you're like. You've got time for a drink before you have to leave so just sit down there. Go on, sit. I'm going to make us a nice cup of tea.'

'Coffee.'

'Okay, okay, coffee. The idea is for you not to move. I'll get everything. I will even open a packet of biscuits, how's that?'

Lou sat down in the armchair. Phyl called out from

the kitchen, 'Is it serious, this thing with Harry? I mean, he's going to Paris with you, so ...'

'I wouldn't break out the champagne just yet, Mum. It took me all my courage to ask him. He was the one, actually. He sort of invited himself when I told him I was going.'

'Just like that? Out of the blue?' Phyl handed Lou her cup.

'No, not really. It was my idea to begin with. I emailed him about it while he was in America. I hinted – well, no, I suppose I did suggest he might like to come with me. For company. Because he likes Paris so much. And then last week he asked me about it. Whether I'd really meant it, so of course I had to say yes. I mean, I was going. I've been meaning to go for ages.'

'Aah ...'

'It's okay, Mum. Separate rooms and everything. He's a friend, and that's it.'

Phyl said, 'Listen, this is the first time since – well, for ages, that you've shown the slightest interest in anyone, so I'm not giving up the hope of a boyfriend so easily. You must like him. Go on, you can tell me. Do you like him?'

Lou said nothing for so long that Phyl began to think she'd overstepped the mark. How long will it be, she wondered, before I don't have to watch what I say? How long before we can all stop tiptoeing round the subject of Lou's love life? Why can't I simply ask her if she fancies him and if it's going anywhere?

'I do like him,' Lou said at last. 'Not sure if he likes me.'

'You're sure to find out in Paris. It's such a romantic city ...'

'It was meant to be you, Mum. You and Dad. I'm so sorry ... it's my fault you two aren't going, isn't it?

The moment I said I was going, he put your trip off, didn't he?'

Phyl smiled. 'It doesn't matter. We'll get there. Your father's always happy to have any excuse for not going somewhere. You know him. And we could never go midweek.'

'Cheaper to do that, and Harry can suit himself when he shows up at the office.'

'Then it's very sensible of you to go now.'

Lou laughed. 'The two of you are totally transparent, you know. You only had to hear the word "Harry" and you're happy for me to go instead of you. You'd love it if I settled down with him, wouldn't you? Or anyone really.'

Phyl frowned. 'You make it sound so ... so unfeeling. It's not that, Lou. We want you to be happy, that's all. It'd be so good for Poppy, too, to have a dad. As long as he's a good man, of course.'

'Harry's good. He's lovely.'

'Lou? You sound – you sound quite keen. Are you keen?'

'I've got to go soon, Mum. You have a good time, you two, okay?'

'Right. Okay. And we will. Poppy and I will be fine. Please don't worry.'

'Of course I shan't. I did tell her this morning that Granny would be picking her up. She understood, I think, but it might be a bit of a shock when she sees you at first. I gave her a special goodbye hug but I'm not sure she knew how special it was. Or why, for that matter.'

'Never mind, I'll cheer her up if she starts to miss you. And I'll tell her exactly where you are and what you're doing. She understands a surprising amount. You'd be amazed! And you'll be back almost before she notices you're gone.'

'Yes, I know. It's getting late, Mum. Gotta go. Thanks so much for agreeing to do this for me. I couldn't manage without you, you know.' Lou got up and went to put her coat on. Phyl followed her to the door. She hadn't said how keen she was on Harry. She'd avoided the question. There wasn't any point pursuing the issue, so she hugged her daughter and said, 'You have a good time, darling. Don't worry about anything.'

She watched Lou pulling the suitcase along the corridor to the lift. As the silver doors slid shut, she leaned forward a little and called out, 'I am, Mum. I really am. Quite keen, I mean.'

Phyl smiled to herself as she went back into the flat. Maybe, she thought. Maybe this Harry was the one, the person who'd bring Lou back to what she used to be like before she met Ray.

'D'you mind, Lou? Trains always have this effect on me. Even Eurostar. My eyelids close. I don't want to be rude or anything.'

'It's fine, Harry. You go to sleep. I'll wake you before we get to Paris. Poppy was up for a bit in the night, so I might have a nap myself.'

'Great,' he said and leaned back in his seat. He was fast asleep within minutes and Lou was further from napping than she'd ever been in her life. She stared at him, sitting opposite her across one of the tables, and felt a little dizzy when she thought of what might be going to happen. They were staying at a hotel together. She didn't intend actually to initiate anything herself, but maybe he'd manage, under the influence of the famous Parisian romance-in-the-air thing (which Lou didn't totally believe in) at least to get as far as a proper kiss. She stared at Harry's mouth and began to imagine what kissing him properly would be like.

The sensations that this line of thought were arousing in her convinced her that her days of being horrified by the very idea of sex were over. That on its own was something to celebrate. I'm over Ray, she told herself. I must be. I can think of him without cringing; without fear.

'I can book us rooms on the internet,' she'd said in the office last Tuesday, casual and nonchalant on the outside and embarrassed and a little jittery on the inside. This was her first time at Cinnamon Hill since Harry's return. 'Just for one night. We can go on Wednesday morning and come back on Thursday night. There's a special midweek deal, I think.'

'Yeah, great – that's a brilliant idea, Lou. I actually have to see someone over there and we can combine it with a bit of sightseeing and so forth.'

'I have to go and visit my great-aunt, though. Great-great-aunt, I mean. That's really why I'm going.'

'Sure. That's perfect. It must be quite a thing for you, meeting up with her after knowing nothing about her. Amazing, really, that you ever found one another. You see her, I'll see my chap and we'll meet for all the fun things. Tell me how much my room is after you've booked.'

He'd assumed that they weren't sharing a room. Well, fair enough, Lou thought. He could hardly assume anything else, not on the basis of where they were at the moment. Where was that? Lou wasn't sure. Harry liked her. He'd kissed her affectionately (though not, it had to be said, passionately) a couple of times. They'd been out for a few meals and then he'd gone off to the USA. Now he was back (and she wasn't about to forget all those emails, which she still treasured) and they were going to Paris. Together. No way he'd agree to that if he wasn't at least a little bit interested.

Harry's head had fallen to one side and Lou was filled with much the same sort of feeling she had when she looked at Poppy sleeping: a tenderness, a wish to protect, a longing to hold him close. How mad was that? She closed her eyes and tried to think of something else. Mme Franchard. Ciaran Donnelly. The screenplay. Nothing seemed to work. Her thoughts kept returning to the hotel she'd found on the internet and a half-formed dream of her and Harry miraculously not in the two separate single rooms she'd booked but together in a bedroom that owed more to Baz Luhrmann's *Moulin Rouge* than the reality she knew was waiting for them.

'Sweetie, don't confuse me with facts!' Ellie rolled her eyes at Justin in an exaggerated gesture that annoyed Nessa. Her mother was a show-off and though this was okay most of the time – quite amusing indeed – in the present circumstances, it wasn't exactly the right reaction. They'd been invited to a restaurant famous throughout the South East for its inflated prices and as far as Nessa was concerned they'd have been better off in the local Indian or Chinese. All the food that had arrived on the table was so beautifully presented and displayed that it seemed churlish to complain about the size of the portions, or point out that the pasta was seriously undercooked. She'd have sent it back in the blink of an eye, but it was Justin's treat and it looked – well, she didn't want to live up to her brother's view of her as someone who was never happy with anything. So she cut and chewed her way through something that couldn't have been in boiling water for more than five minutes and tried to concentrate on what Justin had brought them here to celebrate.

That, too, sickened her a little. Three million pounds,

give or take. It made her queasy to imagine it (she saw it in her imagination as bundles of notes, lined up on shelves, hundreds of them, stretching up and up, as far as she could see) and as for knowing it was sitting in Justin's bank account – well! She'd sort of got over the idea that he owed her anything. Mickey had been pointing out that she didn't have a leg to stand on as far as that was concerned and when she was with Mickey, Nessa was able to believe this and not fret about it. The truth was that when she was with Mickey, she was the only thing of any importance. Nessa was now so in love that for two pins she'd have stolen a bit of the limelight from Justin and told him and Ellie all about it. At the very back of her mind, in a place so hidden that she only allowed herself to think about it when she was entirely alone and uninterrupted, was the dream of a civil partnership between the two of them. It had crept up on her slowly, this thought, but now that she'd allowed herself to think about it, she found herself returning to it over and over again. Nessa wasn't worried about what anyone else's opinion was of this plan, but she didn't want even to mention it to Mickey till her divorce from Gareth was done and dusted. Once that was over, once she was certain of the custody terms for Tamsin, she'd announce their engagement.

Her wedding to Gareth had been straight out of the magazines. She'd wanted the whole caboodle then, the knock 'em dead dress, the take-out-a-second-mortgage venue and menu combo and the trad honeymoon in the South of France in a hotel that hadn't, in her opinion, come up to scratch. It had been fun at the time, and she'd been the one who'd organized everything, because Ellie was in Argentina or somewhere and Phyl wasn't a person you'd want to put in charge of anything that required flair. And of course – this struck her as quite symbolic and appropriate now – that was how she met Mickey and became friendly with her. Mickey had been in charge of the flowers because in those days she worked with the real thing for a posh florist in Brighton. Nessa tried to imagine how different her life would have been if she'd ordered her roses from some other place, and couldn't. She had trouble picturing a life without Mickey in it and that was true, she reflected, almost from the moment they'd met and had nothing to do with this latest discovery of her – Nessa still found it awkward to think, much less say aloud – lesbian tendencies. When she and Mickey married, it would be entirely on their own, with Tamsin the only other person there. She would be a bridesmaid and already Nessa was thinking of what would look best on her pretty daughter. She didn't want to invite anyone else. She didn't want canapés, fancy clothes, a big shiny car – she wanted simply to be with her beloved somewhere far away – America, the Caribbean, Italy – almost anywhere where they could be sure of being on their own in a marvellous hotel with a swimming pool. Five star. No expense spared.

What, though, if Mickey didn't want to marry her? No, that thought wasn't for today. Today she had enough to contend with. Bloody Justin, who didn't know how to stop, who couldn't leave well enough alone. She would have been pleased to put him straight about what her opinion was, but Ellie was in full flow and doing a grand job.

'I can't understand how you can possibly want more, darling. Even if you put it into an ordinary building society, the interest alone would keep you in luxury. It's an enormous sum and I just think you're being stupid. That's my opinion. Have you sought any professional advice, financial advice, I'm talking about?'

'You must think I was born yesterday,' Justin said, taking another sip of his wine. This had cost, Nessa noticed, £50 a bottle, but didn't taste much different from most other wines she'd drunk. Justin went on, 'I consulted Eremount's most experienced advisers. Don't worry.'

'They'd hardly be impartial,' Nessa put in. 'Not if they're trying to part you from nearly three million pounds.'

'Everyone I've spoken to says it's a marvellous opportunity to invest in something really exciting.' He started all over again, then, describing the unimaginably thrilling portfolio that Eremount had persuaded him was precisely the right home for his massive fortune. Nessa tuned his voice out because nothing bored her more than talk of money. She liked the substance; she liked the work that led to the acquisition of lots of cash but the nitty-gritty of how and why and where and what firms and futures and bonds and hedge funds and blue chips, etc., it would take to make it bored her to sobs.

'Anyway ...' Justin was about to end his little lecture. Nessa could tell from his voice. He was coming to what he obviously thought of as the flourishing of his trump card, a kind of triumphant climax: 'Since I put my money in, the shares have gone up more than half a per cent. *Half a per cent*.'

'Terrific,' said Nessa, suddenly wanting to be out of there. Wanting to go back to Mickey's cottage and have egg and chips for supper. The knowledge that she couldn't, that she wouldn't see Mickey till tomorrow, made her feel both cross and sad. She and Gareth were going to Tamsin's parents' evening. Together. Damn and blast. Never mind, I'll phone her from the car, Nessa thought and listened to her mother, still going on at Justin and making not the slightest bit of headway. Sod him, she thought. Let him get on with it. I don't care. I don't care about anything except Mickey.

❋

The hotel (*l'Étoile de Montparnasse*) turned out to be just that little bit less glitzy than it appeared on the internet, but hey, Lou thought, I'm not complaining. Her room was on the same corridor as Harry's. It was clean and quite pleasant and even though the towels were a bit on the thin side, you couldn't moan when the view from her third-floor window was a roofscape of Paris. She could see Nôtre Dame and a bridge whose name she didn't know and at night the lights of the city would be spread out for her, and if she wasn't exactly Nicole Kidman, she certainly felt like a more shiny and brightly coloured version of herself.

Harry had gone off almost straight away. He'd knocked on her door and when she answered, he put his head round it, saying: 'Synchronize watches, chaps. I'll meet you back here at five, okay?'

'Fine. I'll be here.'

He'd waved cheerily as he said goodbye and Lou had gone out to lunch rather tentatively. She had a *croque-monsieur* and a *citron pressé* in a café near the Métro and gave herself a pat on the back for the enormous range of her French vocabulary and the fact that the waiter didn't bat an eyelid at her accent. She set out for Mme Franchard's flat and when she got there, felt quite proud of having found the place all by herself, and, what's more, not in a taxi but after having braved the Métro system on her own. So far, so good.

She knocked on the dark wooden door of number 4, Rue du Treixel and waited for the elderly Solange to open it. This she did in record time, considering how slowly she moved, and on this occasion there was no hesitation. Solange exclaimed loudly at the sight of Lou and even remembered her name.

'*Mlle Louise ... oh, quelle surprise ...*' She began to talk and talk at high speed and as they made their way to Mme Franchard's rooms, Lou managed to land on a couple of important words, as though they were stepping stones in an unending stream of French: *faible ... malade ... joie ... ravie ...* From these, she deduced that her great-great-aunt wasn't feeling too good, but would be delighted to see her.

Solange showed her into Mme Franchard's bedroom. Poor old thing, Lou thought. She really must be *faible* and *malade* if she's in here and not in the paper-filled *salon*. She stood by the open door, feeling a little embarrassed. Mme Franchard's eyes were closed, but Solange went up to her and leaned over to whisper in her mistress's ear while Lou waited, wondering what was going to happen.

'*Approchez, approchez, ma chère Mlle Louise.*' Solange left the bedside and beckoned to Lou to come closer. She brought a chair forward from its position under the window and indicated that Lou should sit on it.

'*Le thé ... j'arrive ...*' Solange was gone and Lou was left alone. What on earth could she say? She took Mme Franchard's hand and held it. It was thinner than ever, covered with veined skin, papery and pale and she didn't know what to do with it once she'd grasped it in hers. If I squeeze it, I might break the bones, she thought and shivered and wished she could let go of it again. Don't be so squeamish, she told herself. She's old and not feeling good.

'You are here,' Mme Franchard whispered. '*Merci, ma petite*, I am grateful you come here. I have thought of you many times.'

'I should have come before, but I've been so busy. I've been writing a screenplay.'

'*Qu'est-ce que c'est que ça?* Screenplay.'

Lou only just caught that remark. She said, 'Oh, I'm sorry. *Je m'excuse.* It's like a play for the theatre, but it's for a film. *Un film,*' she added, and in case that wasn't clear enough, she went on, '*Les mots pour les acteurs dans un film.*'

'*Je comprends.* That must be not easy. And your film is a love story, perhaps?'

Why are we talking about screenplays? When she's so ill and weak? Well, why not? Lou said, 'No, it's a film of my grandfather's novel. *Blind Moon.* The book you read.'

'That is good,' Mme Franchard said. 'I am happy if that will be a film.'

This wasn't the moment to tell her about the intricacies of getting a screenplay optioned, green-lighted and the rest. She said instead, 'My father wanted to come and see you. He will come soon, he says. He sends you ...' She was about to say: regards, but Mme Franchard looked as though she was in need of something a bit more meaningful. 'He sends you his love.'

'I am happy ...' Silence fell as Lou thought of something else she might say. Mme Franchard's eyes closed again and soon the only sound in the room was the rasp of her breathing. Where was Solange with that tea? Lou looked around. A giant chest of drawers stood against one wall, and on top of it, resting on crocheted mats, several small photographs in silver frames were lined up in a symmetrical arrangement. A cupboard made of very dark wood took up most of another wall and the bed was high with an old-fashioned brass bedstead. The pillows behind Mme Franchard's head were edged with crocheted lace, like the mats on the chest of drawers, and there was a table under the window. The upholstery of the chair she was sitting on had been velvet once but the nap and the colour had almost vanished, leaving it greyish and bald and she could feel it wobbling slightly when she moved.

Solange came in then, and put the tray down on the table. Lou moved to help her but she indicated that this was unnecessary. After handing Lou a cup of tea, she then set about lifting Mme Franchard into a sitting position. There followed the enormously complicated and delicate process involved in seeing that the old lady took a couple of sips of liquid. Lou wondered how easy she would find it to look after an old person, however much she loved her, and thought it would be even harder than looking after a baby. How kind Solange is, Lou thought. She found that her eyes were filling with tears and she blinked and took a deep breath.

The drinking of tea was over at last and then she was alone with Mme Franchard again. Perhaps the drink had given her strength, because she began to speak. Not as fluently as the last time they'd visited but still.

'There is a letter, *ma chère*. There ... on top.' She pointed with a skinny hand to the chest of drawers. 'Please go and bring here, yes?'

Lou was glad of the chance to move away from the bed. She could see the letter, propped up against one of the silver photo frames. As she took hold of it, she said, 'This is a picture of your sister, isn't it? Louise?' She picked up the photograph and held it up, as though Mme Franchard could see it from where she was.

'*Bien sûr*. You can bring. I want to see her. Ah, you are like her so much – so much.'

Usually, when people said that someone looked like someone else, they didn't really. You could see a resemblance if you wanted to, but in fact it often wasn't obvious. In this case, though, it was so marked as to be a bit spooky, like looking at a photograph of yourself in costume. The other Louise was wearing a dress with a sailor collar and a straw hat. She was standing next to a shuttered window and smiling into the sun, with her hand held up to the brim of her hat. Lou took the letter and the photograph and gave them to Mme Franchard.

'We speak of the letter but first, I wish you to take with you this picture. Will you take?'

'Really? Are you sure?'

'I do not see so good. Better you have, and you see. I will be gone from here soon. The letter is for you, but open it when I am gone. You will do this, please?'

For a moment, Lou was unclear what Mme Franchard meant and then she understood. The old woman thought she was near death. This was her, giving away her possessions in the expectation that she wouldn't be needing them any longer. What am I supposed to say to that?

'I will keep the letter safe,' Lou ventured, and added, 'for a long time, I hope.' Briefly, she wondered what could possibly be in it that had to wait till Mme Franchard was dead, but that wasn't her business.

'I tell my lawyer what is in that letter ...' Mme Franchard said, and Lou understood that it was probably the old lady disposing of some of her things. What'll I do, she wondered, if she leaves me that black cupboard? Can I say I don't want it? Maybe I could sell it – or anything else she might decide to leave me. Lou already had the only thing in the flat that she wanted: the photograph of John Barrington's mother.

'My grandfather would have loved to see this picture,' she said. 'He never spoke about his real mother, but in the novel, Peter expresses his love so well. I'm sure that must be partly what Grandad thought about his mother.'

'I am thinking since I read the book. Do you wish to know my opinion?'

'Yes. Yes, of course.'

'*Et bien*, I think this book is not a *roman*. Not – how do you say in English – invented. I think it is the truth. The things that happen in the book, in life they happen also.'

Lou thought for a moment. No, it couldn't possibly be true. It would mean ... She tried to speak gently. The last thing she wanted was to offend Mme Franchard. She said, 'But if it were true, that would mean that what happened to your sister ...'

She stopped speaking. If it *were* all true, which was something she'd never considered, that would mean that Grandad spent almost his whole life – no, it must have been made up. She wanted to say something that would bring the conversation to a halt. It wasn't going to be easy persuading Mme Franchard in her present condition. She said, 'One thing that is true is that Grandad never really recovered from the loss of his mother. His real mother.'

'*Évidemment*,' Mme Franchard whispered. 'You do not recover from such a wound.'

The silence returned to the room. Lou glanced down at her watch. Still another two hours till she had to meet Harry. How would they fill the time? She had no idea. Then Mme Franchard said, 'You will read to me, please?'

'Read to you?'

'Please. From *Blind Moon*. It is there, with the other books – do you see?' Every word came out of her mouth with a thick wrapping of laboured breath around it; and Lou could feel the effort required for

Mme Franchard to push each one out of her mouth. 'Please read me a short piece ...'

Lou sat on the bald velvet chair and opened the book. This copy, which Mme Franchard had found in a second-hand bookstall, was battered and worn with no dust-jacket and stains all over the cloth cover. Ink. Coffee ... Something. She looked through the pages for a suitable extract and then Mme Franchard spoke again, so softly that Lou had to strain to hear what she was saying.

'My sister's death. Read where she dies.'

Lou opened her mouth to declare her belief in the fictional content of the passage, but knew that it was pointless to protest. She found the place, took a deep breath and began to read:

Dulcie hardly left his mother's side while the baby was alive. She used to hang over the little wrapped-up body and stare at it and stroke it all the time. She used to cuddle Mary, too, and he remembered what Mummy used to say before they came here, about how Dulcie wanted children of her own and how sad it was that she couldn't have any. 'Why can't she?' he used to ask but no one knew, Mummy said. Some people didn't have children and that was that. Dulcie said to him, after the baby died: 'That's why I'm so fond of you. Because you're the nearest thing to my own child I'm ever likely to have.' But her husband was dead, just like Daddy, and you couldn't have a baby if you didn't have a husband.

He noticed something. His mother couldn't notice it because she was too weak to see, but he knew the truth. Dulcie wanted Mary. She wanted her to be her baby and not Mum's. You could tell by the way she used to hold her and look at her as if she wanted to eat her. As if she was a big bird who wanted to fly away with her and never come back. When the baby died, Dulcie cried and cried. She didn't stop for hours and he said to her, 'Why're you crying, Dulcie? You're crying more than Mummy.'

'I loved her. That's why I'm crying. I couldn't have loved her more if she'd been mine. And I'd promised your mother something, too. I promised her that if ... if anything ... anything bad ... happened to her, I'd look after Mary. As if she were my baby.'

Peter wanted to say it. He wished he could have shouted it out at her, made her listen to his words. He knew. He knew that Dulcie wanted Mummy to die. She didn't say so, but she wanted it to be the other way round: Mummy dying and the baby living and then she really would have carried her off for ever.

Now his mother was ill. Properly ill, not simply waiting to have a baby. Not just starving like everyone else, but burning with fever which made her say mad things and gabble in French. Mummy never spoke French. Never. 'I'm English now, you know. Ever since I married your father.' But now, her skin was hot when he kissed her. Peter didn't want to kiss her, but he made himself do it. He had to, because if he didn't touch her hot skin with his lips, if he didn't take her hand and hold it in his hand, she would think he didn't love her and that wasn't true. He did. He loved her more than anything, all there was in the world, and he also hated her for being so weak and thin and useless and for lying there crying about the baby when he was still alive and needing her to look at him, to look at something that was here now, and not far away and in her mind. In her memory. He needed her to say: I'll look after you, Peter, *but she couldn't and she didn't and there was* only Dulcie who'd started looking after him sometimes. She brought him bits of food. She talked to him. He didn't know what he thought of Dulcie. He used to quite like her but now he was a little scared of her, and thought that maybe he didn't like her very much, because he could see what she was doing. The baby was dead and she couldn't have her so she might be starting to want him instead. Was that possible?

The sun had just gone down, and the whole sky was orange, as if someone had set light to it, and the shapes of the palm trees and the huts of the compound were like black paper cut-outs against the sky. He didn't want to go and see his mother who'd been taken to the hut used for all the women who were too sick to be with the others. She just lay there, silent, most of the time so what was the point? But if he didn't go, she'd be sad. She was sad already, he knew that, but she was sure to be even sadder if he didn't go and sit with her. Peter made his way across the compound. His sandals were so thin now that he felt as though he were walking barefoot on the earth, aware of every stone along the path.

He could see the women's hut ahead of him. There was Dulcie with her back to him. His mother was speaking. She never spoke. Hardly ever. When she did, it was in French and no use to anyone. But she was saying something in English. He stopped and shrank back, not wanting to interrupt and wanting to listen because his mother was crying. Speaking to Dulcie and crying.

'You can. Please. I need more water, more food. Ask the guard. Ask him. A medical officer – someone – there must be ... I don't ... can't die. Can't leave Peter alone.' That was his mother and she *was sobbing so much that all the words came out bubbling, floating in tears.*

'He won't be alone, Annette. He won't. Never. I'll look after him. Promise. Promise, Annette. Don't worry. I'm going, I'll find someone. I know who to speak to. There's someone – one of the guards. I'll bring water ... aspirin even. Just hold on, don't worry about Peter. He'll be with me. He'll be all right, I promise you.' *Then Dulcie came down the four steps to the ground and Peter hid in the space under the hut until she'd gone. He stared after her as she went down the path to the women's hut. Why? Why was she doing that? She'd promised Mummy – he'd heard her – that she was going to find the guard, the one who might be persuaded to give Dulcie some aspirin to make her better. Who'd give her water, maybe, and food – something that'd keep Mummy alive. Perhaps she was going to fetch something she'd need to take to the guards' barracks, though what this might be, he couldn't imagine, but that was it, for sure. She'd gone to get something and when she'd got it, she'd go and fetch help for his mother. Meanwhile, he'd talk to Mummy. Try to cheer her up a bit and after a while Dulcie would be back with some help. Water and aspirin. Maybe some food.*

'Mummy?' *he said, quietly.*

'Is that you? Come here, Peter my darling.'

She took hold of his hand and brought it to her lips and kissed it and Peter hated the heat of her lips and how dry they were and he could feel the tears beginning to prickle behind his eyes and he knew he wasn't going to cry – mustn't cry because he'd been very brave all the time and had hardly cried at all since they'd been brought into the camp, even if he'd wanted to sometimes. Wanted to often, but he hadn't, till now. And now he wasn't even crying for the right reasons. He didn't know what to do. Should he say something? Yes. Yes, he would.

'Mummy, Dulcie's gone back to her hut. She hasn't gone to find a guard.'

'Gone to find a guard. That's right. I asked her ... I might ... if she ...'

He wanted to shout at her: No, no, she wants you to die. She doesn't care if you do. She's wanted you to die always. She wants us, me and Mary. Children. Not you. She doesn't love you. She doesn't want you to live. Don't you understand? *He said nothing. His mother had slipped into sleep.*

'Mummy? Wake up, Mummy! Talk to me. Please ...'

Peter began to pull on her hand and then when she still didn't answer him, he pushed at her shoulder and she wobbled about like a broken doll.

'Mummy! Mummy!' *His voice was louder than he'd meant it to be.*

'Sssh!' *someone said.* 'There are sick people trying to sleep here, you know. Why don't you go away and come back in the morning?'

'She won't wake up. Please. Help me. My mother won't wake up.' *Peter heard his own voice sounding like a baby's voice, rising and starting to shriek.* 'Help ... please someone come and help me.'

One of the women came to sit next to him. He knew her a little. Her name was Magda, or Myra or something like that. She put an arm round him and said, 'Don't cry, darling boy. She's gone. She's not sleeping any more. Can you see? I'm so sorry, my precious. She's dead. She's not suffering any longer. At peace, that's what she is. At peace with the angels in heaven.'

Peter sprang up and began to shout: 'I don't

believe in heaven. It's not there. No angels, no God, nothing. I don't believe in any of it. My sister died and she didn't go to heaven either. I saw where she went. Into the ground over there. And if my mother's dead, it's Dulcie's fault. She killed her. I saw it. I was there and I saw it.'

Some other women gathered round. One had gone running towards the guards' barracks and another covered his mother's face, which was good because Peter didn't want to see her, looking like a skull with hair, a yellow-skinned, horrible skull with stringy yellow hair who wasn't his mother but a monster that you had bad dreams about at night. He sat down by her body, her covered-up face, and started to cry. Didn't matter being brave any longer. There wasn't anyone who'd be ashamed of him. Worse than the skull of his mother, worse than this camp, worse than anything was the aloneness. There wasn't anyone in the whole world who was attached to him. He belonged to no one and it was like standing in the dark and knowing there was a cliff nearby and if he took a step in any direction he might plunge into endless darkness and never come out of it.

'Oh ... oh, Annette ... how can she be dead? I was with her – not so long ago. What's happened? Oh, God, how can I bear this?'

'You killed her,' Peter shrieked. 'I saw you. I heard you. You could have gone to get help and you didn't. You went to your hut and didn't come back. I saw you. I was hiding by the steps and I saw everything. You're foul. You're horrible. You wanted her to die. I know you did. I know it.'

Peter expected everything. He expected the ground to crack open and the whole hut to fall into it. He waited for the sky to fall on his head. He *was ready for Dulcie to hit him. He wanted to hit her. Spit on her for killing his mother, his beautiful mother who loved him and whose hair was silky and long and golden and who had pale, smooth skin and soft hands and who wasn't, who couldn't be, a skeleton under a piece of dirty blanket in a Japanese prison camp and who wasn't going to be put in the ground for the ants and grubs to eat and never speak to him again. He wanted to die. He would have been happy for a bullet from some gun to come and stop the endless hurting.*

Instead, instead of everything he was expecting, he felt Dulcie's arms go round him. Felt himself drawn close to her, hugged, and then she was kissing the top of his head and saying over and over: 'I'll look after you. I promised your mother. She'd want me to. You'll be my boy. My son. I'll take care of you. For ever. My son. You'll be mine.'

'I don't want to be yours! How can I be yours when you killed my mother?'

Dulcie laughed as she turned to the others and said, 'He doesn't know what he's saying. Of course I didn't kill her. How could I? I wasn't here.'

He knew it was pointless. Speaking was pointless. Telling everyone what had happened was quite pointless. Dulcie had turned away from his mother, walked away from her and left her to die. She knew – she must have known – how close her friend was to dying and she chose not to tell anyone. Dulcie was a murderer and his new mother. No one else was going to be a mother to him. Everyone else was dead dead dead and it was just him and Dulcie. She wanted him to be her son. He would be her son if that was what she wanted, but he'd never forgive her. Never.

'That must have been,' Harry said, 'awful. Awfully hard, I mean. Poor old you.'

Harry was holding her hand. He'd taken it casually and they were walking, in the way that couples visiting Paris were supposed to walk, along the banks of the Seine in the evening twilight. The heat had gone from the day, but the air was still warm and fragrant with the special scent of Paris: a mixture of tobacco and French cooking and exhaust smells and some indefinable magic essence that made it so different from London.

'She fell asleep but I didn't mind,' she answered, thinking, We're holding hands, and I can't even appreciate that properly because half of me is still thinking about what Mme Franchard said. Lou went on, 'It's one of the bits of the novel which leaves me feeling shaken. It's so moving, and I'm usually in tears over it, but reading it aloud made it okay. I couldn't cry, which I usually do. Because I had an audience I had to be in control. But it's the most awful death, much worse than the kind of thing you get in thrillers sometimes – you know, the gore and mutilation. And what's worse …'

'You can tell me, Lou. Really. Tell me what she said.'

'She's convinced that it's all true. She thinks Grandad was writing down exactly what happened. I've always assumed – well, I thought he'd used his time in the prison camp simply as background to the story.'

'Maybe he did. Maybe Mme Franchard is wrong.'

'But what if she isn't? It means that my grandfather spent his whole life, almost, believing he was living with his own mother's murderer. That's – I can't begin to think what that must have been like. I'll have to tell my dad. He knew Rosemary had adopted Grandad, but he thought she'd rescued him, not killed his mother in order to steal him. He'll be very upset.'

'Yes, you have to tell him. But Lou, there's nothing you can do about it from here. Right?'

'I know. You're right, of course. And I don't want to spoil our time in Paris. I'll be fine. Really. But Mme Franchard gave me a letter, too. I'm supposed to open it after her death. A bit morbid, don't you think?'

'Not at all. Very Victorian novelish, that's all. She's probably leaving you her jewels or something.'

'Gosh, I hope it is jewels, because there's nothing much in that flat I want, unfortunately.'

Immediately, she felt disloyal to poor Mme Franchard. She remembered how thin and frail she'd looked, snoring quietly as Lou read to her. Harry hadn't seen her, so of course he could make light of it. But she felt as though she'd been disrespectful and vowed not to talk so frivolously about her great-great-aunt again.

Harry said, 'You could open the letter, you know. See what's in it.'

'No!' Lou was shocked. 'I'd never do that. I bet you were the kind of nosy little boy who tried to find the Christmas presents your parents had hidden away, right?'

'Of course. Weren't you?'

'No, I wasn't. I waited like a good girl and I was about sixteen when I stopped having a stocking. My dad would creep into my bedroom and put it on my chair and I'd close my eyes and pretend to be sleeping if I wasn't really asleep and I didn't even look into that stocking till daybreak. I could have got the satsumas and chocolates out the minute he'd left the room, but I never did. Not once.'

'Goody-goody,' Harry said. 'I've always known you were, you know.'

They'd stopped walking and Harry let go her hand and took her by the shoulders and kissed her. Lou closed her eyes, thinking: it's happening, he's kissing me. She started to think through how and what and why and then lost it all, caught up in the kiss. She could feel herself stiffen at first, resist a little and then it was fine and she wanted him to go on kissing her and leaned forward, leaned into him and opened her lips under his and let her feelings run through her body. Something within her was unlocked all at once and a rush of desire made her feel weak. She pulled away from Harry and looked at him, and the mauve sky behind him and the shadow of the great cathedral over his left shoulder. Me, she thought. Me and Harry in Paris, kissing on the banks of the Seine.

'Look at this,' Harry smiled. 'Kissing on the banks of the Seine ... of all the cinematic clichés ...'

'I was thinking the exact same thing,' Lou answered.

Matt told himself he should never have agreed to have a meal with Ellie in her flat. It was a mistake and he knew it as soon as the words left his mouth, as soon as he'd told her he'd be there at eight. As he drove to Brighton, he tried to find a decent excuse for his behaviour and there wasn't one. He ought to have said no, sorry. She'd taken advantage of Phyl's absence – that was the bottom line. Until he'd let on (was that some sort of Freudian slip?) that Phyl was up in London, there hadn't been a squeak about dinner, and looking back on the conversation he knew it would have been easy for her to discuss whatever it was she wanted to discuss over the phone. If there *was* an excuse – and there wasn't, not really – then perhaps it was this: she might have taken it into her head to come over to his house and install herself in his lounge and his dining room and ... No, he wasn't even going to think about the possibility of her entering his bedroom. His and Phyl's. That was out of the question. Unthinkable. I'll only stay for dinner, he told himself and then I'll get out of there at once, as soon as I possibly can.

His mind went briefly to Lou, who would probably already have seen Mme Franchard and be enjoying herself with this Harry person, whoever he was. Phyl had spoken about him but beyond getting the basics – that he was a man Lou worked with, practically her boss – he must have switched off from the rest of the conversation. It was something you fell into when you'd been married a long time. You couldn't possibly attend to every single word, or you'd go mad. More than he wished for any other single thing, he wanted Lou to be happy. If this Harry could make her forget the ghastly Ray, he'd be delighted. More than delighted: thrilled to bits. Mentally crossing his fingers, he parked his car in a side street off Portland Place and walked towards Ellie's house. He saw himself as some kind of gladiator about to enter the arena. His heart was bumping about rather uncomfortably in his chest.

'Hello, darling!' Ellie was waiting at the open door of her flat. She was wearing black trousers and a loose, blue blouse in a floaty sort of material that you could almost but not quite see through. 'Come in and sit down. I'm so pleased you came … much nicer than being stuck in that big house all by yourself. Whatever is Phyl thinking of, running up to London at night?'

'She's babysitting for Lou, who's gone to Paris.'

'Goodness! Paris! How romantic!'

Matt leaned back against the rather too many cushions on Ellie's sofa and realized that he couldn't possibly do what he'd intended to do. He couldn't leave. He'd meant to be very careful about drinking, but Ellie had spent most of the meal waving a bottle at him and urging him to have 'just one more'. And he had. One more and then another and soon it became clear that he was not going to be able to drive. How many glasses had he drunk? Couldn't remember. That, he thought fuzzily, had been her intention. She was sitting next to him now, with her head resting on his shoulder and he didn't have the energy to move away. It was comfortable. He liked having Ellie curled up next to him. Where was the harm in that?

'You need to sleep a bit, Matt. Come with me. I'll cover you up and let you doze off a bit. Then you'll be in a better state to drive home.'

He followed her, and the next thing he knew, he was lying stretched out on her bed. She was pulling a silky cover over him, and as she bent over to tuck it in around him, her breasts touched his chest. He could feel the pillowy softness of them and his nostrils were filled with a fragrance he recognized; he put his arms out almost as a reflex.

Ellie responded. How things would have turned out if she hadn't, if she'd just drawn back a little, there was no way of knowing, but it was ridiculous to think of her pulling away. She'd engineered this. She wanted it. She'd choreographed it. He felt himself falling as she kissed him. *I'm doing this, I am, I'm kissing her and I don't want to stop* went round and round in his mind on a kind of loop, and almost as though he were under anaesthetic, he could feel her undoing his belt, unbuttoning his shirt, kissing his chest, and manoeuvring her naked body (how? When did that happen? He hadn't noticed her taking off her clothes) under the silky coverlet next to him. Suddenly, he was completely awake, and energy was fizzing in him ... he'd been half dead a moment ago. How had this happened? He struggled out of his clothes, with Ellie helping him and murmuring in his ear and he was flat on his back and she was everywhere, all over him and he was engulfed in her, and she was nuzzling his neck and he was dizzy with wanting her and remembering her and wanting to move but pinned down and only able to lie there and feel her above him, her breasts pushed into his face, and he licked them and licked them and knew that he'd been wanting this and nothing but this. Soon, he heard himself groaning as she moved on top of him, unable to stop himself crying out and then falling into such sharp pleasure that he almost fainted.

Later, how much later he had no idea, he became aware of a cheeping sound coming from the floor. What the hell was that? He lifted his head. What time was it? He glanced at his watch and sat up abruptly. Nearly one o'clock, so he must have been asleep for a couple of hours. Ellie was still lying there beside him, her mouth a little open, fast asleep. Her pale skin glowed in the dimness. The room wasn't completely dark because a light was shining in from the lounge. Oh, God, what was he going to do about this? And there was that cheeping again. Now that he was properly awake, he realized what it was: his mobile. Someone must have sent a text. When had that come through? Usually, he heard the shrill signal perfectly well but there was a whole slice of time when the phone could have played the Hallelujah Chorus in his ear and he wouldn't have heard it. He got off the bed as quietly as he could and scrabbled around for his trousers. He found the phone, and opened it. The message read: *Where are you? Pl. text back when you get this. Phyl.*

Three kisses. Three 'x's. Not there. Where were the three kisses? She'd left them off and Matt wondered whether she knew where he was. No, how could she? She'd probably rung him at home … where would he say he was? What could he do? Play for time. He texted: *Hope all's well with Poppy. I'm fine. xxx*.

He walked into the lounge and sat down on the sofa. It felt smooth and velvety against his naked skin and the cushions behind him were like a caress. He tried not to go over what had happened with Ellie, and told himself that if he could have gone back and erased the last few hours from his life, he'd have done it without the slightest hesitation. *Liar*, said a voice in his head, *you loved it. You haven't had sex like that in years*.

The trilling of his mobile came at the right time. He'd been considering going back. He wanted to go into the bedroom, wanted to lie down again, longed to wake Ellie up and turn her to face him, and more than anything wanted to sink again into that rippling pool of pure pleasure. No, that's madness, he thought. I mustn't. He opened his phone, trying to ignore his erection.

Phone me at Lou's in the morning.

Still no 'xxx', not even her name. She must know – but how could she? He'd deny it. He told himself that what he'd done didn't matter quite as much as it might have done because it would never happen again. Never. This was the end of it. The beginning and the end. He had no intention of leaving Phyl, Ellie would probably run a mile if he suggested getting together ... No, this was a one-off. A slaking of appetites, that's all. He was quite determined about that. He had till morning to think of something plausible – perhaps a bridge game – he was a member of the bridge club and Phyl knew he played quite often; too much to drink, stayed the night with Paul. That was it. Would she check? Would he have to speak to Paul and warn him? Better had, just in case. He took a deep breath and tried to concentrate on composing a plausible message to send to Phyl. He sighed and punched the tiny silver buttons. *Too much to drink at bridge. Staying with Paul overnight. Will ring tomorrow xxx.*

He watched the little blue envelope speeding across the screen of his phone and then snapped it shut, feeling released for the moment from any guilt, as though that virtual envelope had absolved him of any wrongdoing. He'd covered his tracks for now, and now was the only time that interested him. He walked back into the bedroom. Ellie was still asleep. Might as well, he thought, be hung for a sheep as for a lamb.

'Ellie?' He turned her towards him and took her in his arms.

'Mmm?'

'It's me ...'

'Hello, you,' Ellie said, and a laugh bubbled up from her throat. 'How lovely to see you again.'

Matt closed his eyes and his head was instantly emptied of every single coherent thought.

It had been, no contest, the evening she'd enjoyed most in the last two years or so since she'd left Ray. If you were designing, choreographing the perfect evening, this would have been it. Even the shock of what Mme Franchard had implied could not dampen her pleasure at being here, now, with Harry.

Lou had no idea how long they'd sat on the bench on the river bank, snogging. Snogging – what a teenagey word that was. She hadn't used it, had hardly even thought it since she was about fifteen. This was how it used to be: kissing and kissing as if you never wanted to stop; as though there was nothing else in the world except your mouths, your breath and the closeness and tenderness of having someone's arms around you again. She hadn't realized how much she'd been missing it.

In the end, it was hunger that put an end to their kissing. They'd walked back from the river to a brasserie called La Coupole, which was famous, apparently. Harry was telling her about the artists who used to go there in the old days. When they walked in, he showed her the tops of the columns that held up the ceiling, decorated by this artist and that one. She gazed at them open mouthed, but her thoughts were already racing ahead to later: to when the meal was over. They'd go back to the hotel and ... what? Go to bed together. He'd make love to her, she knew he would. She wanted him to. That was such a strange feeling after such a long time of dreading sex, of shrinking away from any contact, that it quite distracted her from practical things, like the ordering of food.

'I don't care, really,' she said, when Harry held out the menu to her. She waved it away. 'I'll have what you're having.'

'The *choucroute* here is fantastic ... you know, lovely sausages and sauerkraut and bacon bits, etc. Sound okay?'

She nodded, and watched him ordering the food and two pints of Stella and it was as though everything was going on somewhere far away from her. Later ... that was all she could think about. What would happen. What they'd be doing. She was wearing her best underwear – that must mean something. It must mean I was sort of expecting it this morning. Hoping for it, even. When she'd got dressed at about six o'clock, which was quite a normal getting-up time for Poppy, she certainly hadn't been imagining anyone seeing the lacy bra and knickers set she put on. I chose the best ones because I was going on holiday and it was a special day, that's all. Harry didn't come into it ... or maybe he'd been there at the back of her mind the whole time. Never mind ... she could hear him speaking now, but part of her was still miles away, putting together a kind of scenario in her head. Perhaps he wouldn't see her underwear in the end. Maybe he'd wait till she was in bed and then knock on her door and she'd call out to him and he'd be standing in the doorway with the light behind him and then he'd walk over to the bed and she'd hold back the duvet so that he could slide in next to her ... She shivered.

They ate. They talked. Harry had another Stella and Lou asked for a cappuccino. Then, all at once, he fell silent. The contrast between this and how they'd been, chatting and laughing – Lou couldn't understand it, and she had no idea how to describe it. A shadow had fallen over the table, making everything dark. That was what it was like. Harry was too quiet. So was she. She couldn't think of anything to say. Around them, at the other tables in the crowded brasserie everyone else seemed to be having a hilarious time. The laughter was raucous, harsh. The lights, up in the high ceiling, dotted over the walls, were suddenly much too bright and hurt her eyes. Earlier, when they'd sat down, it had occurred to Lou that their diamond brightness mirrored exactly the way she felt: sparkling, twinkling all over with happiness and excitement.

'Lou ... Lou, are you listening to me? You look as if you're miles away.'

'No, I'm listening, Harry. What's wrong? You seem ...'

He took hold of one of her hands and held it between both of his.

'I've behaved very badly, Lou. I'm so sorry.'

Badly? How had he behaved badly? 'I don't think you have,' she said finally. What could she tell him that didn't sound ridiculous? Why was he making her go through this? He must have known that she'd loved the kissing. Didn't he realize that she'd already rehearsed what they would be doing soon? Very soon. This was like some kind of *Alice in Wonderland* thing – nothing was what it seemed to be. She said, 'You haven't behaved badly at all, Harry. I've had a lovely, lovely time.'

Doh! What a lame way of putting it! Why were they in a public place, separated by a chilly marble table-top? Why couldn't she just get up and go over to him and hug him? Kiss him again. If only she could kiss him again, everything would be okay and return to normal and they could get up and pay the bill and go back to the hotel. She said, 'Why don't we go back to the hotel?'

'In a sec. I have to tell you something first.'

Lou felt cold dread take hold of her. She thought: it's like being on some hideous rollercoaster. She was plunging into black depths, leaving her stomach behind, wanting to faint, wanting it to stop, wanting to go back to normal and not being able to. She swallowed. Her mouth tasted of the garlicky sausages they'd just eaten and she thought she might easily vomit.

'Okay,' was what she managed to whisper in reply. If I speak any louder, if I open my mouth any wider, I'll definitely puke.

'We shouldn't – I mean, I shouldn't – well, I got carried away, that's all. I like you so much, Lou, and you're so pretty and you were all fired up by your visit to Mme Franchard and everything. Plus there was the river. It's easy to lose your head, right? I lost my head. Please say you forgive me.'

What to say? 'There's nothing to forgive,' she muttered at last. What the hell, nothing to lose. She lifted her head and spoke with more confidence, starting to allow a little anger at Harry to creep up on her, making her feel less like crying and more like hitting him over the head with one of the thick white china cups. 'I liked it. I liked it a lot. You have no idea how important it was to me.'

'I know. I felt ...'

'You do not know!' Lou realized that she was almost shouting and looked around, embarrassed. No one was taking any notice. 'I felt, for the first time since I left Poppy's father, that kissing someone, wanting someone, not being scared shitless of what would happen if I allowed myself to enjoy being kissed by a man – oh, fuck it, what does it matter. You've obviously changed your mind between the *choucroute* and the coffee. Never mind. I'm off.'

She got to her feet and Harry caught her by the hand. 'Please don't go, Lou. Please sit down. I want to explain.'

She sank back on to the chair. 'Go on then. I'm listening.'

'I met someone in America.'

'What?'

'A woman. I met her the first day I was in Hollywood. I – we – well, I'm in love with her.' He leaned forward and tightened his grip on her hand. 'You can't help it, Lou, falling in love. It just happens sometimes. Like that. Out of the blue.'

'She's Meg Ryan and you're Tom Hanks. I get it, Harry. Okay? You don't have to explain any further. I totally, totally get it.'

'I should have told you before I got on the train this morning.'

'Why didn't you?'

'I wanted to come to Paris. I wanted to come to Paris with you.'

'Why on earth did you?'

Harry looked down at the table and blushed. 'I like you. I also fancy you like mad. You must have known that.'

'No. No, I didn't. Not till today, not really. I mean, I knew you liked me. Or I thought I did.' Lou sat up straight and pulled her hand out of Harry's grasp. 'Okay, let me get this completely straight: you like me, you fancy me, you thought a trip to Paris would be a blast, but on the other hand you are madly in love with some starlet in Hollywood and so you shouldn't have come. You should have stayed home, after confessing your deep love for the starlet to me the minute you got back. Is that about it?'

'Well, sort of. She's not a starlet. She's a lawyer.'

'Oh, pardon me! Ally McBeal, then. Calista Flockwhatsit and not Meg Ryan. Apologies, really.'

'No, I – I'm the one who should apologize.'

'That's right, you bloody should. But it's a bit late now, right? Still,' said Lou, overcome by a kind of recklessness, 'better late than never, that's what you reckon, isn't it? Having succumbed, having kissed me and enjoyed it and just as you're teetering on the verge of taking me back to our hotel and spending the night with me in a storm of violent passion, you get a conscience and decide that no, that wouldn't be a very nice thing to do: to make love to someone and then tell them you're in love with someone else afterwards. You're quite right. Much better to say something before all that happens. I would agree, only I've ...'

The recklessness had gone. The tears were creeping down her cheeks now and she felt hideous: miserable, disappointed, pissed, too full of food ... she wanted to lie down and hide under a blanket and never come out.

'You've what, Lou? Don't cry. Please don't cry. Let's try and ...'

'Don't say it, Harry. Don't say let's go back to how we were before today.'

'Why not? We were okay, weren't we?' He frowned

suddenly. 'You're not going to leave Cinnamon Hill? I need you. I value your judgement, truly. Please don't go.'

'D'you really think I'm going to let you screw up my job as well? Forget it! I'm not leaving. I like my job. I like reading screenplays.' She shivered. The idea of having to find work all over again especially after what had just happened was too horrible to think of.

'It won't be awkward between us, will it?'

Lou glared at him. 'I don't care if it *is* awkward for you, if you want to know. I don't care. I'm going to try and forget that today ever happened. I'm going back to the hotel and you can wait ten minutes before you leave here. I want to walk on my own.'

The bill. Lou realized as she pushed her way between the tables and out into the night that she hadn't even offered to pay for her bit of the meal. Fuck it, she thought, let him pay. It's the least he can do. He's hurt me. He thought he was being kind and he wasn't. She walked along the pavement and saw nothing: not the streetlights nor the people nor the trees in full leaf. She almost ran to the hotel and up to her room. The old-fashioned key stuck a little in the lock and Lou burst into tears. It was too much, the last straw. In the end, she managed to wrench the door open and almost fell into the room. She slammed the door behind her and locked it. I don't care if I can't get it opened again. Fuck Harry Lang! What a bloody nerve! Coming to Paris under false pretences. Men were – she had no words for what men were. He'd actually almost gone to bed with her; what did that say for his love for this American person? This skinny, well-dressed lawyer woman. If he'd been a different sort of man, he'd have gone ahead with it, and they'd be together right this minute.

Lou sat on the edge of the bed and flopped back

on to the counterpane, staring up at the ceiling. The tears were now flowing down the sides of her face and into her hair. There was a part of her that wished Harry was a two-timing bastard. What did she care if he cheated on his Jennifer Aniston lookalike? She wanted him to make love to her. It was the first time she'd wanted anyone to touch her for months and months and she'd worked herself up into longing for it so much that when the chance vanished, she couldn't take it. Was that what was going on here? Her anger and tears, her misery: was that simply because she was being denied a treat of some kind? No, it wasn't. She really liked Harry. She admired him, agreed with him about movies – she hadn't thought about the future but there had been the odd moment, looking at Poppy, for instance, when she'd seen the three of them together: a family.

Lou sat up abruptly and went to the sink. She ran a basin of cold water and plunged her head into it. She groped for a towel – too thin – and began to rub at her hair, her eyes, her face. Then she went to sit on the chair by the window. That's Paris, she thought. City of a million romantic clichés glittering away in the velvety night. Paris isn't helping. I'd rather be in my grotty little flat, with my baby. Poppy. This morning – only this morning yet weeks seemed to have gone by today – she'd been only too happy to escape from having to look after her, but now she missed her. It would have been a comfort to hold her little body close and kiss her chubby cheeks. She took her mobile out of her handbag and wondered whether it was too late to text her mother. No, it was only ten o'clock in the UK. The message read, *Phone when you find this. Late as you like. If not, will see you 2morrow.*

I'll get up as soon as it's light, Lou thought. I'll go to Gare du Nord and take the first Eurostar I can. She went to lie down on the bed again, though she knew she wouldn't be able to sleep much. She smiled ruefully. The scene with Harry had pushed Mme Franchard quite out of her thoughts. She sighed and turned her mind to *Blind Moon*. How could she ever find out if it was true? And did it matter to anyone other than Dad? Everyone else who might have been affected was dead. If those things really happened, then it explained Grandad's reluctance to talk about his childhood. Also, she could see from the photograph that she looked very like the other Louise. Part of Grandad's devotion to her must have been because of that resemblance. Her head was swimming with tiredness, anger, frustration and curiosity, and she closed her eyes. An image of Harry seemed to be imprinted on her brain. Oh, God. Even a few minutes' sleep would be bliss.

No one ever mentioned this aspect of looking after a small child: you were not allowed to go to pieces while you were in charge of one and the result of this was, whatever happened, however terrible things were, you held it all together till some other time when you could collapse and weep and fall apart at your leisure.

'There you go, precious,' Phyl said, dimly aware that a few hours before, her phone had done its pinging and she'd deliberately left the message unread because she couldn't think of anyone who'd be texting her except Matt and she certainly didn't want to think about him now.

'He's with her,' she whispered to Poppy, sticking down the adhesive flaps of the new nappy, buttoning the baby-gro and covering the baby up again with her fluffy white blanket. She moved a couple of the cuddly toys nearer, so that they stood within reach of Poppy's hand if she needed them in the night, but her eyes were closing already. Phyl left the room quietly, carrying the nappy sack, which smelled faintly of violets (why did the manufacturers think they needed to perfume rubbish bags, anyway?) and there was the noise from her phone again. She didn't know exactly what she felt. What did she know for a fact? Only that Matt wasn't at home. He said he was at Paul's after a drunken bridge game which sounded ... She wasn't quite sure why she disbelieved it, but she did. Paul and Matt were not the sort of men to forget about drinking too much. Matt was the embodiment of obedience to the law. He never drank when he had to drive. That meant he'd decided before the alleged bridge game that he was going to stay the night with Paul. Again, most unlikely. So where was he?

Phyl sat down and covered her eyes with her hands. He was at Ellie's. She was willing to bet money that he'd fixed up to go there, knowing he'd be alone tonight, knowing she was far away in London and preoccupied with Poppy. Ellie ... ever since Constance's funeral, Phyl had been wary of her. This wasn't, she thought, simply a hangover from the way she used to feel about Ellie when she was married to Matt. She might easily have appeared at the funeral and then disappeared, but she didn't. She'd moved into a flat far too close to Haywards Heath, and from the beginning there was something predatory about the way she'd made a point of cultivating Matt. When she appeared at Phyl's house, dressed in clothes that would have been more suited to a cocktail party, on that trumped-up excuse, Phyl had been quite certain that she intended to make some kind of trouble. The only question in her mind at the time was what, exactly.

Now she had a good idea, but she had to make sure. If it turned out that Matt had spent the night with his first wife, Phyl needed to decide what she was going to do about it. But not yet. I don't have to do it until I'm quite ready, she thought. I can leave it for now, till I'm sure. I can do whatever I like. For a few minutes she ran through a scenario that had her walking out. Leaving him. Setting up in a flat in London with Poppy and Lou – that wouldn't be too bad, would it? The moment this image entered her head, she started to cry. Oh, no, she told herself. No crying, whatever happens. Phyl scrabbled around in her handbag and found a tissue. She blew her nose and shook her head and told herself not to be so spineless. But imagining a future without Matt was unthinkable. I won't let it happen, she told herself, before realizing that there was little she could do about it if he'd suddenly taken it into his head to dump her. But he won't do that, she thought. He'd worry, wouldn't he, about how Lou would feel. He'd know she'd be on my side – the worries chased themselves round and round in her brain till she felt as though her head was about to split open. She put her hands to her temples and shut her eyes and squeezed hard. Stop it, she chided herself. You're tired and hysterical and you can't decide anything yet. Wait and see what happens tomorrow.

She went and lay down on the bed in Lou's room and stared at the ceiling. It was getting later and later and she was wide awake. I've got to think what to do, she reflected, but what if I'm wrong? What if he's not with Ellie? What if the bridge story is true? The least she could do was find out exactly what had happened to him: where he was and what he'd been doing. Was still doing, for all she knew. Also, she had to try and sleep, she knew that, or she'd be half dead tomorrow. With Poppy, you never knew when the morning would come. It might turn out to be an extremely short night.

Just as she was about to get into bed, her mobile trilled again. It hadn't stopped making its silly little noises on and off for the last couple of hours, calling attention to itself, saying, 'I'm not going to stop irritating you till you read your message, you know.' Phyl sighed and flipped the lid open. It would be Matt – perhaps she ought to see what he wanted. She stared at the message: it was from Lou, and Phyl's heart turned over in her chest and she was all at once icy-cold and terrified. Why was Lou texting her? Something must have happened. Visions of theft, injury, illness ... every imaginable scenario flashed through her mind as she punched in her daughter's number.

'Mum? Is that you? Oh, God, I'm so glad you've rung!'

She was alive. Phyl said, 'Lou, are you okay? What's happened? What's the matter?'

Instead of an answer, she got a torrent of wailing. She said, 'Lou, stop crying, my darling. I can't talk to you if you're crying. Go and sit down. Are you sitting down?'

'Yes. I'm okay. I'm better now.'

'Tell me what happened.'

'Harry's met someone. In America. He says he's in love with her. I don't know what to do.'

'Oh.' There had to be something more intelligent she could say, but the relief was enormous. Not injured, not ill, not robbed, not damaged in any way, but terribly, terribly hurt. Poor Lou. Phyl said, 'You thought it would be – you reckoned he liked you, and you ... I know you liked him a lot.'

'God, Mum, don't be so – so bloody *bland*! It's not *liking*. That isn't remotely what it is! I really, really wanted it to become something. I wanted to go to bed with him and we nearly, so nearly ... He kissed me, Mum, as though he really meant it, you know? Properly. For ages. And then he backed off. That's it – he just – he told me about his American person and said he didn't want to be unfaithful to her and it was wrong of him to kiss me and everything and I don't know what to do …'

'Lou. Listen to me, Lou. It's no good thinking about anything now. It's late. Very late and you must be tired. Go to bed. Try and sleep. In the morning, come back here. I'll stay a few days with you. I don't mind sleeping on the sofa.'

'What about Dad? Won't he want you back home?'

'Probably. I'll speak to him. He won't object, I don't think. He'll be glad of the peace and quiet, I should expect.'

'Okay. That's kind of you, Mum.'

'It's a pleasure, sweetheart. Now, are you going to sleep?'

'I suppose so. I'll try …'

'And Lou?'

'Yes?'

'It must have been awful for you. I can see that, but you should try and be a little optimistic about it, too. You're obviously ready to start another relationship, aren't you? Remember when you thought you'd never want to?'

Lou's laughter came down the phone sounding tinny and slightly hysterical. 'Can't get it right, can I? No sooner does my sex drive return than the only nice man I've met for ages takes it into his head to fall in love with someone else. Good timing, right?'

'You're very young, Lou. There'll be lots and lots of other men.'

'Don't bet on it, Mum. I'm not going to. Night night.'

'Are you seriously saying,' Nessa frowned at Gareth, who was sitting on the very edge of his chair, as though he was getting ready to get up and flee, 'that you're going to believe Tamsin's version of events?'

'I don't know. She seemed very sure of what she'd seen ...'

Keep cool, Nessa told herself. Don't let him see you're rattled. How was she going to get out of this one? She had worried that Tamsin might have caught sight of her kissing Mickey goodbye rather too enthusiastically the other day, but figured that a) it wouldn't mean much to a child and b) she wouldn't immediately go and tell her father. They didn't see all that much of one another. She said, 'Haven't you two got better things to talk about when you're together than what I'm getting up to?'

'Well, yes, but this clearly made an impression on her. She said you were kissing Mickey sloppily.'

Okay, time to start diversionary tactics, Nessa thought, and smiled at her soon-to-be-ex-husband. 'I was hugging the woman, for God's sake. She's my partner. My best friend. Don't you believe me? I'm sorry if you don't, because if anyone ought to know what I like in bed, it's you, right?'

Gareth blushed and moved to put his hand on Nessa's knee. She wanted to flinch but steeled herself and grinned inanely. 'I suppose so,' he said. 'We did have some good times, didn't we?'

'You're getting sentimental, darling. This isn't the sort of thing you ought to be discussing with your ex-wife.'

'You're not my ex-wife. Not quite yet.'

He sounded sad. For two pins, Nessa knew, he'd be back at her side and grovelling over the Melanie mistake. Well, too bad, chum, she thought. 'Now, now, you're expecting a new baby. I don't think Melanie would be too pleased to hear you talking like this.'

Gareth looked shamefaced and Nessa felt quite

sorry for him. Still, he *had* stopped going on and on about her kissing Mickey 'sloppily'. She felt like laughing. Sloppily didn't begin to describe it, but she made a mental note to be more careful when Mickey and Tamsin were around together. For the moment, anyway. It wouldn't be for long. If her plan came off, if Mickey agreed to marry her, then of course Tamsin would have to know. She'd probably enjoy being a bridesmaid. God, Nessa thought, I've lost it altogether – what's the matter with me? Daydreams of weddings kept popping into her head at the most inconvenient moments, together with visions of herself and Mickey, stretched out on a Caribbean beach ... that was where they'd go for their honeymoon. St Lucia. 'I'm sorry, what were you saying? I was miles away.'

'I noticed,' Gareth said. 'It wasn't important. I was just saying: the lawyers reckon the divorce will come through in the next month or so.'

'As soon as that?' She tried not to sound too delighted, but she felt like punching the air. 'They've been very quick, haven't they?'

'Because we've agreed about everything, I suppose. I didn't fight you in any way, did I? I'd better go. Melanie's expecting me.'

Gareth, it was true, had been good as gold since that night when she'd chucked him out of the bedroom, being cooperative and lavish with the child maintenance and not even putting up a fight about the house. This, it turned out, was because Melanie thought it was 'old-fashioned'. More fool her. They'd bought a property where the paint had only just dried on the walls and they were welcome to it. Nessa's happiness made her feel generous. She stood up to accompany Gareth to the door and kissed him before he left. 'Do give Melanie my best,' she said, and waved as he got into his car and reversed into the road. She waited till she was sure he'd gone and then flew to the phone in the hall. She dialled Mickey's number.

'Darling?' she said. 'He's gone. A bit of a narrow shave. Tamsin told him we were kissing sloppily.'

'That sounds good. Sloppily. We should do that again.'

'Stop, Mickey ... too much to do. I can't start feeling randy now.'

'Later then, okay?'

'Yes ... I'll be there at six. But listen, Gareth said the divorce would probably be through next month. I want to take you out. Let's go up to London. Let's do lunch. Some French bistro in Soho or something, and then go to a ridiculously posh hotel for the whole afternoon and overnight. How about it? A celebration. My treat.'

'We could have lunch here and go to bed for the rest of the day.'

'God, woman, have you got no sense of occasion? I want to have a party. I want luxury. A hotel with a spa. I love you, Mickey. Do you realize that?'

'And I love you.'

Nessa heard her voice tremble a little as she said, 'Then I'm going to book it. Week after next, okay? Thursday.'

'Okay. Gotta go, Nessa. One of us has got to keep the firm going here.'

'I'll see you later. I'm going online to find us a blissful hotel ... Bye.'

She put the phone back on its cradle and went to the computer. She typed *luxury spa hotels + London* into Google and peered at the screen, considering the results. This was going to be huge fun.

A bolthole, Lou thought. That's what this flat is. Grotty, small, not very conveniently situated and undesirable in almost every possible way but still, somewhere to run to when you were feeling wounded. She'd managed to endure a post-mortem that her mother felt would make her feel better and which had actually made her feel worse. She was now in her bedroom, considering the wreckage that passed for her life.

She hadn't even bothered to unpack her case properly, just thrown it into the tiny cupboard to attend to later. She emptied the contents of her good leather handbag on to the bed and then hung it up on the back of the bedroom door in a drawstring cotton bag that reminded her of school. She transferred everything into the rather shabby sack that was her everyday handbag and came across a white envelope with her name on it.

'Oh, God . . .' she whispered. It was Mme Franchard's letter. She'd forgotten completely about it. That shows, she thought, what a state I'm in. Mme Franchard and the time she'd spent with her had been pushed to the back of her mind since she'd got home. Poor Mme Franchard. Tears came to her eyes at the thought that she didn't know whether she'd ever see the old lady again. But I'm not going to cry, she told herself, and went to put the envelope away in a safe place. For a moment, she couldn't think of one, but in the end she placed the letter or whatever it was between the pages of *Blind Moon*. The book lay always on her bedside table. She didn't need to hide it, just keep it in a safe place that she'd remember. No one else was after it.

But what, she wondered, could be in the letter? She lay on the bed, fully dressed. I could have a look. Why don't I? Had she actually promised not to open it till the old lady was dead? Lou could no longer remember. But she wouldn't open it. She mustn't. It was as though there were something magical sealed in with the letter which would evaporate if she disobeyed her instructions. Also – and this was completely ridiculous – she had the creepy feeling that if she tore into the paper, that might cause Mme Franchard's death. Nonsense, of course, but she wasn't willing to take any risks. I'm going to forget all about it, she told herself. But I'll have to ring Dad and tell him what she said.

Tomorrow, Mum would be going home. She looked dreadful and it occurred to Lou that perhaps looking after Poppy was getting to be too much for her. When asked, she'd said it was just being a little tired but it seemed worse than that to Lou. Mum actually looked unhappy, and what's more she obviously didn't want to talk about it.

I can't worry about her, Lou thought. I've got Poppy back tomorrow and I want to just lie here and close my eyes and stay here till I feel better, maybe for a month or two. And I can't. I have to shop and chat and work and smile and do all the things that people do when they're alive.

She turned on to her stomach and buried her face in the pillow. Scenes from the disastrous evening in Paris came into her mind and she tried to banish them, with little success. She'd been snubbed. She'd been willing – longing – to break what seemed like years of celibacy and she'd been rejected. *But you're not in love with Harry*, a tiny voice in her mind said. That was true but it didn't matter. She still felt shitty. Let down. Disappointed. Sad. Who were her friends? How many did she have? Who could she ring up and moan at? There was Margie, but she was more of a babysitter. There was Cath from college, but she was in Scotland now. There were Dotty and Coral from school days but they weren't much good to her as they lived in Haywards Heath. Jeanette from Cinnamon Hill was okay but lived miles away south of the river and anyway, she wasn't a friend so much as a work acquaintance. What was the matter with her? It was unnatural for a woman of her age not to be surrounded by good pals. Even Bridget Jones in the book and the movie had a gang of sorts. Thinking about how lonely she was made Lou feel even more miserable. She totted up all the things she didn't have: a husband, a boyfriend, an income that meant something, friends, a decent flat – even her family wasn't up to much. A useless sister and brother who weren't even proper blood relatives. No grandparents. No aunts and uncles. No cousins.

In the end, the list of woes was so relentless that it made her laugh. It was just completely ridiculous. What happened to counting your blessings, eh? A beautiful daughter, parents who loved her to bits, a job she enjoyed, even though she made no money at it, and above all, herself. I'm young, she told herself. I'm healthy. I've just written a screenplay. I'm okay. I haven't got Harry. That's it. That's the only thing about today's situation that's different from what was happening a couple of days ago. And perhaps having a step-great-grandmother who was a murderer. Oh, how fabulous! She smiled. Grow up, woman, Lou said to herself. Go and wash your face and make the best of a bad job.

She toughed it out all the way to the bathroom, but then seeing herself so blotchy and red-eyed from crying depressed her all over again. Fuck it! she thought. It's no good. I *am* sad about Harry and there's nothing I can do. I'll just have to get used to the fact that he likes me but isn't interested in me romantically. That's it. And while I do, I have to face the fact that I'm going to be miserable at least some of the time. Bloody Harry!

9

'Darling, how lovely to see you! I was beginning to think you were never coming home.' Matt took Phyl's suitcase from her and carried it into the house. Once they were inside, he turned and took her in his arms and kissed her. 'I've been missing you so much.'

'Really?' Phyl was allowing herself to be kissed and for a moment Matt wondered whether she *knew*. No, that wasn't possible. His night with Ellie, which he'd regretted almost as soon as he'd managed to escape from the flat in Portland Place, was beginning to acquire in his mind the status of something between a fantasy and a nightmare, and because there had been no immediate repercussions, he'd assumed that Phyl had swallowed his bridge story whole. He'd been quite good, he reckoned, at the follow-up, ringing her the next day with anecdotes from the evening, messages of good wishes from everyone round the card table and so forth. There had been something in her voice on the phone that slightly put the wind up him, till he realized that it was Lou's situation that was getting to her. It was also on account of poor Lou that she'd decided to stay on for a few extra days in London.

For once, he hadn't minded. It had given him time to regroup. Gather his strength. Ellie had been a ghastly mistake. She always was a mistake. In the old days, it was one that had taken him a couple of years to shake off, but the thing last week ... well, that was never going to happen again and he'd told Ellie so in no uncertain terms. Typically, she'd pooh-poohed the idea of him showing restraint, but he'd been strict with himself and hadn't rung her and certainly hadn't visited her and had managed to be 'out of the office' when she called him there. Not that he'd confided in his secretary, or only partly. He'd made out that Ellie was a nuisance, no more, and after him for business reasons and he'd left instructions that no calls from her were to be put through to him. He regarded Ellie as a kind of virus that had infected his bloodstream. Did viruses infect your bloodstream? Or was that bacteria? Whatever, he was over the fever now, and seeing Phyl again had made him more determined than ever to put his night with Ellie firmly out of his mind.

'Come into the kitchen and I'll make you a cup of tea.'

'I could do with one.'

She followed him and sat down at the kitchen table. Without needing to think, he reached for the decaffeinated Earl Grey, the cups Phyl liked best, and the tin of shortbread that was precisely where he knew it would be. This, he reflected as he wondered what to say next, was what it was about, a life together. A great many years shared. Knowing the person, having the kind of life where things existed in their proper order: the shortbread tin to the left of the top shelf in the second cupboard and always, always *there* and not anywhere else and filled with the same kind of biscuits. This was marriage. Or was he mad? Driven mad by retrospective guilt? Nonsense! He was only being mildly silly and that was on account of the huge relief he was feeling. There was Phyl, same as ever, sitting in her usual chair and looking ...

'You're looking very tired, darling. Is anything the matter?' Matt didn't have to feign concern. His wife looked ghastly. Her skin was greyish, the shadows under her eyes so purple and huge that they gave her the appearance of a panda.

'I am tired,' she answered. She took a sip of tea and sighed and leaned back in the chair. 'Not had too much sleep recently. Poppy's going through a bit of a wakeful period. Teeth, I suppose. Or just being unsettled in general because of Lou. Kids are like animals in that way, they pick up vibes from their parents.'

'How's Lou feeling now?'

'How did you think she was on the phone?'

'Well, she sounded – I suppose trying to be brave just about describes it.'

'She's depressed. She's another reason why I've not been sleeping well. After Ray, she was so low that she could scarcely move, but now she's perfectly okay on the surface and doesn't let on that she really, really cared about this Harry person, but it's clear she did. I saw tears in her eyes every so often, in a quiet moment.' Phyl laughed. 'That's one good thing about little children: they don't leave you many quiet moments to get gloomy in. But she's very hurt, there's no doubt about it. She was going to Cinnamon Hill today for the first time. I must remember to phone and ask her how it went.'

'I don't think it's too sensible of her to work in the very place where she's going to run into him all the time. She could find something else, surely?'

'I know. I asked her about it but she was adamant. It made me wonder why she was so keen to stay on and I reckon she's still hoping. She yelled at me when I suggested that was why she didn't want to leave, really let me have it. You know: why d'you want to define me through Harry? Why can't I be wanting to stay on because I like the work? That kind of thing.'

'Poor you. Never mind, she'll work it out. Here, have a piece of shortbread.' Phyl shook her head. 'No, thanks. Matt, can you sit down a minute? I want to ask you something.'

'Of course. I'm in no rush to get back to the office.' He sat opposite Phyl and patted her hand. She pulled it away, and he was mystified. Something was going on here. She was about to say something grim. Terrible. Please, God, he said to himself, in a formula he hadn't used since the night that Poppy was born when he found he could hardly bear the idea of Lou in pain, let it not be cancer. Not illness. Please, God, let it be anything but that.

'What is it, darling?' he whispered. 'Are you ill?'

'Oh, God, no, Matt, for heaven's sake! Stop looking as though I was about to be marched off to a hospital. No, I'm absolutely fine. Unhappy but fine. Torn apart but nothing wrong with my health, I promise.'

'I can't bear to hear you talk like that, Phyl. It makes me ... I don't know what to do when you say such things. I need you.'

'Is that right?'

'Yes, it *is* right. I couldn't survive without you.'

'Rubbish. Of course you could. Everyone can survive.'

'You know what I mean. I ... I love you, Phyl.'

She stood up, abruptly, moving from the table to the kitchen sink, staring fixedly out of the window at the garden. She had her back to him so that he couldn't see the expression on her face, but he could tell there was a lump in her throat when she spoke. What the hell ...

'Do you?' she said. 'You have a funny way of showing it.'

He stood up. 'What are you talking about? Have you taken leave of your senses?' He was standing beside her and turned her round to face him. She dropped her head and he put his hand under her chin and lifted it up. 'You're crying, Phyl. What's the matter? Oh, darling, tell me why you're crying.'

'You bastard! You dishonest bastard! You KNOW why I'm crying! You've been seeing Ellie. Don't deny it. I know. That night – the night you said you were at bridge – you weren't. I know you weren't.'

'How do you know?' As soon as the words were out of his mouth, he knew what he'd done. How could four tiny little words so immediately wreck completely the elaborate lie he'd constructed and which he thought was standing up so well? A mistake. A dreadful mistake to say that. He knew what he ought to have said, what might have allowed him to carry on lying. Something like *of course I was. How dare you suggest I'm not telling the truth?* That would have been the way to go: white-hot indignation would have been a far better option. Terrified abject guilt, that was what his words meant. He couldn't go on lying now. Part of him wanted to run: just turn and run out of the room and not come back. He was back to being a child. Constance had often made him feel like this. Phyl said, 'I'm right. I knew I was. Okay.'

'Where are you going? Come back, Phyl. I want to talk to you.'

From the door, she said, over her shoulder, 'I don't want to talk to you, though. I'm going upstairs to pack.'

'To unpack, you mean. I'll carry up your suitcase.'

She went on walking, not looking back. Matt didn't know what to do, what to say next. Phyl was on the landing. He called out to her: 'Wait! Don't go! Please come back down ...'

No answer. Should he follow her? Would she be angrier if he followed her and talked the matter out, found out what she knew and what she intended to do about it, or should he stay out of the way? In the end, he opted for direct action.

'Here you go. Here's your case ...' he said, standing in the doorway of their bedroom. Phyl had started to tip the contents of her drawers on to the double bed. She'd already done one and was starting on the second. 'Phyl? What on earth are you doing? Stop it. Please, darling, don't do that.'

'I'm going to need,' she said, putting back the second drawer, now empty, 'some more suitcases. Can you get some down from the attic? I'm not sure how many I'll need. Three or four at least.'

'But why?' Matt knew he was shouting and he didn't care.

'Because I'm leaving you. I'm going to put some cases into storage and live with Lou for a bit till we can find a nice place together. It'll make life much easier for her if I'm there full-time to help her and it must be good for her to leave that poky little flat of hers. I'm sure you'll make some kind of generous settlement, after more than twenty years of marriage.'

Things were going far too quickly. How had it got to this? Matt felt as though a current had swept him along and not only did he not have the smallest clue about how he had got to this point, he also felt as though huge chunks of time must have elapsed when he'd not been paying attention because he had lost the thread of how one thing led to another. He tried as hard as he could to follow a line of logic in what had gone on since she'd accused him of seeing Ellie and he'd said those horrible, fateful four words: *How do you know?* He'd spoken, then Phyl had said she was right and then, seamlessly, she'd started up the stairs to pack. That was it. She knew about him and Ellie and she was leaving.

'Phyl?' he said, tentatively. 'May I come in and talk to you?'

'I don't care. It won't make any difference.' She was on the fourth drawer by now.

'Please stop doing that and come and sit down next to me. Please ...' There was a small sofa under the window and he went to sit on it. She stood, hesitating, by the bed, not crying any longer but with her mouth set tight, as though she never wanted to smile again. In the end, she approached the sofa. Matt felt like a hunter, not daring to move a muscle lest he frighten her away. After she sat down, he started to talk. He didn't stop to think about what would be politic, about what he ought to say, about what might influence his wife ... his dear, beloved, cherished wife ... to change her mind. He only knew he wanted more than he'd ever wanted anything, that she shouldn't go. Shouldn't leave him.

'Phyl, it's true. I *was* at Ellie's. She asked me and I didn't say no. I could have done. I ought to have done. It was a weak moment, that's all. I do not love Ellie. I stopped loving her a very long time ago and that hasn't changed. You were away, I was on my own, and she asked me ... I didn't want her coming round here and she would have done. She ... she'd set her heart on ...'

'On getting you back. I could see that was what she wanted. God, she's ghastly! How *could* she?'

'I don't think she does. Want me back I mean.'

'She wants you, though,' Phyl spoke so quietly that he found it hard to make out what she was saying. 'And you want her.'

'I don't want her.'

'You do! Don't lie to me, Matt, I know you do. There's all that stuff about us not making love often enough ... I know all that, I know I ... Well, doesn't matter. But I know you still fancy her and don't dare to lie to me and say you don't. You do, and you took advantage of me being away and you thought you could get away with it and she asked you to her house and you took a chance that I'd never find out that you stayed the night.' Phyl was crying now, the tears pouring down her cheeks, and her voice had risen so that she sounded mad, hysterical. She was shrieking. Matt put his arms around her and she shook him off with a violence which pushed him back hard against the back of the sofa. 'You fucked her that night and I suppose a few times since and if I hadn't suspected anything, you'd have gone on and on and I ... I ... I can't compete with that. I can't do seduction. I've never been able to and I'm not going to start now. So you can have her and welcome. I'm leaving.'

'Phyl? Please. Calm down. Just for a minute. Listen to me. Please, darling.'

She put her head in her hands and leaned over her knees, sobbing. He put his arm around her shoulders and waited for a moment, expecting her to push him away again but she didn't. She was too overwhelmed by her misery, probably didn't even notice that he was touching her.

'You're right about some things, Phyl, and wrong about others. I *did* fancy her. I was feeling – well, we hadn't been ... you know what I'm trying to say, without me spelling it out. Ellie is so blatant. She's so ... I'm not blaming her, you understand. I could have got up and walked out at any point and I didn't. It's me. My fault. I am not making excuses for myself. But other things are also true and they're more important. I love you. That's the truth and I don't care if you do come back at me and say my behaviour shows the opposite. It doesn't. It shows stupidity. Recklessness.

Greediness. Randiness. All sorts of unworthy things but not that I don't love you. She made sure of me. Got me drunk. Okay, okay, I could have said no to the booze too, but I didn't. I am not going to deny it. I wanted to go to bed with her and so I did. And that's it. I've regretted it ever since. It only happened once and it's not going to happen again. Not ever, I promise. In fact, I'm going to avoid seeing her at all and if I do have to meet her, for some family thing, I'll make sure you're there too. I will never, I swear, be in the same room alone with her as long as I live.'

Matt paused, waiting for Phyl to say something. Were his words having any effect? The silence went on and on. In the end, he spoke again, just to break it.

'Please don't leave me, Phyl. I'll never ... We can start again. We can be happy. I'll take you to Paris. I know I've been saying that for months but I will. We can go whenever you like. I love you, Phyl. Please look at me. Say something. Say you won't go. This is our house. It'll just ... it'll die without you. I will. I'll die without you.'

'You won't,' she said. 'Why would you?'

'You know what I mean,' Matt whispered, hardly daring to hope, but feeling his heart lift at her words. At least she was speaking to him. 'I may not stop breathing, but I won't be able to function. I'll be so unhappy that I'll just ... shrivel. Wither. I'd go mad from loneliness. I couldn't cope. Really.'

'You'd cope admirably. You could hire a house-keeper.'

'Oh, God, Phyl, you're misunderstanding me deliberately! I know I could do that, but I'd be empty and dead inside without you.' Another thought occurred to him and he felt suddenly icy cold all over. 'You haven't said anything about all this to Lou, have you?'

'What? That I was leaving you? Getting ready to

move into a bigger flat with her and Poppy? No, I haven't. Not yet.'

'Then please, Phyl. Think about it. Our whole life … I … Don't you believe that I love you?'

'I do. But is that enough for you? If you don't fancy me any longer, what kind of a sex life will you have?'

'Not fancy you? Wherever did you get that idea? Of course I fancy you. I always have. Nothing,' he added, taking her in his arms, 'has changed about the way I feel about you. It won't. Not ever.'

She was allowing herself to be kissed. The relief he felt as her mouth opened under his was so enormous that he found himself on the point of tears. I can't cry now, he thought, I have to convince her. I have to start all over again. I have to make her know how much I love her. She was pulling away from him now and he frowned at her.

'I'm going out. I'm going for a walk. I have to think about this, Matt,' she said, and left the room. He sat on the bed, wondering where she would go. He heard the car starting. Brighton. She'd go and walk on the beach and Matt knew he wouldn't be able to relax until she returned. Her belongings spread all over their bed made him feel almost sick and he wondered how long it would be before Phyl began to put them back in the drawers. *If* she put them back in the drawers.

Cinnamon Hill Productions was uncharacteristically quiet. Summer schedules meant, Lou knew, that there'd be a desk free for her when she came in. She was sitting at it now, angry because Harry wasn't going to be coming in even though he wasn't on the rota as being on holiday. Damn and blast him! She'd been rehearsing for more than two weeks exactly how she'd be when she saw him: nonchalant, insouciant, funny, happy, completely and utterly normal and moreover drop-dead gorgeous. She'd picked up a couple of new tops and a skirt in the sales, had a haircut and applied her make-up with a care and attention she hadn't lavished on her face since she was about sixteen. In those days, when she still believed in the magical transforming power of lipstick, eyeshadow and mascara, she used to study articles in magazines with obsessive attention, committing to memory every one of their pronouncements.

'Where's Harry today?' she asked a deeply tanned Jeanette. She had clearly just come back from somewhere very hot. 'He's not on holiday, is he?'

'No, but he's gone down to Sussex today to see Malcolm Boyd. Wish I could have gone with him.'

Malcolm Boyd was the pin-up hero of several of what Lou now also called 'broken-glass movies' and the UK's answer, according to the celeb mags, to Johnny Depp. Why would Harry be talking to him? It crossed Lou's mind that he might actually be avoiding her. If he was, what did it mean? Not that he'd thought better of his Paris declaration. He'd have been in touch: by phone, by email, in person even, if he'd wanted anything about their relationship to change. All she'd had, since that awful night was one sheepish email. Lou knew it by heart: *I'm so sorry about last night, Lou. Please let's still be friends. Harry x*. She'd written back even more briefly. *No worries. See you soon. Lou*. No kiss. What was that x about on his part? It was certainly deliberate and she read it as a pathetic attempt to ingratiate himself, make himself feel a bit better for ruining their romantic trip. She prided herself on being over the worst of what she'd felt, coming back home in such a rush after getting up the very next day after that awful night and taking the first available Eurostar out of Gare du Nord. But even now, remembering it made her shrink and cringe.

She opened her email account. Nothing there apart from a few spam items. Harry wouldn't see the need to write to her but the fact that he'd buggered off to Sussex when he knew she'd be coming in meant – what did it mean? Precisely nothing. Ciaran Donnelly – she hoped against hope, every time she logged in to her email, that even though it had only been a few weeks since she'd delivered *Blind Moon* into his hands, there would be a message from him. She fantasized about it. Sometimes she imagined him reading the script and being so bowled over that he rang her at once on her mobile. There were days when she checked her voicemail and text messages over and over. At other times, mostly in the middle of the night, she imagined a terrible rejection: *Don't ever try writing a script again – you just haven't got what it takes – better to be honest than to raise your hopes only for them to be dashed over and over again* ... Thinking such things was enough to make her weep, so she tried to keep away from them and concentrate on the happy daydreams. What was the point of fantasies if they didn't cheer you up? That was what they were designed to do, right? Take you from your grotty little world into a better one. A more glamorous one. A world where the credit line: *Screenplay by Louise Barrington. Based on the novel by John Barrington* was blazoned across an enormously wide screen in curly letters of deepest scarlet.

She began to type a message to her mother. That had been the condition of Phyl leaving and going back to Haywards Heath. Lou had promised to email every day and let her mother know how she was. In detail. Happy as she was for Phyl to help out with Poppy, she wanted, more than anything, her little flat to herself. She wanted the luxury of being miserable without having to submit to questioning and attempts at cheering her up. Was she properly miserable? Lou wasn't even sure about that.

She arrived pretty quickly at the conclusion (after a couple of days of moaning and weeping on and off) that what she was feeling was simply an acute case of deep disappointment. She sort of came to her senses. Harry had failed to give her the treat, the boost, she was expecting, but actually, he'd not done anything that dreadful. He'd snogged her. He had a girlfriend. So bloody what? Men were always doing stuff like that. They were all, if they could possibly get away with it, two-timers. He'd have said he behaved in an exemplary manner and hadn't two-timed anyone. Hadn't he stopped himself from going to bed with her in a most restrained and gallant fashion? Bully for Harry and full marks for gentlemanliness and all-round good behaviour! Lou, for her part, wished she'd had at least one night of passion with him, but what would have been the point of that? How would she have felt, hearing about the American girlfriend, if she'd already been to bed with Harry? A hell of a lot worse, is how. So okay, well done, Harry, for drawing the line when he did. Still, the thought of what she'd missed out on sometimes made her grind her teeth in frustration. On the plus side – and she forced herself to consider a plus side, even when she felt a long way from positive – she was clearly no longer terrified of being touched by a man. She would have welcomed it and that had to be a good thing.

What to say to her mother? It occurred to her, now that she'd managed to poke her head out of the accumulated rubble of her own feelings, that she hadn't asked Phyl the right questions. Or even enough questions, come to think of it. Her mother had definitely not been her usual cheerful, chatty and placid self.

Now that Lou thought back on the time they'd spent together, she'd been too quiet and she looked like hell. She'd done her best, true enough, to make Lou feel better but you could see her heart hadn't been in it. It was as though she was doing it in her sleep, or while being really preoccupied with something else. There were dark rings under her eyes and an expression of unexplained misery when she thought you weren't looking. Why didn't I ask her before she went home? Because I was too caught up with what I was feeling. She sighed and began to type *Here at Cinnamon and not much going on. Harry away, so no need for embarrassment. Sorry I put you through all that, again. And you didn't look as though you were feeling great. Is anything wrong? I feel bad not asking you when you were here. But pl. tell me if it is! Lots of love, Lou xx.*

The phone in her handbag began to trill. That'll be Mum, she thought, not bothering to press 'send'. I can ask her straight out what's wrong.

'Hiya!' she said, in the tone of voice she always used when she knew it was Phyl at the other end.

'Is this Louise Barrington?'

Shit! Not Phyl at all but someone – oh, God, that Golden Ink man. Jake Golden. She must have sounded ridiculous. She said, 'Yes, this is Louise Barrington. So sorry. I was expecting it to be someone else.'

'I'm sorry to disappoint you!'

'No, no, not at all ...' When was this dancing around going to stop? Why didn't he come straight to the point? He sounded much less eloquent than the last time they'd spoken. She paused and waited for him to say something sensible.

'Hello? Are you still there? I'm ringing to see whether you're free for lunch sometime this week. Thursday? Or Friday?'

'I'm busy on Thursday, but Friday's fine.' She was perfectly free on Thursday as well, but one thing she'd learned from the same magazines that had taught her all she knew about make-up was that you never accepted the very first date offered. You never let on that you were sitting in your flat staring at the walls and wondering whether it was worth microwaving a potato for lunch. You invented dates. Appointments.

'Friday, then. Do you know La Bergerie? It's very near Tottenham Court Road station. I can send you the map reference on email if you like. About twelve-thirty okay for you?'

'Yes, that's fine. And I'd love some directions. My email is *loubar@hotmail.com*.'

'Okay! I'll send it straight away. I'm looking forward greatly to meeting you. Goodbye.'

'Bye' Lou put the phone away, wishing she'd had the presence of mind to ask how she was supposed to recognize him. Google Images, she thought. Thank heavens for Google and all its works. She pressed the right buttons and there he was – always, she noticed, turned away from the camera. And in group shots, always in the back row, half hidden behind someone else. So, modest and also tall. Fairish hair and glasses. Well, she'd find out soon enough. And the one thing the Google Images couldn't provide was his birth date, so she had no idea how old he was. She left Images and Googled Golden Ink. There was plenty of stuff on the internet about the firm and the books they published but nowhere could she find his date of birth. Never mind. Why should she care how old he was? He was maybe going to reissue *Blind Moon* and that was the only thing that mattered.

'Champagne and strawberries for dessert!' Mickey smiled. 'I wish your divorce came through every week. What a treat!'

'The champagne is only the beginning. We're booked at Devere Lodge in Mayfair. A spa, and I thought room service tonight, although I feel as if I never want to eat again after what we've just had. Is that okay?'

Nessa watched Mickey nod, her mouth too full to speak. This is it, she thought. I should say it now, if I'm going to. Did men go through this kind of panic when they were about to propose? She'd thought and thought about what she'd say, and how she'd do it, and whether it would be all right to show Mickey the pair of rings she'd found in one of the antique shops in Bath last week and bought at once. They were beautiful: Victorian half-hoops, one set with garnets and the other with moonstones. She imagined Mickey with sparkling dark red gems on her hand and herself wearing the glowing blue-white stones. No, she wasn't going to bring them out here. They'd be for later on.

'How did Gareth take it?' Mickey asked. 'Is he okay?'

'Fine, really. Tamsin's got used to the new arrangements and she's getting quite excited about having a little brother or sister. That'll be in a few months and I reckon it'll distract her. She's with Gareth and Melanie now. She seems fine, I have to say. It's a huge weight off my mind.'

Nessa didn't add that she'd found herself a little hurt at the ease with which her daughter had adapted to Melanie. Mostly though, she was pleased, of course she was. She wanted Tamsin to be happy more than she wanted any other single thing. And besides, she and Mickey didn't need a weepy, distressed, anxious kid around when what they wanted (Nessa wasn't in the habit of deceiving herself) was freedom from responsibility so that they could spend as much time together as possible. For one reason or another, including Mickey's trip to Prague for a trade fair, it had been more than two weeks since they'd managed a night together. Nessa had to stay behind because of the finalizing of the divorce and various meetings with Gareth that she'd arranged, and while Mickey was away she'd tormented herself so thoroughly with visions of other women in her lover's arms that she found it hard to sleep, and rang and texted Mickey so often that her bill was going to be astronomical. Never mind, it had been worth it to hear her, to hear her saying things ... Now, looking across the table at Mickey, Nessa felt so overwhelmed with desire that it was all she could do not to lean over and kiss her, then and there, in front of everyone. The table was small enough. She could easily have done it. She contented herself with taking Mickey's hand and holding it between both of hers.

'Mickey – darling Mickey. There's something I want to ask you ...'

Mickey still said nothing, but nodded. Nessa wondered if she knew what was coming. Could she have had the same thoughts herself, and not dared to say anything? Better to get this over quickly. She took a deep breath and stared down at Mickey's hand in her own. 'I want you to marry me. A civil partnership, or whatever it's called. I just ... I want us to be together for ever.'

'Me too. That's what I've been thinking.'

'You have? Honestly? Why didn't you say?' Nessa wondered if the frantic beating of her heart was audible.

'I was waiting for the divorce. I didn't want to ask you before I knew about that. We're done here, Nessa. Shall we get the bill?'

'Yes, of course.' Nessa could scarcely contain her

joy. Mickey had said yes. I want to get to the hotel, Nessa thought. I want her to make love to me. Now. She turned to find the waiter and signalled him to bring the bill. Her eye was caught by a couple sitting near the window. Was that – could it be? It was. It was Lou and some man. Have they noticed us? she wondered. Me and Mickey? She didn't care if they had. She had nothing to hide. She presented her credit card to the waiter and said to Mickey, 'There's Lou, in the window. Amazing coincidence, isn't it? I'll have to say hello. We're going to pass very near her table.'

'Who's that she's with?'

'Never seen him before in my life. Nothing to write home about, really.'

'Just not your type, Nessa. I think he looks sweet.'

'Who needs a man who looks sweet? Who needs a man, period?'

This struck them both as hilarious and they started to giggle. 'Control yourself, Nessa,' Mickey said. 'You don't want Lou to think you're a drunk as well as a dyke.'

'She'll never put two and two together. She'll just reckon we're having some sort of office lunch, or something. Let's go and say hi.'

They made their way to the table at which Lou and the unknown man were sitting. Nessa adopted her polite social voice. 'Hello, Lou. What an amazing coincidence! How lovely to see you – it's been weeks and weeks, hasn't it?'

'Hello, Nessa. Yes, it is a coincidence. I noticed you and Mickey – hello, Mickey – over there but I didn't … Anyway, how are you? Oh …' She blushed, realizing she ought to be introducing the mystery man. Nessa stepped into the slightly awkward pause.

'I'm sorry – I'm Vanessa Williams. Lou's sister – well, sort of. It's complicated, but I'm sure she'll explain if you ask her nicely. And this is Mickey Crawford, my partner.'

'How d'you do?' The man rose to his feet and shook hands with her and with Mickey. 'I'm Jake Golden. Good to meet you.'

American, Nessa thought. I wonder where she met him. They exchanged a few more words and then she and Mickey said goodbye and left. She looked back at them, sitting in the window and tried to work out how long they'd known one another, but they weren't giving anything away. What was that Lou had said? That she'd noticed them, her and Mickey. Did she see me take Mickey's hand? I don't care if she did, Nessa thought. In fact, I'll phone her when I get back home and tell her – tell her everything. That might be an excellent way of breaking the news to Matt and Phyl.

They'd reached the edge of the pavement. The traffic lights were against them. As they waited, Nessa turned to Mickey and kissed her on the lips. The kiss went on rather longer than was decent in a public place. Nessa reflected that she used to have strong views about people – anyone – kissing in public but that had all, it seemed, gone out of the window. She clung to Mickey and the London traffic roared and surged around them and she didn't give a damn who saw them.

'What did your sister mean, it's complicated?' Jake Golden asked. He might look shy and quiet, Lou thought, but he was clearly both nosy and outspoken. She put it down to his being American.

'Well, her mother used to be married to my father. We're not related by blood but we were brought up together. My parents made a point of referring to the three of us as brother and sisters. That's me and Nessa and her brother, Justin. But we don't see very much of one another now that we've grown up. Just birthdays and funerals and so on. My dad's birthday will probably be when I see her next.'

Jake said something non-committal and turned his attention to the menu. Lou felt too nervous to want to eat anything, but had decided she'd ask for a mushroom omelette. La Bergerie was exactly the kind of restaurant she'd imagined she'd be going to in Paris with Harry. Small, panelled in dark wood, with checked cloths and baskets full of French bread on each table. Proper French advertisements on the walls. There were also, she noticed, framed photographs of famous people everywhere: Jonathan Miller, Alan Bennett, and a good few others who looked as though they dated from ages back and whom she didn't recognize. Still, it was obviously a place approved of by a certain kind of celeb. She'd refused wine because she wanted to keep a clear head and they were sharing a bottle of sparkling water.

The waiter came to take their order and while Jake was giving it, Lou gazed out of the window. Was that Nessa and Mickey? Yes, they were on the pavement, waiting for the lights to change. Nessa suddenly turned and so did Mickey and they were kissing. Could it be? She craned her neck to see better and sure enough, there they still were, clinging together, kissing passionately. The traffic lights changed and they went on standing there, with their arms around one another. Lovers. It was obvious. Lou blinked and then they'd crossed the road. Jake had finished the ordering and was saying something to her, so she tore her thoughts away from what she had seen. Nessa and Mickey. How long had that been going on? She'd heard from Phyl about Gareth's other woman, but had it been Nessa's affair with Mickey that made Gareth turn to someone else? Lou was determined to find out. I'll ring her later, she thought. I have to concentrate on Jake Golden and what he's saying. I have to think of Grandad's book.

'I'm sorry ...' she smiled. 'I was miles away.'

'It's okay. I was just asking whether you knew about us. Golden Ink, I mean.'

'Everything it's possible to know from Google,' Lou said. 'But I noticed that you don't publish very much fiction.'

'No, that's right. Mostly memoirs, travel, a bit of poetry ... that kind of thing. And always things from the past that have been allowed to go out of print. I guess I'm not a great lover of fiction. One of the reasons I liked *Blind Moon* so much was because it struck me as thinly disguised memoir. D'you think it was?'

'Really? Did you think that? It never occurred to me till recently when someone – well, my long-lost great-great-aunt – told me the same thing. That Dulcie was just another name for Grandma Rosemary. She really did adopt him and bring him back to England after the war. And in the book, Peter makes it clear that Dulcie is responsible for his mother's death. But I've been thinking about it and wondering: would he have lived with his own mother's murderer? Because if it's true, then she *did* murder her, didn't she? I mean, Peter's mother might have died anyway, but Dulcie made sure of it. How could something like that happen?'

'John Barrington may not have had an option. He was all alone with no one to take care of him. I don't think he had a choice. He knew – he must have known – that Rosemary? Is that her name? was offering him a chance of survival, of education, of life.'

'He could have left her later on. When he was older. If she really was a murderer, that is. If he didn't invent that to make things more dramatic. No, I'm going to tell my father what Mme Franchard, my great-great-aunt, told me, but I think it's fiction. A novel. After

all, other things in the camp truly *were* horrible. So
many people died. And his mother had just had a baby
– she must have been very weak, weaker than many
of the others. She could easily have died from natural
causes and Grandad might have simply made it more
dramatic by inventing a murder.'

Jake had nearly finished his bowl of onion soup.
'What about that baby? Was that true? Could he have
invented that as well?'

'No, that was true. I remember him speaking to me
about his sister – to me and to my father.'

'None of it matters, actually. Whether it's true or
not. It works as a novel. A very truthful-sounding
novel. And I want to bring it back. Reissue it. If you'll
give your permission. You're the copyright holder,
right? I'm afraid I can't offer a very big advance ...
we're such a small operation. How does £2,000 sound
to you?'

It sounded to Lou like an enormous amount of
money. Most of what I've had till now, she reflected,
hasn't been mine at all, but Dad's. This would be the
most I've ever earned in one lump sum. Jake was still
talking. 'You could have £1,000 now and £1,000 on
publication. D'you have an agent?'

Lou shook her head. 'Should I get one?' Where did
one begin to look for an agent? She was starting to
feel a little giddy. All this was happening much too
fast. She said, 'I'd like some time to discuss this with
various people. My father ... he doesn't know much
about books, but he's a solicitor. And my boss.' Harry
would know about agents, she was almost sure. He'd
help her, and she wouldn't mind. She'd put aside her
personal feelings towards him for this, because it was
important to get it right.

'You don't need an agent at this stage,' Jake said. 'I
won't cheat you, I promise. And you can always join

the Society of Authors and let them have a look at the contract for you. I'd want to publish next year. I'll consult you about how the book should look but I have to warn you, I'm a bit stubborn where things like typefaces and covers are concerned.'

He smiled and Lou thought: his whole face changes when he smiles. She'd recognized him at once when she arrived at the restaurant, not only because he resembled his Google image but also because he was sitting in the window clearly on the lookout for someone. He had a long thin face, with fair hair cut very short. His horn-rimmed glasses were those ultra-modern ones that were the same shape as 3-D goggles and his eyes behind the glass were a sort of pale greenish-blue. You couldn't exactly call him handsome, but when he smiled his face was completely transformed and you just wanted to smile along with him. He dressed in a way that Lou wasn't used to, more plainly than anyone she'd ever seen before: a white shirt and dark grey trousers and brown loafers. Perhaps the garments were amazingly expensive but Lou couldn't tell when it came to men's clothes. And how old was he? He could be a very young-looking thirty-five or still in his twenties and making himself seem older by what he wore. Could he be as old as forty? She doubted it, but she was a very bad judge of people's ages. His voice was the best thing about him. He did sound like Clint Eastwood and Lou would have been happy to have sat there for ages just listening to him.

'There's something else,' Jake said, and Lou stopped thinking about what he looked like and concentrated instead on what he was about to ask. 'I'd love it if you could write an introduction. I'd pay you £500 for that, a straight fee. What do you think?'

'I couldn't ... what would I say? I've never written an introduction before, how long would it have to be?'

Her heart was suddenly pounding. She didn't know whether she was terrified or excited. Perhaps a bit of both. She'd just written a whole screenplay, but this was a proper commission.

'I thought you could write a piece about how you remember your grandfather. Personal stuff. Nothing too intellectual. Just what he was to you. It's the sort of thing our readers love … Would you consider it? About two thousand words.'

'Well, if you're sure. Anyway, how do you know I can write?'

'I'll take a chance. If it doesn't work, we'll think again. Can you?'

'Write? Yes, I think I can. But it'll be a challenge. I've never done anything like this before. D'you think it would make the book better?'

'I do. And there's something else. You'd have your name on it. Have you considered that? Can't I appeal to your vanity?'

There was that smile again. 'Okay. I'll try. I'll write something and email it to you.'

'Great. Let's have a pudding, okay?'

Suddenly, Lou felt hungry again. The book would be there, in the bookshops with her name on the cover, under Grandad's. For an instant she wished more than anything that he were alive to see it, but this was still fantastic. *Blind Moon by John Barrington with an introduction by Louise Barrington*. She said, 'Yes, I'd love something. Thanks.'

When the waiter arrived, Jake said, '*Tarte au citron* for me.'

'And for me, please,' Lou added.

'Coffee?'

She nodded. She didn't really feel like coffee, but it seemed the right thing to have at this moment. Sophisticated. A writer's drink.

'Now,' Jake said, 'that we've dealt with business, I'd like you to tell me about yourself.'

He sounded as though he meant it. Lou folded her napkin and laid it on the table.

'I've wanted to be a writer ever since I can remember,' she began and saw him lean forward. He was interested. He wasn't pretending to be. He really, truly was.

Nessa sighed into the phone. 'No, Justin, I'm not at home. I'm in London.'

'That's amazing. So am I. Please tell me where you are, Nessa. I need to talk. I'm in a car. I'll come straight round to wherever it is.'

How irritating was this? Why did he need to talk? Surely it could wait. Everything had to be immediate with Justin. He was the Emperor of Instant Gratification – now, now, everything now. She glanced sideways to where Mickey, stark naked, lay on the bed with the satin coverlet wrapped round her. They hadn't even got as far as getting in between the sheets, but then it was only four o'clock. She could hardly say it was too late … she did some quick mental calculation. If he came round now, they could get rid of him reasonably quickly. She could make some excuse. They'd still be able to have another swim and then supper and then come back to bed. Thank God for small mercies. Justin might have phoned fifteen minutes earlier. She wouldn't have been able to answer the phone. Wouldn't have wanted to. Just thinking about what they'd been doing only a few moments ago, she and Mickey, made her feel aroused all over again. Now she had to concentrate on her silly brother who was obviously in some trouble.

'You haven't done anything stupid, have you? Drugs or something?'

'God, Nessa, give me credit for some sense!'

Sense was precisely what Nessa did not give him credit for, but she said only, 'Okay. Be in the lobby of the Devere Lodge Hotel in fifteen minutes. Can you do that? It's in Mayfair, just round the corner from the American Embassy in Grosvenor Square.'

'I'll find it, don't worry. I'm in the area. I'll be there. What are you doing somewhere like the Devere? Are you alone?'

'No, as a matter of fact. Not that it's any of your business. I'm getting ready now and I'll see you soon, okay?'

She snapped the phone shut before he could ask any more questions.

'Bloody nuisance, my brother,' she said to Mickey. 'Do you want to come down with me and see what he wants?'

'No, it's okay. I'll wait up here. He might not want to confess whatever he has to confess in front of me.'

'Maybe you could come down later. Give me half an hour or so and then just appear. Okay? Will you do that?'

Nessa was at the dressing-table mirror with a good view of Mickey on the bed behind her.

'Okay, no problem. I'll be down soon.'

Nessa made her way to reception. It would be a pleasure to sit here for a while and wait for Justin. This hotel was complete bliss. The sofa she chose was red velvet and sinking into it was like burying yourself in the petals of a rose. Justin would spend the entire time till he saw her wondering *How come Nessa's in London? Who's she with? What's the story?* He knew about the divorce of course, but not in detail. For a moment, she felt a little nostalgic about how they used to be, she and Justin, when they were kids. Close. Telling one another everything. She dismissed

346

this vague feeling of regret as nothing but sentimentality. The truth of the matter was she'd adored her little brother when that was all he was, but when he grew up into a rather selfish and, in her opinion, not terribly intelligent man, she'd gone off him. As simple as that. She wondered how many siblings, parents – relatives of one kind and another – went on pretending to love one another because of convenience, what was expected and so forth, when in truth love had disappeared out of the equation long ago. She'd have put good money on it being most people. For instance, she asked herself, how much love does Phyl have for us now that we've left home? We'll all troop down there next week to celebrate Matt's birthday in the traditional way, but I bet if I cancelled and Justin cancelled it would make not a jot of difference to our Non-Wicked Stepmother. Lou was a different matter. Where Matt and Phyl were concerned she was the bee's knees and little Poppy of course could do no wrong. So maybe it was the blood is thicker than water thing, but that wasn't entirely it, because how to account for her not really loving Justin any longer? She sighed. The love she felt for Mickey had pushed most other emotions into a small corner of her being. And she'd go to the dinner in Haywards Heath because Matt, oddly enough, did genuinely seem to want to keep in touch. He does love me and Justin, she told herself, and wondered fleetingly whether it was because they reminded him of the blissful days when he was married to Ellie ... that was a possibility. The drag about this particular birthday was the fact that Matt insisted on Gareth coming too, and Tamsin. She'd asked him why on the phone, pointing out that a divorce was a divorce. He'd replied, mildly but firmly, that Gareth was still Tamsin's father and it was a family event.

'And besides,' he'd added, 'I'm not divorced from

Gareth. Surely you can spend one evening in his company?'

And she'd agreed because, above all, she wanted to be thought of as civilized and doing everything she could to keep things normal for Tamsin. But it was a drag, because for a long time she'd imagined that perhaps Matt's birthday would be a suitable occasion for her to arrive with Mickey as an obvious couple. She'd even kidded herself that she could just *be* in her new situation without having to explain anything to anyone. No such luck. That would have to be done quite separately. Perhaps we should host a coming-out ball, tee hee. She was smiling at the thought when she saw Justin coming through the revolving doors. She waved at him.

'Hello, Justin,' she said. 'I can't get up, this sofa's too comfy. Come and sit down. You look like hell.'

'Always so kind, Nessa darling.' He sank down beside her and gave her cheek a perfunctory kiss. 'But you're right for a change. I look like hell because I feel like hell.'

'Tell me about it.'

'It's hard to know where to begin ...' Justin said. 'Can we order something to drink? I need something ... how about a glass of wine?'

Nessa stood up and went to the bar. She ordered two glasses of white wine and while the barman was getting them, turned to look at Justin on the sofa. He had an expression on his face which she recognized from childhood. This was how he looked when another kid had taken something of his and not given it back: wounded, aggressive, and on the verge of a tantrum. This, she thought, is going to be interesting.

'It's always good to see you, Lou, you know that. Even with a piece of information like this.' Matt smiled at his daughter. 'And your mum's always happy to see Poppy, even for a few hours. Can't you stay the night?'

'No, not really, Dad. There's stuff I have to do, but I'm so grateful to you for this idea. And I'm sorry to have sprung it on you. I was upset when Mme Franchard told me. I've thought about it since, though, and I don't know what I believe any longer. It might all be made up. I just felt – well, Rosemary was the only grandmother figure you had, even though you weren't very close, I know.'

Matt stared down at the slightly worn leather that covered his desk and fiddled with his letter-opener. 'Come along, then. Let's have a look and see what's in the files.'

They made their way down the stairs to the cellar, which had been converted many years ago into a storage room.

'I had no idea this was down here. So many files! What's in them all?' Lou stared around her and Matt laughed.

'Old wills, property-searches, papers of every kind. Some people think it's a pile of junk but I prefer to call it an archive. A fantastic filing system in any case, which Rosemary's husband set up and we're still grateful to him for it, believe me. Right. Let's see.'

'What are you looking for exactly?' Lou wanted to know. She was peering at the labels as they walked between free-standing shelves crowded with box files.

'I know it's down here somewhere. Yes, here you are. Rosemary's papers.' He pulled the file off the shelf and opened it. 'Not much in here, really. I can honestly say I've never opened this before. Let's take it upstairs and have a look. I'll get someone to bring us a cup of coffee.'

Seeing Lou sitting in the client's chair made Matt feel strange. He'd hidden from his daughter the shock he'd felt when she broke her news: that his adopted grandmother might have murdered his father's birth mother. He was used to hiding his feelings and concentrated on keeping his voice even as he searched methodically through Rosemary's effects.

'Birth certificate, marriage certificate, will. Various bits and bobs. I thought as much,' he said at last. 'And there are letters in here. From my father to Rosemary. Nothing of much interest. This is her prayer book. She went to church every Sunday of her life as far as I know.'

Matt picked up the leather-bound book. A small piece of blue writing paper fell out of it as soon as he opened the front cover and he picked it up and read aloud what Rosemary had written on it in her spidery hand:

Dearest John,
    This letter will be kept with my will. When you read it, I will be dead. I am ready to meet my Maker and if I have any fear, it's of an afterlife in which what I've done will be punished. I have, I hope, been a good mother to you, but I can't keep the truth hidden any longer. When we were all in the prison camp together, your mother fell ill. I did nothing to save her life. I could have done and I didn't. That makes me no better than a murderer. She might have died anyway, but I could have made an effort to prevent her death and I chose not to. What I did was unforgivable, but I ask you to understand how desperate I was for a child. You have been that child and I've loved you with

all my heart, though I realize that I have never been a real mother and may not have shown this very well. I've done my best and that is all any of us can do. When I see my beloved friend Louise in God's presence, I will beg her to understand my motives.

With my love,
Rosemary Barrington.

Matt could feel himself turning cold. When he finished reading the letter, the silence grew, filling the room, and then he spoke again. 'My father must have hidden this letter after Rosemary died. Folded it into a book he knew wouldn't ever be looked at again. Filed it away in the cellar assuming no one would ever come across it. And look at the date: 1963. Two years before the publication of *Blind Moon*.' He sighed and buried his head in his hands. 'It's as though this letter gave him permission to write the book. To tell the truth. And to hide the fact that he was doing so by pretending it was a novel. Making up names for all the characters.'

Lou sprang up and went round to Matt's side of the desk and threw her arms around him. 'Oh, Dad,' she said. 'This must be such a terrible shock for you. I'm so sorry ...'

'No, no, it's all right.' Matt hugged his daughter. 'It oughtn't to make any difference and yet ... d'you think he knew all the time? From his days in the camp? From his early childhood?'

Lou nodded. 'Yes, I think so. I think he saw her die. His real mother. It's very – very vivid. You'll have to read it, Dad. Now that you know it's not invented.'

Matt laughed. 'That's a bit of a thing, isn't it? I never read my dad's books when I thought they were an invention and now this one turns out to be true, so I've got no excuse, have I? Have to find out what he went through. Poor bugger.' Tears came to his eyes and he blinked them away. 'He had to live with that his whole life. Why couldn't he have told me? Or my mother?'

'Constance wouldn't have been the most sympathetic person, I shouldn't think. And Grandad wouldn't want her getting on even worse with Rosemary than she did, would he? He'd have pushed it all down, deep inside him. Hidden it until he came to write the book.'

Matt put the sheet of blue paper back into the prayer book. 'Let's go home. I want to talk to your mother. And thank you, Lou, for telling me this. I won't pretend it's not a shock, but it's always better to know the truth.'

Even as he said the words Matt was wondering whether he really believed them.

10

Matt's birthday was in the second week of August. Phyl couldn't quite remember when celebrating it had turned into a major family event but they'd had a party of some kind ever since Lou was about five or so. The character of the occasion had changed over time, but nowadays it was generally a dinner on the second Saturday of the month. This year, by a happy coincidence, the day of the celebration was Matt's actual birthday: August eleventh.

In the past, she'd loved preparing the meal. She used to spend ages thinking about possible menus, and there was nothing she liked better than shopping for whatever she'd decided to cook. What used to make it special, she thought now, was the fact that this was the one day when Constance would deign to come down to earth from the heights of Milthorpe House and sit at her table. Phyl smiled. And every year I made such an effort to see that everything was perfect. It was a kind of challenge, and most years she succeeded in wringing a few words of praise from her hypercritical mother-in-law. There had been the odd occasion when compliments had not been forthcoming and once or twice Constance had actually cancelled *because I'm not really feeling up to it, darling – you understand, I'm quite sure* but, for the most part, she was sure that Matt had nothing but happy memories of his own birthday.

There was, of course, no possibility of Constance attending this year. Phyl smiled at the thought of the old woman appearing like Banquo's ghost at the head of the table. That'd be something to see! For her part, she couldn't help feeling relieved that her mother-in-law wouldn't be there ever again. She'd never have dreamed of confessing to Matt that those years when his mother hadn't made it to the table were more comfortable for her. She didn't have to feel as though she were competing in some kind of *Masterchef* event in her own home. That was the thing about Constance – she was the embodiment of judgemental. She judged every single thing that appeared before her. Clothes, people, food, jewels, books, films – she had an opinion on everything and in the case of books or films, didn't even feel she had to have read or seen the work in question. No, it would all be much more relaxed without her, though there were a few ... what could you call them ... stumbling blocks? Pieces of grit in the sandal? Irritants, in any case. Things which might go wrong.

There's me, for one thing, Phyl thought. It was now three weeks since she'd agreed to stay with Matt and she still sometimes woke up in the night full of dread ... *what if?* What if he was just saying that about not going back to Ellie? What if he still went round to the flat in Brighton and they ... her mind filled with such horrible images once she started on this tack that she'd had to get out of bed on several occasions and go downstairs and have a cup of tea in the kitchen till she came to her senses. She hated watching Matt like a prison warder, but couldn't help it. She knew the password on his email account and checked his messages, but Ellie, she was almost sure, didn't do email.

And Matt wasn't a fool. He'd delete any incriminating texts from his mobile phone. Did Ellie know about texts? She couldn't ask him.

It's all nonsense, she told herself as she began to make the pasta sauce. She'd decided on a starter of field mushrooms with a chick-pea stuffing, followed by linguine with a fresh crab and saffron sauce. Then they'd have the pavlova – a spectacular affair with meringue and fresh berries which had been ready since this morning. Matt was sincerely sorry. He really does love me, she thought. She remembered how distraught he'd looked when she was threatening to leave and allowed herself to be slightly consoled. The sex ... well, she'd done her best to please him and he'd done his best to be attentive and loving and it was okay, but there was something – a shadow – over them both. It would maybe disappear over time, but just at the moment it seemed to her that Ellie was a sort of ghostly presence who managed to slip between them. I'm thinking about her, Phyl thought, every time Matt takes me in his arms. He knows I'm thinking of her. He knows I'm thinking he's thinking of her ... and so it goes. The complications made her feel sick, as though she were staring into some kind of giddying spiral and she tried hard not to bring them to mind during the day. You are never content, she chided herself. He's *not* with her, he's with me. He didn't want me to leave. He loves *me*. How many times does the poor man have to say it before I truly, truly believe him? When she was being strictly honest with herself, she knew that in her heart of hearts she never would entirely believe it. *Given the choice, no one would choose you over Ellie.* That was what Phyl thought in her most secret heart and no amount of factual evidence would convince her otherwise, but she'd lived with the thought so long that she'd managed to squash it down and squash it down till it was no more than a paper-thin wisp of an idea that clung to the edges of her mind.

'Lou for you,' said Matt, coming into the kitchen with the phone in his hand.

'She's still coming, isn't she? Poppy's okay?'

'Nothing bad, darling, honestly. I've already said it's fine. Got to go.'

Phyl took the phone from Matt, who left the kitchen at once. 'Hi, love,' she said.

'Hello, Mum. I did ask Dad to explain but he says I've got to ask you ...'

'Ask me what?'

'Whether I can bring someone with me tonight – an extra person. Dad reckoned you always make too much food anyway.'

Phyl relaxed. She had no idea why she assumed every single phone call would be bringing her some bad news, some difficulty, something she had to deal with. The relief she felt when it turned out to be good news, or at least not a disaster, was ridiculous.

'Of course, darling. It's no problem. Gareth can't come, it seems. Nessa's asked if Mickey Crawford can come instead and I said yes. Who're you bringing?' For a wild optimistic moment, Phyl wondered whether Harry might possibly have ...

'It's Jake Golden, the publisher who's going to re-issue Grandad's book. He wants to meet Dad because of him being John Barrington's son. He's totally into everything to do with Grandad. He wants to meet you too of course, but it's mainly Dad. Jake's very nice. You'll like him.'

'I'm sure I will. Okay, got to go, darling. Lots to do still. When do we expect you?'

'About five, if that's okay. I want to be able to feed Poppy and get her settled down before we start eating.'

'Right. See you soon, then.'

Phyl went to replace the phone on its stand in the hall. She calculated numbers in her head ... how many were they going to be now? Only seven because Tamsin was with Gareth this weekend so she wasn't coming either. Not exactly a full house. Briefly, she wondered about Justin. He'd sounded not quite himself when they'd spoken on the phone. And how come, she wondered as she'd often wondered before, he was so beautiful and still unattached? People were very mysterious, she decided. She'd brought Justin up but wouldn't have said she knew him at all nowadays.

You couldn't really call it a wine cellar, even though this was where Matt kept the wine. It was a large underground space, a couple of rooms under the house which were always cool even in the hottest weather. The garden furniture lived down here and so did the folded-away paddling pool and lots of cardboard boxes in assorted sizes which Phyl insisted on keeping even though, as far as Matt knew, they'd never, ever used one of them. But what if we decide to move? she'd said the last time he moaned about the boxes taking up too much space. To which his answer had been *we're not moving. Not ever.*

Phyl thought he was joking, but he wasn't. He liked this house, his work was here in the town and why would he move? Even when he retired, he intended to stay exactly where he was. He'd never understood the desire people had to rush away from their lives to somewhere where no one knew them and where they had to start all over again from scratch. Now he looked carefully at the wine bottles, stored in racks against the wall opposite the pile of boxes. He knew what he was going to take up to the table – a 1996

Puligny-Montrachet – but he wasn't in a rush. He sat down on one of the garden chairs and put the bottles on the floor next to him.

Ellie. That was a narrow squeak. Since that night, the night he'd spent with her, he'd been feeling as though a bulldozer were moving over him. He'd been churned up. Turned over and over – shaken. Everyone he loved: Phyl, Lou, Poppy, Nessa and Justin (and yes, he really did love them, even though they frequently exasperated him beyond measure), his friends, his colleagues, his practice, his home ... all of that had been on the point of disappearing. He imagined the separate components of his life as though they were sweets in one of those old-fashioned glass jars common in his childhood. Sleeping with Ellie had twisted open the lid. Suddenly, everything was on the point of sliding out. He was about to lose every bit of what was precious to him. *Phyl had been packing to leave him.* Whenever he wavered, whenever he felt (and he wasn't in the habit of deceiving himself – he *did* occasionally feel it) overcome with a retrospective desire for Ellie, this sentence was enough to make him come to his senses. *Putting her things into a suitcase.* She would have gone. She would also, he was quite sure about this, have managed much better without him than he would without her. She would have gone to Lou at first and then they might have found a bigger flat together. He envisaged an idyllic life for the three of them: Phyl, Lou and Poppy getting on perfectly well without him.

Matt closed his eyes, and shuddered. He ran through the scenario that would have followed: Lou would be on her mother's side. She might have wanted not to see him again; she might have kept Poppy out of his life for ever. He couldn't even think about such a possibility without breaking into a cold sweat. His life, his comfortable, easy, pleasant life, would turn into a nightmare. He would have the house, although if the matter came to a divorce, a judge may have insisted he sold it and gave Phyl half the proceeds … all kinds of consequences might have followed.

The worst of these was that he could well have found himself saddled with Ellie again. That was the real horror. She'd drive me mad, he thought, if I went back to her. She drove me mad years ago and it's even worse now. I could never, ever trust her for one moment. Life would be the very opposite of peaceful. She'd be discontented, demanding, difficult. He closed his eyes. The sex, he had to admit, would be spectacular. Never mind, you couldn't have everything, and the days when he would have thought the world well lost for a good fuck were long gone. He picked up the bottles of wine at his feet and left the cellar, locking it carefully behind him.

'Some people,' Jake said, 'say a thing's fine when it's really not. Is your mom like that? I hope it really *is* okay for me to invite myself to your family celebration.'

'It is, honestly. I was the one who told you about it. I needn't have mentioned it. And you could still stay overnight in the house. There's plenty of room.' One of the things that Lou admired about Jake was his quiet efficiency. He'd gone online and booked himself into the Hilton Park Hotel, which wasn't far away, as soon as Lou had assured him he was welcome at Matt's birthday dinner. She glanced at Jake's profile as they drove. Poppy was asleep in the child seat in the back of the car.

'Well, between you mentioning that it was happening and me saying I'd like to come – that's a huge gap.'

'But you should let me pay for the child seat,' she

said. 'I can't believe you just went out and bought one and had it fitted and everything.'

Jake didn't take his eyes off the road as he spoke. He was a careful driver, as Lou had known he would be. He was careful about everything, but it was odd, because being that kind of person often went with ... with what? A sort of lack of passion and you couldn't say that about Jake. He was very obviously passionate about all sorts of things, mainly to do with books, but he was – she sought the right word – measured. Unsensational. Calm.

'Look, Lou, I don't know how to say this because it's kind of vulgar to talk about money, and so forth, but it's truly okay. You don't have to pay. I guess what I'm saying is putting a child seat in a car is no big deal for me. I wanted to come and meet your dad – and your mom of course – but mainly I'm very interested to meet John Barrington's son, and a car seat just makes it easier, that's all. We could have gone down on the train but hey, this is better, right?'

'Much better. Thanks, Jake ...' They could, she realized, go on other trips. Lou wondered if he had that in mind.

'We can go other places with Poppy, too, now that I've got it. Had you thought of that?'

'That's really kind of you,' Lou said.

'I like Poppy,' Jake smiled. 'She's cute.'

Lou came to the conclusion that she didn't know much about Jake, considering how much he knew about her. That first day in the restaurant, only a couple of weeks ago, they'd sat over coffee till after three o'clock and she seemed to have told him every single thing about herself. He was easy to talk to: unthreatening and interested. She'd had to rush to fetch Poppy and mentioned getting a taxi and he'd said, 'No, that's okay, I'll take you,' and he'd driven her to

360

the nursery and then all the way home. She'd sat in the back of the car with the baby on her lap that time and her part of the conversation had been directed at the nape of his neck.

Poppy loved riding in the car. And she liked Jake, grinning at him as she got out and making all kinds of happy sounds. He'd driven off with a wave and a smile. Lou had thought that was it. She reckoned she'd write the introduction and email it to him when it was finished, but he'd started to email her and phone her about this and that, mostly to do with the book and Lou found that she looked forward to his messages. When she'd told him she was going down to Haywards Heath for her dad's birthday party, Jake had asked her straight out whether he could, as he put it, 'come along'.

It occurred to her that he was simply a very straight-forward person. If he wanted something, he asked for it. If he could get it, fine. If not, he went on to the next thing with no repining. But he asked, and wasn't embarrassed about asking. He also didn't think twice about buying stuff that would make his life easier. The car seat – that was a bit – Lou didn't know what to call it. Excessive, perhaps, or presumptuous, even cheeky. What did it mean? First, that he was rich enough to get it installed in his car without a second thought. It was, she noticed, exactly like the one her parents had bought for their car. Not cheap. What she had to work out was what else it might mean. Was he telling her something? Was this a subtle way of letting her know he was interested in her? It would have been easier, surely, to ask her out if that were the case. Maybe it was no more than his way of ingratiating himself with John Barrington's family ... but why would he need to do that? He was about to pay her an advance and the right to reissue *Blind Moon* was his. Perhaps that was it. Maybe he felt as though he were in some way related to her through the book.

'Mind if I put on some music?'

'Not a bit.'

Lou didn't recognize the sounds that filled the air around them. Almost everyone else she knew had some sort of rock or pop music playing in their car. Her father always listened to Radio 4 as he drove. This was opera.

'Mozart,' Jake said. '*The Magic Flute*.'

Lou nodded. It wasn't Midlake's *The Trials of Van Occupanther*, which was her current favourite, but it was okay.

So here we are again, Nessa thought, gathered round the family table. She tried calculating how many of Matt's birthday dinners she'd attended, but she'd had too much to drink already and her head was in a muddle trying to integrate the various strands of conversation going on around her. Mickey had volunteered not to drink tonight, which was good of her, but, as she pointed out, 'They're your family not mine, so you're the one in need of alcoholic assistance.'

Mickey looked stunning. She was wearing a plum-coloured wraparound dress in some clingy material and very high-heeled shoes. She'd nearly forgotten to change into the shoes until Nessa reminded her, preventing her from appearing in public wearing her driving loafers. Phyl was in black, with her good jewellery (a string of pearls, pearl earrings) and Nessa knew that she'd chosen this outfit because she thought it would make her look less chubby. She wasn't exactly fat, but worried constantly about how she could appear thinner than she was. She didn't look too bad, but there were dark, puffy bags under her eyes, ill-concealed by make-up.

Lou had made an effort, too, in a kind of pastel-coloured chiffony top and a brownish skirt. She had a good figure and was quite tall and had a kind of natural elegance. She could, Nessa thought, look amazing if she tried. Or had money. Or both. Maybe I should help her out. Be her style counsellor or something. The bloke she'd come with was a bit of an enigma. Jake Golden, who apparently was going to reissue that book of Grandad's. He didn't look like her idea of a publisher but Nessa didn't really know what that was. Someone older. Someone fatter than this Jake person, who was very slim and youngish and wore ultra-modern glasses which almost made you not notice that he was quite good-looking. He was rich, too. She could see that. His white shirt was pure silk, she was willing to bet on it, and his shoes were Italian but so understated that you'd have to be an expert to know this. Clearly he was someone who didn't need to be looked at. He was also very quiet and sat next to Lou, taking in everything that was going on, but Nessa was an expert on body language and it seemed to her that he was keener on Lou than she perhaps realized. They hadn't got it together yet, because there was nothing about the way she was behaving that betrayed a huge passion for this man. Interesting, in any case.

They'd started eating quite late, because it took some time for Lou to settle Poppy down. Nessa hid her irritation and helped herself to more pistachios while everyone waited to get to the table. She knew that Lou had to bring her daughter with her, not having anyone she could easily leave her with overnight, but it was a drag. Very small children and grown-up dinner parties didn't mix well. Then once they'd sat down and begun to eat, Justin appeared. He was always late for everything and this was something about her brother which really, really pissed Nessa off and always had done.

First, there was the drama of the arrival (which was probably why he did it. He liked to make an entrance and adored being stared at), then the apologies, sliding into his place at the table, being introduced to Jake over the starter and then (this always happened with latecomers) everyone wanting to know the reasons for the lateness which, in Nessa's experience, never turned out to be in the least interesting.

'You're looking a bit harassed, Justin,' said Matt.

'I am. I am. Harassed. Troubled. You name it.'

Nessa stared at him. He was surely – *surely* – not going to tell Matt what he'd told her at the hotel? She'd warned him against it and she had the distinct impression that he'd agreed to keep quiet about it, at least until after the birthday. She raised her eyebrows at him in what was meant to be a warning signal and he smiled angelically back. Of course, Matt rose to his remark.

'Troubled? What's the matter?' he said. 'I hope you're not in any kind of difficulty, Justin.'

'No, and in any case it's not something I want to talk about at a party, with a guest present and everything.'

Jake Golden opened his mouth to say something and thought better of it. Matt stared at Justin. 'Very well, Justin. But may I have a few words with you after dinner?'

'Absolutely,' said Justin and proceeded to help himself to salad.

Nessa spent the rest of the meal trying to work out what Matt would say when Justin told him what had happened. For her part, she'd been very sympathetic and understanding, but she couldn't help an impulse from childhood surfacing now and again. Serve him right, was the first thing that had come into her mind. It was a bit of a disaster, but it did sort of serve him right, and try as she might Nessa couldn't work up any truly heartfelt sorrow on Justin's behalf.

'Are you quite sure you want to discuss this now, Matt? I mean, it's your birthday and so on ...'

They'd gone into Matt's study after dinner. Matt indicated a chair and watched his stepson sit down and fold one leg elegantly over the other. He said, 'It's perfectly all right. That's almost over. Nearly ten o'clock. I didn't like your mention of trouble.'

'But I could have come to see you at the office. We don't have to do it now if you don't want to.'

'But I do want to, Justin. It seems to me you're trying to put off telling me. I'm reminded of your schooldays. You never told me about detentions and so forth. I always found out from Nessa or your teachers. The more you indicate you're unwilling to talk about it, the more anxious I become.'

'Okay ... you asked for it. I've lost a bit of money.'

'Do you mean from the sale of Milthorpe House?'

'I've lost a lot of that. Yes.'

Matt felt winded. It was true, then, that this kind of news, often described as a punch in the stomach, did have exactly that effect. There was a pain somewhere beneath his ribs. He was short of breath. He tried to steady himself by counting to ten in his head and that didn't work. The numbers simply wouldn't take hold and he gave up at about four.

'As I understood it,' he said, going into lawyer mode purely in self-defence, 'you'd sold the house to Eremount. Isn't that right? I imagined you'd invest the money in something. Possibly even Eremount, who seem to be taking over the world.'

'Yes, well. I didn't.'

'You didn't invest?'

'No, I bought – well, I didn't invest in Eremount. I was advised by someone I know – a perfectly legitimate broker – to put the money into something … well … a bit more speculative.'

'I see.' Matt thought he did, too. Did he really want to know all the grisly details? Now, tonight? Perhaps not, but better find out the worst. 'How much have you lost?'

'Almost all of it. There's about twelve thousand pounds or so left – maybe a bit more. The company I bought into, which is called Kiteflyer Holdings, has just gone into receivership and there's nothing anyone can do. I'm totally fucked.'

Matt ignored the obscenity. If he'd felt breathless before, he was now almost sure he was about to have a heart attack or a stroke. Had he heard correctly? He could actually feel the blood rushing away from his heart … or was it *towards* his heart, flooding it and making him cold and sweaty at the same time? 'Let me get this straight. You've lost more than two million pounds. *Two million pounds! Is that right? I can't believe it.'

'I know, I know. I felt – when I heard I felt so gutted I nearly – very nearly, actually, threw myself off a high building. Or pills. I thought of pills, seriously I did.'

Matt knew what he ought to say: that he was glad Justin had thought better of killing himself, but he was so overcome with uncomprehending rage that he couldn't bring himself to utter the words. For two pins he'd have picked up the paperweight on his desk and thrown it at the silly bloody fool in front of him, who made him want to scream with frustration. Was there no end to his stupidity? Obviously not. Matt said, 'You didn't think to consult me about this? I might have warned you it was an insanely stupid thing to do: to invest in something so fly-by-night. So clearly unsafe.'

'But it wasn't. That's the point. It looked brilliant. Amazing rates of return on your investment.'

'You've never heard the thing about the value of your shares can go down as well as up?'

'Course I have. I just never thought that this particular firm would go bust.'

'You don't have to tell me that! Thinking is the last thing you've been doing.'

'I don't actually know what business it is of yours, Matt. I mean, it's very good of you to be concerned on my behalf, but I'll just soldier on and hope for the best. It's done now and I have to move on. Move on to something else. It's unfortunate, that's all.'

Matt stared at Justin. Was it possible he didn't realize what he'd done? First of all, he'd sold Milthorpe House. Almost immediately after the funeral. That had hurt Matt though he hadn't known quite why. True, it had been his childhood home but he'd managed to persuade himself that it was only a house when all was said and done and if it turned into a posh spa, why should he care? Since the sale had gone through, this thought had given him some comfort.

When he'd heard how much Justin had got for the place, it had surprised him. Not that it was more than the property was worth – it may even have been less – but the thought of Justin in possession of millions of pounds when Lou had nothing had upset him. Was this a kind of justice? Justin losing his money wouldn't help Lou, so why did he obscurely feel it was a kind of balancing of the books? No, it was a disaster whichever way you looked at it. Justin would be moaning about it. He'd given up his estate agent's job when he found himself in possession of so much money and now he'd probably have to go back to them and beg them to take him on again. Justin was speaking and Matt tuned in to what he was saying.

'Mum and I are thinking of going abroad. She's got connections in Argentina – well, you know that. We talked about going over there and seeing what the opportunities are.'

Matt leaned forward. 'Really?' he said.

'Oh, yes. I'd have thought Mum might have been in touch with you about it. She's put her flat up for sale.'

'Right. Well, I'm sure she'll let me know eventually. Perhaps when it's sold.'

'Can I go now? I could do with another cup of coffee.'

'Yes. There's nothing more to say, I suppose. You've been a bloody fool but I imagine you know that already.'

Matt couldn't bring himself to offer any more sympathy. He wondered, briefly, what Ellie had said to her son. Probably clutched him to her ample bosom and told him it wasn't his fault. Even though it was. No one else's fault but Justin's. He stared at the phone. Was Ellie really leaving? It looked as though that might happen and he sent up a prayer of thanks to any divinity who might be listening. It was beginning to look as though the night he'd spent with his ex-wife wasn't going to have any of the awful repercussions he'd imagined. Phyl was here, Ellie was going, and that was the way he wanted it. He was happy. It was his birthday and he had much to be grateful for: a good wife, a lovely daughter, a beautiful granddaughter, a house, a job, money, health, good relations with his stepchildren, even though one of them was a complete prat, and if there was a certain lack of colour and fire missing from the picture, well, that was a small price to pay for contentment. A fleeting vision of Ellie in the throes of passion, naked, open, swallowing him up completely came into his head and he pushed it away at once. He was not going to go there. Definitely, absolutely not.

'D'you know what Justin's talking to Dad about?' Lou was loading the dishwasher in the kitchen. Nessa had come with her, carrying a tray with all the last bits and pieces from the dinner on it. She probably, Lou thought, wants a fag and outside the back door is the best place to have one. To her surprise, Nessa started bustling around the kitchen doing a pretty good imitation of a traditional housewife, clearing up what Phyl had left undone before serving the dinner. She hadn't brought a handbag with her, so no fags for the moment. Lou had been meaning to ask her what the matter was with Justin, so she was happy to have Nessa's company, whatever her real reason was for helping.

'I do, as a matter of fact.'

'Are you allowed to tell?'

'Well, Justin hasn't said I can't tell you. And he's speaking to Matt so of course it'll be common knowledge in about ...' she glanced at her watch '... ten minutes or so.'

'Go on, then. Spit it out.'

'He's broke. Well, not broke exactly but he's lost the money from the sale of Milthorpe House.'

If Lou had been holding any crockery, she'd have dropped it for sure. As it was, she whirled round to face Nessa, gasping. 'Lost it? How lost it? I can't believe it. It was zillions.'

'Not really. A measly just over two million or so. Barely enough to keep body and soul together.'

They started giggling. The wine must have had something to do with it because before long, they were clutching one another, helpless with laughter. In the end, it was Lou who broke away. 'Stop!' she said. 'You must stop – I can't laugh this much. And I don't know why we're laughing anyway. It's awful. It's not funny. It's unbelievable. *Two million pounds*. What did he do?'

Nessa tore off a piece of kitchen towel from the roll hanging near the cooker and wiped her eyes and blew her nose. 'No, I don't suppose it is funny, not really, but you have to laugh or else you'd just – I don't know – cry, I suppose. He invested in a dodgy firm who've gone bust. That's it. I think he wishes it were something more dramatic or dangerous. I think he'd have loved it to have been the Mafia or something. Such a drama queen, our Justin. Oh, God, I don't know. It just makes me cross when I think of what we could have done with some of that dosh. Me and Mickey.'

Lou remembered what she'd seen when she was having lunch with Jake for the first time: Nessa in a clinch with Mickey. She couldn't mention that, so she said, 'Paper Roses, you mean? You're not in financial difficulties, are you?'

'Difficulties? No, not at all. The business is doing very well. I just meant – never mind.'

Lou glanced at Nessa. She'd sat down at the kitchen table and Lou sat down opposite her. Nessa was blushing. Suddenly, Lou realized why. A confession was on the way, she was sure of it. Should she say something? Lou was wondering about this when Nessa said, 'Who's this Jake then? Are you two an item?'

'No, no, of course not. Whatever makes you think that? He just came down to see Dad, really. He's interested in everything to do with Grandad and his writing. In fact, I was going to ask Justin if he could pull strings with Eremount so that Jake can go up to Milthorpe House to have a look at the actual study and all of that, before they pull the place apart.'

'It shouldn't be a problem, I'd have thought. It's going to be some time, I reckon, before actual work begins on the site.'

'I hate the thought of Milthorpe House being a spa.' Lou made a face.

'Can't think why. It's a bit sentimental to think of it as some kind of ancestral family home.'

Lou didn't answer. Part of her knew Nessa was right but she couldn't help what she felt. She'd promised to take Jake to look around it tomorrow morning, before they set off for London. Mum and Dad had agreed to look after Poppy for a couple of hours. It was going to be strange but at least Jake would get some idea of what the house was like when Grandad was alive. The builders and workmen hadn't moved in yet, and it would be a while before they started on the conversion. She said, 'Why did you think Jake and I were an item?'

'Well, he's rather dishy, isn't he? In a sort of undernourished, Gary Sinese kind of way.'

'Is he?'

'You hadn't noticed?'

'He's okay. He's very nice, that's the thing. He's as keen on *Blind Moon* as I am.'

'Aha! Common interests. Very important. That's what all the agony aunts say, isn't it?'

'Shut up, Nessa. I'm not going to think about it. Okay?'

'Hmm. Are you still – I mean, after Ray – are you still off sex?'

'Bloody hell, Ness. It's none of your business.'

'But I'm dying to know and you can tell me. How about … if you tell me, then I'll tell you a secret. How's that?'

Lou looked at Nessa. Whether it was the wine working its magic, or whether Nessa had really changed, it seemed to her that for the first time since she was a child and in awe of her older sister, she was feeling something like a proper connection between them. Was there any reason why she couldn't talk about Harry? Not really. She said, 'I *was* keen on someone. Someone at my work. Harry. We went to Paris together for the weekend, but it didn't work out. I got the signals wrong. He was involved with someone already. In America. That's it.'

'That's bad. Poor old you. Still, you were up for it, right? You assumed you were going to bed with him?'

Lou nodded. Nessa grinned and said, 'No harm done then – you're still up for it. I'd consider Jake, if I were you.'

'He's much older than I am,' Lou said.

'How much older?'

'I don't know.'

'You don't know how old he is?'

Lou shook her head. 'I haven't asked him.'

'Right, then. You'd better find out.'

'Stop it, Nessa. You're just trying to avoid telling me your secret.'

'No, I'm not. Honestly.'

'Have you got one? Truly?'

'Oh, yes …' Nessa looked vaguely around. She was thinking, Lou knew, of ways of escaping. Of running away from the kitchen, of not having to spill the beans. 'I've become …' She stopped and said nothing for so long that Lou prompted her.

'You've become what?'

'I'm in love. I'm madly in love. That's the secret.'

'Who with? Why the fuss? Does that count as a secret?' Now that she'd started by pretending she didn't know anything about Mickey, she couldn't do anything but be surprised.

'Well, nobody knows yet. I haven't told anyone.'

'Then I'm honoured, but that's only half a secret if you don't say who it is. You haven't exactly hung around. You've only just got a divorce.' A thought occurred to Lou. 'Or had you been having an affair for years and years that no one knew anything about?'

'As if! No, this is – well, it's a bit – I don't know how to tell you.'

'He's married. Do I know him?' (God, she was doing well at this cover-up!)

'No, that's not it. Not it at all – oh, God this is hard.'

Lou laughed. 'He's much younger than you are. You're afraid people will say you're cradle-snatching?'

'No, no ... nothing like that. You know this person.'

'I do? Oh, go on, Nessa, just say the name.'

'It's Mickey.'

'Mickey?!'

Nessa nodded. She was blushing again. Lou looked at her and opened her mouth to speak, and then thought better of it and took a deep breath. I have to be careful what I say here, she told herself. Now that Nessa had told her, she was trying to work out the ramifications of what she knew. She had to say something, or Nessa would think she was shocked. Well, she was, a bit, if she stopped to think about it. Could you just become a lesbian overnight? Was that what had happened to Nessa? Could she ask her how it happened? She said, 'God, Nessa, I don't know what to say. Have you ever ... I mean ... how did you know ... Oh, this is ghastly. I don't know what I'm supposed to say! Tell me about it. Go on. I just want to know how you feel. What happened?'

'I fell in love. That's what happened. I wasn't, I've never – I mean I never thought I'd ever be attracted to a woman. In that way. But I found I was. I am. And,

373

well, it's great. I'm so happy, Lou. She's so – I can't explain it. It's like we fit together. I'm like – well, it's a bit like being a teenager again, I suppose. I just think about her all the time. We're going to ... this bit really *is* a secret, so don't say a word to anyone, okay? We're going to have a civil ceremony. At Christmas.'

'But, who knows about Mickey?'

'No one. Well, Justin might have put two and two together, but no one else. I couldn't say anything before the divorce came through because I didn't want Gareth throwing a wobbly.'

'Would he?'

'I didn't want to take the risk of him getting complete custody of Tamsin. And you'd be amazed at how many people there are who'd raise an eyebrow if they thought a child was being brought up by a couple of dykes.'

'Don't say that, Ness. It's horrible. But what'll happen now? When you get married, for instance?'

'I'll wait a bit before I tell Gareth. We're getting into a custody routine. Melanie's baby will be here soon and he'll have his work cut out coping with that. Melanie will see to it, I promise you. My relationship with Mickey will be a *fait accompli* by then.'

'When are you going to tell Mum and Dad? And Ellie?'

'I've no idea. Maybe tonight. No, I'm only kidding. Dad'll have enough to think about with Justin's revelation. Don't want to knock him out entirely. You'll keep quiet, won't you? Don't tell a soul. Okay?'

'No, I won't. I promise.'

'Right ... gotta go. Mickey'll be wondering what's happened to me. Jake'll be wondering what's happened to you.'

'No, he won't.' Lou smiled at her. 'Tell them we've been clearing up and that I'll be there any minute.'

374

When Nessa had gone, Lou took a damp cloth and began to wipe the work surfaces. Nessa and Mickey. She tried to imagine what it would be like to make love to another woman and failed. Did this new passion of Nessa's mean that she'd given up men altogether? She might be bisexual. That must be nice – gave you many more chances of finding a soul-mate. Would she consider it? Lou thought about the young women she knew and decided that no, she truly, truly didn't fancy a single one of them. So I'm not bisexual, she told herself. What about Jake, though? Nessa thought they might be an item. It was true that Lou had been thinking about him quite a lot recently. She had admitted to herself that she fancied him, but only in a general sort of way. Not seriously, because he'd never shown any sign of fancying her, but maybe … he'd put a child seat for Poppy into his car. *Actions speak louder than words*. Well, perhaps they did, but there hadn't been any words. None. The fact that he'd never flirted with her had to be weighed against the things he had done. And she ought to try and find out exactly how old he was. Not that it would make much difference if she decided that – oh, for God's sake, grow up. Nessa being in love and seeing everything through rose-coloured spectacles was getting to her. That was all this was. Paper Rose-coloured spectacles! I must be a bit drunk, Lou thought, smiling at her own silly joke as she went back to the sitting room.

Nessa and Mickey and Justin left the house some time after ten o'clock. Nessa's story was she had to get up early to meet a supplier who was flying over from Germany. Lou suspected that what she really wanted to do was be alone with Mickey. Justin had probably fled the chilly atmosphere that seemed to have sprung up between him and Matt after their chat. I must find out from Dad what he thinks about all that stuff with the money, Lou thought. Out of the corner of her eye, she watched Jake and her parents talking quietly together. You could almost, she thought, see them relaxing as he spoke. He had that effect on everyone. Calming them down, and giving them the kind of attention that made them eager to talk, to confide in him, instead of running away in horror at his rather un-English directness.

'Lou told me what you found in Rosemary Barrington's prayer book,' Jake said. 'That must have been very upsetting for you. Did you know your grandmother, Mr Barrington? Rosemary Barrington, I mean.'

'Do call me Matt, please. Oh, yes – I was already grown up by the time she died. She was a difficult sort of woman. I never got on very well with her, actually. That was probably my mother's doing. She didn't like her a bit. And my father – well, he had a strange relationship with his mother.'

'Do you think that might have been because she wasn't his real mother?'

'Possibly, but he seemed ... well, resigned at least, to being her son. He was always very dutiful but I never saw much affection between them, but then my father wasn't one to show his feelings. Apart from Lou. He adored Lou.'

Lou smiled and Jake turned to her and smiled too. To Matt he said, 'If he knew what had happened, it must have been a little hard for him to show affection to someone he regarded as responsible for his mother's death.'

'Yes, I suppose so.' Matt leaned forward. 'I feel very guilty, never having read *Blind Moon*. I've glanced at the beginning.' He looked shamefaced. 'I'm not much of a reader, actually. I can remember when it came out.

There were a couple of articles in the paper. A few reviews. Dad was a small kind of celebrity for a bit, but I was young then and getting on with my own things. You know how it is. You don't really pay that much attention to what your parents are up to.'

Lou said, 'When Grandad first read it to me, he left out all that. I used to think it was a kind of boys' own adventure. And completely fictional.'

'I'm not saying what I've learned about Rosemary isn't terrible,' Matt said. 'But I've been thinking and perhaps … well, I'm making excuses, but it's more than likely that Louise would have died anyway. That doesn't make what Rosemary did any more under-standable, but just – well, perhaps it's not quite as bad as murder. Maybe there's a case for saying Louise was spared days of unnecessary misery. I still find it hard to take in her motive.'

'She wanted her child,' Jake said. 'She'd wanted the baby for herself – Mary, the girl baby who dies in the book, but Peter – your father, Matt – was the next best thing. It's very important in the novel, Dulcie's longing for a child. You're led to believe that she'd do anything. As indeed she does.'

Matt said, 'Still, after all, a Japanese prisoner-of-war camp – people were dying there all the time from dis-eases and hunger and what have you. That's true, isn't it? Mightn't he have – I don't know – dramatized the situation to make it more exciting? More of a shock to the reader?'

'Perhaps, I guess,' said Jake. 'But there's Rosemary's letter. The one you've just found.'

'Sometimes people …' Matt paused, 'dramatize things that have happened to them, or around them, to make themselves look more important. Perhaps Rosemary was mistaken?'

Lou shook her head. 'No, you'll see if you read the

book, Dad. It's so carefully described. Every single thing.'

'In any case,' Jake added, 'I don't think it makes any difference to the book. The story is there, in black and white, and soon everyone's going to be able to read it and the biography won't really come into it.'

'I'm rather relieved that my father didn't live to see his work revived,' said Matt.

'How can you say that, Dad? Grandad would be so thrilled,' Lou exclaimed.

'Well, yes and no. Nowadays the press would have been all over him, asking him all sorts of intrusive questions: was your mother deliberately murdered by your adoptive mother or was that just something you made up? You can imagine the sort of thing I mean, I'm sure. He'd have hated all that.' Matt stood up. 'I hope you forgive me if I go up now. I'm very tired suddenly. It's been a super evening, even if a little more, well, serious, than I'm used to on my birthday. And thank you, Jake, for the champagne, that was a kind thought. I'm delighted to have met you – and please don't feel you have to hurry off to your hotel. Do stay. Have another cup of coffee or something.'

Jake stood up to say goodnight. Lou waited as her mother, too, said her farewells and followed Matt upstairs. Jake said, 'I'd better go too, I guess, but your dad's right … I wouldn't mind another cup of coffee, if that's okay.'

'Me too. That crab sauce always makes me thirsty.'

'I cannot believe,' Jake was saying as they went into the kitchen, 'that your father didn't read the book years ago. Amazing.'

'I know. I'd always assumed, when Grandad first read bits out to me when I was a child, that he'd made the story up. And now I think I remember – well, it was a long time ago and to be honest I'd forgotten about it till just a moment ago – isn't it strange how things come back to you? Like scenes from a film suddenly coming into focus.'

'Remember what?'

'Grandad sort of alluding to it.' Lou prepared the coffee and put it on the table as she spoke. 'One of those conversations that start out being hypothetical. You know: there's a bear chasing two of you and you have to decide whether to run away as quickly as you can and save yourself or stay with your companion who isn't so fast and risk becoming the bear's dinner. That kind of thing. Grandad was always clear that he'd stay. He'd never, he said, abandon a friend. And then he said something I didn't understand at the time, but which ... well, he said *unless that friend had something I really, really wanted and could only get if he died. That would make things different, I suppose.* I was about nine or so and I was very shocked. I argued with him. I said if he did that, it would be a kind of murder and he agreed with me, that was the thing. He smiled at me and said *of course you're right. It is murder, isn't it? Very well, I wouldn't do it whatever happened. Satisfied?*'

'And that's it? No more than that?' Jake took a sip of his coffee. 'This is delicious. Thank you.'

'No. No more than that. Maybe what Dad says is true about Rosemary dramatizing her role. Even if she didn't actually murder Louise, even if Grandad made that bit up, he makes it obvious in the book that Dulcie – Rosemary – is obsessed with having a child, almost any child. The way he describes the events when they all come out of the camp; the way Dulcie takes him over, almost smothers him – that's true, I'm sure.'

'Then there's this: would a child consent to being adopted by someone they reckoned killed their beloved parent?'

'You've read it, Jake! It's made quite clear why he submits to that. What's the alternative? An orphanage? Being sent to live with someone he's never heard of? Rosemary was his mother's best friend. Before his mother's death he liked her. Admired her. He thought she was pretty and kind. Surely some of those feelings would survive? I don't think it matters. Not to the novel. Maybe to my dad. He might not like the idea of his grandmother being exposed as a murderer, so perhaps we'd better not emphasize the autobiographical element too much. I don't think Dad would like the press all over him any more than Grandad would have done. Let's just say it's a fantastic novel, that's all.'

'And that's how I'm going to publish it. You'll be the one, as you're the copyright holder and a lot prettier than your dad, who'll answer any questions from the press.'

'Will there be any, d'you think?' This hadn't occurred to Lou. Well, she wouldn't mind. She'd spend some of the advance on a few new clothes. That remark about her being prettier than her dad didn't mean he thought she was actually pretty, did it?

'I hope I can drum up some interest. I'll do my best. There,' he finished his coffee in one long gulp. 'I should go now. It's getting late.'

'Okay. I'll come and see you out. It's a bit tricky reversing down that drive.'

The house was silent as they walked through the hall and out of the front door. There was a three-quarter moon in the sky and the air was quite warm. Jake opened the car door and turned towards her.

'I'll come by and fetch you and Poppy tomorrow – if you really want to go back to London. It's so pleasant here. I think I'd spend every weekend here if I could.'

'No, I have to get back. A friend of Poppy's from

380

nursery is having a party. Can you believe it? A birth-day party for a one-year-old!'

'Start as you mean to go on. When is Poppy's birth-day?'

'She'll be two just after Christmas.'

'Right. I'm going now, Lou. I'll see you tomorrow. It's been great, really. Thanks.'

He took a step towards her, and before she'd understood exactly what was happening, his arms were around her. He didn't say a word, but kissed her. Nothing about this kiss reminded her of Harry, and how she'd felt about him. This was something completely different. It was over too quickly, before she'd had time to process what it had been like, how she felt about how it felt, what she thought about Jake ... Fragments of incoherent ideas chased one another through her head during the few seconds that she'd stood there with his arms around her, and she could smell his skin, and taste his rather cool lips and, most of all, be aware of his hands, one on her neck, hold-ing her face close to his, the other on her lower back, caressing her as they stood there.

Then he was gone, with a grin and a wave and she was left on the drive with the honeysuckle that grew in profusion against the garden wall spilling its fragrance into the air, and making her feel a little drunk. I *am* a bit drunk, she told herself. Maybe it was a thank-you kiss. *Thanks for inviting me down to your parents' house. Here's how I do thanking.* I don't, she reflected, know anything about Jake's love life. Perhaps he's got someone, just as Harry had, and this was just ... just something that might have been a handshake, if she'd been a man. For her part, she thought her relationship with Jake was a bit like the ones she'd had with her tutors at uni – the younger ones at least: a mixture of awe, deference, friendliness and admiration for their intellect. The ones who were fanciable she'd sort of fancied at a distance, without ever considering that anything might come of it and that was the way she'd been with Jake. Until tonight. Now she'd have to think again.

She turned to go into the house and was suddenly overcome by tiredness. Better get to bed fast. Poppy would be up no later in the morning than she normally was. Play it by ear, that's what I'll do, she decided. She would pretend it hadn't happened till she saw an indication from Jake that it had. But it had. She was still aware of how it had been to have his hard, slim body touching hers. What was he thinking about now, on the way back to his hotel? And how old was he? Suddenly, it became important to know.

Phyl was snoring slightly and Matt got out of bed as quietly as he could. He stood at the window looking out at the drive. The moon was not quite full, but he could see Jake's car clearly. He and Lou were in the kitchen, probably having a cup of tea. He wished he could go and join them, but knew it was out of the question. That crab sauce of Phyl's was delicious but it did seem to raise a thirst. There was a bottle of water on his bedside table and he fetched it. As he drank, he heard footsteps crunching in the gravel and returned to the window. Jake was kissing Lou. Had he been expecting that? Were they involved? The thought had crossed his mind a couple of times tonight, when he'd intercepted a smile between them at the dinner table, and once when he'd noticed how Jake was looking at Lou while she was talking to Nessa: intently, with a kind of wonder on his face. What about Lou, though? How had she been with Jake? Matt hadn't spotted anything he could have put his finger on, but he had seen that she was comfortable in his company. If they did have a relationship, was that a good thing? Would he hurt her?

The car had gone now and Lou was still standing there in the drive, staring after it. Matt looked down at her. He would, he knew, do anything, anything at all, to guarantee her happiness. If he could be assured of that, he'd want nothing else in the world. The conversation he'd had with her and Jake about his own father's novel came back to him, and he wondered if John Barrington had ever felt about him as strongly as he felt about Lou. Certainly, he'd never shown it, but then he was a reserved man and Constance had been so much more in evidence as a parent, so much more *there* in his life, that it had scarcely ever occurred to the young Matt to wonder whether his father really loved him.

Children – even when they weren't your own flesh and blood – never stopped worrying you. There was never a time when you could relax and say let them get on with it, it's nothing to do with me. Look at bloody Justin – what he'd allowed to happen to Milthorpe House, to his mother's money – and the ghastly provisions of that last, mad will Constance had seen fit to draw up without consulting him: these things were still robbing him of sleep. No sooner had he more or less got used to a *status quo* he found hard to bear than something else happened.

What had irked him more than anything was the notion of Justin strutting around in possession of that property. Matt hadn't approved of the sale of the house, but at least it had meant that, in future, there was no chance of Lou having to visit her brother there as some kind of poor relation. So he'd made the best of the sale and after that what annoyed him was the fact that Lou was barely scraping along while Justin had millions in his bank account.

He wondered why he wasn't rejoicing now. He should be, by rights. Justin was no longer a millionaire, even though he wasn't quite down at Lou's level of income, so there was some justice in the world after all. And yet Matt found that he couldn't be happy about it. There was something stupid and wasteful about putting your money into something that went bankrupt. It showed exactly the sort of financial carelessness that he deplored. Never mind – Justin would have to work his own way back from that *débâcle*.

His thoughts turned to what Jake had asked him about his own grandmother. He'd told Lou that he intended to go back and read *Blind Moon*, even though he often wondered what it was about fiction that got people so involved with it. The few novels that he'd read seemed to him to take for ever saying things which could have been conveyed in half the time. He knew this was a failing of his, but he couldn't help it, any more than one could help colour blindness. Factual matters were different. If something was true, then it was worth learning about, worth consideration. Now that he had learned that his father was no more than a reporter, Matt could read it to find out what actually happened in the prisoner-of-war camp. Perhaps he could ask Lou to help him; ask her to find the specific pages about Rosemary and the death of his real grandmother – save him the trouble of reading the whole thing. No, that was cowardly. He needed to read every word. He sighed and contemplated getting into bed again and then decided against it. He wasn't going to be able to sleep, and he didn't want to sit here in the dark. He left the bedroom and tiptoed downstairs. He noticed as he passed that the light was still on in Lou's room and almost knocked at the door, but then thought better of it. She'd be getting ready for bed and Poppy would doubtless wake her in the early hours. Better let her get some sleep.

In the kitchen, he helped himself to a glass of milk and sat at the table to drink it. He tried to recall his early memories of Rosemary Barrington but nothing very interesting came to mind. She was a bossy woman, rather boring to a small boy, and she seemed always to be at odds with Constance. He remembered a row between his parents which was about Rosemary, and the reason it stayed in his mind was because it was so rare for them to shout at one another in front of him. He hadn't thought about it for years, maybe not for decades, but tonight's conversation had brought it back to him. Generally speaking, the Barringtons had managed to keep their discord to themselves, hissing at one another behind closed doors, leaving Matt holding his breath in the hope of overhearing something. He rarely did.

This was the fight he remembered because they'd been in the car. There was no way they could have avoided Matt overhearing what they said and, looking back, it seemed to him that they'd forgotten about him altogether. His father had been driving and his mother's sharp profile was turned towards him so that she could lambast him more easily. Dad had failed to do something – what it was Matt had no idea – but it was clear that his mother had objected strongly to something Rosemary had said to her.

'You never stand up for me,' she shouted. 'You're always so preoccupied with *her*. With your mother. I'm sick to death of it. You have a duty to me. Whether you agree with me or not, it's your business to defend me from Rosemary, not go along with her version of events.'

'That's not what I did,' Dad had replied. 'I just …'

'You shut up! You said nothing! That's what you

always do. Just my luck to be married to someone so spineless that he can't even utter a squeak when his mother launches into one of her tirades ...'

'She is NOT my bloody mother!' Dad was shouting, and Matt remembered shrinking back against the leather upholstery, praying for him to shut up. His father rarely raised his voice and hardly ever swore, so the effect of this fury was enormous. Matt almost stopped breathing. His father went on, 'She's nothing to do with me.'

'She *is* to do with you,' Constance shrieked. 'She might not be your birth mother but she's brought you up since you were eight. And in any case, her relationship to you or the lack of it has absolutely no bearing on what you should have done when she attacked me. You should have told her what you thought of her behaviour. She *is* your mother to all intents and purposes. She's brought you up since childhood.'

'She took my mother from me.' Matt could see from his seat in the back of the car that his father's neck was red. It always went red when he was angry: scarlet patches covered the skin from his collar to his hairline. His voice rose to a shout as he went on speaking: 'She robbed me of my mother ... *robbed* me.'

'What nonsense!' Constance laughed. 'Your mother died of starvation, and probably malaria and God knows what other ghastly illnesses, in a prisoner-of-war camp. It's frightfully sad and all that, but you ought to have got over it by now. It was years and years ago, John. Talk about living in the past! You're a real expert at doing that, aren't you? Well, I'd be grateful if you stopped worrying about your mother, who's been dead for donkey's years, and took a little more notice of *me*.'

Matt drank the last of the milk. His father hadn't answered, or if he had, the memory of what he'd said had gone. What remained, what came back to him now as he sat in his own kitchen, an adult, well able to deal with unruly emotions, was the utter misery he'd felt then in sympathy with his father. He'd recognized – how old had he been? Not much older than ten, certainly – the depth and complete hopelessness of his father's sorrow. I knew, Matt thought, even at that age, that he and Constance were always going to be at odds with one another. They ought to have separated. There were some boys at his school whose parents were divorced. It wasn't completely unknown, but Matt dreaded it more than anything. For years and years he'd gone to bed praying that his parents would stay together and his prayers had been answered. He should have specified some happiness in his fervent, whispered chats to the Almighty. For someone who didn't know whether he believed in God or not, he did make a lot of demands on His time. Just in case ...

Matt rinsed his glass and left the kitchen. *She robbed me of my mother.* The novel was a truthful account of what had really happened and remembering those long-ago words of his father's made Matt believe this properly for the first time. Until now he'd been uncertain, but that memory had returned unbidden to convince him. He would tell Lou about it tomorrow. The light was out now in her room and he offered up another prayer, for his daughter's happiness. And Poppy's. Their health. Lou's success. He wasn't going to take the risk of leaving anything out.

Without curtains, without carpets, Milthorpe House was echoey and cold. Jake had picked her up early and here they were, walking round a place which Lou thought she knew better than anywhere, but which suddenly looked like nothing so much as a stage set waiting for scenery, props and, especially, actors to come and make it live again. The house felt dead. There was nothing in it that Lou could point at and say, I used to love this when I was small …

'It's horrible,' she whispered. 'I wish you could have seen it when Constance was alive. She wasn't a nice person, but she did know how to make a house beautiful.'

'I just feel so – well, it's good to see where he used to live. Can we go and look at his study? Will it worry you? You can stay down here if you like and just give me directions …'

'No, I'll come too. I haven't been in there for years. Without Grandad there, I never wanted to. Constance didn't change anything about the room but it wasn't the same after he died.'

They went up the stairs together, Lou leading the way. She'd not slept well: a combination of Poppy and then being unable to fall asleep again, and part of that disturbance was to do with Jake. That kiss last night … he'd made no reference to it this morning and Lou interpreted that as meaning it was due to the lateness of the hour, the scent of honeysuckle: whatever. When something caught his attention, he focused on it completely. Now, he was totally absorbed with John Barrington, trying to imagine how it was for the writer to sit in this room and put down the words that would become his novels.

'Tell me how the room was arranged,' he said.

'The desk was here. Grandad didn't like looking out of the window while he worked. He told me once that the blank wall was like a screen and he could see the scenes unfolding on it – like a movie. We loved movies. We used to watch them together all the time. There was a sofa there, and a small television over in the corner and they used to show old black and white movies in the afternoons sometimes. The curtains were tobacco-coloured – velvet I suppose they must have been, but they were very worn and old. I don't know how Constance allowed it. She wouldn't have stood for worn curtains in any other part of the house ...'

Suddenly, there were tears in her eyes.

'I'm sorry, Lou,' Jake said. He looked stricken. 'I wouldn't have asked you to come if I'd known it'd be so hard for you. Let's go, I've seen enough.'

'No, no – I'm fine. Really. I just felt sad for a moment, that's all. Not about Grandad. Or not really. Just a sort of regret that he couldn't be alive to see his book reissued. That's all it is. And tiredness. Poppy woke up last night. She mostly sleeps through these days but last night, well, sod's law, isn't it? Kids always wake up when you go to bed late. Let me tell you about the desk. He had a rolltop desk which I loved. He let me keep my pencils in one drawer. My grandmother got rid of it when he died, and that makes me so angry whenever I think about it. I'd have loved that desk ...'

'That's too bad. That kind of thing really gets to you, but it's so cool. To be here, I mean. To look out of his window. I really get off on stuff like this, you know. Writers' houses. I love them. I did all the tourist things when I first came over here. Stratford, the Lake District, Hardy's Dorset, even Brontë country. And modern writers ... it's harder with them, so I'm lucky to know you. And very lucky to have got here before they turn it into something else.' He smacked his hand against the wall. 'It makes me mad, to think this is disappearing. How can you stand it? A health club!'

'Grandad's not famous enough for anyone to turn this place into a shrine.'

'I know. It's sad, that's all I'm saying. I'm glad your brother didn't run his cock-eyed idea past me. I'd have been – well, I'd have found it hard to be polite to him. It's … I dunno … Philistine, I guess.'

'Justin does his own thing. He always has. He never thinks about anyone else, and he's so good-looking that people don't seem to mind. They indulge him.'

Jake smiled. 'I've noticed that. The beautiful get away with stuff, that's true.'

The study seemed crowded all of a sudden. Jake was leaning against the wall by the door. Lou was on the other side of the room. Suddenly, he came towards her, holding out his hand. 'Come on, Lou. We're out of here.'

He held her hand as they walked downstairs. She felt as though she were being led out of a dangerous maze. He knows the way out, she told herself and that thought was followed by another: you're mad. *You* know the way out. *You're* the one who's been here before, not Jake. Still, the feeling persisted that he was looking after her; guiding her out of somewhere that used to be a happy place and wasn't any longer. She'd been about to cry, about to sink into memories that made her sad, and Jake had been there to take her back into the sunlight. The study had always been on the dark side of the house, and the sun never reached it till late in the afternoon, but now, coming out at the front, there was the warmth and brightness of a clear August morning and her spirits lifted.

Once she was in the car, once they were on their way to Haywards Heath to fetch Poppy, she began to feel tired and slightly depressed again.

After a while, Jake said, 'You okay? You're very quiet …' He shot her a quick look and a smile and then turned his eyes to the road.

'I'm fine, just tired.'

'Go to sleep. Really. We've got at least half an hour.'

390

'I think I will. Thanks, Jake.'

She closed her eyes and leaned back against the seat. As she drifted into sleep, she became aware of a hand moving over her hair, softly, very softly and then adjusting the cardigan that was draped over her shoulder, covering up her bare arm. Did he think she was asleep? Did he want her to know he'd touched her? Lou didn't care. He'd stroked her hair ...

11

'I think it's very kind of Mummy to ask us out to dinner. We can have a ... well, a bit of a celebration. Have you told her about your new little brother?' Gareth grinned at Tamsin and, like a human lighthouse, turned his head and the beam of his happy smile on Nessa too. She smiled back. Well, he *had* just had a son and whatever anyone said, men did go all gooey when a male child was born. Nothing you could do about it but disapprove and have another glass of wine to show how delighted you were. He was here in the restaurant, ready to hand Tamsin over for the weekend. Melanie, naturally, had sailed through the entire process with no trouble at all, and everything surrounding the birth was positively jubilant and positive and life-affirming, quite unlike her own painful experience, which still made her shudder in horror even after eight years. It was quite true that the whole thing had been worth it in the end because of Tamsin, but the actual process itself hadn't been a pleasant one.

'Congratulations, Gareth,' she said. 'And you, Tamsin, sweetheart. You're a big sister now! Isn't that lovely?' She found that she, too, was doing the beaming thing, and added, 'I think we'll go and find a nice cuddly toy for him tomorrow. Okay? Have you decided on his name yet?'

'Barnaby,' said Tamsin. 'Barney for short.'

'Lovely!' said Nessa, while privately believing the name would be very much more suitable for a teddy bear.

The waiter came with their pizzas, and for a few moments they chewed away in harmony. Nessa looked around. The restaurant wasn't too crowded but there were a few people sitting at tables quite close by: probably enough to stop Gareth from making a scene. She'd gone over and over it in her mind. She'd decided to break the news about Mickey to both of them together, and though of course she could have done so in private, she knew that being in a restaurant meant that Gareth wouldn't be able to have any kind of row with her. She looked at Tamsin happily eating her pizza and took a deep breath. Here goes, she thought, and smiled at her ex-husband and her daughter.

'I'm glad you're both here together, you two, because there's something I want to tell you. I've got a bit of good news of my own that we can celebrate. I'm ... well, I've fallen in love.'

'Good for you, Nessa! Who's the lucky fellow?' Gareth asked and he sounded genuinely pleased.

'I'm afraid it's not a bloke, Gareth. It's Mickey. Mickey Crawford,' she added, smiling, making sure they both knew who she meant.

'But Mickey's a lady,' Tamsin said. 'Ladies can't fall in love with other ladies.'

'Yes, they can. It's ...' Nessa thought for a moment. 'It's not what most women prefer, but some do. They fall in love with other women.' Let's not, Nessa thought, turn this into a sketch from *Little Britain* with talk of 'laydees'. She had been so taken up with Tamsin, with her reaction, with seeing that she had absorbed the information and not been, at first sight anyway, completely traumatized, that she'd hardly glanced at

Gareth. She turned to him now, because Tamsin had gone back to her meal. She looked okay, but Gareth ... he was clearly about to have some kind of fit. His face had turned dangerously red and he was opening and shutting his mouth like a goldfish. Nessa smiled at him encouragingly and said, 'Relax, darling. No need to throw a wobbly!'

'That's not what I'm doing,' he spluttered eventually, wiping his mouth with a paper hankie. 'I'm just ... I cannot believe what you've just told me. We can't discuss it now, anyway.'

'Why on earth not?'

'Don't be ridiculous, Nessa. It's not – it's not suitable for our daughter to hear and I don't want the entire clientele of this restaurant listening in on what's a very private discussion.'

'What nonsense, Gareth! There's nothing whatsoever to discuss. Mickey and I love one another and now that the divorce is through, I'm going to start making arrangements for a civil ceremony.'

If he'd been purple before, what colour was he now? Nessa saw the blood rise in her ex-husband's face and was amazed at how much of it there must be in his body to produce this strange red and white blotchy effect. She waited for him to return to normalish, which he did after a few moments. He said, 'You mean, one of those stupid gay marriages.'

'Isn't there some kind of law where you're not allowed to say offensive things like that? I must look into it. Dad'll know.'

Gareth seized on the mention of Matt. 'Have you told them? Your parents? They will be thrilled to bits to hear the news. I don't think!'

'Lou seemed pleased for me. I was really chuffed at her reaction. And no, I haven't told Matt and Phyl yet. I don't imagine they'll be delighted, but whatever they

394

might feel privately they'll behave properly. I'd also like to remind you that you're not related to me any longer. We're totally separated. By law.'

'That's as may be. However, we're Tamsin's parents. We're bound by her ...'

'I'm not bound by anything to sit here and be insulted. Is that really the best you can manage – sneering at my forthcoming wedding?'

'Wedding?' Tamsin spoke up, her attention caught by one interesting word shining out from a whole lot of what must, Nessa supposed, be boring ones. It was Tamsin's turn to grin now. She said, 'Dad's having a wedding soon. Melanie says as soon as she's got her figure back. I'm going to be a bridesmaid. She said I could.'

'Well, that'll be lovely, won't it?'

Tamsin nodded. Nessa went on, 'How would you like to be a bridesmaid for me and Mickey as well, when *we* get married?'

'Silly! Ladies don't marry other ladies.' Tamsin looked indulgently at her mother.

'They do sometimes. They're allowed to now. And men can marry men.'

'Shut up, Nessa! She doesn't need to know all of that. She's only eight, for God's sake.'

'No reason for her not to know it, though. It's true. It's going to be happening more and more.'

'Worse luck. Bloody ridiculous, the whole thing. World's gone mad.'

Nessa was going to wade in and say something but then stopped herself. Was it mad? There were certainly some people, maybe a few of the business contacts she'd built up through Paper Roses, who might think badly of her and Mickey for coming out, and if they actually declared their love in a civil ceremony, well – that could just be too much for them. I can't help it, she told herself. It's right, and it's good and if anyone can't come to terms with it, then that's their problem. They will in the end. They'll get used to it. And the more it happens, the easier it will be for other women. Or men, come to that.

'Can I really be a bridesmaid, Mummy?' Tamsin brought her out of her musings. At least she had her priorities right. 'I could wear the same dress I'm wearing at Daddy's wedding, couldn't I?'

'I couldn't get married without you for my bridesmaid, Tamsin. And we'll get you a whole new outfit too. Push the boat out. We'll find you the most beautiful bridesmaid's outfit in the world.'

The last thing she wanted was a wedding that was anything like Gareth's. She reckoned she could predict pretty much what that would be like but she'd have to check nearer the time.

'Cool. Can I have some ice cream, Daddy?'

Gareth passed Tamsin the menu with bad grace.

'I don't know what I'm going to say to my friends,' he muttered. Nessa smiled at him. 'They'll love it. Think of the sympathy you'll get.' She leaned over to whisper in his ear, not wanting Tamsin to hear what she was about to say next. 'They'll be wondering whether I was what they'll undoubtedly call a dyke while I was married to you.'

'You bloody weren't!' he exclaimed. 'That's what makes all this so crazy. I find it impossible to believe, if you want to know the truth.'

'I'm afraid you'll have to get used to it, darling. It's how things are now.'

Lou manoeuvred the pushchair over a rather rough piece of ground and made sure that none of the cuddly toys Poppy insisted on taking with them had fallen out as they walked along. She was in Highgate Wood, which wasn't exactly smooth underfoot, but which was a lovely place to stroll about in and a much pleasanter way of getting to Jake's house than struggling up the busy main road which sloped rather steeply. Finding ways of avoiding exhaust fumes, which she always imagined puffing straight into Poppy's face, was something Lou did all the time.

Jake had offered to meet them at the Tube station. They were invited to tea. It was good of him to include Poppy in the date, but Lou thought she'd have preferred to be *tête-à-tête* for a change. Since that night at her parents' house, he'd been in touch by email in a very friendly manner and they'd been to the movies a couple of times. He'd taken her out to lunch, but with some other people from his office, so that she could meet them. He behaved, for ninety-nine per cent of the time, like the person who was publishing her grandfather's book. But there were occasions when she caught him looking at her and she was knocked back by the emotion she saw, or thought she saw, in his eyes. The other thing about him was, he didn't speak about himself. At first, this was refreshing. It was fun to be asked about what *you* thought for a change, and Jake always seemed very eager to hear her opinions about everything. He asked her questions, too, about her youth and especially about her memories of Grandad, and Lou loved talking about those. No one had ever been as interested in him before and it was a relief to Lou to be able to express all the feelings that she'd been unable to share with anyone until now.

'But,' she said to Poppy's back in the pushchair, 'it's not fair, is it? Hey? He doesn't tell me anything. For all I know he's married with three children. I'd never know. Well, maybe we'll find out when we get to his house. D'you reckon he's ready for you, Poppy? You're going to be on your best behaviour, aren't you?'

'Ducks!' Poppy said. 'Quack!'

'No, we're not going to see the ducks today, darling. We're going to tea. A tea party.'

'Party!' Poppy was mollified. Parties were even better than ducks in her world view and Lou immediately felt guilty.

'Not a real party,' she said. 'A nice man. A nice house. Cake!'

'Doggies!' Thank heavens her daughter's eye had been caught by a couple holding the leashes of three dogs who gambolled and barked and frisked in a way specifically designed to entertain a child. She hoped that Poppy would have forgotten the promise of a party by the time they got there.

Jake's house turned out to be a white-stuccoed semi-detached. From the outside, it didn't look any different from its neighbours: a small paved bit in the front, with a few shrubs growing in pots under the window and a front door painted dark blue. Jake was waiting on the doorstep.

'You made it! I nearly came to find you in the wood.'

'We got a bit sidetracked. There were dogs we had to look at. Sorry ...'

'No, it's okay. I knew it was probably something like that. Did you like the dogs, Poppy?' He was crouching down, undoing the straps on the pushchair. Poppy held her arms out and shouted, 'Yake!' at the top of her voice. She really likes him, Lou thought, folding up the pushchair. Does that mean anything? Probably not. Poppy liked everyone who wasn't positively unkind to her and so far she hadn't met any of those. Fleetingly, Lou wondered what life would be like if you never, ever met any horrible people, nor anyone who was nasty to you. Dream on, she thought. Doesn't happen. One of these days, even Poppy would discover the truth that not everyone wished her well, but till she did Lou was happy to let her think the world was nothing but sweetness and light.

'I hope,' Jake said over his shoulder as he carried Poppy into the house, 'that your kid likes my toys. I've put out all my best stuff.'

'Wow! Look at that, Poppy.' The carpet was covered with so many wonderful things that Poppy was silenced for a moment. Jake set her down and she looked around her, trying to take in what was spread out on the carpet: a set of Russian dolls, a wooden Noah's ark with about twenty pairs of creatures to go in it, a collection of coloured cardboard boxes, a basket full of painted wooden eggs and a whole lot of plastic bowls of various sizes in pretty pastel colours which Lou recognized as Tesco's cheapo barbecue range from last summer.

Poppy settled down to play and Lou sat on a nearby armchair, near enough to scoop her up if she got it into her head to attack Jake's more fragile possessions.

'This is amazing, Jake. Are they really all yours?'

'Yup. I had to go up to the attic to fetch the Noah's ark down, but it's good to have it out where I can see it. I loved it when I was a kid. My family thought I was crazy to bring all this stuff over here to the UK, but I didn't see a reason to leave any of it behind. As you see, I'm a bit of a hoarder.'

'Lucky for Poppy. She's in heaven. You're very good with babies, Jake. Have you got children of your own?'

As soon as the words were out of her mouth, Lou regretted them. She bent towards Poppy, helping her to put an elephant into the ark.

'Kids? Me? No, of course not. What made you think that?'

'Well ...' Okay, Lou thought. Now that the subject's come up, I'll forge on. 'You might be married.'

'*Married?* Don't you think you would have noticed?'

'Not necessarily. You've never said either way. For all I knew, till today, you might have had a wife in the USA – or even here in England. Or an ex-wife. It wasn't really my business to ask you, only now ...'

'Now what?'

'I'd like to know.'

'No, Lou, I'm not married. Never have been. I'm single.'

'Right,' Lou said. All the fanciful things she'd been thinking about Jake disappeared in a moment. She'd imagined him a romantic widower, with a wife and child killed in a terrible accident. She'd thought he might be divorced, with a terrible harridan in the background, busy sucking every penny out of him. She'd wondered if he might be gay, but then dismissed this thought when he kissed her, though that didn't necessarily mean anything. Or did it? Anyway, whatever she'd dreamed up, the truth was much simpler. He was single.

'May I ask you something else?'

'Sure. No secrets here. Ask whatever you like.'

'How old are you?'

'How old d'you think I am?'

'I've no idea. I've wondered ... I reckon,' she looked at him carefully, 'mid-thirties?'

'Spot on. Thirty-five.'

Twelve years older than she was – why did she think of his age in relation to her own? She was surprised that Jake, to all intents and purposes the most eligible person in the world, had managed to avoid getting hooked for this long. She was longing to ask him. He'd asked her directly about herself and she'd been only too happy to tell him her entire life story in detail. He knew about Ray. She'd even told him about Harry. The only thing she hadn't mentioned was the screenplay she'd written. That was too private to talk about until she knew what Ciaran Donnelly thought of it.

'I'm surprised you've managed to stay single,' she said in the end. 'You like children ... I'd have thought ...'

'Just because I'm single doesn't mean to say I haven't got a tragic past.' He was smiling as he spoke.

'Of course not. I'm sorry ... do you have one? A tragic past, I mean.'

'Not an operatic sort of tragedy. Common enough story, I'm afraid. I had a long relationship with a married woman. My stupidity. My youth. Anyway, she didn't leave her husband for me and since then, well, it's been a few years and I've been busy setting up Golden Ink. You know how it is ...'

'You moved to the UK. Was that because of her?'

'Partly, I guess. But I've always wanted to live in London. Early exposure to Dickens. You don't get over that. I love it here. And I go back and forth a lot to the States.'

Poppy was being too good. She appeared totally absorbed in the Noah's ark and wasn't going to provide any immediate diversion. Lou would have to continue with this conversation and she had no idea what to say next. This had never happened to her before with Jake. There always seemed to be plenty to talk about and discuss but now that kiss – very carefully not referred to during the last couple of weeks – seemed to loom in front of her. Perhaps she'd blown it up out of all proportion ...

'Lou?' Jake's voice broke in on her thoughts.

'Sorry, Jake, I was miles away.'

'Bet I know what you were thinking.'

'Bet you don't.'

'Bet I do. I was thinking the same thing.'

Lou smiled. 'How d'you know?'

'I do, that's all.'

'Go on, then. What was it?'

'The night we were at your parents' house. I kissed you. You were thinking about that and so was I.'

'No, that's wrong. I wasn't.'

'You're lying. You were.'

Lou covered her face with her hands. 'How did you *know*? I was fibbing, of course I was, but how did you know?'

'You're blushing. Don't you know that you are?'

Lou nodded. 'I s'pose so. I do know I am really.'

'Why are you?'

'Because I'm embarrassed.'

'Why?' he repeated. 'Have you been thinking about that kiss?'

'Yes. Yes I have.'

Jake said, 'Me, too.'

'What have you been thinking?' What she wanted to say was: it can't have come into your mind too often or you'd have found some way of kissing me again.

'I didn't want – I was concerned. I didn't want to rush into anything that might hurt you. I was also nervous.'

'You? Nervous? I can't believe it. I've never seen you being nervous.'

'I hide it.' Jake smiled. 'I didn't want … I wanted … oh, heck, I wanted to be sure. Of my feelings. You're very young, Lou.'

'I'm not that young! I'm twenty-three.'

'Very young, like I said. I wanted you to be … well, I didn't want to pressure you into anything you might regret.'

Lou looked across the carpet at Jake, sitting forward on the sofa. If she wasn't careful, this moment would pass and Poppy would start mithering and demanding attention and that would be the end of this conversation. She got up and went over to sit next to him. Poppy didn't even look up from her play.

'Jake,' she said, 'you might be older than I am, but you think too much. Please just stop talking and kiss me again.'

She leaned towards him and put one hand on his shoulder. At once, his arms were around her and his mouth was on hers. She closed her eyes. Let it go on, she thought. She clung to Jake as though she never intended to let go.

'Mama ... Maaam ...' Poppy wailed. The kiss ended, and Lou and Jake sprang apart.

'What's the matter, darling? Don't cry. Nothing's wrong. Look ... look at this doll.'

Jake smiled at her as she slid down to Poppy's level on the carpet. 'I guess she thought I was attacking you.'

'It's okay,' Lou said. 'Don't worry about it.'

'She's going to have to get used to it. So are you. I'll get the tea stuff. We all need some cake, right?'

He left the room and Lou picked Poppy up and hugged her. 'Oh, Poppy,' she said. 'Don't you just love him? Jake? Say it. Jake!'

'Yake!' Poppy shouted, caught up in the excitement. 'Yake!'

'Do you mind?' Lou smiled up at Jake, who was leaning on one elbow in her bed. This was probably not, she thought, how he'd intended it to be. To be woken up at five o'clock by a shouting toddler demanding light refreshments after a night spent in a small, rather shabby bedroom in a flat that could no way be described as desirable wasn't what Lou would have dreamed of either, but now it seemed to her completely blissful.

When she'd come back about an hour ago from dealing with Poppy, Jake was fast asleep. She slipped in beside him, breathless at the sight of his slim, pale body in her bed. In *her* bed. She lay there, conscious of his quiet breathing, and went over the last few hours in her mind. He'd brought them back from his house in the car and helped Lou to carry all Poppy's stuff upstairs. And then he just stayed. She'd fed and bathed Poppy and Jake had helped. She'd put her baby to bed. Then she'd made them a risotto. They opened a bottle of wine that Dad had insisted on giving her after his birthday. They'd drunk too much. She'd shown him the photograph of John Barrington's mother, which lived on the shelf above her table.

'This is the first Louise – my great-grandmother.'

He'd held the wooden frame in his hands and stared down at the picture. 'She's ... she looks exactly like you. That's amazing. Don't you think that's amazing ...?'

'I know. It's spooky.'

'Where's it taken? By the sea, it looks like. You can just see it, there, behind her head.'

'I think it's the house in Brittany. You can see how thick the walls are. I suppose they need to be, with the sea so close.'

'It's beautiful. She's beautiful.' He'd leaned forward then and kissed her, putting his arms around her and drawing her down into the depths of the sofa. 'I can't drive home,' he added, whispering the words into her neck. Lou had felt her bones melting, her whole body frantic with longing for him. 'And it's late.'

'Stay. Stay here,' she'd said.

He'd followed her into the tiny bedroom. He undressed her and she lay naked on the bed and closed her eyes while he tore off his clothes and came to lie beside her. She could see him by the light left on in the lounge. 'Kiss me,' she whispered and he did, oh, God, he did. He touched her all over. He licked the hollows of her neck and spoke words to her that she heard and didn't hear and understood and repeated back to him and then he was there, inside her, moving inside her and she thought she might faint and didn't faint and moved with him and cried out with him and lay next to him afterwards, panting and laughing and he was kissing her again and telling her he loved her, he loved her, he always would and he loved her and he wanted her and she was his love his only love and kiss me, he said and she did and she didn't want to stop, not ever. Then he woke up and said,

'Hi, Louise. Hi, my darling,' and she wondered about him calling her Louise and what it meant and she nearly asked him and then decided not to and whispered, instead, 'Do you mind?'

'What are you talking about?' he said sleepily. He lay down again on his side, and put an arm around her naked body. 'Mind what?'

'Well ... this flat. It's grotty. Not your sort of place at all.'

'I have no idea what you're saying. Any place you're in is my kind of place.'

'But you ...'

'I love it. I love this flat. Ssh ...' Gently, he pulled her on top of him as Lou whispered, 'Poppy could wake up at any moment. I'm not sure we should.'

'I am. I'm sure we should. Sssh ...'

'Feels as though autumn's on its way with a vengeance, doesn't it?' Matt smiled at his secretary and wondered, not for the first time, how social wheels would be oiled without the wonderful weather clichés which could be trotted out for every occasion. And since he was holding a dripping coat at arm's length as he spoke, Matt felt that today he was more than entitled to comment on the weather. He'd been soaked, just walking from where he'd parked in the tiny car park behind the office for use of Barrington employees only.

'I'll make some coffee, shall I?'

'Thanks, that would be wonderful. And a couple of biscuits, I think, as well.'

Once he was in his place, behind his desk, Matt began to feel better. In the three weeks since his birthday, he'd felt like a recovering patient, conscious that he shouldn't take too much for granted, but still telling himself that things were looking up. Yes, that was the way he put it when he was thinking about it. Things were improving on all fronts.

Ellie wasn't being difficult, Justin wasn't nagging him for help, and Nessa seemed happy now that the divorce was a *fait accompli*. The best thing of all, as far as he was concerned, was what had happened to Lou. It looked, from things she'd said, as though she and Jake Golden were – he never knew how to put it. An item. A couple sounded too formal and lovers too flowery and romantic. In any case, pleased as he was for Lou, he didn't like to think too much about her being someone's *lover*. But it was a good thing, there was no doubt about that. Lou sounded more positive than she had for ages and, apparently, Jake was very fond of Poppy. He knew that Poppy's mere existence would put off a lot of men. He hadn't been like that. He'd been perfectly content to accept Ellie's children by another man, but he knew that most people would run a mile before taking on an infant who wasn't theirs.

Don't get ahead of yourself, Matt thought. He's not

proposing marriage. And there's still the problem of Lou's lack of money, that awful flat and her complete obstinacy when it came to accepting help from him and Phyl. The advance on *Blind Moon* was welcome, but it wasn't much, and privately Matt wondered whether the book would go on to make money. He doubted it. Never mind, Lou was okay for now and he was glad about that.

'There's someone just arrived to see you who isn't in the book,' Mrs Beaumont said, coming in with the coffee and biscuits. 'He had an umbrella, thank goodness. He's French ... a Monsieur Thibaud, or Thebaud, or something ... You're not expecting anyone from France, are you?'

'No, I don't think so, but you'd better send him in.'

Monsieur whoever he was entered the room rather tentatively. First he put his head round the door, and then the rest of him followed.

'Come in, come in. The English weather is behaving in just the way people think it always does, I'm afraid. Come and sit down. I'm sure you could do with a hot drink. Is coffee all right, or do you prefer tea?'

'Coffee is very good, thank you so much.'

M. Thibaud settled himself in the chair in front of the desk as Matt phoned through for another cup and saucer. Mrs Beaumont brought it in and while she busied herself with handing out the coffee, Matt had a chance to assess his visitor. A middle-aged man, bald and quite small, with a pair of rimless glasses enlarging already quite protruberant blue eyes. Reasonably well dressed in a conservative style, he carried a very old-looking briefcase.

'It's very good of you to see me, out of the blue like this,' he said. Matt wondered how it was that foreigners didn't seem to have any problems speaking English, whereas he'd have had a struggle in any European language. M. Thibaud went on, 'I left a message on your machine.'

'I'm very sorry. I don't seem to have received that. It's easy to dial the wrong number, I think, when you're calling from abroad. But there's no harm done. I've no pressing engagements till after lunch.'

'Thank you. My name is Jules Thibaud. I am the attorney of Mme Manon Franchard. I regret very much to say that Mme Franchard passed away ten days ago. I have only just found your address and other details among Mme Franchard's papers. I am deeply sorry to be the bearer of such news.'

'Oh!' Matt didn't know what to say. Finally, he spoke. 'That is very sad. I only met Mme Franchard once but she was my great-aunt and I'd have liked to know her better. I feel badly about it. I ought to have made sure to see her more often ... to bring her to England, perhaps. I'm very sorry to hear this, and I know my daughter will be too. She'd only met Mme Franchard twice, but I know she liked her. Lou ... that's my daughter, Louise ... she's the one who's interested in our family history ... I must phone her and tell her the news. She'll be very sad.'

M. Thibaud coughed and opened the flap of the briefcase. 'Mme Franchard was a client of mine and a good woman in every way, but order in her papers was unknown to her. I have found a letter she has written to me, in which she tells me that your daughter, Louise, possesses a letter Mme Franchard gave her on the occasion of her last visit. Is this so?'

'Yes, she brought a letter back with her from Paris ... that was in August. I can telephone her, if you like?'

'That would be very kind of you, if it is convenient.'

'Absolutely.' Matt dialled Lou's mobile and smiled at M. Thibaud as he waited for her to answer. 'I often wonder how we managed to do anything before the advent of mobile phones ... Lou? Can you talk, darling? Good ... thanks. Are you at home? Right. Right ... it's okay, only I've got a piece of rather sad news, darling. Mme Franchard has died ... Yes, yes, I know. Of course ... her lawyer is here. M. Thibaud. He's been going through Mme Franchard's papers and as I understand it, she's told him she gave you a letter. Is that right? It is? Good ... then let me put you on to him now. Are you ready to speak? Oh, quite right. Okay. I'll wait for you to ring back. Bye, Lou.'

Matt turned to M. Thibaud. 'She's going to ring back very soon. She has to find the letter and read it herself. Mme Franchard apparently made her promise not to open it until after her death. Please have another biscuit. I'm sure Lou won't be long.'

Lou sat down on the sofa. That thing that people said about having the stuffing knocked out of you was right, she thought. That's just what I feel like. Sort of sad, but not really, truly, terribly sad because I hardly knew Mme Franchard. And I'm surprised even though I shouldn't be, because when I was in Paris, she looked very weak and ill. And she gave me a letter to open when she died ... this isn't a shock. Not really. I was expecting it, but also, because of everything that's happened, I'd forgotten all about it. Now that I've been reminded, I'm stunned and I have no right to be.

She stood up and went to find the letter, fearful for a second or two of opening it. She wondered if she ought to phone Jake, but that wasn't unusual. She felt like phoning him about every ten seconds and found the time when they were apart difficult. I'm in love, she thought. Amazingly, she'd found that she could repeat these words to herself in her head over and over without feeling a fool. She had never imagined it could be like this: as though there were a thin thread of something or other pulling her towards him at all times. Whatever she was doing or thinking, wherever she was, every part of her was drawn in his direction. She imagined what he'd be doing: reading something or other in the office. Talking to someone on the phone and leaning back in the chair, and whatever he was doing she knew with absolute certainty that he was thinking of her in exactly the same way. We yearn for one another, she thought and almost laughed. What kind of language was that, for God's sake? *Yearned* – but that was exactly right, and when they met after a few hours apart they clung together as though they'd been in imminent danger of being separated for ever. Bloody ridiculous, Lou smiled. I've lost my heart. *My true love hath my heart and I have his* ... there was no doubt about it, reason and normal behaviour had gone out of the window.

Since that night three weeks ago, when they'd made love for the first time, Lou had spent part of every day with Jake. It was the thing with the car seat all over again. He'd gone to John Lewis the very next morning, bought a cot for Poppy and proceeded to turn one of the small rooms in his house into a nursery. He'd taken Lou to help choose pictures and bedding for the cot and a small chest of drawers. She'd watched him do this in a daze. What was the etiquette about letting a man buy stuff for your baby? Was it the same as letting them buy you perfume and lingerie?

'Don't you need to think about this for a bit?' she asked weakly, as they came out of the shop with so many carrier bags that they were both staggering.

'No. No, I don't. I want to spend every night with you. I want you to move in. You won't, for some reason, so I need to make it easier for you to stay over sometimes. I'm betting it'll happen one day, right? You want it to happen, don't you?'

She'd nodded. Of course she wanted it, but everything was so sudden, so quick, so overwhelming that she felt that one of them had to keep their feet on the ground.

'What if it doesn't work out?' she said.

Jake had stopped in the middle of the pavement, and stared at her. 'No question in my mind. Tell me if there is in yours and I'll take all this stuff back to the shop.' He'd been grinning as he spoke, so what could she say? They'd gone back to his house and spent a couple of hours putting up the cot and hanging the butterfly mobile and unpacking all the soft, fluffy, white and pink checked bed linen – cot linen – and then he'd taken her into his bedroom for the very first time and undressed her and they'd made love till it was time to go and fetch Poppy. When she got up from his bed she was weak and trembling with satisfied desire and just wanted to stay there in that bed for the rest of her days, with Jake kissing her and touching her and taking her to such extreme edges of feeling that she found herself crying out and clinging to his hair, to his back, wanting to fold every bit of him into herself. It was completely exhausting and yet she was always ready for more … He had a habit of waiting till she was out of bed, on the way to the bathroom, on her way to getting dressed and then he'd come after her and stop her and carry her back to the bed, to the warm sheets they had just left for one more kiss, one more caress. Often Jake took her to the nursery to fetch Poppy in the car but there were times when she had to go on her own, and leaving the house when he was in it became harder and harder. She used to sit on the Underground and throb all over with longing, wondering whether everyone else could guess at what she was remembering.

Even now, when she was supposed to be sad for poor Mme Franchard and opening her last letter, most of her thoughts were with Jake. Okay, concentrate, she told herself. Open the damned thing:

My dear Louise,
  If you read this, I am dead already. I think that you and your father are my last relations who are still living. I am very happy that I met you in my life to remind me of my beloved sister, called by your name. M. Thibaud, my lawyer, has my will, but I wish now to add this small gift for you. It is my house in Brittany. Not my father's big house, which was sold after the war, but a much smaller property where we spend our holidays when I was young. My sister, Louise, loved it very much. I do not live there for many years. It is by the sea in a village near Penmarc'h. The house I have neglected and it is closed now, but the location is most beautiful. It is all I have to leave for you, dear Louise, but I will be happy to think of you there. Please tell M. Thibaud to do all that is possible to make this go with speed.

Lou picked up her mobile. She punched in her father's number, feeling a little giddy. First the announcement of Mme Franchard's death and now this. Was it true? Would it happen? She was finding it hard to take in. Dad would know what the legal position was.

'Dad? Yes, I've found it. I think Mme Franchard has left me a house ... Yes, okay. I'll read it to M. Thibaud. Right ... Hello, M. Thibaud. Are you ready for Mme Franchard's letter? ... Okay.'

The page lay open on the table and Lou read out

what was written on it, feeling a bit of a fool, her voice sounding unnaturally loud in the empty room. When she'd finished, she was almost ready for M. Thibaud to say something along the lines of *well, these are the ravings of an old lady and we can't take any notice of them*. To her amazement, he asked only one question:

'Is the letter signed and witnessed?'

'Yes ... Mme Franchard has signed it and Solange Richoux has witnessed it. And there's a date: twenty-fifth of July 2007.'

'Excellent. That will make everything easy. There are no competing claims on her will, so there will be no problem, I think. I will have to find out about the details of this house. I did not know of it. Your great-aunt is – how do you say in English? A black horse?'

'A dark horse.'

'*Exactement*. A dark horse. She tells me very little about herself. I think you will have to come to France, when I have discovered what is to be done, to sign the papers and of course you will wish to see the property, is that not so?'

'Yes, thank you. I don't know what to say. Thank you!'

'I have to thank you, Mademoiselle. Without this, there is only one bequest. To Mme Richoux, your great-aunt had left all her furniture and effects. There is very little money. Very little savings.'

'Oh,' Lou said. 'Right.' What else could she say?

'You are fortunate that she has not told me of this house. I would have advised her most strongly to sell it, if I had known about it.'

'Perhaps that is why she didn't tell you?' Lou said.

'*En effet*,' said M. Thibaud, chuckling at the other end of the line. 'That is quite true. She was a clever woman, I think.'

As she listened to the Frenchman talking, Lou began

to take in what had just happened. She had been left a property in Brittany. I'm a property owner, she told herself. I own a house. Neglected, Mme Franchard said, but I can do it up. A vision of herself and Jake and Poppy in Brittany flashed through her mind, in which they looked like something out of a TV property programme – designing features in blond wood and whitewashing a picturesque cottage. She'd be in denim dungarees but still look beautiful – stop it, she told herself. That's mad. Denim dungarees – where did that come from? She'd been watching too many reruns of *The Good Life*. And I refuse to count my chickens till I've signed all the papers. But I must tell Jake. I wish M. Thibaud would stop talking. I need to talk to Jake. Oh, God, I wish he could be here now ...

12

What am I letting myself in for? Phyl wondered. There was no way she could have refused to come to this lunch. Nessa had made a point of saying she needed everyone in the family to be there. There was something she wanted to share with them, that was the way she put it and all sorts of possibilities had gone through Phyl's mind since she'd received the invitation. There was an actual, physical written invitation: that was unusual. She couldn't recollect anything more formal than a telephone call on other occasions when Nessa wanted them to visit her at home. This must be something important. Could she be pregnant? Who by? There had been no evidence that she had seen another man since her divorce from Gareth.

'Has Nessa said anything to you?' she asked Matt. He was humming under his breath as they drove.

'About what?'

'About this lunch. I'm dreading it.'

'Why? There's nothing to dread, Phyl, truly.'

'You're being stupid, Matt. Ellie will be there. I'm going to feel most uncomfortable.'

Matt said nothing for a while and Phyl was working up to shouting at him for not being sensitive to her feelings when he suddenly turned into a lay-by and stopped the car. He turned to her. 'I couldn't say what I wanted to say while I was driving. There's nothing to be uncomfortable about. Ellie's the one who might feel that, though of course she won't. You have to realize something, darling. She doesn't attach importance to sex. That's the truth of the matter. It's just – well, like going for a swim, or having a nice meal. Not an activity which has any emotional significance to it.'

'You don't know that. I think she wanted you for herself. I think she'd have loved it if you'd left me and asked her to marry you again.'

'Maybe. Or maybe she thinks she would. I know, and I think if she's honest she knows as well, that it would be an even greater disaster than it was last time round.' Matt took her hand. 'You're my love, Phyl. Okay? Really, truly, for ever. Do you believe that?'

Phyl nodded. He said, 'Then just remember that. Hang on to it. This lunch is about Nessa in any case and Ellie will have plenty of distraction. Don't worry. And we can leave as soon as you like. Just give me a signal. Okay? Ready?'

'As I'll ever be.'

'Well, you look fantastic. So no worries there.'

That was kind of him. Phyl had never been sure of herself where clothes were concerned, but today she reckoned she looked okay. She'd decided to go for a more formal version of what she normally wore because the one thing that she *did* know was that she looked her best in casual clothes. Dark grey tweedy trousers, a very expensive cream silk shirt, a long string of malachite beads to set it all off and a cashmere cardigan which was exactly the same colour as the necklace. Black suede shoes with a patent leather wedge heel. She'd even gone to the hairdresser and looked, she reckoned, as good as she ever would. Bring it on, Ellie, she thought as they went up the drive of

Nessa's house. I can take it. She took a deep breath. Even with her new-found confidence, she would be delighted when the lunch was over and they were on their way home again.

Nessa had certainly pushed the boat out. The table was laid with a white tablecloth and the white, pink and dark red roses in the gloriously over-the-top centrepiece were obviously proud to be made of silk and didn't pretend for a moment to be the real thing. The food had been provided by a firm called Simply Natural. Lou knew this because she'd seen the logo on the van delivering the grub earlier that morning. She and Jake had been the first to arrive. Nessa had asked them to come early, because she wanted what she called 'ballast' against her own mother and Matt and Phyl.

Tamsin had been put in charge of Poppy and was doing a very good job too. Lou hoped that having someone dance attendance on her every second of the time wouldn't go to her daughter's head. Poppy had only to indicate that she wanted something and Tamsin rushed to provide it. She cuddled her, she talked to her, she read stories to her and now the two of them were in the kitchen. Poppy's meal had been heated in the microwave and Tamsin was tucking into what looked suspiciously like fish fingers and chips. To each his own. There were a couple of members of Simply Natural's staff overseeing the serving of the meal, and they'd promised to keep an eye on the children.

'Call me if she's any trouble,' Lou had told Tamsin before she sat down at the table, but so far so good. Occasionally, she tuned out of what was being said around her and listened to the sounds coming from the kitchen, but there'd been nothing untoward and so she began to relax. Nothing had been said so far, but Lou knew what this lunch was about. Nessa was going to tell Ellie and Matt and Phyl (and Justin, too, if he didn't know already) about Mickey. She'd clearly thought carefully about the seating. A round table made things a little easier. Mickey was on Nessa's right. Then, going anti-clockwise round the table, Matt, Phyl, Jake, Lou herself, Justin, and Ellie on Nessa's left. Lou felt like blowing a fanfare or something, to herald the announcement that was surely due any minute now.

They'd eaten smoked salmon, a delicious Greek pie made from filo pastry with a filling of cheese and spinach and had just tucked into a chestnut and brandy trifle which was quite the most delicious thing Lou had ever tasted. She wondered fleetingly whether she could get the recipe from someone at Simply Natural but dismissed the thought almost at once. She wasn't a cook and had no real intention of becoming one in the near future.

The talk, all through the meal, had been general. Topics covered included America and the pros and cons of living in Britain rather than in the States. Justin told them about a new scheme of his, which sounded even more dodgy than the last one. He was going to Argentina with Ellie to look into setting up a property business there. Dad, Lou thought, looked as though the less he heard about this plan, the better he'd like it. Argentina! That was a long way to go to start over again. Mum was very quiet and Lou wondered why that was. Could it really be that she hadn't got over being Dad's second wife, after Ellie? Was it possible that she still felt unconfident after all these years? That would be astonishing, but it was quite true that Ellie did put everyone else to shame when it came to OTT showbiz-type glamour. Even Jake was mesmerized by her, though she could see from his expression that part of the fascination was amusement at her outrageousness. The scarlet silk thing she was wearing would have been more suitable on some yacht on the Riviera … long and flowing and kaftan-like, but embroidered round the neck with so many sequins, bugle-beads and other assorted gems that she gave the impression of having turned into a kind of Christmas tree decoration. You could do worse than have Ellie on the top of your tree, Lou thought, and smiled. Nessa was as smart as she always was, in a clinging silky dress in shades of rust and beige with long amber earrings. Mickey wore a moss-green velvet jacket over a white satin camisole. Lou felt her own black skinny jeans and cream shirt were only just okay, but Jake had bought her a long Missoni scarf in about thirty shades of red which she reckoned was easily the most beautiful thing in the room. It made her feel as though his love was wrapped round her throat. What a soppy thought, she told herself, and took another sip of wine.

'Okay, everyone,' Nessa said, tapping her glass with the edge of her knife. 'I'm sorry to stop the conversation and it won't be for long, but you must all have been wondering at the reason for this lunch. Some of you may have guessed. Others of you know already, but I thought I'd make a formal announcement so that we can all, well, get it out of the way.'

Dad was pale. Ellie was leaning forward and Lou could see the tops of her breasts and wondered how many garments in her wardrobe had buttons up to the neck. Mum looked bemused and you could just see that Justin had an eyebrow ready to raise. Jake was sitting quietly, wearing what Lou thought of as his poker face: the one that gave nothing away.

'Here it is, then. You are all of you invited to our wedding. Mickey's and mine. We'll be married in a civil ceremony on the twenty-second of December and then spending our honeymoon in St Lucia – Christmas in the Caribbean.'

Lou thought: Ellie will be the first to break this silence. She was right. Nessa's mother, to give her credit, gathered her wits more quickly than anyone else and raised her glass in the general direction of Nessa and Mickey. It was obvious that she'd already had a fair amount to drink, but she staggered to her feet and said, 'I propose a toast to the happy couple! Girl-on-girl action isn't my kind of thing, sweetie, but the very best of luck to you both and take no notice of what anyone thinks or says. I never have!' She chortled and took a sip of wine and sank back down again. Lou smiled. *Girl-on-girl action* was a bit off, perhaps, but the sentiment was a sound one. Bully for Ellie.

Mickey said, 'Thanks so much, Ellie. We intend to be very, very happy.'

What was Matt going to do? Lou had noticed her father's mouth falling open at the news but he'd managed to recover himself just in time and, as soon as Ellie had sat down, he raised his own glass to Nessa and Mickey and said, 'Yes, that's marvellous news, Nessa. Thank you for telling us in such a splendid way as well. This has been a delightful lunch. We're all – I think I can speak for everyone, can't I? – we're all looking forward greatly to the ceremony. All the best to you both!'

One day, Lou thought, I'll speak to him and see what he really thinks. He'd never make a scene and he'd never spoil an occasion like this, but was he so relaxed about Nessa becoming a lesbian? What were his views on such things? To her surprise, Lou realized that she'd never discussed it with him. She and Jake had talked it over, of course. He'd been to so many civil ceremonies that he was totally used to it and didn't bat an eyelid, but Lou had to confess that it would seem a little – well – unusual was the word – to watch Nessa coming down the aisle, or whatever you did at a register office, with another woman. She was so consumed with thinking about their own love-making, hers and Jake's, that she'd long ago given up trying to imagine what it must be like to go to bed with a woman. Nessa, she thought, loves Mickey and that's what counts. Maybe she feels exactly the same way that I do with Jake when she's making love to her. Lou realized that every single person, every single couple, was different, so obviously Nessa and Mickey would be too. She wasn't the same person with Jake as she'd been with Ray. Her half-sister must have enjoyed making love to Gareth once upon a time. I must stop thinking about this, Lou thought. I'm seriously tipsy. I'm confused. There's only one thing I know and that's that I love Jake. And he loves me. She raised her own glass and said, 'That's the best news, Nessa. I'm really, *really* happy for both of you.'

Children made very good babysitters, Phyl reflected, but they did get fed up quite quickly. Tamsin had done brilliantly, looking after Poppy both before and during lunch. Now, quite understandably, she was bored, and had gone off to her room to do something or other and Phyl had jumped at the chance of leaving the table and taking care of her granddaughter. She decided almost as soon as the baby was in her care that they'd go for a walk in the garden. It wasn't too cold and the sun was shining in an autumnal way.

'Come on, Poppykins,' she said, very pleased at the idea of escape from the company. Ellie hadn't presented a problem and it occurred to Phyl that Matt may not have told her the full truth. Oh, he'd have let his ex-wife know that there was no future in their relationship, but he could easily have hidden the fact that she, Phyl, knew what had gone on between them. It would have been typical of Matt not to have told her. He'd have reckoned that there would be fewer chances of embarrassment if the story was *Phyl knows nothing*. Okay, if that was the way he wanted to play it. Ellie must be feeling smug, and that annoyed her. She must be thinking *I know something she doesn't know* and revelling in her superior knowledge of what Matt was really like.

'Never mind, eh, Poppy? I don't care. I *do* know and she doesn't know that I do and that makes me the winner!'

'Ganny!' was Poppy's response. 'Gardin!'

'Let me button up your coat. It's chilly outside.'

Nessa and Gareth's house (but now Nessa's alone and maybe soon Nessa and Mickey's) stood in about an acre of well-cared-for garden. There was a pond near the wall at the back of the property, and Phyl and Poppy made their way down to it. Phyl gave up trying to keep Poppy off the rather damp grass and thought, it's only clothes and shoes. If they get a little damp, they'll get dry again.

'Yoo-hoo!' Phyl turned round and there was Lou, waving at her from the French window of the sitting room. She'd opened it, which can't have been what Nessa would have wanted, in this weather. 'Can I come and look at the fish as well?'

'Mummmeee!' Poppy cried and took off in Lou's direction, wobbling a little as she stumbled over the grass towards her mother. Lou picked her up and together they came to stand by the pond.

'Typical of Nessa to have a nice clear fishpond with no mud to spoil the fun,' Lou said. 'Look at that big fish, Poppy. It's a big goldfish.'

'Fish!' Poppy agreed and struggled to get down for a

closer look. She peered over the stone rim of the pond and gazed at its inhabitants as they glided in and out of the plants with which Nessa had decorated their habitat: water lilies and reeds and ferns.

'What do you think of Nessa's news, Mum?'

'I'm ... well, I'm thrilled for her of course, but I have to say, I find all that ...' Phyl didn't know how to put it. She didn't want to appear old-fashioned, but there was a part of her that shrank slightly at the thought of gay marriages or civil ceremonies, or whatever they were called. There wasn't anything wrong about it, nothing like that, but in her most secret heart, Phyl was of the opinion that it was a bit – well, *strange*. Her whole mind shied away from even thinking about what went on in bed when two women were together, but nowadays you saw enough lovers of the same sex kissing passionately on television to know that even seeing that much did make you feel *peculiar*. She'd long ago made a decision not to dwell too hard on the nitty-gritty of such relationships, and that was in general. When it came to a woman she had known since childhood and had raised since she was nine years old, then matters were even more complicated. Phyl couldn't help wondering whether it was anything she'd done ... or perhaps it was the result of Nessa's mother running off and abandoning her ... her head was aching with the weight of the knowledge and she hoped very much that she'd grow more used to it by the time the wedding – the civil ceremony – came round. She wasn't about to tell Lou all this, so she just said, 'I like Mickey a lot. I hope they're happy together.'

'She's certainly prettier than Gareth,' Lou said, and for some reason this struck Phyl as very funny and she burst out laughing. Lou joined in, and then so did Poppy.

'God, I'm sorry, Lou,' Phyl said. 'I think I've drunk a bit too much.'

'Me, too ... but can I tell you something?'

'Not if it's going to be a shock. I can't take another shock today.'

'You're supposed to say surprise. Not shock. That's a bad thing.'

Phyl smiled. 'Okay, I understand what you're saying. Surprise, then. Tell me yours.'

'Jake. I'm in love with Jake.'

Her happiness was obvious. Phyl recognized the wide grin from childhood, from those times when Lou was at her most joyful.

'Not a surprise at all. I knew ages ago.'

'You're just saying that. Hindsight's twenty-twenty.'

'Just because you're in love with an American, you don't have to use expressions like that. Twenty-twenty, indeed. And you're wrong. I knew you liked him when you came down to Dad's birthday. I could see. And he loves you.'

'He does! He really does, Mum. I can't believe it ...' Lou flung her arms round her mother. Phyl hugged her daughter and found that there were tears standing in her eyes.

'What's the matter, Mum? You look as though you're about to cry. You should be happy for me.'

'Oh, I am, I am. Really, I am. I just – when I think of all that's happened to you, I'm just so – I suppose relieved is the word. The world is so full of bastards, isn't it? I think you're very lucky to have met Jake. And he's lucky to have met you.'

'Destiny! That's what it is!' Lou burst out laughing again.

'That's right. Kismet. Fate. Things like that. And he loves Poppy. That's the most important thing. I knew he was the one as soon as you told me about the car seat for Poppy. You should have known then too.'

'Part of me must have done, I suppose, but I didn't want to let myself hope. Especially after Harry. That dented my confidence a bit.'

'Are you and he okay now? At work, I mean.'

Lou nodded. 'Fine. I'm taking some time off, though, in the spring. We're – Jake and I are going to do up the house in Brittany. That's the plan, anyway … fingers crossed.'

'You haven't even seen the place yet …'

'That's what I came out here to ask you, really. Will you and Dad take Poppy for the weekend, when we do go?'

'Of course. Nothing I like better than having her to stay. You know that. Any weekend except the seventeenth of November. That's when we're off to Paris. Even though poor Mme Franchard is dead, your father promised me. Now we've booked the hotel and it's all set.'

'Lovely! You deserve it. I was thinking of next weekend, actually. Will that be okay? It's such short notice, only Jake just told me on the way here that he could manage next weekend.'

'Fine – no problem at all. I'll check with your dad, but I'm sure he'll be all for it.'

'Mumeee …' Poppy was sounding peevish for the first time that day. Lou picked her up.

'Come on, Madam, you're a tired little kitten. Time for a nap. You can sleep in Tamsin's room. That'll be nice, won't it?'

The two of them went up the garden path together to the house and Phyl looked after them. I'm happy, she thought. And then this was followed by another thought: I'd better remember how this feels, right now, because things can change so quickly. Please, God, don't let them change for Lou and Jake. Let them be happy. Please let them be really, really happy. She closed her eyes tightly, just as she used to do when she was in primary school, saying the Lord's Prayer. Somehow the tighter you closed your eyes, the more fervent the prayer seemed to be. This prayer, she told herself. I want *this* prayer to be answered.

❋

'Aha!' Ellie giggled. 'This is where you've got to! You're hiding from me, Matt, aren't you? And now I've found you, so there!'

'Not at all. I simply thought I'd help Nessa by taking out some of the glasses.' He pointed to the tray he'd just put down on the work surface. He was perfectly able to load a dishwasher but hadn't dared to do so in Nessa's house without her permission. Still, he'd wanted to help in some way and so he'd taken charge of clearing the table. And Ellie was right. Part of his intention was to escape from her. He squared his shoulders, and told himself that there was very little she could do or say to him here in the kitchen with so many people around and liable to come in at any moment. He knew Phyl was in the back garden with Poppy because he'd seen them going down to the fishpond, but still, she could come back at any moment. Get rid of her, he told himself. Send her back to the lounge. Now.

'Aren't you amazed at Nessa's news? I am. If I hadn't heard it from her own lips I'd never have believed it. Well, Mickey's a nice woman, and whatever turns you on, as they say.'

'Quite,' Matt answered, trying to achieve a difficult balance between being friendly and being cool. It was proving very hard. Ellie had come right up and planted herself too near him – smiling up at him, letting him become aware of her perfume, making sure that he had, if he wanted it, a good view of her cleavage.

'Ellie,' he ventured, moving away from her. 'This is – I'm not sure why you've come after me, but there's nothing else really for us to say to one another. I told you on the phone. I'm ... I'm sorry about what happened but it was a one-off.'

'Hmm. Well, yes, I know that really, but admit it, Matt. It was something special, wasn't it?'

'Very nice indeed.' (God, what did he sound like? Someone describing biscuits and cheese he'd just eaten. But he could hardly enthuse about it. Give Ellie an inch and she'd take about a yard and a half.)

She laughed. 'You've always been a master of understatement. Well, I can take a hint, and I think Justin and I will do very well together overseas. I've been finding the UK a bit – well, a bit unadventurous, if you must know. But if you ever change your mind, Nessa will know where to find me.'

She put her arms around Matt's neck. He couldn't get away. His back was pressed up against the sink. She's going to do it, he thought. I can't move. Better to get it over with and then make a dash for the door. Oh, God, please, please don't let anyone come in and find us. She's mad. She's incorrigible. Ellie's mouth was now on his. He could feel the heat of her body through his shirt and it took all his willpower not to respond. What if Phyl came in now? he thought. I can't, I mustn't! He let her kiss him and stood as stiffly as he could while she did it. He kept his lips firmly closed too. Then he moved firmly and definitely away from her.

'I can see,' Ellie laughed, 'that I'm wasting my time. Never mind, darling. Don't let it worry you.'

'Absolutely. I'm fine. I do wish you luck in Argentina, Ellie. I'm sure you'll have a terrific time there. And you can keep an eye on Justin.'

She stepped back. 'Justin's hopeless. He's only coming out for a few weeks, to see how the land lies. Renting out his flat in Brighton to a friend, I believe. Maybe that will generate a bit of income at any rate, while he's not getting his usual salary. I'd better go back there and see what's going on.'

'Right,' Matt said, relieved to see her leaving the room. He exhaled, unaware until that moment that he'd stopped breathing naturally the minute Ellie walked into the kitchen. The danger was over. He walked over to the window to see what Phyl was up to and found her talking earnestly to Lou. Poppy was trailing her hand in the pond and running around the rim, obviously following one of the fish as it swam along. He smiled. He remembered Tamsin doing the same thing, exactly.

The truth of the matter was, he did still think of that night with Ellie. It was something he'd tried to eradicate from his memory with no success at all. He couldn't help it. He fancied Ellie like mad and always would and that night with her was ... what was it? Amazing. Unforgettable. Marvellous. He felt guilty that his own wife didn't make him feel like that, but it couldn't be helped. He loved her. He could no more envisage living without Phyl than living without his right arm, but it was thoughts of Ellie which made his pulses race; Ellie he fantasized about; Ellie who came into his mind at inopportune moments, and there didn't seem to be anything he could do about it. He sighed and wondered how long this effect would last. Maybe as time went on, as the memory faded, he'd forget how it was, that night. How he'd felt. How he'd almost passed out from an overdose of pleasure. Phyl was waving at him from the garden, smiling at him and he smiled back and felt like a rat. But I'm not a rat, he thought. I'm here. I've sent Ellie packing. I love my wife. I love her. There's nothing wrong with having a fantasy life. Show me the man who doesn't.

Harry was on the phone when Lou came into the room to talk to him about a script she'd just read about two sisters working in a supermarket. It made her laugh, though the title, *Special Offers*, obviously needed work. Harry nodded at her and indicated that she should sit down, so she did, wondering why he was smiling so hard into the handset. Why was he looking so pleased with himself? She looked at him as he spoke, comparing him to Jake and feeling happy. She had a lot to thank Harry for, she decided. If he'd become her boyfriend, she'd never have become involved with Jake and how dreadful that would be ... even though she hadn't been going out with Jake very long, she found it hard to imagine a life without him and the moment she thought this, she suddenly felt herself turning cold. What if something happened to him? To her? What if he grew tired of her? What if it didn't work out? What if, all sorts of ghastly things ... No, I'm not going to think like that, Lou thought. I'm going to be positive. Look on the bright side. Harry was looking directly at her and nodding and saying, 'Yes, yes, she's right here as a matter of fact – sure. No, I'll go and get us a coffee while you speak to her. Okay ... be in touch. Ciao, Ciaran!'

Ciaran? Could it be? Harry was holding the handset out so that she could take it. He was grinning all over his face.

'Hello? This is Lou Barrington.'

'I've found you. I'm so sorry. This is Ciaran Donnelly. I owe you an apology – you must think I'm so rude. The fact is, I've only just read your script. Would you believe it got buried under some files? I'm sure you would. You've been to my house, have you not?'

Lou nodded and then realized that he couldn't hear her nod and said, 'Yes, yes, I have.' What was he going to say? Why had he rung Harry? What was happening? She could feel her heart pounding in her chest and breathing had turned into something she found difficult.

'I love it! It's great ... I'm going to option it. Not a lot of money, I'm afraid, in an option, as you know, but I do think it's a grand little screenplay you've written and I don't want anyone else getting wind of it. I'll try and raise some finance now – you know how it works, don't you? No guarantee that it'll be made, but a first step.'

'Yes. I'm so sorry to be so – tongue-tied. I don't know what to say. I'm ... I'm overwhelmed ... completely knocked out. I didn't think for one second that you'd like it. I used to dream about it at night ... how you'd look at it and throw it across the room in disgust ...' Lou stopped speaking, aware that she was babbling. Talking nonsense in all probability. And in her head, like a pulse, beating and beating were the words *grand little screenplay, grand little screenplay*. She wanted this conversation to go on for ever. And she wanted it to be over so that she could phone Jake, and Mum and Dad and tell them. If only Grandad were alive! He'd have been so pleased: *Blind Moon* coming out again, for everyone to read and now maybe – *maybe* – a movie. A movie she'd written. Lou was finding it hard to believe this was happening.

'Not at all, not at all. No disgust, I assure you. We should meet soon, I think. I'd like to meet you properly now that I'm investing in you – does £2,000 sound very stingy?'

'No, not at all. That's fine.'

She had no idea whether that was fine or not, but

she'd have sold him the option for much less than that. He wasn't just anyone. He was Ciaran Donnelly.

'I'll be in touch soon, then. Goodbye to you, my dear.'

'Goodbye. And thank you very much.'

'My pleasure!'

Lou put the handset down in its cradle just as Harry came back into the room. He patted her on the shoulder as he went to sit at his desk. Then he grinned at her.

'You're a cagey thing, Lou Barrington. You never said a word. You might have given me first look.'

'I didn't want to. You know me. It would have been difficult for you to be honest, wouldn't it? You'd have wanted to let me down easily.'

'Apparently, it's great. Well, no more than I'd have expected. When can I see it? Will you email it to me? I really, really want to read it, Lou.'

'Okay. And I'd like to know what you think. I'm a bit scared to be honest, but I would like to know.'

'You went to his house? Really?'

Lou nodded. Harry said, 'I never would have guessed you had that kind of nerve. Well, it paid off. I reckon your chances of him finding the finance for it are better than average. He's obviously very keen.'

'He did sound keen, didn't he?'

'Yup. And you've changed, Lou, since the summer. Are you in love? That's the only thing I can think of that would account for that – well, that glow. Tell me about him.'

'How d'you know it's a him? It could be a her.'

'NO! Really!?'

'No,' Lou laughed. 'It's a him. My sister's in love with a woman, though. They're having a civil ceremony at Christmas.'

'Blimey! What did your family say?'

'Nothing much, really. You have to accept it, don't you? No one is going to bust up with someone for life just because of who they're sleeping with.'

'Not everyone's as broad-minded ... Tell me about the him, then.'

'He's called Jake Golden – of Golden Ink.'

'You're kidding me!' Harry's eyes were wide open, and so was his mouth. 'Talk about landing in the jam. Do you have any idea of how rich that guy is?'

'Well, I haven't asked him but I'd assumed he was quite well off. He's got a publishing house ...'

'Publishing house is peanuts, Lou. His dad is Morton Golden – internet and communications wizard. They are in the stratosphere as far as the spondulicks are concerned. I reckon you can take me out to lunch on the strength of that. And I want to meet him. Make sure he's good enough for you, Lou.'

'What a cheek, Harry! I will take you out to lunch for sure, but you've got a nerve, asking if he's suitable. Well, you can relax. He's lovely, don't worry. Really, really lovely.'

She rose to her feet and left the room.

Harry called after her, 'Are you going to give up your job now you're a screenwriter?'

'No, of course not.'

'But with such a rich boyfriend? You could lie on satin sheets eating caviare all day long.'

'He's not my husband, you know. His money has nothing at all to do with me.'

She knew she wasn't quite telling the truth even as she spoke. There were all sorts of ways in which Jake's wealth had made a difference. If the truth were told, she was still trying to take in this new information. I knew he was rich, she thought, but this. This was a bit overwhelming and Lou made up her mind to deal with it later on, when she was alone. I ought to have guessed ages ago, she told herself. She took out her mobile and dialled Jake's number.

'Jake? Can I buy you lunch? Yes, Dolce Vita is fine – my treat. I've got a marvellous piece of news ... What? No, I'm not telling you over the phone. You be there at one.'

As she made her way to the Underground, it occurred to Lou to wonder what Jake would be imagining – could he possibly think she was pregnant? She nearly dialled again, just to save him the worry. Would that occur to him, even for a moment? No, of course not, but he might wonder. She hadn't confided in him about the screenplay. Was that wrong? Would he mind? No, he'd understand. She was sure of it, as sure as she could be of anything. Jake was too level-headed, too easy-going, too. And it wasn't such a big deal anyway. Lots and lots of screenplays got optioned and not made into movies. A huge majority of them, in fact. *Blind Moon* wouldn't be a movie – she had to start telling herself that to avoid disappointment. She wouldn't mind. She was happy now. About Ciaran Donnelly and what he said. About Jake, especially. And there was a tiny part of her that was happy to see Harry looking slightly wrong-footed. That was mean of her, she supposed, but she couldn't help it. Serve him right if he was jealous – only a tiny bit maybe, but still jealous – of Jake.

The house was more of a ruin than a house. Lou had hired a car at Rennes airport and driven to the edge, almost, of a high, white cliff at what felt like the end of the earth – Finistère was a good name for it, she thought. It was a stormy October morning. The wind was whipping the navy-blue ocean into crests of white and the village she'd driven through was not much

433

more than a street. She had found the place after asking in the local café which was called Les Naufragés. A bit of a strange sense of humour, she thought, calling something The Shipwrecked.

Jake would have come with her if he'd been able to. He'd been just as keen as she was to see the house, but a last-minute business meeting in New York had suddenly come up and couldn't be postponed.

'It's okay,' he said, making the best of it. 'I'll come with you later. As soon as I can, and we'll fix it up together and spend holidays there together and it'll be great, but the first time, I reckon you ought to be by yourself, Lou.'

'That's nonsense,' Lou had said. 'It'd all be so much easier if you came. Am I really going to have to deal with French lawyers and real-estate people and so forth, all on my own?'

'Sure. Why not? You're not scared, are you?'

'No, but—'

'There you go. I'll help you book your flight and hotel on the internet and that's it. You'll be fine.'

And she had been fine and of course Jake had been right. M. Thibaud had come down from Paris to meet her flight and guided her through the legal stuff with the local notary or whatever he was called, and he'd even offered to accompany her to the house. She'd refused, as politely as possible, so he'd agreed to provide her with directions and leave it at that.

I'm glad, she thought, that I did come by myself. This place will be lovely in the summer. The landscape seemed a bit savage at the moment, but that made her feel strangely excited. Lou loved the whole idea of a house perched on a cliff. She loved the thought of looking straight down to the sea. She'd studied the photograph of the first Louise, as she thought of her, for clues as to what the house might be like and imagined a solid building, planted firmly in its foundations and four-square to the winds coming off the ocean.

The *patron* had told her where the Franchard property was: about a hundred yards further than the last house in the village, he said, on the cliff side of the road. She wouldn't be able to miss it, because it had no roof and the door was painted red. Red, it turned out, was the colour of the bits of paint still clinging to what remained of the warped wood that must once have taken up the entire doorway.

Lou parked the car in front of the house, which stood with its back to the cliff, separated from the road by a small garden full of overgrown trees all bent low as a result of the wind. She got out, and pushed open a shutter that was hanging off its hinges and peered inside at what seemed more like a deserted barn than a house real people had once lived in. The room she could see, which must have been the kitchen, was big, but beyond that, there was an even bigger room.

She went in past the splintered wood of the door and looked around her. Two large rooms on the ground floor. An ancient wooden table, wobbly on its legs, stood in the middle of the kitchen. Lou went up the rickety stairs to the first floor and examined the three bedrooms, each one exactly like a whitewashed cell. Then she went downstairs again and walked over to the back window, which she recognized at once. This was where Louise Franchard had stood as a young woman, smiling and with the sea behind her. The place was completely empty and the table was the only sign Lou could see of human habitation. Milthorpe House, when she'd gone round it with Jake, was empty as well, but you knew it had been lived in recently. Ceiling roses, dado rails, working light bulbs, pale rectangles where paintings had hung: everywhere there were signs of human attention. Here there was nothing, and yet Lou could imagine what it had been like when the Franchards were living here: spartan, but comfortable. There would have been lamps. Floor coverings. Curtains at the windows. Beds on the upper floors with fat quilts on them, probably stuffed with the feathers of seabirds.

Every house is haunted, she told herself, every single one, whether someone is living in it or not. Ghosts of ordinary people doing ordinary things drift through the rooms. She could envisage the sisters, Manon and Louise, sitting by the fire – there was the kitchen fireplace – and what? Knitting? Reading? Talking to one another? Whatever it was, part of them was still here, because she'd thought about them. Remembered them. Ghosts, it occurred to her, owed their existence to the long memories of the living. The reason most ghost stories were scary, rather than simply sad, was because sensational murders were remembered for far longer than normal domestic events and by people who had no family relationship with the dead person.

Lou shook her head. What a time to be philosophizing! If Jake were here, he'd be sizing up the space in the kitchen to see whether an Aga might be fitted into the spot where the fire once burned. She looked out of the window again at the back garden, which was entirely overgrown and wild and seemed to stretch to the very edge of the cliff. We're going to have to put some kind of fence up there, she thought, for Poppy. She shivered. A very strong fence – but, God, what a fantastic view! She took out her phone to take some photos of the sea. Then she snapped the fireplace and the front garden and went outside to capture the battered red front door. She would send them to Jake's phone as soon as it was morning in New York. He slept with his mobile on the bedside table and she didn't want to wake him up. Suddenly, she wished more than anything that he was here with her, seeing this. Next time, for sure. And what about after that? They'd been together almost all the time for the past few weeks, but Lou was ashamed to find herself thinking more and more about the future. I'm getting to depend on him, she thought, and so is Poppy. She loves him. I love him. She laughed and the sound of her voice was very loud in the empty house.

'I want to marry him!' she called out and the only answer was a seagull, crying outside the window. She giggled. Love had made her soft in the head, but it was true. Or a version of it was true. She wanted to live with him for ever, married or not. She put the phone back in her handbag and opened the front door and as she did so, it started to ring. She scrabbled around for it and found it almost at once.

'Hello?' she said.

'It's me, Jake – why don't you ever look at caller ID?!'

'Jake! You're supposed to be asleep. It's the middle of the night where you are.'

'Five a.m. Woke up early because I'm missing you so much.'

'Me too. I miss you like mad. Jake, I'm in the house. In France ...'

'I know. I'm so curious. What's it like? Have you taken photos?'

'I'll send them to you now – it's beautiful.'

'Figured it might be. If the hotel's okay, book us in for the weekend in a month. A family room. We'll bring Poppy. Okay?'

Lou nodded. 'Okay, that'll be lovely – oh, Jake, I can't wait to see you.'

'Not long now, but listen, I've been thinking. Your flat – what about giving it up?'

'And moving in with you?'

'Yes, with me. There's so much room and it seems ridiculous to go backwards and forwards when we want to be together, right?'

'I suppose so. Yes, right.'

'So you'll give your landlord notice, or whatever you have to do?'

'Yup.'

'Fantastic. Okay, I'm going to get up now. I'll speak to you again later. Lou?'

'Yes?'

'I miss you so much ...'

'Me too.'

'And I love you. D'you know that?'

'Yes. I love you too.'

'That's good. Okay, bye.'

'Bye ...'

He was gone. She ended the call and then spent a few moments sending the photos of the house through to his phone, marvelling, as she did every time she thought about it, about the magic that enabled Jake in New York to get a message from the other side of the world. She'd put her phone back in her handbag and left the house, closing the red door behind her. Just as she was getting into the car, she heard the beep of an incoming text message. Jake – reacting to her photos. She flipped open the lid. The message read, *Fantastic! If I let you share my house, will you let me share yours? Xxx.*

Lou laughed. She texted back: *What do you think?*

Then she shut the car door and leaned against the headrest and closed her eyes. She listened to the sound of the waves crashing against the cliff, far below her, and wondered whether this was how the first Louise had felt: that she was ready to leave everything, her house, her family, her life, everything she knew, in order to follow her lover wherever he wanted her to go. That's how I feel, she thought. I would have done exactly that, exactly what she did. She turned the key in the ignition and started to drive. She glanced back briefly at the square white ruin of her house, then turned her attention to the silver, twisting road that led to Penmarc'h.